# PRAISE FOR HILARY DARTT

"Author Hilary Dartt's debut novel – The Dating Intervention – contains every essential element that a fantastic, page-turner type book should contain: a deep sense of character, a near-tangible sense of place, and a captivating plot that moves quickly and fluidly throughout."

RACHELLE SPARKS

"I didn't want it to end! Hilary Dartt is a real talent!"

AMAZON REVIEWER

"Dartt's writing style is distinct, witty, fun, and heart-felt. She creates characters that feel like real people … Love it!"

BLOGGING & WRITING BLOG

# ALSO BY HILARY DARTT

**The Seedling Homestead Series**

*The Composition of Order*

*The Structure of Perfection*

**The Intervention Series**

*The Dating Intervention*

*The Marriage Intervention*

*The Motherhood Intervention*

**The Garden Club Series**

*Jasmine's Pact*

*Studying Sequoia*

*Just Holly*

# THE ARCHITECTURE OF VISION

VISION

HILARY DARTT

# PROLOGUE

MARGARET MILLER'S first mother gave her two things during their short time together: she gave Margaret life, and she also gave her a single piece of advice, one for which Margaret was eternally grateful: "Take care of yourself."

The phrase became lyrics to a song that formed the soundtrack for Margaret's existence. And, those words were some of the last coherent words Margaret's biological mother ever said to her. As such Margaret applied great importance to them. She considered taking care of herself a kind of religion.

The first time she heard the phrase, Margaret was six years old. She loved snails and french fries from Burger House, although she hadn't yet realized that when Mama offered her "leftover" fries, they were actually someone else's trash.

The two of them lived in a tiny second-story apartment in Cheyenne. They kept mostly to themselves, except when Mama had a "visitor."

These visitors always stayed about an hour or so, and Margaret learned early on to make herself scarce when they came over. She'd wander the apartment building. Sometimes she stopped to pet Mr. Jingles, the stray cat that lived under the Dumpster out back. Sometimes she played with the giant leaves that fell off the tree out front, using them to make patterns and pictures on the sidewalk.

It used to be that when Mama's visitors arrived, she'd say, "Hello," and then go off on her own. And although most of them were nice enough, things changed when one man asked Mama if Margaret could give him a "blowie." Margaret didn't know what that was. She imagined blowing on the man's face, or maybe blowing some dust off his hands. The man seemed friendly, and Margaret didn't think she'd mind.

But Mama came unglued. She glared at Margaret, as if she'd been out of line, and then pointed at Margaret's bedroom. Margaret knew better than to argue or ask questions. She marched right in there. When the screaming started, she put her pillow over her head. All she could discern were snatches: "Six years old, for God's sake!" "Disgusting!" and finally: "Get out! Out! And don't bother coming back!"

Then the door slammed, and Margaret heard, with clarity she'd never forget, a wail.

When she crept out of her bedroom to see what was wrong, Mama was standing by the front door, looking out the window. Below, on ground level, the man walked through the apartment building's tiny parking lot, glancing back up at them every couple of seconds. Mama, with both arms crossed at her waist, looked like she was holding onto herself so she wouldn't fall over. Tears stacked up on her lower eyelids, and her mouth was a funny shape.

The man had reached the edge of the parking lot, now. A couple more steps and he was out of sight.

Mama turned towards Margaret and, in a gesture that was quite uncharacteristic, she hugged her. Margaret froze for a few seconds before giving into the embrace. In a voice thick with tears, Margaret's mama said, "Promise me one thing, Margaret. Promise me."

Margaret, her face squished into Mama's stomach, nodded. "I promise."

"Take care of yourself. Go to college, get a good job, and never rely on anyone."

Again, Margaret nodded. She squeezed her mama tighter and said, "I promise."

## CHAPTER ONE

—————

IT HAPPENED GRADUALLY ENOUGH that Margaret Bradley pretended it wasn't happening at all, until circumstances forced her to admit it. She was losing her vision—which was the most important thing in the world to her, and to her clients.

She literally couldn't go without it. How many times had someone said, "I love your vision," or, "This is Margaret, our architect. She has amazing vision"? Too many to count.

It was also the one thing that allowed her to keep her promise to her first mama. She'd gone to school and gotten a great job, and now she didn't have to depend on anyone. Ever.

And that's why it was impossible for her to lose her vision.

Driving in the dark became difficult, and then impossible. One night, as she returned home after the grand opening celebration for a building she'd designed—it was the new library in the City of Pine Bluff, Arkansas—she realized she could barely make out the street signs or the edges of her lane. She could see the light from the traffic signals, but just barely. Everything blurred together as if her window was fogged up. Only, it wasn't. She blamed it on the wine, even though she'd had half a glass at most.

But somewhere deep in the recesses of her mind, as she crept along the road at fifteen miles per hour, she knew it wasn't the wine. She knew it wasn't the cold medicine she'd blamed the week before when she drove home from a late meeting in Steamboat Spring, Colorado.

So, Margaret stopped driving at night. She took taxis whenever she needed to, and although this put a slight dent in her pocketbook, it didn't hinder her social life too much … and it allowed her to have a few glasses of wine on a date.

"Silver lining," she told herself on more than one occasion (especially the occasion where she'd needed to take the edge off a particularly strained dinner conversation with a certain Carl the Cryer, whose eyes leaked throughout the meal while he talked about his ex-wife. Margaret downed three healthy glasses of pinot noir with her spaghetti).

Then, her peripheral vision started to disappear. Not that she needed that for work, or for her social life, which is why she ignored it for such a long time. She became accustomed to swiveling her head all the way to the right and all the way to the left.

Until that day in Seattle, when she almost died.

As always, she was in the city for work. She had a seven a.m. meeting with the owner of a building on Pike Street, downtown. He wanted to turn it into—what else?—a coffee shop. She'd grabbed a coffee from her hotel lobby, and was walking down the street with her folder under one arm, taking in the scenery. She stepped off the curb to cross the street at 6th Avenue.

As she always did before an initial meeting with a client, she was going over her plan, thinking about her vision—yes, there was that word again. The coffee shop would have high ceilings with a row of windows running along the tops of the walls. The counter would stand along the back edge of the space, and she was still working out how to ensure maximum flow as people ordered, waited for their drinks, and then sat down. Deep in thought, Margaret didn't actually turn her head to the left to look for traffic as she started to cross the final intersection before she arrived at the new location.

The next several seconds—which actually lasted moments or even hours, in Margaret's mind—happened in slow motion: someone shouted, tires squealed on pavement, a car horn honked and Margaret finally turned her head, swiveled it all the way to the left, to see a gray sedan quickly approaching. She reacted, still in slow motion, her arm coming up (spilling her coffee) and her body scooting away from the car, which came to a screeching halt just inches from her left leg.

She dropped her folder, to brace herself on the hood of the car. Her drawings scattered all over the ground.

Of course, her first instinct was to gather up those papers. She knelt down right there at 6th and Pike, dirtying the knees of the designer slacks she'd bought at Nordstrom the evening before.

"Geez, lady, I almost ran you over."

Of course, she hadn't seen the driver of the gray sedan get out of his car, but here he was, helping her scoop up the contents of her folder. Now that she was touching the papers, she realized some of them had fallen into the puddle of coffee she'd created.

"Shit." Her face burned with shame, and she said, "I'm so sorry. You don't have to help me pick these up. Really, I'm fine."

"Lady, I gotta get you off the street before you endanger yourself again. Did you even realize you were walking against the light?"

Margaret looked up at the crosswalk signal and realized she couldn't even make out which symbol was illuminated.

"I'm really sorry," she said. "I'm just distracted, that's all. Important meeting."

"Nice drawings," he said, as he handed her the stack he'd collected. "But, lady, nobody's going to see them if you don't snap out of it."

He was right.

She thanked him for his help. Then, with a forced chuckle, she thanked him for not running her over. She thought she made out a smile before she stepped back onto the curb to wait for the next opportunity to cross.

This time, she paid attention—to the sounds of people talking next to her, the flow of traffic—and when those people started walking, she did, too.

Margaret feigned confidence as she walked along the sidewalk, but tears stung her eyes and made their way down her cheeks.

That was the moment. It was the moment when Margaret Bradley, independent professional, architect of great vision, social butterfly, finally had to admit she needed help. She could no longer take care of herself.

As soon as her meeting was over, she walked outside and leaned against the wall.

When the receptionist at the ophthalmologist's office picked up, she burst into tears.

---

"SO TELL ME, Margaret. What brings you in, today?"

Dr. Thomas Lane looked at Margaret from under bushy eyebrows. The lighting conditions here were nearly perfect. Margaret knew because she could make out the color and round shape of Dr. Lane's bright green eyes.

They were sitting in the exam room, and Margaret leaned her head back against the head rest. She'd always thought these huge chairs and all the eye doctor's equipment looked like torture devices.

"I'm having some changes to my vision."

"What kinds of changes?"

Margaret's lips had gone dry, and she licked them. She wondered, for a fraction of a second, whether she had to answer the question. Keeping this problem to herself had kept it from being a problem. Sort of. He waited. She cleared her throat.

"At first, it was my night vision. I couldn't distinguish shapes, you know? I couldn't quite read the street signs or see other cars, in the dark. I stopped driving at night. And then, my peripheral vision went. It seemed like I didn't have any, all of a sudden. That's when I started taking taxis. And now, my regular vision—it's just—blurry. Not all the time. Some days, I wake up, and I can see almost normally. And some, I can't."

"How long have you been noticing symptoms?"

She looked down at her lap, and then up at the two mirrors on the opposite wall. They looked more like blobs against the white background.

She inhaled and answered on the exhale: "A few months. Maybe twenty-four."

"Twenty-four months?" Dr. Lane was incredulous. "Twenty-four months is more than a few, dear. It's two years."

"I know. I just—it just—I didn't think it was serious, you know? And like I said, I can still see clearly sometimes. Plus, it's the twenty-first century. Surely, anything, or almost anything, is fixable, right?"

"I wish that were true," Dr. Lane said. "Do you have a family history of vision loss?"

"I don't know." Margaret shrugged one shoulder.

"Your mother, your father, perhaps a grandparent?"

"It's not that," Margaret said. "I'm adopted. My biological mother is dead. And I don't even know who my father is. Last I saw my mother, she had pretty good vision—and pretty good aim. Anyway. That's the long answer. I don't know if anyone had vision loss."

Dr. Lane nodded. He leaned forward, his elbows on his knees. "I suspect you have a condition called retinitis pigmentosa."

"Sounds like a doozy," Margaret said, because she didn't know what else to say and she wanted to keep the mood light. And because it sounded like a doozy. "Or something out of a magic spell book."

This didn't even earn a chuckle from Dr. Lane, who said, "It's a degenerative eye disease, Margaret. It causes severe vision impairment. Do you know what the retina is?"

"Yeah," Margaret said, dread forcing her to slog through the recesses of her memory for the information she'd learned in high school biology. "It's at the back of the eye, and it converts light into images?"

"Right," Dr. Lane said. "It's a thin piece of tissue lining the back of the eye. It contains photoreceptor cells, rods and cones, which convert light into signals the brain interprets as vision. In retinitis pigmentosa, those photoreceptor cells degenerate. They stop working effectively. People with retinitis pigmentosa *usually* begin experiencing symptoms —similar to the ones you've experienced—in early adulthood. Most of them lose their vision gradually over time. Some cases are more severe than others."

Margaret wondered if this torture chair reclined because she thought she might pass out.

"What's the treatment?"

"Let me get you some water," Dr. Lane said.

Margaret hardly noticed he was gone but a moment later, he was pressing a water bottle into her hands.

"It's open," he said. "Why don't you have a drink?"

She nodded and took a sip. "Don't you have anything stronger?"

This time, he did chuckle. "Not at the office, dear, unfortunately."

A few seconds passed, and Dr. Lane spoke again. "Research is promising when it comes to treatment in the future," he said. "But right now, options are limited."

"Options are limited. What does that mean?"

"Unfortunately, there's not too much we can do."

"So, I'm losing my vision."

"Yes, I think so. I'd like you to see a specialist, to be sure; a doctor who has the equipment to get a really good look at your retina, and your photoreceptor cells."

Margaret started to speak, but Dr. Lane held up a hand. "Now, keep in mind that some cases are more severe than others. Depending on lighting conditions, you may be able to see just fine, at least for a while. Some people with this condition continue to have daytime vision."

"I don't think you understand," Margaret said. "I'm an architect. I can't lose my vision."

"I know this information may be difficult to process."

"It's impossible," Margaret said. "I need my vision to draw plans, to see buildings, to see spaces. To *see*."

"If this were a debate, you'd win," Dr. Lane said. His voice sounded so kind she almost cried. "But, I'm sorry to say, it's not."

"I'm going to get a second opinion." Her hands were shaking. She knew. She knew she could get a second opinion, and that it would be the same as Dr. Lane's opinion. Because, as he'd said, this wasn't a debate. It wasn't about opinions. It was fact. She was losing her vision.

"Like I said, I'm going to refer you to a specialist. She can give you a more detailed exam and, hopefully, advice about how to move forward."

"Where can I possibly go, if I can't *see*?"

Dr. Lane rolled his stool toward Margaret and took her hands in his own. He leaned in, so their eyes were on level, and he said, "Margaret, this isn't a death sentence. I promise you, you still have the opportunity to live a rich and full life, even with retinitis pigmentosa."

"My life can't be rich and full if I can't see," she said. "You don't understand."

Her career was everything. In using it as a vessel for self-sufficiency, she'd foregone all the things other people did: finding a partner, having children, buying a house. All so she could focus on her career.

"I'm sorry, Margaret," Dr. Lane said. He gave her hands one final squeeze, and then rolled over to the desk.

"I'm sending out a referral right now. It's Dr. Marie Rossi. She's good. Very good."

The lying started the next day. It wasn't outright lying, but it was lying by omission. Margaret had already scheduled a trip to Arizona. Her niece, Amelia, was graduating from high school, and she'd promised to be in the stands with pompons.

If the trip weren't specifically for graduation, Margaret would have postponed it until she was able to go to the specialist. Or find some witch doctor who could perform some kind of voodoo and bring her vision back.

But Amelia was one of her favorite people. Her favorite person, actually. And Margaret didn't want to let her down.

Typically, she'd fly into Phoenix and then grab a rental car and jet up Interstate 17 to Flagstaff, where Amelia lived with Margaret's youngest sister, Sarah, and her husband, Donny. Not this time. She paid an exorbitant fee to ride an airport shuttle from Phoenix to Flagstaff, and then called for a taxi to take her to Sarah's house.

The process was cumbersome and—well, whatever the opposite of empowering was. Luckily (or unluckily), Sarah was so distracted by her marriage problems that she didn't even question Margaret's taxi arrival.

They went out for lunch, which, under normal circumstances, would have been a fun activity. But Sarah took her to a trendy little Italian place where low lighting was part of the ambience and for the first time, Margaret couldn't read the menu. The letters blurred together, tiny gray smudges.

Margaret kept Sarah talking. She went as far as to talk about Sarah's sex life, and to insist on going to The Big One, a boutique sex shop a few doors down. Then she ordered bottomless martinis.

And it worked. Sarah didn't notice anything was amiss; at least, not at first.

Then Margaret said, "What are you getting? What's good here?"

"The ravioli," Sarah said.

"I'll have the same," Margaret said.

"You don't eat pasta. It gives you gas."

"I know. I'll get a side salad."

Which didn't make sense. But it, too, worked, because Sarah was distracted. Margaret could see the blob that was her sister shrug one shoulder, as if to say, "Suit yourself," and they moved on to a different topic.

The next day, as they were driving to Amelia's graduation, she and Sarah received a text, simultaneously. Margaret could barely read her text messages, which was why her phone was lying at the bottom of her purse on the floor between her feet. But the only person who would text them both at the same time was their older sister, Hannah.

Sarah didn't move to look at her phone, even though the notification was deafening. She was behaving so strangely that Margaret dug out her own phone, angling it away from Amelia so Amelia wouldn't see the super-sized font Margaret had started using.

Sure enough, the text was from Hannah, and as Margaret read it, her blood practically froze.

*Mama just collapsed. Taking her to the hospital now. I know it's Amelia's graduation day … text me later.*

For a few moments, Margaret debated whether she should break this news to Sarah. Then she decided it was better to do it now. She'd hate for Sarah to see the message if she used her phone to take pictures during the ceremony. She had to say Sarah's name several times before her sister responded.

"I just got a text from Hannah," Margaret said.

"And?" Sarah said.

"Mama's sick," Margaret said. "Hannah's taking her to the hospital."

Amelia gasped. Donny cursed.

"What kind of sick?" Sarah said.

"Not sure," Margaret said. She used voice-to-text to ask Hannah for details, and Hannah's response came back quickly. "Unconscious. We won't know anything right away. Possibly a stroke."

They rode the rest of the way in silence. And while Margaret was horrified at this news, she couldn't help but also feel the tiniest bit relieved. Now Sarah and Donny would be too busy thinking about Mama Katherine to notice Margaret's strange behavior.

During Amelia's graduation, Margaret was in the stands, just as she'd promised she would be. And she waved those pompons, even though she couldn't even make out which gowned-and-capped teenager was her niece.

Of course, Sarah and Donny picked her out right away, and when they pointed her out to Margaret, Margaret just waved, hoping her palm was facing the right direction.

And then, midway through the ceremony, Margaret had a terrible realization: if Mama Katherine was sick, she'd have to go see her. She had no choice but to go to Wyoming. And even if she was sick, Mama Katherine would know something was off.

There was absolutely no way Margaret could continue acting like things were normal, she thought as she watched the sea of maroon-clad high school graduates become taller as the kids stood up.

Then, as they threw their caps—maroon dots—into the air, Margaret felt a tear slip down her cheek.

---

MARGARET SAT on a comfortable chair in Dr. Marie Rossi's office. The cushions were covered in leather and Margaret was almost positive they were filled with goose down.

While music had played in the waiting room, the only sound in here was the ticking of a clock. Margaret drummed her fingers on her thighs. Is this what it felt like to wait for an executioner? Under different circumstances, she would have laughed at herself. Even she knew she was being dramatic.

Finally, *finally*, the office door opened. Dr. Rossi came in, and

Margaret could smell her perfume—floral with a hint of vanilla. She sat down in a chair across from Margaret and leaned forward, her elbows on her knees. Fortunately, she didn't try to make small talk or ask how Margaret was. She cut right to the chase.

"I've just finished reviewing the exam results. Dr. Lane was right. You have retinitis pigmentosa."

Margaret inhaled and then held her breath. She'd gone against her own advice and performed hours of Internet research after seeing Dr. Lane. None of the websites had anything good to say about this condition. She was going to lose most, if not all, of her vision.

This was impossible. She couldn't go blind. Not now. She was too young. There were so many things she hadn't seen. The petroglyphs in Utah, the beaches in Belize, the waterfalls in Costa Rica. And although she'd never wanted a husband or children, she realized with a start that if she did fall in love, and start a family, she'd never see their faces.

She clenched her fists, digging her fingernails into her palms.

"It's genetic." Dr. Rossi's voice was calm, but Margaret didn't feel soothed by it. "Does anyone in your family have retinitis pigmentosa?"

"I don't know," Margaret said. "I'm not in touch with my biological family."

"How long did you say you'd been having symptoms?"

Dr. Rossi leaned back in her chair. Margaret could guess what the woman was wearing, just from what she'd gathered during their conversations: a pencil skirt with high heels and a cardigan set. Her hair was perfectly combed and she probably had that air of authority. She was, undoubtedly, beautiful, with one feature that was just a tiny bit too big. Probably her teeth.

"A while," Margaret said. "I could tell from Dr. Lane's response that he thought I should have come in sooner."

"How long is a while?"

Margaret sighed. "Does it matter? Isn't the prognosis the same?"

Before Dr. Rossi could answer, though, Margaret realized she was acting like a spoiled brat. If she were in the other chair, giving a consult, she'd be offended. She rubbed her eyes, sighed, and spoke. "I'm sorry. I started noticing symptoms about two years ago. At first I thought it was just, you know, allergies or something. Making my vision weird. I kept putting it off because deep down, I was afraid it was something serious. I was afraid it would mean I couldn't work."

When Dr. Rossi said, "I understand," Margaret believed that she did. "What do you do for a living?"

"I'm an architect."

Dr. Rossi took a long moment to respond. "Lots of people with vision loss continue to work full-time," she said.

"Not as architects, though, right?"

"Margaret, I know it may feel like it, but this isn't a death sentence. First of all, as your symptoms continue progressing—and in most cases, they, do, unfortunately—then you'll have good days and bad days. You'll have days where you can see almost as well as you always have, and you'll have days where you can barely see anything."

"And at some point, the bad days will outnumber the good," Margaret said. "And before long, I'll lose my vision completely."

Dr. Rossi made a humming noise. "You still have the opportunity to live a really full life. Yes, it may be different from what you've had, or what you imagined you'd have. This is going to be a transition, but I'm confident that with your determination, you'll be able to do many of the things you want to do."

"I just hate that this is happening. I feel like I'm living a nightmare."

"I understand. It won't always feel this way. Give yourself some time to get your feet underneath you. There are tons of great resources available, and before you leave today, we'll make sure you know how to access them."

"My mother's sick."

"And you're worried you won't be able to take care of her."

"Right."

"Do you have siblings?"

At the thought of Hannah and Sarah, Margaret blanched. They'd insist on taking care of her. Hannah would already be taking care of Mama Katherine. And with Amelia leaving for college, Sarah was finally going to be able to focus on herself. This was so unfair.

"Two sisters," Margaret said.

"I'm going to be honest, here," Dr. Rossi said. "You're going to have to let your sisters take care of your mom. Just for now. Just until you get your feet underneath you, like I said. And then, once you learn how to navigate the world without your vision, you'll be able to help, too. This is going to require a lot of patience, Margaret. Patience with yourself. But I promise you, you're going to get through this."

Then, in a gesture that was completely unexpected, Dr. Rossi stood up, pulled Margaret to standing, and gave her a long hug.

Margaret left the office a few minutes later with a binder full of resources and a tiny bit of hope (which she hadn't had when she walked in). Next step: visit Mama Katherine.

# CHAPTER TWO

Margaret Bradley was going to go broke before she went completely blind. Having to take taxis everywhere—especially all the way to rural Wyoming—was costing her a small fortune.

Her other worry—telling Mama Katherine about her impending blindness—weighed heavily, too, and she spent the entire drive to the Seedling Homestead with her hands clasped together and her stomach churning. The scenery passed in a series of shadows and bright spots, and the taxi driver played tour guide, unaware that Margaret couldn't see the bison in the nearby field or the geese flying overhead.

She wondered if she'd always remember what those things looked like. Would she be able to recall the way the sunlight sparkled off the rivers or the way the waterfalls churned down the sides of a canyon?

As they approached Mama Katherine's farm, the taxi driver whistled.

"Beautiful place," he said.

"I know," Margaret said. "Takes your breath away, doesn't it?"

"Sure does."

They stood there for a long minute, and then the taxi driver said, "I'll get your bag, ma'am."

She tipped him well, and he got into the taxi and drove away, leaving her alone to remember the first time she'd seen the property. It was shortly after her first mother had given her that sage advice.

Margaret sat in the backseat of the social worker's station wagon, terrified after what had just happened with her mama. Every time she thought about that, she closed her eyes tight, as if that would stop her remembering. But it didn't. This time, she looked out the window, focusing extra hard on the way the sun, low in the sky, was slanting through the trees at the side of the road.

The social worker said she was going to live with a new mom and a sister.

"How do you like that? A sister!" the social worker said. Margaret could tell she was expecting a positive reaction. She smiled and nodded, still staring out the window. Deep down, she was scared: what if the sister didn't like her?

But then, they'd arrived. They were turning off the main road onto a long dirt driveway, and the social worker said, "Almost there, now."

Margaret looked out her window and the first thing she noticed was a weathered sign: *Seedling Homestead*. Then she noticed the landscape. Margaret was accustomed to being inside most of the time. Other than sending her out during those special visits, her mama rarely let her outside of their apartment. They mostly slept during the day, and they almost always kept the shades down when the sun was up.

So, starved for sunlight and the outside, she'd thought the farm looked like a place where magic happened. The social worker put the car in park just before sunset, when the light was golden and pouring over everything.

"Is this where the unicorns live?" Margaret said.

The social worker laughed, but Margaret recognized it as a sad laugh.

"Well, I suppose you can make it so, with your imagination."

The house itself sat low to the ground and had porches all the way around. There was a huge garden there, with tall corn stalks shooting up towards the sky, watermelon vines rolling along the ground, and rows and rows of green plants Margaret didn't recognize. Just across the way, there was a barn.

"A real-life barn!" Margaret said.

By now, the social worker had opened the car door, and was helping Margaret out.

"Get your things," she said.

Margaret grabbed the garbage bag she'd brought, which held everything she owned: clothes, shoes, a single stuffed teddy bear.

When she stepped out of the car, a dog raced up to greet her. She'd never seen a dog, except on TV, and she was immediately charmed.

But she didn't get a chance to pet it because a voice boomed towards her from the direction of the house: "Butch Cassidy, you get back here this instant."

The dog's ears perked up and it did a quick about face, charging back to the source of the voice; a woman so tall she could probably reach the cereal boxes on top of the refrigerator without scrambling up onto the counter. She could probably even touch the ceiling.

The adults talked for a moment, their voices lowered.

Margaret heard the social worker telling the tall woman about her mama. "Drugs. Three days, they were in that apartment. Just the saddest story."

The dog sat next to the tall woman, watching Margaret and trembling. Margaret wandered over to the garden and realized some of the plants held something that looked like tomatoes, only they were green.

She had never eaten a tomato, but she'd seen them on TV. She wondered what they tasted like. The leaves on the plant were surprisingly fuzzy, and the green fruits were smooth and cool. Before she realized what was happening, she'd reached out and plucked one, right off the plant.

Margaret panicked, then, her memory immediately flashing her images of the time she'd taken a soda off the counter. She'd reached out, picked it up, and taken a long drink of it—and her mom had lost control, yelling and screaming and throwing things.

Would it be the same with the tomato? Would this tall woman become angry? Would she throw things? Margaret looked around for throwable objects and spotted them everywhere. There was a shovel and a bucket and a little stool.

Just as the tomato rolled off her palm and onto the ground, the tall woman approached. "You dropped your tomato."

Margaret froze. She felt her breathing stop.

Most of her mom's tirades started this way. With a short statement, in a quiet, calm voice.

"Well, don't you want it?"

Margaret nodded. She knew that you always answered when someone asked you a question. Always.

"Go on and grab it, sweetheart. And we'll go in and cook it up."

Mama Katherine walked next to Margaret, and the dog trotted along behind them as they went up the path and through a door on the side of the house. When they did, an older girl bounded up from where she was sitting at a table. Squealing, she wrapped her arms around Margaret, who immediately dropped the tomato and her garbage bag. The dog barked and wagged its tail.

"I'm Hannah," she said, holding Margaret at arm's length. "And you're my new sister. Margaret."

As Hannah held onto Margaret's shoulders and studied her with serious gray eyes, Margaret realized she may not pass inspection. If that were the case, would the tall woman send her packing? Put her back in the social worker's station wagon?

Hannah's inspection didn't last long. She pulled Margaret in for another hug. While Margaret was noticing that Hannah smelled like syrup and some other funny scent she couldn't identify, Hannah said, "I'm glad you're here."

Margaret's body relaxed against Hannah's, and she put her head on her new sister's shoulder.

So, from that first moment, Mama Katherine's farm was a magical place. They fried up the green tomato and shared it off a single plate, Hannah chattering away about all the things they'd do together.

They spent the entire next day exploring the farm and playing in the creek, and Margaret realized that's what Hannah had smelled like: the mud on the edge of the creek. At the end of that day, when they walked back to the house, Margaret was so, so tired (in fact, she fell asleep sitting up at the dinner table), and so, so happy.

As she looked at the ranch house then, she thought, this is home.

And it felt the same way, now, thirty years later. This was her refuge. No, she wouldn't stay here forever. But the fact that she could come back whenever she needed to was comforting beyond measure. She needed her mama.

A thought crept in, then—Mama won't be around forever—but she squashed it quickly. It wouldn't do for her to start thinking about that now.

Just then, Mama Katherine emerged from the house. The side door slammed behind her. And there was John Wayne, Mama's fourteen-year-old heeler, walking stiffly beside her, his tail wagging. Butch Cassidy had died when Margaret was eleven, and then there had been Ringo, a chocolate lab. Margaret felt some of the tension slip away as John Wayne bumped the top of his head against her palm.

Mama's voice voice rang out across the driveway, as loud and strong as ever.

"Margaret, sweetheart! I didn't even realize you'd gotten here. I didn't hear you pull up. Where's your car?"

"I took a taxi," Margaret said, and then blurted out the story she'd rehearsed: "I wasn't sure how long I'd stay, and I didn't want to deal with a rental. The taxi was a Prius. You know how quiet those things are. Gas efficient, too."

And then she was in Mama Katherine's arms, and tears were slipping out from under her eyelids. Mama Katherine probably assumed those tears were related to her own health, because she said, "Oh, honey, I'm fine. I just had a little dehydration, that's all."

"I know, Mama. I'm just glad to see you."

"Come on in. Hannah's run into town to buy some flowers. She'll be back soon."

Margaret hadn't planned on telling Mama right away, but someone had moved the furniture in the dining room. The big buffet that had always been on the far wall was now on the wall just inside the door, and Margaret swung her bag into it, hard, when they walked in. It would probably leave a scratch in the wood, but Margaret couldn't see it to check. Obviously.

Then, because her eyes weren't adjusting to the difference in lighting between outside and inside, she couldn't make out the chairs around the table. Someone had forgotten to push a chair in, and she ran into that, too, almost knocking it over.

"Margaret! Honey! Did you overdo it on cocktails on your flight? Take a few nips on the taxi ride here?"

Margaret, irritated at her own clumsiness, huffed out a sigh. She didn't know how long she could get away with keeping her failing vision a secret. "No, Mama. I wish I had. Where'd you say Hannah was?"

Telling Mama was one thing, but telling Hannah was a whole different thing. Hannah was a worrier, an embracer of The Worst Case Scenario.

"She ran to the market to buy flowers. Oh, and then to the store to get stuff for dinner. What's the matter, honey?"

"Mama, I have to talk to you."

"Well, sit down. I'll make you some tea. There's no use talking without a good, strong pot of tea."

"I'll just put my things in the bedroom."

A few minutes later, they sat at the dining room table. Margaret had made her way slowly to the bedroom, where she dropped her bag on the floor just inside the door. Then she'd come back through the house, walking with her hands out in front of her so she wouldn't run into anything else.

"How was your trip?" Mama Katherine asked.

"Oh, you know," Margaret said. She slid into a chair. "It was fine."

"Was it?"

It was now or never. Hannah would be back soon. And putting this off wouldn't make it hurt any less.

"Mama, I'm going blind."

Margaret heard Mama Katherine's sharp intake of breath. And then she heard silence. She filled it. "Please don't tell Hannah and Sarah just yet, okay? I need to figure out what I'm going to do. I don't want them to worry. The doctor says there are lots of resources. I'll be fine."

"Of course you'll be fine, sweetheart." Mama Katherine covered Margaret's hand with her own. "Of course you will."

"I'm scared, Mama."

"Oh, honey."

If Margaret was still a little girl, Mama Katherine would be pulling her into her lap right now.

"I won't be able to work."

"Nonsense. A girl as bright and talented as you?"

"Thanks, Mama. But not as an architect."

"We'll find a way."

"I wish I could say that with as much confidence as you have," Margaret said.

Mama Katherine pushed a cup of tea across the table, and said, "Tell me what the doctors said."

Margaret told Mama Katherine the whole story, starting with the loss of her peripheral vision, throwing in the near-miss with that gray sedan in Seattle, and ending with her visit to Dr. Rossi's office.

"She said I'll have good days and bad, but ultimately, I'll be completely blind."

"Did you get another opinion?"

"Well, the evidence seems pretty clear," Margaret said. "My regular eye doctor and the specialist agree I have retinitis pigmentosa. That's two opinions."

"True," Mama Katherine said.

"I don't know what to do."

"You'll just do what you've always done. Kick ass and take names."

Margaret sighed. "I guess so."

"Did they give you any information about how to move forward?"

"Tons. Almost too much. There are classes I can go to, of course. Mobility training, braille reading, computer courses, you name it. The doctor said I actually have an advantage, since I grew up sighted. That's what they call it—sighted."

Now Mama Katherine was rubbing the top of Margaret's hand in slow circles with her thumb. "Remember that time, when you first arrived here, and Hannah was teaching you how to use the rope swing to cross the creek?"

Margaret couldn't help it: she laughed. The series of events that day hadn't felt humorous at the time, but the older she got, the funnier it seemed.

"I remember."

"You came into the house mad as a wet hen. You *were* a little wet hen. You were spittin' mad! You stomped right in through that door, your face all twisted up, your hair matted to your head."

"And I said, 'Hannah's pickin' on me'."

Yes, Margaret thought, she'd dropped her g's and become a country girl instantly upon moving here.

"That's right," Mama Katherine said. "And when you explained what happened, it was all I could do to keep from laughin'. But we walked back out there, and poor Hannah was in tears. She just wanted to teach you how to cross the creek."

"And I wouldn't *listen*, she kept saying," Margaret said.

"Right. But we convinced you to try again."

"And I fell into the creek again, and bruised my butt."

"Right," Mama Katherine said. "But you tried again. And again and again and again. And then what happened?"

"I did it."

"You did it. And you were so excited. You were thrilled. Elated, even. Remember that?"

Margaret nodded. "I do remember that, actually. I had blisters on my hands from all that rope swingin'. And then I crossed that creek every chance I got, just for fun."

Mama chuckled. "Right. You did. In fact, I remember Sarah coming in the next summer, complaining that you were hoggin' that darned thing."

"I loved that rope swing," Margaret said. "Did you take it down? I didn't even think to look."

"It darned near fell down. That new family moved in, you know, across the way. At the Miners' old place."

"They did?"

"Yeah, Matthew and Heidi Sutton and their five boys. The oldest one's a teen, maybe Amelia's age. But there are a few younger ones that would probably love a rope swing. I had Matthew take it down so they wouldn't get hurt if it broke. But maybe while you girls are here we can hang up a new one for them."

"That sounds good, Mama. I'm glad I came. Thank you for talking me down."

"Any time, sweetheart. And let me know what I can do to help you, okay?"

Margaret nodded. "For now, can we just wait to tell Sarah and Hannah? I don't know if I'm quite ready for that."

"Of course, honey. But you know you're going to have to tell them eventually."

"I know. Just not yet."

Hannah came in through the front door, then, and when she saw Margaret, she squealed the same way she had when Margaret walked into the dining room the day they met.

"You're here! I didn't see your car outside and I was disappointed you weren't here yet."

Instead of answering, Margaret stood up and hugged her sister. It felt so good to be home. Maybe everything really *would* be okay.

---

MARGARET JUMPED at the chance to go to the farmer's market with Hannah the following morning. She loved the little white booths with their fresh lettuce and melons and handmade soaps and crafts, and she wanted to see it just one more time.

As Hannah drove them, in Mama Katherine's old pickup truck, she reached over and patted Margaret's leg. "You look beautiful, as always," Hannah said. "How do you never age?"

Margaret raised an eyebrow. "Oh, I'm aging."

"Well, you don't look like it."

"Well, thank you."

And what was Margaret to say? *You look beautiful, too, Hannah. Although, I can't actually see your face. It's wonderful to see you.*

This was ludicrous.

"I've missed you," she said. "It's wonderful be with you."

There. That was accurate. Hannah turned on the radio, and Margaret rode in silence, allowing herself to get lost in thought. It would be impossible for her to see all the things she wanted to see, just one more time. The farmer's market was a good start. What if she had to make a list of her Top Five things to see again? What would they be? The ocean, for sure. She didn't care whether it was the Pacific or the Atlantic, or the Mediterranean Sea, for goodness' sake. And she'd really like to see some of the old castles in Scotland. And what about the cherry trees blooming on the east coast? Or the fall colors there? The redwood forest! She loved that place. That was five. And she could think of countless others.

And Hannah had said she looked beautiful. Which was nice, but what was beauty if you couldn't see it?

"You're quiet," Hannah said, then.

"Just recovering from a long travel day," Margaret said.

Hannah snorted. "You usually bounce right back. Maybe you *are* aging."

Margaret slapped Hannah on the arm. Hannah laughed and turned up the radio, then shouted over the music: "I love this song!"

It was "I Want to Hold Your Hand," by the Beatles, which they'd listened to as kids—too many times to count.There was nothing to do but sing along, and that's what Margaret did. Hannah joined her, and rolled down both windows as they sped down the road. Margaret felt the wind in her hair and on her face, and they were still belting it out, imaginary microphones in hand, when they pulled into the parking lot at the farmer's market.

Margaret heard Hannah shift the car into park. "Wait," she said. "Just finish the song with me."

If she'd thought about the possibility of people watching them, she probably wouldn't have finished out that last line with such reverence.

"*Now* you can turn off the truck," Margaret said.

She was smiling as she climbed down from the passenger seat, but felt her expression fall when she heard a man's voice coming from a few feet away.

"Wow." He whistled. "Talented duo, there."

His voice was deep and rumbly. It had that mountain-man quality she liked. She wished, wished so hard, that she could see his face. She imagined a beard (which she adored) and twinkling eyes.

"The Bradley Sisters," Margaret said. "At your service."

The man laughed, and that, too, sounded rumbly. Margaret had always been an observer of men, and this one probably had big hands. They were probably very skilled. She shivered and then shut the door of the truck. And when she would have expected the man to walk away, she realized he was coming closer. She could see the shape of his body approaching her. He was tall and broad, and she felt smug satisfaction that she'd likely guessed correctly about the size of his hands.

"Leroy," he said. Margaret could just make out the movement of his arm extending, his hand reaching out to shake. *Leroy?!* That wasn't what she'd been thinking. Completely by accident, she froze.

Then the man laughed, a loud, boisterous sound Margaret thought belonged partnered with a strong Irish whisky.

"You should see your face," he said. He slapped his thighs; she heard palms against denim. "I'm totally kidding. My name's not Leroy. It's Ethan."

Now he grabbed her hand and shook it, still laughing.

"I was right, you're a city girl. I knew it! You'd never be able to get past my name if it were Leroy, would you?"

Margaret shook her head, while simultaneously noticing that his hands *were* big and enveloped hers quite nicely. "I have no idea what you're talking about, Ethan, but you're very funny. Quite charming. Nice to meet you. I've got to go. My sister's waiting."

She didn't withdraw her hand from his.

"Wait," he said. "Which Bradley sister are you? You didn't say."

"Margaret," she said. She hoped she was looking in the general direction of his eyes.

"Quite nice to meet you," he said.

"Likewise."

Margaret trailed her fingertips along the truck, using it as a guide to find Hannah, who was leaning against the grill.

"Well, that was entertaining," she said. "Ethan seems like a very nice fellow."

Margaret linked her arm with Hannah's and as they began walking through the parking lot, Margaret hoped there weren't any obstacles on the ground. She was dying to know what Ethan looked like.

"What would you rate him, on a scale of one to ten?" she said.

"Oh, back to our junior high shenanigans, are we?" Hannah sounded amused.

Margaret said, "Absolutely."

"What would you rate him?" Hannah said.

"Oh, no you don't," Margaret said. "You always want to hear everyone else's ratings before you give yours."

"Fine," Hannah said. "He was an eight. He'd be a ten if he'd shave that beard."

"I kind of like a beard on a man."

"You like anything on a man, as long as it's accompanied by a—"

"Hannah!"

"Well, it's true. Here we are. What shall we shop for?"

"Let's just browse," Margaret said. The farmer's market—any shopping experience, actually—was going to be a whole new ball game now that Margaret was losing her vision. She wondered if it would ever be quite as fun, since she actually couldn't browse.

By paying careful attention to shadows and light, she could tell where the rows of tents were, and the other shoppers. No, she couldn't make out facial features or patterns on shirts, but she could navigate without killing herself.

"Ooh, look at those flowers," Hannah said, then. "I just love peonies, don't you?"

"I do," Margaret said. "I also love churros. I think I smell cinnamon. Do you see someone selling churros?"

"Um, right in front of your face," Hannah said. Margaret laughed it off, and hoped Hannah thought she'd been joking.

They bought churros, and then Hannah wanted to look at the soaps. While she did, Margaret stood with her back to the table, pretending to look around, although all she could see were blotches of color and variations in the light.

"Fancy meeting you here."

It was Ethan. Ethan of the Sexy, Rumbly Voice. Margaret couldn't help but smile as he stood next to her, his back to the soap booth. She felt him cross his arms.

"Did you get what you came for?" Margaret said. "I got my churro."

"I love those things," Ethan said. "Haven't had one in ages. I got my soap."

"No you didn't."

"No, I didn't," he said. "I came for salad fixins."

"Salad fixins?"

"Yeah. You know, kale, radishes, carrots?"

"Fancy salad," she said. "You sound pretty highfalutin for a Leroy."

She felt his body shake as he laughed.

"That's right. That's me, a highfalutin Leroy."

"Who are you cooking for?" she said. She had nothing to lose. Once she left Wyoming, she'd never see Mr. Highfalutin Leroy again.

"Do I have to say?" Well, this was interesting.

"No," Margaret said. "But now I'm even more curious."

"You were curious?" he said.

"I asked, didn't I?"

"If you must know—"

"I must," Margaret said.

"I'm cooking for my parents."

He sounded sheepish. She imagined a little boy looking down at the ground, hands clasped behind his back, one foot behind him, toes digging into the dirt.

"Aw, that's sweet," Margaret said. "I don't know why you're ashamed of it."

"I'm not," Ethan said.

"Are, too."

"Am not."

"Children!" Hannah was back. "Do I have to break up this fight?"

"Ethan, this is my sister, Hannah."

"Ah," Ethan said. "The other Bradley sister. I can't decide which one is prettier."

Impressed that he'd remembered their last name, Margaret found herself leaning against him like they were old friends. His arm really did feel massive against hers. She wished she could read Hannah's expression. Actually, maybe she didn't. Hannah was always implying Margaret was too flirtatious.

"Margaret's prettier," Hannah said. "Always has been."

Margaret shook her head, rolled her eyes. "Ethan's getting salad fixins. He's cooking for his parents. And he's embarrassed about it."

"Not exactly," Ethan said.

"I'll let the two of you work this out," Hannah said. "I've got to get some salad fixins, myself. You want that fresh lavender, Margaret? I know you like that stuff."

"Oh, sure," Margaret said. "I do like that stuff."

"I'll be right back," Hannah said.

"Lavender, on a salad?" Ethan guffawed. "That sounds like some kind of hippie nonsense."

Margaret shrugged one shoulder. "It's good. I like it. The first time I had it was in downtown Chicago. Trust me, I thought it sounded weird, too. But I promise you, it's good. With a little goat cheese? Delicious."

"Hmpf. Maybe I'll try it sometime."

"So, tell me about your dinner. What are you getting to go with the salad?"

"I got a couple of nice steaks," Ethan said. "And I was debating between baked potatoes and mashed potatoes."

"Baked are easier," Margaret and Ethan said at the same time.

Margaret wondered why she was standing here, doing this, with a man she'd likely never talk to again. He was really charming. She loved his voice. But it's not like anything between them could go anywhere. Not only did he live here, in Wyoming, but she did not live here, and didn't plan on it. And, the whole losing-her-vision fiasco wasn't going to be conducive to starting a new relationship.

Out of habit, Margaret started to scan the area for Hannah, but then she remembered she couldn't distinguish between the shapes and colors that were swirling around like beads in a kaleidoscope. She hadn't even paid attention to which direction Hannah went.

"Ah, now I've bored you," Ethan said.

"No, it's not that," Margaret said. She felt like she might have a panic attack. The stirrings of fear were just setting in around the edges of her consciousness. "I just realized I forgot to start the cake. We're having cake for dessert and I planned to bake it before we left, to give it time to cool while we were gone. And now I'm panicking."

That last part was true, anyway. Was this what her life was going to be like from now on? Where she was constantly feeling lost—or at the very least, on the verge of being lost?

"Are you okay?" Now he'd wrapped one of his massive hands around her bicep, and he was crouched down, looking right at her.

"Yes, I'm fine. It's just—I'm fine." Margaret's mouth felt dry. She licked her lips. "Do you see my sister anywhere?"

"Here she comes, now," Ethan said. "See her? Are you sure you're okay?"

"Yes!" Margaret said. "Absolutely. I'm fine. I just hope I didn't mess up the timing on that cake."

"What cake?" Hannah said.

So much for that lie. "That cake I was going to make for Mama Katherine."

"Oh," Ethan cut in, saving her. "You're cooking for your mom, too."

"You are?" Hannah said.

Why was she being so dense?

"Yep," Margaret said. "That chocolate cake, remember? I meant to bake it before we left to give it time to cool by the time we got home. But I forgot. We'd better get going."

Under normal circumstances—or normal-weird circumstances—she'd grab Hannah's arm and steer her back to the car. But she couldn't actually tell where Hannah's arm was. Instead, she turned toward Ethan and smiled up at him, hoping her eyes were looking into his. "Lovely to meet you, Leroy. And now we must go."

"Well, that was weird," Hannah said the moment they were in the car. "At first, I thought you were going to jump that guy's bones right then and there. And all of a sudden, you went cold. And why did you call him two names? Was his name Ethan, or Leroy?"

The hilarity of the situation hit Margaret then, and she found herself overcome by a case of the giggles.

"Ethan," she said, her voice high-pitched. "It was Ethan."

"What's so funny?" Hannah said.

Margaret managed to calm down enough to speak normally. "He told me his name was Leroy. I think he was testing me, trying to gauge my reaction to a country name, or something."

"That's weird," Hannah said.

"You're too serious," Margaret said. Then, because she couldn't help herself, and because she had to know, she said, "Anyway. What did you think? Was he good-looking?"

"I didn't think country men were your type, Margaret. I thought you liked the city slickers. The guys—what do they call that? Metrosexuals? The ones who wear skinny jeans and smell *fantastic* and put on jewelry. Anyway, I thought you thought feminine was sexy."

"Oh, my God," Margaret said. "You thought I thought that?"

"Well, yeah," Hannah said. "You always—"

"Wait," Margaret said. "You're getting off topic. I just wanted to know if you thought Ethan was good-looking."

"Oh," Hannah said. "Yes. Ethan was good-looking. I'd tap that."

"Hannah!" Margaret said. She turned to face her sister, her mouth open in surprise. "You never talk like that. Do you actually tap that with men?"

"Of course I do," Hannah said. "I mean, I was joking. Just now. When I said 'tap that,' but of course I date. And, um, you know."

"Screw?" Margaret felt a wicked sort of delight. Hannah never opened up about her dating life. In fact, Sarah and Margaret had often wondered if she even had a dating life.

Margaret knew that if she could see the details, she'd see that Hannah had both hands on the steering wheel, probably at eleven and one. Her elbows straight, her head locked at the twelve o'clock position, and her mouth set in a firm line. Her cheeks were probably as red as ripe, ripe tomatoes.

A laugh bubbled up from somewhere deep in Margaret's core.

"Don't laugh at me," Hannah said.

"I'm not," Margaret said. "I'm just delighted, that's all. I love hearing you talk about men."

"This is why I don't," Hannah said. "I've barely said anything and here you are!"

"Here I am, what?"

"Here you are embarrassing me."

"I'm not embarrassing you," Margaret said. "I'm just enjoying having a conversation with my big sister. About sex."

"We haven't even had a conversation, yet," Hannah said.

"So, tell me, Hannah," Margaret said. "When's the last time you did it?"

"When's the last time *you* did it?" Hannah said.

Her driving was becoming herky-jerky, which meant she was exasperated. Margaret felt her own lips twitch.

"Hm," Margaret said. "It's been a while, actually."

"So you have some pent-up—"

"Hannah!"

Hannah laughed. "Let's change the subject, okay?"

---

SARAH, Amelia and Donny arrived that night, bringing as much excitement to Mama Katherine's house as a funeral. When Margaret visited them for Amelia's graduation the week before, she'd known something was off, and it appeared as if things were still tense.

Donny, usually engaging and charismatic, didn't speak more than a couple of words. Amelia, who radiated excitement every time they were all together, was subdued. And Sarah's whole countenance screamed exhaustion.

Margaret didn't have much time to study the trio, though, because her phone rang shortly after they slogged onto the porch. She hoped no one noticed the way she held it just inches from her face to see who was calling, or the way she ducked inside like she was smuggling stolen objects. She waited to answer until she was out of earshot.

"Margaret, this is Sandy from Dr. Rossi's office. Dr. Rossi would like you to come in again. She got some more test results back, and she'd like to discuss them with you."

By now, Margaret had made it into her childhood bedroom. "Um, okay," she said. "Sure. I'm in Wyoming right now, but I can fly back home, no problem."

"Great," Sandy said.

After they made the appointment, Sandy cleared her throat. "Also. Dr. Rossi was wondering if you'd like her to set you up with a mentor."

"A mentor for what?"

Typically, Margaret would be looking around the bedroom, running through the memories the various objects sparked. Would she always be able to envision the trophy on the bookshelf in that corner? The one she'd earned for winning the two-hundred-meter race at the state track meet? And what about the poster Mama Katherine had given her? The one that showed the silhouette of a hiker climbing a mountain: "Determination is power." Over there, on the opposite wall, was the huge picture holder Margaret had filled with photos from high school: junior and senior prom, her sixteenth birthday, the sleepover she'd had with school friends where they gave each other makeovers.

"Well, another—" Sandy cleared her throat again.

Margaret could tell she was nervous, which, in turn, made Margaret nervous.

"Another successful, professional woman who has lost her vision. In case, you know, you have any questions, or just need someone to talk to."

"I appreciate it," Margaret said. "But I think I'll be fine."

"Are you sure?" Sandy said. "We have one patient in particular who we thought would be a good match for you."

It might be a good idea, Margaret thought, but it would only take her feelings of humiliation to another level. Going blind was erasing the confidence and sense of capability Margaret had always felt, and she didn't need an audience for that.

"I'm sure," she said. "Thank you, though."

"Okay," Sandy said. "Dr. Rossi thought you might say that."

"Did she?"

"Yeah," Sandy said. "And she told me to tell you that the offer stands. Any time. You can just call us. Talk to me, and I'll make it happen. Dr. Rossi wanted me to say that a mentor can provide a lot of peace during this—um, this time of transition."

"Hmm," Margaret said.

Somewhere on that picture holder, there was a photo of Margaret driving her first car: a convertible. She was sixteen and grinning at the camera like she owned the world. And she'd really felt like she did. How quickly life could shatter that illusion.

*A mentor probably would be helpful,* Margaret thought, but she wasn't quite ready for that. "I'll get back to you," she said. As an afterthought, she said, "Thank you very much, Sandy. And will you please tell Dr. Rossi I really appreciate her thinking of me?"

When Margaret re-emerged from her bedroom, she could hear Donny and Amelia in the kitchen, chatting at the sink. They'd picked up dish duty, which meant Donny was avoiding Sarah. If he wasn't, then Sarah would be in here, too. Mama Katherine was making tea; Margaret recognized the bight coral shirt she'd been wearing.

None of them noticed Margaret, which gave her the chance to observe—as best she could—for a few moments. Donny and Amelia's movements were quick and efficient. They made a good team, Margaret noticed, as Donny rinsed dishes and handed them to Amelia to put in the dishwasher.

Mama Katherine moved slowly. When she reached into the pantry to get the tea, her arms stayed raised for way longer than necessary. She struggled to get the lid off the teapot—Margaret could tell from the way her posture changed. Donny took it from her, without saying anything, and handed it back after he'd removed the lid.

Margaret cleared her throat, and Mama Katherine jumped. "Margaret! I didn't see you there. Why don't you put some teacups on the tray for us ladies? Oh, and the sugar bowl."

"Sure," Margaret said, hoping her voice didn't betray her panic. Where was the tray? And where was the sugar bowl?

Amelia and Donny were still at the sink.

When Amelia was little, Margaret would whisper to her, "I have a secret mission for you. Go get me another cupcake," and Amelia would run off, snickering, and then return to deliver it, incognito.

Maybe Margaret could do something similar now. Ask Amelia to find the sugar bowl and the tray. But Amelia wasn't a toddler any more. Not only would she think it was bizarre that her aunt was asking her for help in this way, but she'd also wonder if something was wrong. And she wouldn't be afraid to make a big deal out of it in front of the other adults.

Margaret sighed. She knelt down in front of the cupboards where she remembered the tray being, and opened the doors. Using her hands, she searched for the tray. There were a few baking dishes, with their smooth glass sides. And there was a casserole dish, thick and with looped handles and its lid, tucked upside down into its opening. Yes, this was the right place. But where was the tray?

Margaret ran her fingers along the edges of the shelves, hoping she'd feel the cool silver or the intricate handles. But she didn't.

"Whatcha lookin' for, Aunt Margaret?"

Ah. Maybe Amelia could help her, after all.

"I can't find the tea tray."

There was a beat of silence. This couldn't be good.

"You mean … *this* tea tray?" Amelia said.

Of course, Margaret couldn't tell what Amelia was pointing at or referring to. She just laughed and shrugged.

"Oh! I don't know how I didn't see it."

"Huh," Amelia said. "I don't, either."

Then she stood up and walked away, leaving Margaret in the same predicament she'd been in a moment ago. Margaret had a thought: maybe Mama Katherine had already set the tray on the counter. She lifted her hands and placed them there, and sure enough, her fingertips bumped against the tray. Perfect. Now where was the sugar bowl?

"Here you go," Donny said.

He plunked the sugar bowl down on the tray, and Margaret smiled at him with way more gratitude than the gesture was probably worth.

"Thank you," she said. Then she turned and started walking towards the living room.

"Um, Margaret?" Donny said. "Aren't you forgetting something?"

"Huh?" she turned around slowly, taking extra care not to tip the sugar bowl right off the tray.

"Aren't you supposed to bring cups?"

"Oh," Margaret said.

Now she was flustered. She could walk back into the kitchen and hope to find them by feel, stacked helter-skelter amongst the coffee mugs. Or she could retrieve Sarah and have her get the cups. Or, she thought as she heard clinking sounds coming from the kitchen, she could wait and Donny would bring them to her.

"You're such a gentleman," she said. "I was just thinking my hands were full and it might be a pain to come get the cups."

He probably gave her a strange look; not that she could see his expression, but they'd known each other for so long that there was pretty much no way he didn't notice something out of the ordinary was going on. But without saying anything, he loaded the cups onto the tray.

"You're good to go," he said.

"Thanks, Donny," Margaret said. Then she turned around, tripped over her own foot, and fell forward. She managed to grip the tray, but she felt the cups and the sugar bowl fly off the front of it as her elbows hit the floor.

Surprisingly, she didn't hear the hard sounds of anything breaking —everything must have shot straight onto the carpet. Donny was at her side, then, and judging by the proximity of his voice, he was kneeling down next to her. "Are you okay?"

"I'm fine," she said, getting up slowly. She held up the tray. "Saved the tray."

"Well, you did do that," he said.

Out of habit, her eyes cast about for the cups she'd dropped. Of course, she couldn't make them out against the carpet. She stood there dumbly waiting for Donny to collect everything.

"I guess we're going to need the vacuum," she said.

Mama Katherine, Hannah, and Sarah must not have noticed any commotion, because none of them had come over just yet. But Margaret's face burned as she headed for the closet where Mama stored the vacuum, listening as Donny collected the cups.

And to think this was only the beginning. Things were only going to get worse from here. Margaret stifled a sob as she reached for the vacuum, and then took a deep breath as she wheeled it back to the scene of the disaster.

She'd been hoping Donny would take it from her, and he did. A few moments later, he said, "There. The evidence is gone. I'll refill the sugar bowl for you."

He did, and returned with the tray. "Enjoy your tea."

Did Donny *know*? There was no time to ponder it—everyone was waiting for tea.

# CHAPTER THREE

MARGARET COULDN'T HELP but see the parallel between Mama Katherine's life and her own. Mama Katherine was losing her independence, too—but that was the natural course of things. She was in her mid-eighties. Margaret's independence was being torn from her hands.

It was before five a.m.; Margaret had found an app where she could get her phone to speak to her—to tell her the time at the press of a button. She couldn't sleep. It was late enough now that she might as well get up and start the coffee.

When she went to lift the coffee pot off the machine, it was already hot.

"Could't sleep?" Mama Katherine's voice startled Margaret, and she jumped.

Once she recovered, she grunted.

"There's a mug next to the pot. Left side."

Margaret reached out and found it, and mumbled her thanks. Then she made her way to the table and sat down. Normally, she'd sit right across from Mama Katherine, but the light was too dim for her to tell where that was.

"You couldn't sleep, either?" she said.

Mama Katherine sighed. "It's another gift of old age. I wake up with the sun. Or sometimes, before the sun. I could stay in bed, toss and turn, but I realized a few months ago that getting up is a better option."

"And then you sit here alone?"

Mama Katherine chuckled. "You know, when you girls were

younger, I would have given anything for a moment of peace and quiet. Just one day to drink my morning coffee in silence. Or even near-silence. But now that it's just me and Hannah here, I miss those days. I really do. I loved raising you girls."

"I loved being here," Margaret said. "From that very first day when you helped me cook that green tomato."

"Ah, yes," Mama said. "The green tomato. The look on your face after you'd picked it, that nearly broke my heart."

Now Margaret chuckled. "Poor little waif that I was."

"You really were," Mama said. Margaret heard her sip her coffee. "It's wonderful having you all under the same roof again."

"And now I'm going to be just as helpless as a six-year-old. Only, I'm approaching forty."

"Oh, nonsense," Mama said. "You're going to be just fine. If anyone can handle this, it's you."

"Not true," Margaret said. "Mama, I met a man."

"What? Is it serious?"

"No!" Margaret said. "No, it's not serious. I just meant, I met a man, at the farmer's market. When I went with Hannah. Now, as you know, this is where I'd gush about how good-looking he was. Or otherwise. But I actually don't know."

"True," Mama said. "But maybe it doesn't matter."

"Of course it matters," Margaret said. "I mean, how can I know whether I'm attracted to someone if I can't get a good look at his eyes or his hands or his shoulders?"

When her memory stirred up the sound of Ethan's voice, though, her body gave an involuntary shiver, and she smiled. Maybe that's how.

"You'll have to rely on your other senses, I guess," Mama said. "Margaret, your life is about to change in ways you probably can't even imagine, yet. But that doesn't mean it's over. Losing your sight is an obstacle. Of course it is. And it's going to require you to have a lot of patience with yourself as you learn to navigate the world in a new way. But it doesn't mean you can't enjoy the same things you've always enjoyed. Men included."

"I can't enjoy sunsets. Or beautiful views."

"No," Mama said. "Certainly not in the same way."

Suddenly, Margaret felt selfish. How could she possibly complain about losing her vision when Mama Katherine was, most likely, facing the end of her life? Mama Katherine was going to say good-bye to everything.

"I'm sorry, Mama," Margaret said. "I know I shouldn't complain. I'm just scared, that's all. But you're right. I'm sure I can handle this. Let's talk about you. What are your plans for the day?"

"Oh, you know," Mama said. "Working in the garden, feeding you girls. That kind of thing. Just enjoying a full house."

*Just enjoying a full house.*

Mama had always been able to put things in perspective. Margaret should practice enjoying the small things. Right now that meant being here, in her childhood home, with her family.

Tomorrow, it meant navigating back to the airport and through downtown Seattle to see Dr. Rossi.

NAVIGATING an airport wasn't as easy as using her other senses. Margaret ended up asking a stranger—a woman with a kind, loud voice that had announced she was going to Seattle—to guide her to the right gate. Then she asked a gate attendant to guide her to the right seat.

Would going blind mean she'd forever have to rely on the kindness of strangers to get from Point A to Point B?

Mama Katherine had always called Margaret, "an independent little cuss," and Margaret had always taken pride in that. But, she reminded herself as the plane lifted off, things change.

During the trip from Cheyenne to Seattle, Margaret dozed off. When she did, she dreamed of her first mama.

It was nighttime, and the two of them had just woken up. The last of the light was leaving the sky, draining down toward the horizon like water being drained from a pot.

"How would you like to move, Margaret?" Mama said.

She was lying on her back, looking up at the ceiling.

"Move?"

"Yeah. To a different apartment. Or a different town. Or a different state."

"Could we move to a different planet?"

Margaret's mama laughed. "No. Maybe by the time you're an adult, people will be able to travel between planets. But not right now."

"Do *you* want to move, Mama?"

Now, Margaret's mama turned on her side and looked at Margaret. They shared the same intense green eyes, the same curly black hair.

Margaret, Mama said, got her freckles from her dad. But Margaret had never met him.

"I don't know, Margaret."

Margaret thought about Mr. Jingles and the tree with the beautiful leaves. She thought about Mama and her visitors and the way she always seemed agitated just before they arrived.

"Why would you want to move?"

"Just a change of scenery, I guess. Sometimes a change of scenery is exactly what the soul needs."

Margaret startled awake when the flight attendant announced they were starting their descent. She wasn't sure whether she'd been dreaming or remembering. Margaret and her mother hadn't moved.

Her words, though—*sometimes a change of scenery is exactly what the soul needs*—echoed with such clarity now. Margaret didn't remember much about Life Before Mama Katherine, but there were these moments, moments when her first mama had given her what she now thought of as sage advice.

And maybe that *was*. There was nothing like losing your vision to create a change of scenery.

---

"AFTER HAVING a look at your test results," Dr. Rossi said, "it looks like your disease is progressing quickly."

Margaret thought—but didn't say—that she could have stayed in Wyoming and received this news by phone.

"I know what you're thinking," Dr. Rossi said. "You're thinking you could have stayed in Wyoming and received this news by phone."

"Ha," Margaret said. "That's exactly what I was thinking. How did you know?"

"Your expression gave it away."

And there was yet another adjustment Margaret would have to make: she wouldn't be able to read expressions. She'd have to listen to tone of voice and emphasis.

"Well, you're spot on."

"I wanted to talk to you about meeting with a mentor," Dr. Rossi said.

"Yeah," Margaret said, drawing the word out. "Sandy mentioned that when she called to set up this appointment. I appreciate it. I really do. I think I can manage just fine on my own."

"I know you can," Dr. Rossi said. "I have complete confidence that you can manage on your own. I just want to make the transition as easy as possible for you. And I believe having a mentor will do that. I'm sure Sandy told you, we have a specific patient in mind. In fact, I reached out to her, and she said she'd be happy to talk with you. Why don't you schedule a coffee date?"

"A coffee date? You've got to be kidding. And then what? I walk into a crowded coffee shop and try to find a woman I can't see?"

Dr. Rossi sighed. Margaret imagined she wore an exasperated expression, lips pressed together.

"I understand it's intimidating," she said. "But you're going to have to do it eventually. You're going to have to meet people, order food, go places. Other patients who have met with mentors have been very successful at doing all of these things. They've become confident more quickly."

"I think I'll just stay home and use the Internet to meet people," Margaret said. "Come to think of it, I can order food online, too."

"Your choice," Dr. Rossi said. "Please let me know if you change your mind. Meanwhile, Sandy and I have put together a folder and an audio file for you. Both files contain the same information. We like to give patients the hard copies in case their families want to read up on the resources. Sandy can help you load the audio to your phone. Once you've gone through everything, we can help you get started."

"Get started?"

"You'll hear in the audio that there are schools you can go to, trainings you can complete. Mobility training, for one, so you can still get out and about. You may want to learn Braille. And there are special devices you can use with your computer. You may want to learn how to set those up."

As Margaret made her way down the hall between the exam room and the entrance, Sandy caught up with her and pressed a folder into her hands.

"I've already emailed you the audio file," she said. "You can listen to it from there."

Margaret nodded. "Thank you, Sandy."

She was tempted to throw the folder in the trash can she knew stood outside the door, but she refrained. She'd told Dr. Rossi that she would manage, but the truth was, she didn't know if she could.

# CHAPTER FOUR

Margaret had never been a secret-keeper. She was terrible at it. Her expression always gave her away. In fact, her sisters had learned early on to keep her in the dark about any secret plans until the last minute.

But as she was quickly learning, some things changed. A couple of days had passed since her most recent visit with Dr. Rossi, and she was back in Wyoming.

She sat down to breakfast with her sisters, Amelia, and Mama Katherine, and Amelia proposed what she obviously thought was a great idea.

"I think we should have a Fourth of July party."

Her voice was infused with enthusiasm, and everyone else seemed to approve. But fear flooded Margaret's veins right away.

"I don't know," Margaret said. She poked a piece of pancake and swirled it in her syrup.

Hannah and Mama Katherine said, "Well, I think it's a great idea."

Margaret, struggling to find a solid reason why she, the Queen of Parties, didn't want to have a party, said, "It just seems like a lot of work, is all."

"But, Aunt Margaret," Amelia said, "you're, like, the queen of parties."

"I know," Margaret said. "I know I am. But there's just so much to do around here."

"Has an alien Aunt Hannah taken over your body?" Amelia said.

"Body swap," Hannah said. Her tone said she was trying to sound like she was joking, but it didn't quite get there.

"No," Margaret said. "It *is* a great idea. It's just—it's a great idea. Let's do it. It'll be fun. And Farmer Eddie can come."

"It doesn't have to be big," Mama Katherine said. "We'll just invite Eddie, and the Suttons, and maybe a few other families. And that's it. Okay?"

"And Donny, Amelia, and I will do most of the work," Sarah said. "Okay? You just be here, sharing that sparkling personality with all of our guests."

"Okay," Margaret said. She looked at each of them in turn, giving them a smile she hoped was at least somewhat convincing.

ONCE THE BRADLEY sisters started planning a party, there was no stopping them. The excitement level began to build, to the point where Margaret couldn't help but feel infected by it. When Hannah said she was going to the farmer's market to buy party supplies— locally brewed beer and handmade flower pots—Margaret volunteered to ride along. She told herself it was because she wanted to help Hannah, not because she wanted to run into Ethan again. Then she told herself to stop lying to herself.

Hannah, driving them to the market in Mama Katherine's old truck, said, "You're hoping to run into that—what was his name? Larry? Leroy? Aren't you?"

"What?" Margaret asked, all innocence.

"Don't pretend like you don't remember meeting him the last time we were there."

Margaret smiled, and Hannah said, "I knew it!"

They rode in silence for a few minutes, and then Hannah said, "Are you okay, Margaret?"

"What? Of course. What do you mean?"

"I mean, you're acting really strangely. You're uncharacteristically quiet. You don't want to have this Fourth of July party. That's not like you."

"I'm just worn out, is all. I've been working a lot, you know. Life has been just nonstop. I was looking forward to some rest and relaxation."

"Are you sure?" Hannah said. "It seems like more than that. It's not just the party."

Even while Margaret was thinking that Hannah was very astute, and she was going to have to tell her about the blindness soon, she said, "I'm fine. Promise."

"Well, okay," Hannah said. "But if there really is something else, you can talk to me about it. You know that, right?"

Margaret nodded, thinking of the countless times she'd confided in her oldest sister: when she lost her first tooth and then misplaced it, and thought Mama Katherine would be mad and the Tooth Fairy wouldn't come; when, at seven, she broke the sugar bowl Mama Katherine bought at a street fair in Mexico; the time she'd thought she was pregnant—it had turned out to be a false alarm.

And every time, Hannah had been the perfect confidant. Although she did have a tendency to go worst-case-scenario, taking action to fix a problem seemed to soothe her. She never panicked or tattled. She always listened calmly, and usually came up with a solid plan of action to right the situation. She'd coached Margaret on how to draw a picture of her tooth for the Tooth Fairy, and write a note to go with it. They'd walked through the apology speech Margaret would make about the sugar bowl. And without batting an eye, Hannah had driven them to the store to buy a pregnancy test before Margaret went into panic mode.

"Right," Margaret said. "Thank you."

She wanted to reach over and give Hannah's hand a squeeze, but the best she could manage was a quick pat on the leg, which probably seemed sarcastic. Hannah didn't say anything about it.

"So," Margaret said. "What are we buying today, besides beer and flower pots?"

Hannah cleared her throat. "Salad stuff. And that's it. And I was hoping we'd run into Leroy. For your sake."

Margaret felt an involuntary smile lift the corners of her mouth, and she didn't try to stifle it. "Well, let's find out."

Margaret had always believed in serendipity. But it was a lot easier to take advantage of serendipity when your vision cooperated. She stuck close to Hannah, who led her between rows of white tents in search of the perfect garlands to use as decorations for the Fourth of July party and the perfect greens for the salad. And she perked her ears, hoping to catch the sound of Ethan's voice.

The last time she'd met him, he was buying salad supplies, too. Maybe he'd be at one of the booths where they sold spinach or kale or lettuce. It was almost certain that if Hannah saw him, she'd say something. That assumption, Margaret thought, was based on past behavior. A memory—one saturated with embarrassment—came rushing in.

"Hey, Hannah," Margaret said. "Remember Tucker Brown?"

Beside her, Hannah snorted. "Of course I do. You talked about him continuously for eons."

"Eons? Really?"

"Okay, not eons. But for months, it seemed like."

"Remember that time we saw him at the drug store?" Margaret said.

As she'd expected her to, Hannah laughed. "Boy, do I. You were so mad at me."

"Not really. I was exaggerating."

"No," Hannah said. "You were mad."

"Well, you practically announced, right then and there, that I had a crush on him."

"You should have been thanking me."

"You humiliated me!" Margaret said. Hannah shushed her. "Well, you did."

"Why are you laughing?"

"It's funny, now. Twenty-something years later, whatever it is. I was embarrassed. Humiliated. We were shopping for anti-diarrheal medicine for Sarah, remember?"

"Oh," Hannah said. "I remember."

"And Mama Katherine sent us into the store to get it while she waited in the car with Sarah. And as we walked down the aisle, you're saying, loudly, 'Now where would the diarrhea medicine be?' Remember that?"

Margaret imagined Hannah's expression: eyes crinkling at the corners and lips pursing the way they did when she was amused.

"I remember," Hannah said.

"And then—"

"We spotted him," Hannah said. "Tucker Brown. The subject of many late-night conversations. The protagonist in countless made-up love stories."

Now Margaret was hysterical. "And you said—"

Here and now, it wasn't Hannah's voice that finished the sentence. It was a deep and rumbly voice, one tinged with humor: "What do we have here?"

Margaret and Hannah responded simultaneously.

"Ethan," Margaret said.

"Leroy," Hannah said. "How did you know? That's exactly what I said."

Ethan laughed. The sound was husky, and made Margaret shiver.

For just an instant, arousal took over, but then the hysteria consumed her again.

"Geez," Ethan said. "If I'd realized I was so funny, I would have become a standup comedian."

"It's not you," Margaret said. Her voice came out in a squeal.

Hannah said, "We were reliving one of Margaret's most embarrassing moments from junior high."

"Ah," Ethan said. "That's a brutal time."

Margaret had regained her composure, and she kept it with no small effort as she said, "Tucker Brown."

She hoped Hannah wouldn't elaborate, because Ethan seemed like a smart guy and would probably put two and two together and realize he was Margaret's modern-day Tucker Brown. But apparently, Hannah couldn't resist.

"And you should have seen Margaret's face," Hannah said. "It was bright red. She must have felt like she was on fire."

Margaret shook her head. "I'm sure it's just as red now, as it was then."

"Not quite," Hannah said, elbowing Margaret. "But close."

"You're still beautiful, though," Ethan said.

That silenced Hannah, and Margaret, too.

"You know," Hannah said. "I'll just leave you two here for a minute. I just spotted some flower pots over there."

She patted Margaret's arm and was gone.

"*That* was pretty embarrassing," Margaret said. She turned away from Ethan and began running her hands over the base of a lamp on the table next to her. It had a beautiful silhouette.

"Margaret," Ethan said, "will you have dinner with me?"

Margaret wanted to say, "Yes. A resounding yes. Yes, a hundred times over."

But she froze. Having dinner with a man—a stranger—when she couldn't see made her feel vulnerable. What if he was a murderer? What if he asked her to go for a walk after dinner, and he led her straight into the woods and killed her? Well, obviously that was ridiculous. Murderers did not hang out at the farmer's market and make highfalutin salads for their parents. But what if he offered her a bite of his food, and she didn't even realize what was happening? What if she made a mess of her own meal because she couldn't see? She'd always been comfortable in dating situations, but now, fear gripped her.

Where she'd normally say, "Yes," this time, she said, "Wow. You cut right to the chase."

Then she wondered whether that was a nice thing to say.

Ethan chuckled. "I didn't know how long we'd be alone together."

"You were afraid my big sister wouldn't approve?"

"Of course she'd *approve*," Ethan said. "I was afraid she'd want me for herself, and a fight would break out between the Bradley sisters, right here at the farmer's market."

"Huh," Margaret said.

"What's happening, here?" Hannah said. So, she was back.

"This very nice, highfalutin man has just asked me to dinner," Margaret said. "And he's afraid you'll want him for yourself and the two of us will get into some sort of catfight, right here. And probably, I'll hit you with this lamp."

"Obviously, that's true," Hannah said. "And what a shame to ruin that beautiful lamp. But you know what, Margaret? Since I ruined your chances with Tucker Brown when you were in the seventh grade, I will step aside now and let you have dinner with Leroy. And if, for some reason, things don't work out between you, I'll go ahead and have dinner with him, next."

"It's settled, then," Ethan said. "How about next weekend?"

"Oh!" Margaret said. "I'm not sure I'll—"

"You'll still be here," Hannah said. "That's right after the Fourth of July party."

"Let me get your digits," Ethan said.

Margaret assumed he was pulling out his phone, and she hoped she waited an appropriate amount of time before rattling off her phone number.

"I'll call you," Ethan said.

Again with the shivers, Margaret thought. She did love the sound of his voice. And judging by the (very limited) time they'd spent together thus far, it would be nice to spend a whole evening with him. There had a be a way to do it. Blind people dated all the time, right?

She put out a hand to shake Ethan's, and he took it. But he didn't shake it. Instead, he pulled her in for a hug. At first, her body stiffened with surprise, but after that initial shock wore off, she relaxed into his arms. He smelled good, like pine trees and soap and outside. And even though he held her gently, his body was rock hard. *Wow.*

Before she realized what was happening, she was hugging him back. Hannah cleared her throat. Margaret giggled. Ethan released her.

"Well," Margaret said, resisting the urge to straighten her shirt. "I guess we'd better go."

Ethan's husky laugh rang out behind them as they made their way to the parking lot.

"Well," Hannah said, once they were on the road. "You two certainly took care of a lot of business while you were alone."

Her voice sounded the tiniest bit disapproving, and not for the first time, Margaret wondered what went on in Hannah's own love life.

"And that's just the start of it," Margaret said in what she hoped was a raunchy tone. "You didn't leave us alone for very long."

"Ha," Hannah said.

"Why do you have that tone of voice?" Margaret said.

"What tone of voice?"

"You know."

There was a long pause, and Margaret imagined Hannah shrugging a shoulder. Then Hannah let out her breath and said, "I don't know. You just met the guy, that's all. And you're going to have dinner with him."

"And?" Margaret said.

"And, I don't know. I mean, it seems kind of sudden. What if he's a creeper?"

"What if he isn't? He seems like a perfectly nice guy."

"What if—"

"Hannah," Margaret said. She held up a hand to stop her. "When is the last time you went on a date?"

"What?"

"You heard me."

"I don't know. Um—"

"You know," Margaret said.

Hannah laughed, high and breathy.

"I know that laugh," Margaret said. "You're embarrassed to say. How long has it been? A month? Six months? A year?"

The sounds of the truck's engine, the tires on the road, the air rushing past the cab, filled the space where Hannah's answer should have been.

Finally, after a mile or two had passed (by Margaret's estimation, anyway), Hannah said, "I don't know."

"You don't?"

"I mean," Hannah said, "I actually can't remember. This is the end of June. And I remember meeting a guy during the school year. Must have been early in the school year. Maybe even September."

"And?" Margaret said.

"And we went on a weekend date," Hannah said. "We went on a hike and had a picnic."

"That sounds lovely," Margaret said. "Did you see him again?"

"Oh, no," Hannah said.

"What? Why not?"

"Oh, I don't know," Hannah said. "He seemed a bit too—a bit too *something* for me. You know?"

"Nope. I don't know. What does that mean?"

"I don't even know," Hannah said. "I think he moved away."

And that was that.

A few more miles passed, and Margaret's phone rang. Of course, without holding the phone inches from her face, she couldn't read the display to see who was calling. So she said, "Oh, I'll call them back," and pressed the button to send the call to voicemail. A few seconds later, her phone signaled that someone had left a message. She used a voice command to check her voicemail, and smiled when she heard the recording: "It's Ethan. I see that you're already avoiding my calls. Now you have my number. Save it. I'll be sending you dirty photos later."

He chuckled, and Margaret ended the call.

"I heard that," Hannah said. "Is he really going to send you dirty photos? Did you guys talk about that?"

"No!" Margaret said. "Learn to take a joke, Hannah. You're far too serious."

Using voice-to-text, she responded: "Got your message. Anxiously awaiting said photos. Make sure the lighting is sufficient."

Hannah gasped, scandalized. Margaret laughed. And her phone dinged with a picture message.

# CHAPTER FIVE

The Fourth of July dawned hot and just one humidity point short of unbearably sticky. Margaret hadn't even gotten out of bed yet, and as she lay there, the sheets clinging to her skin, she felt a strong sense of dread. She wasn't dreading the party itself, she thought, but all the related activity: cleaning, cooking, setting the table. Typically, she loved parties. But she had a feeling she wouldn't get through today—a day they'd spend all together—without revealing her secret.

She'd undoubtedly do something clumsy, something that proved she was losing her vision. And she didn't feel quite ready to admit it. Not to herself, and not to her sisters. What if Dr. Lane and Dr. Rossi were wrong? What if they'd both made a mistake, and she didn't actually have retinitis pigmentosa? This was the kind of thing that happened to someone else. She didn't want to worry Hannah and Sarah until it was absolutely necessary to do so.

She dug the heels of her hands into her eyes and rubbed, hard, wishing some miracle would occur and her vision would clear up.

Maybe she could fake sick and hide in her bedroom all day like she had in second grade. It was the day when all the students had to turn in their family trees. Only, Margaret's family tree looked more like a single stick with a single name on it: hers. Yes, she could use Mama Katherine's name, and Mama Katherine's relatives, but everyone would know they weren't Margaret's ancestors. Some of her friends had already told her what their family trees would look like: lush and complicated, with grandparents, great grandparents, aunts, uncles, cousins, and second cousins. Branches reaching towards the sky.

Margaret wanted so badly to miss school that day that she'd told Mama Katherine she had an upset stomach. Mama Katherine popped a thermometer in her mouth at the breakfast table and then went to gather eggs. While she was outside, Margaret stuck the thermometer into one of the fresh muffins Mama Katherine had left on the counter to cool, and let the mercury rise to one hundred and two.

When Mama Katherine came back in, Margaret held up the thermometer. "A hundred and two."

"Oh!" Mama Katherine said. "You *must* have an upset stomach. Back to bed with you."

Feeling relieved and a bit smug, Margaret had followed instructions. She stayed in bed all day, reading. Mama came in every hour to check on her, and she tried her best to look fatigued. Come to think of it, she'd never admitted to Mama Katherine that she'd faked being sick.

Unfortunately, the kind of schemes that worked at age seven didn't necessarily work when you were in your thirties, Margaret told herself. She'd have to suck it up. Maybe she could get out of being assigned any tough jobs by feigning a headache. That would allow her to keep her secret while still attending the party.

And maybe she'd actually enjoy it.

She got out of bed and stretched, and for some reason, at that moment, her thoughts flashed to Ethan. If things were normal, she might have invited him to join them. But things weren't normal. She put on her shorts, and before heading to the kitchen for coffee, she checked her phone for the time. Eight thirty. She'd overslept. And, speak of the devil, there was a message, in the extra-large font she'd found, from Ethan: *Have a great time at your party today. I'll be thinking of you during the fireworks show. And decide where you want to eat. I'll call you tomorrow to make plans.*

When she realized she was smiling, she said, "Get a grip, Margaret. It's just a text."

Still, several times throughout the day, she found herself grinning as she went about her chores.

Margaret's focus on her own impending misery had made her forget to think about Sarah and Donny's marriage; specifically, the speed at which it was disintegrating. They could be divorced before the end of the year. Yes, Donny had already said he planned to leave Sarah after they took Amelia to college. Margaret losing her vision might be inevitable, but this split wasn't. Not yet, anyway.

Margaret decided she'd enlist Hannah's help, and maybe together, they could reignite the flame. When Mama Katherine assigned Hannah to the task of picking up paper plates, Margaret volunteered to go to the store with her.

"So," Hannah said as soon as they were both in the truck. "What's going on?"

"With what?" Margaret said.

"With you," Hannah said.

"What do you mean?"

"You're acting weird," Hannah said. Then, as if it had just occurred to her, she said, "What was that picture message Leroy sent you?"

"Could you just call him Ethan?"

"Nah. What was it?"

"It was a picture of the cucumber he'd just bought," Margaret said. A bubble of hilarity rose in her throat.

She didn't know why she'd found Ethan's picture so funny, but she had.

And when Hannah said, "Oh, my God. Is he in junior high?" Margaret knew Hannah wouldn't understand, and she also knew she wouldn't be able to explain what she found amusing. She laughed. She couldn't help it. When Hannah didn't join in, Margaret stopped abruptly and changed the subject.

"I'm worried about Sarah," she said.

"What?" Hannah said.

"I think we need to intervene in her marriage."

"Isn't it too late?"

"It's never too late for love, Hannah," Margaret said.

Hannah sighed.

"I'm not talking about you, Hannah."

"It was one of those subconscious, Freudian things," Hannah said. "You guys are always trying to get me to fall in love."

Well, that was true. Margaret shrugged and said, "What do you think we should do?"

"I have an idea," Hannah said.

THE FOURTH of July party was in full swing, and Margaret and Hannah stood next to the outdoor dining table, on surveillance.

"Here," Margaret said, grabbing Hannah's shoulders and turning her toward the grill where Donny was taking care of the steaks. Sarah was supposed to be delivering him a bottle of water. Margaret positioned herself facing Hannah, which served two purposes: first, it would appear that they were engrossed in conversation and second, it would seem natural when Margaret instructed Hannah to give her a play-by-play.

"Oh, my God," Hannah said, her voice barely registering as a whisper. "She's making such a weird face right now. She looks like she has something in her eye."

"Wait," Margaret said. "Did you try to give her flirting lessons again?"

Silence.

"You did, didn't you?" Margaret said. "Hannah! You're terrible at that. Go fix this."

Now Hannah was laughing. "Okay. I'll go fix it. But you have to come over in one minute. Okay? Count to sixty and then come over. Count slowly. You always count too fast."

"Are we in elementary school again?"

Hannah said, "We're acting like it, aren't we?"

"I suppose so," Margaret said. "Okay, go. I'm counting."

Margaret turned around to watch Hannah's shape walk towards the grill. When she got to sixty, she saw that Hannah and Sarah stood some distance from the grill. She finished counting and made her way toward them. As she approached, she heard Sarah say to Hannah, "Okay, but stop watching me. You're making me uncomfortable."

"How can I coach you if I don't watch you?" Hannah said, and Margaret had to bite her lip to keep from laughing.

"Hey, Sarah," Margaret said. "Remember that time when we were in high school, and Hannah wanted to coach me as I flirted with Jackson Riverdale. Remember that?"

Instantaneously, the three of them were laughing, half-collapsed, hands on each other's shoulders.

"That was just awful," Margaret said, her voice a squeal, and Sarah said, "I can't believe you were doing what she said to do! You just followed right along while she marched you to your grave."

"That was downright mean," Margaret said, and Hannah, tears streaming down her face, said, "Well, you used up all my hairspray that morning and I couldn't fix my hair. I was upset."

"You—" Margaret gasped for air, still laughing. "You humiliated me."

"You deserved it!" Hannah said.

It hadn't been funny at the time—at least, not to Margaret—but within a few days, the three sisters would tell the story for anyone who'd listen. Margaret's face would twist into an angry expression (save for the slight quirk of her mouth) and the other two girls would be in hysterics.

"And she told me to copy everything she did," Margaret would say.

"And then," Sarah would say, her voice a crescendo of hilarity, "she started rubbing her hands all over her body."

Hannah would nod and demonstrate, her hands roaming from her throat to her shoulders to her neck, and then, of course, right down her torso.

"And she just *did* it," Hannah would shriek.

"She was just talking away, to Jackson Riverdale," Sarah would say as Margaret's face became redder and redder. "And rubbing herself."

"Ah," Mama Katherine said now. She had walked up just as Margaret had recreated the body-rubbing moment. "Reliving the Jackson Riverdale experience, are we? Again?"

"Now that's all I'm going to be thinking about when I'm talking to Donny," Sarah said.

"Perfect," Margaret said. "And if you want, I can stand behind him and tell you what to do."

"Oh, please do," Sarah said. "Since apparently Hannah here, expert that she is, thinks I'm failing."

"I don't," Hannah said. "You just seem unnatural, that's all."

"As unnatural as rubbing her hands all over her body while she talks?" Margaret said, putting herself into hysterics again.

"All I can do now is to walk away," Sarah said.

"Just act natural," Mama Katherine said.

This was the kiss of death: all three girls hooted with laughter. Sarah left them and walked back over to where Donny stood at the grill.

Margaret wasn't sure whether their advice had worked until later on that evening.

During dinner, Sarah suggested that they play charades. Sudden silence blanketed the table, and Margaret imagined everyone exchanging shocked looks.

When they were younger, they'd played charades at every family gathering. Sarah and Donny made an awesome team. No one ever wanted to play against them because they seemed to have this deep psychic connection. It was the most fun. Until Sarah became this ultra-serious mom who had to get Amelia to bed right after dinner. It had been years since Sarah had played charades, and even longer since she'd actually enjoyed it.

Truth be told, Margaret had spiked Sarah's beer with tequila tonight. (And Donny's beer, too. And while she was at it, she'd spiked her own.)

But it was still surprising that when Sarah pulled the Romeo and Juliet card, she planted a big, solid kiss on Donny's mouth before plunging an imaginary dagger into her heart. Margaret watched the whole blurry scene play out, and she felt happy tears filling her eyes when everyone else applauded. Then, Sarah topped the night off with a smaller—but equally significant—act: she had a root beer float, which she hadn't done in forever.

Fourth of July party, Margaret thought: Success.

THE MORNING after the Fourth of July party and the epic Romeo-and-Juliet kiss, Margaret sat with Sarah, Hannah, and Mama Katherine at the kitchen table after breakfast. Since the four of them had cooked, Donny and Amelia went outside to feed the chickens and collect eggs. As soon as the door shut behind them, Margaret asked Sarah if Donny had said anything about the kiss.

When Sarah said he hadn't, Margaret felt her own eyes go round, and she imagined everyone else's did, too.

"He didn't say a word?" Margaret said.

"Not a word."

"What did you talk about when you took Farmer Eddie home?" Hannah wanted to know.

"Root beer floats, mostly. Alien invasions."

Mama Katherine gave a little chuckle. "You haven't had a root beer float in years."

Sarah said, "Believe me, I heard about it. I don't know what I was thinking."

"Thus, the alien invasion," Margaret said. "A health-conscious alien invaded your body."

"That's right," Sarah said. "I don't take any responsibility for my lapse in root beer float drinking."

"What else did you talk about?" Hannah said.

"Nothing, really," Sarah said. "Do you think I should have brought up the kiss?"

"Let it lie," Mama said.

"Yeah, let it lie," Margaret and Hannah said.

After a beat of silence, Sarah said, "Okay. It just feels strange to not say anything."

"You'll get over it," Hannah said. "Speaking of not saying anything, Margaret, why don't you say something now about all the sneaking around you've been doing?"

Margaret's heart responded right away, beating hard and fast. She sat up very straight. "Me?"

"You're the only Margaret in here," Sarah said.

"You've been sneaking around?" Mama Katherine said.

Even though she'd run out of coffee several minutes ago, Margaret raised her cup to her lips.

"You've never been much good at hiding things," Mama Katherine said. "And you're not getting up from this table until you tell your sisters what's going on. Out with it."

Margaret's expression was always a dead giveaway. She took a fake sip of coffee from her empty cup, and held that cup in front of her face.

"I've got all day," Sarah said.

"Me, too," Hannah said.

"I don't," Mama Katherine said. "You all know I'm going to have to use the toilet soon. I can't go more than an hour without peeing these days. Ah, the joys of getting old."

"It's nothing," Margaret said. "I don't want to worry you."

"So it *is* something," Hannah said. "Otherwise you wouldn't be worried about worrying us."

Sarah said, "Good point," and Margaret said, "Well, that's true."

"Go on, then," Mama Katherine said.

"Well, they're not sure, exactly," Margaret said. It was a white lie.

"Who aren't?" Sarah and Hannah said at the same time.

"The doctors," Margaret said. "I've got to get a third opinion."

"A third opinion about what?" Sarah said.

Margaret looked at the tabletop. "Dr. Lane, my eye doctor, thinks I may have retinitis pigmentosa."

"What's that?" Hannah said. "Is this the part where we should get worried?"

"Probably," Margaret said, her voice cracking just the tiniest bit. "I am."

"What is it?" Sarah said.

Margaret took another deep breath, then looked at each of them in turn before saying, "I'm going blind."

The sequence of events that followed Margaret's announcement made her wish she'd kept her impending blindness a secret forever, even though she knew that was impossible. Rooms went quiet whenever she entered. Her sisters went out of their way to help her, pulling out chairs, dishing up food, and talking way too loudly, as if an increase in volume would help her navigate their world.

It's not that she didn't appreciate the sentiment, but each of these small things felt like one step down the side of a slippery slope; one where she'd wind up depending on everyone else for every need. Pretty soon, someone would be in the bathroom with her, tearing the toilet paper off the roll.

One morning just after the Fourth of July party, Margaret woke up to a quiet house. After having her coffee, she wandered outside to find everyone. She heard voices coming from the direction of Sarah and Donny's RV, and walked that way.

When she approached the open door—she could see the gray smudge in the middle of the white siding—she heard Mama Katherine talking.

"It's a solid idea. I think it's going to take some convincing, though. I think Sarah's right that Margaret will want to start researching as soon as possible."

Margaret found herself thinking, *What in tarnation?* even though she hadn't used that phrase in ages. It was one of Mama Katherine's, one that Margaret herself had ditched when she moved away from podunk Wyoming. She stopped, several yards from the RV, and listened as Mama kept talking.

"You're right that she's adventurous, Hannah," Mama Katherine said, "but still, I think it's going to be tough to get her to agree to taking a kind of vacation when she's going to want to dive right into the learning and planning. We'll just have to bring it up to her and see what she says."

A vacation? What was going on, here? Margaret decided that since this conversation was obviously about her, she should join in.

As she climbed up the RV steps, she said, "Wow, is there a party going on in here? I didn't get an invitation."

She motioned for Hannah to scoot over. As she sat down at the dinette, she could practically feel her mom and sisters holding their collective breath.

"Wait," Margaret said. "I know what's going on, here. This is a pity party, and I'm the guest of honor."

"Well, there's no time like the present," Hannah said to Sarah and

Mama Katherine. "Don't look alarmed, Margaret. We just wanted to talk to you about something."

Margaret put her head in her hands. "Bunch of busybodies. But I do love you."

"So," Hannah said, "Sarah thinks we need to focus on the practicalities. Like where you're going to live and whether you want a guide dog."

Margaret wanted to say that she had a home and the last thing she needed was a guide dog, but instead, she pressed her lips together.

"And Hannah," Sarah said, "Wants to go on a road trip. To give you a chance, to, you know, see nature's beauty."

"Awesome stuff," Hannah said. "Nature's awesome stuff."

"Right," Sarah said.

Margaret was stunned. She looked from one sister to the other, her mouth open. "You guys. I really appreciate the gesture. I do. I am beyond grateful you want to be involved, here. But right now, we're not even sure what's going to happen. I may not even be able to see nature's awesome stuff. It might be a waste of time. And you're both so busy."

"Not true," both Sarah and Hannah said at the same time. Hannah said, "I'm still on summer break."

"And I just have to take Amelia to school and then I'm fixing to be a single woman, so…"

"And I've got nothing but time," Mama Katherine said. "As you know. Besides. You know your sister won't leave me home alone, anyway. And didn't the doctor tell you that you'd have good days and bad? Nature's lighting is great stuff."

"You guys don't have to do this," Margaret said. "I'm perfectly capable of getting this all figured out on my own. I don't want to stress you out."

"I'm not stressed," Sarah said. "Are you, Hannah?"

"I'm not stressed," Hannah said. "Are you, Mama?"

Mama Katherine chuckled. "No. I'm not, either. That's settled."

"But you all have things to do," Margaret said.

"Nothing as important as this," Hannah said.

When Sarah didn't speak, Margaret pinned her with a direct stare. "I'll go," she said. "But, Sarah, you have to patch things up with Donny before we leave."

"Fine," Sarah said. "I will. So. When do we leave?"

"Give me a week," Margaret said, not because she needed more time, but because she was formulating a plan of her own.

"You always have been an independent little cuss," Mama Katherine said.

The words they didn't say—that Margaret couldn't do much of this on her own, that her independence was already slipping through her fingers—hung in the air, even louder than the ones they did.

***

BEFORE ANY LEAVING TOOK PLACE, Margaret had a date to go on. She had dated—a lot. Why, then, was she nervous about this date with Ethan? Was it because she was losing her vision? Was it because he was different from the other guys she'd dated? Was it because she was in her home state again?

She told herself she shouldn't be nervous—this was probably a one-time deal, and it was very unlikely that she'd see Ethan again, ever.

In the bathroom of her childhood home, Margaret applied mascara. With all the lights turned on, and the bright afternoon sun filtering through the window, she could see just well enough. Going through the ritual of preparing for a date, it was hard not to remember the romantic ventures of her youth.

Jackson Riverdale—the one who'd been the unfortunate spectator to Margaret's rubbing her hands all over her body at Hannah's direction—ended up being a sweet guy and the first one to pick Margaret up in his parents' car when they were both sixteen ("A real date!" Sarah had said as she sat on the edge of the tub, watching Margaret get ready. "Can you believe it?").

As an adult, Margaret's constant traveling for work meant she'd met men in almost every major city in America. It was just for fun, to provide herself with company and find great new hot spots, approved by locals in each destination.

She'd developed a kind of rhythm for these trysts: she'd select an outfit, which was an almost-scientific process. The shirt should bring out the green in her eyes and be appropriately cosmopolitan for whatever city she was in. The pants should accentuate her curves and be comfortable enough that she could eat a burger and fries without feeling like she would pop off the button. And the shoes should make a statement. What that statement was depended on her mood. They might say, "Don't even think about it, Mister." Or they might say, "I'm a sex kitten." Margaret chuckled now, remembering the time in

Cincinnati when she'd wondered which pair of shoes said, "Tread lightly. I'm on my period."

After outfit selection, Margaret laid her clothes out in the bathroom. Then she'd shower, and apply a body cream with a light scent. These days, city guys had countless sensitivities, and she didn't want to send one home with his eyes watering from a strong perfume. She'd get dressed, hair in a towel, and then put on her makeup before drying her hair with a diffuser.

But this evening was different.

Truth be told, she hadn't anticipated dating while she was here. She hadn't packed any shoes that had anything even remotely sexy to say. Never mind the clothes. There had to be some rule against wearing a plaid shirt on a first date. And now, here she was, in the bathroom in one of Mama Katherine's robes, putting on makeup before getting dressed. She'd already thrown off the rhythm of this evening, and it hadn't even started.

Maybe Amelia had something she could borrow, she thought. Her niece had been spending quite a bit of time with one of the new neighbor boys—Luke—and she'd brought most of her clothes on this trip since she was heading to college afterward.

Margaret followed the sounds of Amelia's laughter to the kitchen. The evening sunlight streamed in through the window, and Margaret could make out the silhouettes of two people at the counter. The silhouettes joined, and the laughter ceased. Which shirt was Amelia wearing now? Margaret should borrow it. It seemed to do the trick.

She chuckled to herself, and the sound startled Amelia and Luke, who jumped apart like they'd been caught doing something much more scandalous than kissing.

"Aunt Margaret!"

"Hi, guys," Margaret said. "Whatcha doing?"

Amelia said, "Um, we're just—"

"Getting some lemonade," Luke said.

"Is that what they're calling it these days?" Margaret said.

Amelia laughed.

"I've come to you for help," Margaret said.

"Us?" Amelia said.

"Well, you, specifically," Margaret said. "I don't think Luke has a date-worthy shirt I can borrow."

"You're going on a date?" Amelia said.

"Stop squealing," Margaret said. "I didn't say I was getting married or adopting a puppy or anything."

"Tell me about him," Amelia said.

Margaret sighed. This wasn't going to be as simple as she'd hoped. And she hadn't left time in her schedule for talking.

"I'll tell you while we walk," she said, linking her arm through Amelia's. "I'm going to be late."

"Luke," Amelia said, "We're on a mission. I'll be right back."

They started walking towards the back of the house, and Amelia said, "Okay, Aunt Margaret. Dish."

Margaret told Amelia about how she'd met Ethan at the farmer's market, and how Hannah had said he was good-looking. It was fun, she thought, now that Amelia was old enough to understand the humor in the situation—including Ethan sending the picture of the cucumber.

"He sounds fun," Amelia said. "I think you'll have a great time. But what if you like him?"

"What if I do?" Margaret said.

"I mean, you're not planning to stay here, are you?"

"No," Margaret said. "But I can like a man for an evening, can't I? That doesn't mean I've got to marry him."

"Do you think you'll ever get married, Aunt Margaret?"

"Nah," Margaret said. "I'm an independent woman."

*Or, I was.*

"Speaking of that," she said, filling the silence. "Do you think I could talk you into being my driver tonight? Maybe you could drop me off at the restaurant and pick me up a couple of hours later?"

Within thirty minutes, Margaret had put on a coral tank top and matching sandals, and Amelia was stopping the pickup truck alongside the curb in front of the restaurant.

"Is that him, sitting on the bench next to the entrance?" Amelia wanted to know.

"Does he have a deep, rumbly voice and a great sense of humor?" Margaret said, unbuckling her seatbelt.

"Judging by the plaid shirt and the huge beard," Amelia said, "yes. He does."

Margaret froze, her hand on the door handle.

"He does not have a plaid shirt," she said. "Or a big beard."

"No," Amelia said. "He doesn't. I was totally kidding. He has a short beard. Manly. Anyway. You'd better go. He's standing up. He's really tall. He's coming this way."

Margaret's door opened, and Ethan grabbed her hand to help her down.

"Wow," he said. "You've got your own chauffeur. Is that because you plan to get drunk and take advantage of me in the bathroom?"

Margaret could hear Amelia cackling as Ethan shut the door. The truck pulled away.

"Very funny," Margaret said. "That's my niece, Amelia. She wanted to use the truck tonight, and she asked if she could drive me. She'll be back in three hours, which means she'll know if you kidnap me."

"Smart," Ethan said. "You look beautiful this evening."

"Why, thank you," Margaret said. "I'm relieved you're not wearing a plaid shirt."

"A gentleman never wears a plaid shirt on a first date. Next time, though."

She didn't bother telling him there wouldn't be a next time. She was enjoying herself too much already. He'd chosen Jack's, a casual but upscale steakhouse, and as they entered, she could smell fresh bread baking.

"I've always loved this place," she said. "But it's been years since I actually ate here. Mama always wants to cook for us, you know?"

"My mom's always demanding that I cook for her," Ethan said. "That's why I couldn't wait to go out."

When they stepped inside, Margaret noticed the restaurant was a bit dark. She worried she wouldn't be able to read the menu. Ethan gave the hostess his name, and just as Margaret was thinking she wouldn't be able to see as they walked between tables, he took her hand and tucked it into the crook of his elbow. Her first reaction was to pull her hand away—the contact seemed a little too intimate for a first date and she didn't want to rely on a stranger to lead her around.

But her second reaction was gratitude. He seemed to know just what she needed. She decided to enjoy this moment. She could feel Ethan's bicep through the soft fabric of his shirt, and following his lead removed some of the stress.

In what Margaret assumed was a stroke of good luck, the hostess sat them at a table right next to the window at the back of the restaurant. Because it was summer in Wyoming, the early evening sun was still bright and provided more than enough light for Margaret to read the menu. She hoped Ethan didn't hear her sigh of relief as she sat down.

"So. What's good?"

"I mean, pretty much everything's good," Ethan said. "Especially this view."

Automatically, Margaret looked towards the window.

"I didn't mean that view," he said. "I meant you."

She smiled. "That's a pretty bad line, coming from someone who claims his name is Ethan and not Leroy. Now, if you were a Leroy, I'd understand."

"What can I say? The first time I first spotted you, I said to myself, 'Now there's a girl who could give me a run for my money.'"

"What does that mean, exactly?"

"With me being so attractive and all, it's hard to find a woman who can measure up."

Margaret didn't know whether to laugh. The very sound of his voice sent feelings zipping around from one corner of her body to the other, which was definitely something. But was he for real?

Now he laughed. "Geez, Margaret. I'm only kidding. You're a deer in the headlights right now. Here's the server. Want wine?"

Amused, Margaret shook her head at him before turning toward the server. "I would love some wine," she said. In this light, she could see the server, as she pulled the cork and poured the wine.

"And for you?" the server said to Ethan.

"Yes, please," Ethan said.

"I was only kidding," he said, again, when the server walked away. "The first time I saw you, I thought you were beautiful. Stunning, actually. And the way you carry yourself, with such confidence. I find that attractive in a woman. Not to mention your sense of humor."

"Yes," Margaret said. She slid her fingers along the top of the table until they touched the base of her wine glass, and then she picked it up and took a sip before adding, "I'm pretty much the whole package."

Ethan asked what she did for a living, and Margaret found herself tacking the phrase, "for now," onto the end of her answer. She'd never done that before, and the words left an empty, hollow feeling in her chest.

"For now?" Ethan said. "Onto bigger adventures?"

"Not exactly," Margaret said. "What about you? What do you do?"

"Pig farmer," he said.

"No you're not," Margaret said.

"No, I'm not. I'm a computer programmer."

"Here? In Timbuktu, Wyoming? Do they even know what computers are in these parts?"

"Ha," Ethan said. "I'm sure they do. But I work remotely. I'm a contractor, and my clients are all over the country. Probably even in your hometown."

"Seattle?"

"Yep," Ethan said. "Blue Sky Systems."

"No way," Margaret said. "I designed the building for their headquarters."

"Small world," Ethan said, and for the first time, Margaret wondered if brushing this off as a casual one-time encounter was a mistake. Maybe they had more in common than she realized. They chatted for several more minutes, and the server came to take their order.

As soon as he walked away, Ethan said, "So, when did you start losing your vision?"

In what was a rare occurrence, Margaret was speechless. Even as she said, "What? How did you—" her thoughts were all over the place. How did he know? Was it that obvious? And if it was, then why did he still want to take her to dinner?

"Never mind," she said then. "I don't really want to talk about it, if that's all right."

"Sorry," Ethan said. "Off limits?"

"Not exactly," Margaret said. "It's just that I haven't even started coming to terms with it, myself. I don't know how to talk about it. It's still new. And even though it's progressing quickly—much more quickly than I'd like—I don't know what it's going to be like."

Her voice cracked, and she realized she was talking about it. She took another sip of her wine.

"You know," he said, "Beethoven was deaf."

"I did know that," Margaret said. "But it's not really the same thing, is it?"

"Isn't it?"

The direction this conversation was taking made Margaret extremely uncomfortable.

"How'd you get into computer programming?"

"Oh, you know," Ethan said, his voice friendly. "I was that goof-off kid in school, hiding out in my bedroom with my computer all day, programming games. For as long as I can remember, I've just been drawn to it. Computers don't ask too many questions. They don't talk back. They don't make fun of your freckles. They don't argue with you, or change plans or deadlines on you. I like that."

"If you don't date women, what are we doing here?"

"Ha," Ethan said. "I date plenty of women. I just prefer the meek ones."

"You do not."

"No, I don't. Anyway. How long are you here for?"

"I haven't decided," Margaret said. "To be honest, I don't know what I'm going to do. Obviously, the city is going to have more resources for me. But I'm scared to navigate a place—even a place I know well—without being able to see it. It's like my own personal horror film: *Seattle in the Dark*."

She'd meant it as kind of a joke, but she realized even as she said it that it was true. She was terrified of living on her own in the city, without being able to see. This time, Ethan didn't laugh, and she wondered why she was opening up to this almost-stranger about her actual feelings. She never did that.

"Anyway. Enough about that. It's depressing."

"Why'd you become an architect?" Ethan said, then.

"I've always been fascinated by beautiful buildings," Margaret said. "Even as a little girl. Mama took us to New York City one summer—I was ten—and we did all the touristy things. We saw the Statue of Liberty, went to Coney Island, visited the Empire State Building. We saw a show on Broadway—Cats. But my favorite part of the trip was just being downtown, you know? In Manhattan. Just standing there on the sidewalk, dwarfed by these huge old buildings. They were big and sturdy, and at the same time, they had all these delicate details. I just couldn't stop looking up. It drove my sisters crazy. Hannah was so busy herding Sarah and I that she didn't see anything. She must have told me, 'Watch where you're going, Margaret,' a million times. And Sarah loved the people watching. But I couldn't get enough of those buildings. And when we got home, I drew them. I drew exact copies, and I changed things up. I drew and drew and drew. And eventually, I started making my own creations. The rest is history."

As she spoke the words, she felt her body going cold. Was her career as an architect history? It was her life. Without it, what would she be? Who would she be? She couldn't even remember what she'd liked or been interested in before that New York trip. Puppies, probably. She felt like she was going to be sick. How was it even possible that the very thing she'd built her life around was going to be taken from her?

"Are you all right?" Ethan's voice was all concern and kindness, which made Margaret feel like she was going to cry.

"I'm fine," she said. "It's just a lot to think about."

Their food arrived and Margaret ate robotically, spearing the salad on her plate with precise movements, removing the spinach and berries and goat cheese from the plate in a clockwise motion. While they ate, Ethan talked. He told her why he'd chosen to remain in small-town Wyoming and how he lived down the street from his parents. She nodded and smiled in all the right places. And even while she felt grateful for this dinner with this very nice man, she couldn't help but feel a little sad that they wouldn't see each other again.

# CHAPTER SIX

MARGARET DIDN'T KNOW why she wanted a third opinion on what was happening with her vision. She trusted both Dr. Lane and Dr. Rossi. Still, she wanted them to be wrong. Both of them. That happened, didn't it? She scheduled an appointment with a Dr. Robert Lincoln in Jackson Hole.

She'd always prided herself on being ultra-efficient, and she used her time in the taxi to carry out the plan she and Amelia had been formulating: an overnight date for Sarah and Donny. A river rafting adventure, a fancy dinner, an expensive bottle of wine and a hotel room with views would almost certainly reignite the romance between the two of them. Margaret felt very self-satisfied when her driver announced they'd arrived at their destination: she'd made rafting and hotel reservations, arranged for a bottle of wine to be delivered to the hotel room, and shared the details with Hannah, Mama Katherine, and Amelia.

She thanked the driver and went inside.

Dr. Robert Lincoln's voice reminded Margaret of a movie character's: deep and self-assured, with strange intonations in strange places.

"Well," he said, drawing out the *L* sound. It was almost comical, the way the room vibrated as she waited for whatever he'd say next. If this had been any other situation, Margaret probably would have laughed. But today, after her third comprehensive eye exam, all she could do was sit in the chair, hands folded tightly together in her lap, and wait.

"Retinitis pigmentosa," he said, finally, his teeth coming together hard on each T sound. The whole phrase was almost musical. "Yes, I'd say it's a textbook case."

He spoke as if this sentence was the opening to some grand piece of classical music, and then he paused, probably for dramatic effect. Margaret closed her eyes. She heard Dr. Lincoln shut her patient folder on his desk, which suggested finality.

"It's a—"

"I know what it is," Margaret said. Her voice escaped in a whisper. "This is the third time I've heard the diagnosis."

"Your third—but—three?"

"Yes," Margaret said. "My first doctor thought that's what it was, and he sent me to a specialist. And she—Dr. Rossi—confirmed my first doctor's suspicion. And now, here we are."

"Here we are," Dr. Lincoln said. "I usually offer a further explanation." He emphasized the last syllable of *explanation*, and Margaret opened her eyes.

"Not necessary," she said. "I've heard it twice, now. And I've done my own research."

"May I offer you some resources?"

That very afternoon, Margaret was back in Walker, Wyoming. She found Sarah and Donny chatting outside, and sauntered up to them, hoping her smile wasn't too smug.

"I have a surprise for you two," she said. "I booked an overnight for you."

Sarah was glaring at Margaret; Margaret could just feel it.

"Didn't you tell her—" Donny said. His voice trailed off. Margaret knew he was talking about the road trip.

"Oh, I told her," Sarah said.

"She told me," Margaret said. "But one of my final wishes is for you two to spend an overnight together. I'd like to see you together one last time. That's why you're leaving tomorrow morning."

"You're not on your deathbed," Sarah said. "I'm not sure it works like that."

"My vision is on its deathbed," Margaret said. "It absolutely works like that. Because I said so."

Donny cleared his throat. "Where is this overnight?"

"What about our road trip?" Sarah said.

"We'll go after. Your overnight is in Jackson Hole. Just a hop, skip, and a jump from here. I rented you a car. And I booked a hotel room.

And a river rafting experience. You'll be back before our road trip. And it's all nonrefundable, so…"

"We have to go," Donny said. "Or *you* have to go."

"I already gave your names for the reservation. I used your credit card. There is no turning back."

"Wait. You used my credit card?" Donny said.

"Just to hold the reservation. I stole it out of your wallet. I'll give you cash to pay for everything."

Margaret pulled the card and several hundred-dollar bills out of her pocket and held them up. "This is to pay for the room when you get there. And the rafting."

Donny had always had a soft spot for Margaret, and she knew it. She was using that to her advantage right now, grinning up at him as sweetly as she could.

Now Donny said to Sarah, "Did you know about any of this?"

"Nope."

After handing Donny the wad of cash, Margaret waltzed into the house. She squeezed her body into her favorite childhood hiding spot, the coat closet, and listened. Sure enough, Sarah came scurrying in a few seconds later.

"Impossible," she said to herself. "She's like a ghost."

Margaret heard her walking quietly from room to room.

"She did this on purpose," Sarah said.

Still, the two of them embarked on their overnight date without any arguments, which Margaret took as a sign things were improving. Based on the direction her own life was taking, though, she should have anticipated the event would end in disaster.

None of them heard from Sarah and Donny all day, and Margaret hoped that meant they were engaging in deep, healing conversations, or that they'd pulled off the side of the road to perform marital duties. This thought had her chuckling several times throughout the day.

Then it happened: just about eleven p.m., Margaret was slipping into bed to listen to a book (and wait up for Amelia, who was out with Luke) when she heard the front door open.

She felt a little self-satisfied, thinking all was well: Amelia was back by curfew, and now Margaret could go to sleep. There was a quiet knock on the door, and, assuming it was Amelia coming to report on her evening, Margaret said, "Come in."

She saw immediately that there were two bodies in the doorway, and she pulled the covers over her chest.

"Aunt Margaret."

Amelia's voice was strained.

"What's wrong?"

"I don't want to alarm you," Amelia said, "but I hurt my arm. I think it's broken."

(*Oh, thank goodness*, Margaret thought. For a moment she'd feared an unplanned pregnancy, and what better time to announce it than when Amelia's parents were gone?) "What?"

"I fell off Lucky Charm. The horse."

"We went for a nighttime ride," Luke said.

He sounded nervous, which Margaret found endearing.

"I thought we could wait 'til morning to go to the doctor, because Aunt Hannah's asleep. But Luke made me tell you."

"It's bad," Luke said. "It's at a weird angle. It doesn't look right."

Margaret sighed, already dreading Sarah's reaction. She'd been reluctant to leave Amelia in the first place.

"Don't call Mom," Amelia said. "I don't want to ruin their date."

Margaret sighed again, her wheels turning. "Okay," she said.

Amelia flew to Margaret's side and hugged her with one arm. "Thank you, Aunt Margaret. *Thank* you. They're finally on a date and I don't want to ruin it. This is no big deal, it'll be fine. We'll just go to town in the morning."

"I think we'd better go in now," Margaret said.

"That's what I told her," Luke said.

"But—"

"Go get Aunt Hannah."

"But—"

"Go get her," Margaret repeated, hoping her voice sounded mom-like an authoritative. It must have, because Amelia climbed off the bed and walked out.

"Shit," Margaret said, to herself more than anyone else. As Luke walked down the hall to follow Amelia, though, she heard him say, "No kidding."

Sure enough, the bone was broken. The doctor reset it, and where Margaret would have been perfectly happy to take Amelia home and tell Sarah the next day when she returned, Hannah practically forced Amelia to call her. Sarah, of course, insisted on coming back to Walker. When Amelia hung up, Hannah whispered to Margaret, "She ruined it. I can't believe her. I thought they were on the mend, but she just can't let go. Amelia's practically an adult."

Margaret nodded, disappointed. When Sarah and Donny showed up a few hours later, the two of them looked stressed and strained, she worried that all the time she'd spent on planning a romantic getaway was for naught.

So, she was pleasantly surprised a few days later when Donny drove up the driveway in a new truck, a stack of papers in hand. The papers were a kind of offering: they contained information about dividing Mama Katherine's property into several parcels so they could build two more houses there: one for Sarah and Donny, and one for Margaret. Hannah, Margaret supposed, would stay in the main house with Mama Katherine, long into her spinsterhood.

They joked that it would be like a commune, and everyone else thought it was a great idea. They could share the responsibilities of taking care of the property and Mama. They could share the garden's harvest and the eggs. They'd celebrate holidays together again.

Margaret knew they had good intentions, but she felt a bit like she was being tamed, put on a leash, or corralled. If she agreed to the plan, was she condemning herself to a long life of being taken care of? Was she giving up her independence?

Even after three separate diagnoses, Margaret was still holding onto a shred of hope that she didn't have retinitis pigmentosa, that she wasn't losing her vision, that she wouldn't be forced to rely on help for the rest of her life.

What if she agreed to move back to Wyoming, onto Mama's property, and then her vision came back, clear as glass? Then she'd be stuck here, in this podunk town with barely anything to do. No movie theaters, no shows, no real restaurants to speak of.

Her sight was going to come back. It had to.

<hr>

IN REALITY, Margaret's vision showed no signs of coming back, and she and her sisters prepared for their road trip.

"This is going to be so fun!" Hannah said, for what must have been the hundredth time.

Margaret rolled her eyes, for what was probably the ninety-second time.

"Come on, Margaret," Hannah said. "You're getting away, seeing the sights, taking your mind off things. Right?"

"Right. I mean, if I can actually see the sights."

"Margaret. It's all outside. Bright, beautiful lighting. You'll be able to see the sights. And if not, you can just enjoy our company."

Hannah descended the stairs of Donny and Sarah's RV again,

taking her millionth trip into the house. Margaret sighed. This was all too much to take in. As an expert packer of suitcases, she'd gotten ready in mere minutes while her fellow travelers ran around the house like hens being chased by John Wayne. There was some fluttering, some squawking, some pecking. And here Margaret sat, serene, at the dinette, her sisters and mother having refused her offers to help.

Mama Katherine stepped into the RV, her tall frame occupying the doorway. Margaret could tell from the tilt of her shoulders that she was—finally—carrying a full suitcase.

"Want me to get that?" Margaret said, standing up.

"Nah, thanks though, honey."

Mama Katherine hoisted her bag and stepped all the way in. "You okay?" she said.

Before Margaret could answer, she said, "This is going to be fun, I promise."

Margaret felt like snorting or making some kind of snarky comment. But she knew better. Her sisters and her mother were doing this for her. They were giving her the chance to get a look at points of interest they deemed worthy. None of these points of interest were towering buildings or intricate bridges. None of them could give her a double shot of espresso. But Hannah had ordered an espresso machine online and promised that every morning during this trip, she'd make Margaret the best coffee she'd ever tasted.

The machine was rolled safely into a towel in the cabinet above the sink. Margaret had double-checked, herself, and been impressed by the smooth, heavy feel of the handles and carafe.

Mama Katherine slid into the dinette, opposite Margaret.

"What's taking the girls so long?" Margaret said.

"Oh, you know," Mama Katherine said. "Hannah feels like she's got to batten down the hatches since we'll be gone. She's checked the chicken coop about a dozen times. And I don't know what Sarah's up to. Maybe she and Donny are getting in a last-minute screw before we go, now that they're reunited."

"Mama!"

Mama chuckled, and Margaret found herself smiling despite her sour mood.

"Mama? Do you think Hannah will ever have a relationship?"

Now, Mama sighed. "I wish she would. But I just don't know. She feels so darned responsible for me. I love her for it. But at the same time, I feel like she misses out on a lot. You know? But maybe she just doesn't want it."

"Maybe," Margaret said.

"Speaking of relationships," Mama Katherine said. "Hannah mentioned you met a very nice young man at the farmer's market."

Margaret felt her face flush, and Mama Katherine laughed again.

"A very good-looking young man," Hannah said, huffing out a breath as she climbed the stairs into the RV. "And Amelia agrees. After chauffeuring Margaret on her date, she said he was good-looking, too. She even wiggled her eyebrows. Which means a lot, coming from a teenager. Also she said that when she picked you up from your dinner date, you kept smiling. She said, 'And Aunt Margaret was just looking out the window, with this silly smile on her face.'"

With no retort at the ready, all Margaret could do was shrug and nod.

"Well, well, well," Mama Katherine said. "I must say, it's fun to hear this. I've always secretly wondered about your dating life."

"It's no secret, Mama," Margaret said. "You're always asking about it."

"I am?"

"You are," Hannah said. "Mama, you try to pretend you're sly, but you're pretty obvious. I've heard you ask Margaret strange questions about companionship too many times to count. And let's not forget about all those times you've asked me innocent questions like whether there are any male teachers these days, and whether I have plans this weekend."

"I'm a romantic, what can I say?"

There was a beat of silence, during which Margaret was positive she and Hannah were thinking the same thing: Mama Katherine was most certainly *not* a romantic. They'd recently discovered she'd been married once—nearly forty years ago, to Hannah's father—and she'd left him after their first child died in an accident on their orchard. As far as they knew, she'd never gotten in touch with him again. And because she'd left when she was just a few weeks' pregnant with Hannah, it was entirely possible he didn't even know he had a daughter. Plus, she'd never dated or remarried. She never watched romantic movies or read romance novels. She always went for action and adventure. She hadn't even teared up at Sarah's wedding.

"If you're a romantic," Margaret said, "then why didn't you ever get back in touch with Hannah's father?"

Again, silence. Margaret couldn't decide whether blurting that out was courageous or stupid.

Mama Katherine recovered first. "That's is a road trip conversation," she said. "I'll tell you when we hit a boring stretch of road."

"No time like the present," Hannah said. "Mama can navigate, since Sarah's the designated driver. And I'll make us some cocktails."

"You drink cocktails?" Margaret said.

"Sweetheart," Hannah said, "there's a lot you don't know about me."

*Well,* Margaret thought. *This is going to be interesting.*

To Margaret's surprise, Hannah followed through: she mixed each of them a strong Bloody Mary, and she made a virgin one for Sarah, who'd finally given Donny a satisfactory good-bye and was climbing into the RV.

There was a little bit of chit-chat, and Margaret and Hannah sat at the dinette, sipping their spicy drinks. Just about the time Margaret felt the vodka hitting her bloodstream, Sarah buckled herself into the driver's seat.

"Where do you want to go, Margaret?" she said. "What's something you've always wanted to see?"

For a moment, Margaret thought she might cry. But she took a deep breath and said, with decision, "Zion National Park. Let's start there."

The RV rumbled to life, and as the tires crunched over the gravel driveway, Mama Katherine said, "Girls, I'd like to tell you a story."

Beside Margaret, Hannah sighed. "Is it about my dad?"

"It is," Mama Katherine said.

Margaret had always assumed that Hannah and Mama Katherine having deep conversations was a natural by-product of the two of them living together. While Margaret was off galavanting around the country, and Sarah was in Arizona, being the perfect mother and wife, Hannah was in Wyoming. There was probably lots about Mama that she'd learned as an adult, that neither Margaret nor Sarah knew.

That's why Margaret was surprised when Hannah said, "You've told us before that you didn't date or get married because you wanted to take care of us. But now we know what really happened. Haven't there been times when you wanted to reconnect with my dad?"

"Oh, honey. I mean, there were times, yes. There were times when I thought, or knew, that I should tell him about you, certainly. And of course, it would be convenient to have a man around the house. An extra set of hands to unroll that damned chicken wire on the coop, or another body for harvesting the corn or the tomatoes. Things get done a lot faster when there are two people involved. But the more time that passed, the harder it seemed. I imagined that he'd be too angry with me to have any sort of relationship—even a friendship. I felt like I'd ruined things between us—that they were irreparable."

She sipped her drink.

"Irreparable?" It was Sarah who spoke. Sarah, whose own marriage was in the early stages of overcoming what had seemed to be irreparable damage.

"No, not you and Donny, sweetheart. That's fixable. You two have been in love forever. But Philip and I—maybe it was doomed from the start. As you know, it was an arranged marriage. Our fathers wanted to control the apple industry in California, and our marriage created the largest orchard merger in history."

She sighed and took a sip of her drink. "We were practically strangers when we stood at the altar. Afterward, we settled into a kind of friendship, making small talk and sleeping in separate rooms. And at first, that's what I thought I wanted. He was nice enough to me, and I to him. He seemed to respect that I wanted a career, and I respected his passion for the orchards and the business. Slowly, though, I realized it wasn't enough for me. I imagined growing old with Philip—he, working at the orchards and me, working at the advertising firm—the both of us leading separate lives indefinitely. There had to be more, didn't there? So, as you read in my old journal, I devised a plan. To fall in love with Philip and make him fall in love with me. And it worked. At least, I thought it did. But then our first child, Benny, was born. And although I was a sufficient mother, I never fell head over heels for him the way some mothers do. Then he died. And if Philip and I were really in love, we should have come together after our son died. But it tore us apart." Her voice had become thick. She cleared her throat. "Anyway. I was just fine on my own. And I think I did a pretty damned good job of raising you three without a man around to tell me how to clean my kitchen or bake my bread."

Margaret thought there must be some metaphor in there, but she wasn't quite sure what it was.

"What if we found him?" Hannah said.

"Found him?" Mama said.

Margaret couldn't quite tell, but she thought Sarah was sitting up extra-straight in the driver's seat, ears perked.

"Yeah," Hannah said slowly. "Found him. And reconnected the two of you."

"Oh, I don't know," Mama said. "That has disaster written all over it. I'm positive he hates me by now, and I deserve it."

"Maybe not," Hannah said. "Surely he played a role in whatever happened between you."

Silence.

"I guess I'd rather you waited until I was dead and buried."

Hannah gasped. "Mama!"

"Anyway," Mama said. "Let's change the subject."

"But we have lots of questions," Sarah said.

"And I'll answer them, in due time."

"Hmpf," Hannah said.

"Tell us about your date, Margaret," Mama said.

"Ooh," Hannah said, before Margaret could answer or point out that she'd made a quick recovery after hearing Mama's story. "Sarah, she's grinning like a—well, I don't know what. But she can't wipe that smile off her face."

"Ooh, do tell, Margaret," Sarah said.

Margaret knew it wouldn't do any good to resist. They'd be cooped up in this small space for the next week or so. "Okay," she said. "Fine."

Hannah clapped and squealed, and Margaret laughed. "You're the exact same Hannah you were in junior high, you know that?"

"I know," Hannah said, "and I love it! I just love being here with my sisters, all of us in one place, that's all. Go on. Tell us about Leroy."

"Leroy?" Sarah said.

"Ethan," Margaret said. "When we met him at the farmer's market, he told us his name was Leroy. But he was just joking. Anyway. First of all, that was a one-time deal, okay? Don't get attached to him, because I'm certainly not. This isn't the time in my life when I should be getting myself into a romantic relationship I can't sustain."

"Why can't you sustain it?" Mama said.

Margaret thought that was obvious, but since it was Mama who'd asked, she bit off any impending comments and said, "I just need to focus on getting myself oriented and situated, you know? And plus, if I do go back to Seattle—"

"I thought you were staying here," Hannah said. "Donny's working on the plans for our commune."

The truth was, Margaret was afraid to stay here, in Wyoming. She was afraid that doing so was giving up the life she loved. But she didn't want to get into that, now.

"I know," Margaret said. "I'm just still getting used to the idea, you know? Like when you first get into a pool, and you have to get in gradually, let the water rise a little bit at a time."

*Until you drown.*

"Okay," Hannah said, sounding anything but convinced. "Tell us why you can't sustain the relationship with Ethan?"

"Well, I just have a lot to learn right now. I just need to focus."

"Wouldn't it be nice to have that support?" Hannah said.

"Until it's not there any more," Margaret said.

"Tell us about him," Mama said.

Margaret sighed. "He's got this amazing voice. I mean, it would be a baritone if he started singing. And when he laughs, there's seismic activity."

"Like a vibration?" Hannah wanted to know. "No wonder you liked him. He makes you vibrate."

"Oh, Lordy," Mama said.

"What else?" Sarah said. "Since Hannah has taken us to the gutter."

Margaret took a deep breath. "He's encouraging without pitying me."

"Wait," Sarah said. "You told him?"

"I didn't tell him," Margaret said. "He already knew. He said he could tell from the way I acted at the farmer's market. There was a moment, when Hannah walked away, and I almost panicked. I think that's when he noticed. And—"

"I'm sorry, Margaret," Hannah said. "I—"

"You didn't know," Margaret said, waving a hand. "Anyway, when we walked into the restaurant, he tucked my hand into the crook of his arm and led me to the table. It wasn't until later that I realized he'd done it because he knew I couldn't see very well. He'd obviously asked for a table with lots of light. And then whenever the server came up, he said, ultra-casual, 'Here's the server. Want some wine?'"

The way Ethan behaved that evening was a huge indicator that he was a kind and thoughtful man. But he deserved someone whole and vibrant, not broken.

"Wow," Hannah said, and Mama Katherine said, "I think you should see him again."

"We did have a nice time," Margaret said. "He's funny and smart and he has really nice biceps. But I just don't know. This is absolutely the worst time to start a romantic endeavor."

"Or," Sarah said, "it's the best time."

"Remember that teacher we had in high school?" Hannah said, and Margaret and Sarah said, "Mr. Lopez."

"Yeah," Sarah said. "Remember what he would say?"

"He would say, 'Just—just open your mind to the possibility that this could be true,'" Margaret said.

"Exactly," Hannah said.

"Well, well," Mama Katherine said. "I didn't know they taught that kind of stuff when you girls were in high school."

"He was the philosophy teacher," Hannah said. "And we all thought he was pretty dreamy."

"Did we?" Margaret said. "Because I seem to remember you having a crush on that Tanner Lucas guy. The same one who'd always debate with you in your college classes. You only had eyes for him."

Margaret didn't answer, and Mama Katherine said, "Wow, Hannah. If your face were any redder, it'd be on fire."

Margaret snickered.

"I wonder what ever happened to him," Sarah said.

"I don't," Hannah said. "He was a thorn in my side."

"Oh, I'll just bet you wanted him to be," Margaret said, and Mama Katherine clucked in fake disapproval.

"You've never looked him up?" Sarah said.

Hannah scoffed. "Why would I?"

"Um, because he was totally hot," Margaret said. "Mega-hot. And I, for one, always wonder whether those guys hit their prime in high school, or remain, you know, good-looking into adulthood."

"Then *you* look him up," Hannah said.

"I just might," Margaret said.

Then two thoughts struck her in rapid succession: first, she wouldn't be able to tell what Tanner Lucas looked like now even if she did look him up. Second, what did good looks even matter, when a woman couldn't see? Not being able to see her romantic partners really changed the game. How would she know how they ranked on the scale of good looks? Did it even matter?

The weather cooperated on the day the women visited Zion National Park, and Hannah and Sarah forced Margaret to admit she was glad they'd suggested the road trip. The color was spectacular: mountains of red rock rising into a sky the color of lapis lazuli, shamrock-green moss dripping down from the sides of natural tunnels, shining rivers cutting through the earth.

Bryce Canyon didn't disappoint, either, with its otherworldly rock formations and impossibly wide views. Sarah drove them straight across Utah to Arches National Park. Just outside Arches, they found ancient petroglyphs scratched into rock walls, and they visited Moab, where all-terrain vehicles crawled up and down and over steep granite boulders.

After they went to the Grand Canyon, which made Margaret jittery as she looked over its edge (the gaping expanse was big enough even she could see it), she came to a realization that had been dawning since they set out on this adventure: maybe her life wasn't over. Maybe losing her vision wasn't akin to a death sentence. No, things would never be quite the same for her, but seeing all these majestic landmarks gave her a new sense of possibility.

They were driving the long, dry stretch between Arizona and New Mexico when Hannah said, "Here, Margaret. Let me see your phone."

Used to following commands issued by her big sister, Margaret handed it over.

"I'm buying you an app," Hannah said.

"I use free apps," Margaret said.

"Not this time," Hannah said.

Margaret shrugged and settled back against the window, her legs stretched out across one side of the dinette.

"Here," Hannah said a minute later, handing the phone back. "Let's practice."

A beat of silence passed, and then Margaret's phone chirped.

"Well, that was exciting," Margaret said.

"I think you have to unlock your phone. Can you see the message box on the screen?"

Margaret unlocked her phone, tapped the message box, and a robotic woman's voice said, "Message from Hannah. Hello. Are you enjoying the RV trip so far?"

"Ha!" Hannah said. "It worked. I am amazing."

"You *are* amazing," Margaret said. She couldn't help but smile. "That's pretty cool."

"Wonders never cease," Mama Katherine said. "If you'd have told me even ten years ago that we'd be able to send messages with a few taps on a screen, I'd have said you were crazy."

Just then, Margaret's phone chirped again. Without thinking, she unlocked it and tapped the message icon.

The robotic voice said, "Message from Ethan slash Leroy. I really enjoyed dinner the other night. Next time, we should try dessert."

Margaret gasped. Hannah gasped. Sarah said, "Wow," and Mama Katherine gave a whoop.

"Well, I can tell this app is going to be fun," Hannah said.

Not for the first time in recent days, Margaret felt her face heating up.

"What are you gonna say back?" Sarah said.

"I'm going to say, 'It's none of your beeswax, Sarah,'" Margaret said. "Just don't listen when I do voice-to-text because I'm going to tell Ethan just how much I love his dessert idea."

Then, they were all laughing—until Margaret's phone made another notification sound.

Into the silence, the phone said, "Message from Ethan slash Leroy. What do you like for dessert?"

"You know," Sarah said, her voice high-pitched with hilarity, "you should probably change that thing's voice to one that sounds more manly, if you're going to start sexting. Especially if you're going to start sexting when we're all together."

This had Hannah practically shrieking.

Margaret, her own lips twitching, told her phone to activate voice-to-text. Then she said, "I like cucumbers."

This stumped the other passengers in the RV, and they fell silent.

"He sent me a picture of a cucumber," Margaret said. "The other day."

"Then you should add something like, 'Covered in chocolate,'" Hannah said.

"No!" Sarah said. "Something like, 'But only when they're in my mouth.'"

"Well, I never," Mama Katherine said. "I am truly scandalized. I had no idea I was raising a bunch of harlots."

"It's not me," Margaret said. "I'm still a proper lady."

Then she activated voice-to-text and replied to Ethan: "I'm willing to try anything once."

A few seconds later, his reply came in, the feminine voice of the application breaking through the road noise: "Well. This should be interesting. I'll get a menu together."

# CHAPTER SEVEN

A ROMANCE BREWING and a great new adventure with her family ...
Margaret knew she should be over the moon. But the adventure was
over. It was time to go back to her apartment and pack up her things.
Someone had decided that Sarah would fly with her from Wyoming to
Seattle, where they'd rent a moving truck and drive back. As if their
road trip hadn't involved enough driving. Although Margaret
protested—insisting the could make the trip alone—Hannah made the
flight reservations and Sarah packed her bags.

And, truth be told, Margaret thought, it seemed like the most
logical idea. They couldn't really incorporate the apartment-packing
into their road trip. There was no way to fit everything into the RV
with all of them sleeping in it, and Mama Katherine had to get back
home, anyway. Something about minding the chickens, even though
the neighbor boys had volunteered to feed them. Margaret suspected
Mama wanted to get back to Farmer Eddie, but she wasn't quite brave
enough to say so.

On the plane, Margaret planned to feign exhaustion. She loved
spending time with her sisters and mom, but she also needed alone
time to recharge and she hadn't gotten a lick of that for several weeks.
She surprised herself by actually drifting off to sleep, not waking
again until the plane touched down—which made her jump and
curse. Sarah giggled, and Margaret elbowed her, gently.

A half-hour later, they stepped out of the taxi outside Margaret's
apartment building, which she'd selected in part because of its architecture, which combined contemporary lines with historic details.

Margaret turned her face towards the sky and inhaled the scents of the city: swollen rain clouds overhead, exhaust from the cars going by, the sauerkraut from a hot dog vendor's cart.

"I love it here," she said to Sarah. "I mean, just listen to it."

"The honking, the shouting, the noise," Sarah said. "What's not to love?"

"It's a bit much for you, I know," Margaret said. "But I love the hustle and bustle."

"I know you do," Sarah said. "Let's walk."

As they did, Sarah said, "You don't have to move, you know. You could stay here."

Margaret could hear the doubt, the lack of conviction, in her sister's voice.

"Here we are," Sarah said. "Want me to open the door?"

Margaret gave her the code. Inside the foyer, the familiar feel of the tile under her feet brought tears to her eyes. She loved this entry with its high ceiling and white marble walls and crystal chandelier. The elevator slid open as they approached. Sarah pressed the button for the tenth floor, and Margaret swallowed the lump in her throat. She'd bought an apartment up high for the view, obviously. Was that even important now? Obviously not.

The elevator started up with a hitch and a creak, and Sarah grabbed her arm.

"How old is this building?" she wanted to know.

"About four centuries," Margaret said. "The elevator, too. I'm sure they'll crumble at any moment."

"Shut up," Sarah said.

Even though she wouldn't be using this particular elevator (which, along with the rest of the building, was only a decade old) again, Margaret wondered how she'd ever know which floor she was on. Usually, there were plaques at each floor, with Braille on them. Only, she couldn't read Braille.

The elevator jolted to a stop, and Sarah's grip tightened on Margaret's arm. Sarah cleared her throat and released her grip. "We're here. Thank God."

Her apartment door swung open, and the scent of her favorite cinnamon vanilla candles hit Margaret, along with innumerable memories. Oh, how she loved this place. She'd hired a designer to help her give it a cozy, yet cosmopolitan feel, and together, they'd dressed the space—which was all concrete floors and brick walls—in black and white with bright pops of color.

The parties! Margaret loved hosting a good party, and often invited colleagues over for drinks or coffee or hors d'oeuvres. People would gather around the island in the kitchen, with its smooth, black and white granite, and they'd laugh and talk and sometimes sing. There was always music, and usually, dancing.

And then there were those quiet nights, when she would sink into the cushy sofa, dig her toes into the faux bearskin rug and light a fire. Always with a glass of wine.

One of her favorite things to do was to sit next to the window when it was raining, and watch the cityscape become a kaleidoscope through the raindrops.

Now, she pressed her palm against the window. The sky was post-rainstorm beautiful, puffy gray-and-white clouds separating to let the sun streamed through. Margaret wondered if she'd forget the way the clouds looked, at once dense and airy, all the different shades of gray, and the spears of sun illuminating the scene below. She could see it clearly; partly from memory and partly as a blurry version of what her mind knew was there: miniature cars on black streets, miniature people walking on the sidewalks.

At least once a day, Margaret would make up a story about one of the people below. She imagined them now: a man, with the long tan jacket and matching hat. He worked at the accounting firm down the street but trained as a magician on the side. He was perfecting his disappearing coin trick. And a woman there, passing by the magician. She had just landed a new job—at the button factory. Margaret chuckled. Okay, not the button factory. The library. Although it was nearly impossible to see what the woman was wearing, Margaret went ahead and dressed her in a pencil skirt and a plaid button-up shirt under that red coat.

"You hungry?" Sarah slipped an arm around Margaret's waist, bringing her out of her fantasy world. "I could make you a PB and J."

Margaret smiled and leaned into her sister.

"That's *my* specialty," she said. "I suppose we should start packing, and we're going to need fortification for that. I don't have any food here, but we could order in."

They chose pizza, and Margaret paid the delivery guy twenty bucks to go pick up a couple of bottles of wine.

When Sarah *tsked* at her, Margaret said, "I'll tell you what. I'm either going to be drunk or blubbering while we pack up this apartment. I choose drunk. Why don't you open the wine while I start folding the boxes?"

Sarah didn't *tsk* again, and Margaret noticed that her disapproval wasn't quite strong enough to stop her from sharing the wine.

The two of them had packed up the spare bedroom and the bathroom when Margaret's phone, in its robotic voice, announced: "Text from Ethan slash Leroy."

Margaret felt her whole body go still—except for her heart, which beat noticeably faster.

"Well, that's one thing about Hannah's fancy app," Sarah said. "Doesn't give you much privacy, does it?"

"That's true," Margaret said. "And you may as well hear what he has to say."

"Yes, please," Sarah said. "My curiosity's piqued."

Margaret unlocked her phone and tapped the screen, and the robotic voice said, "Dinner again? And maybe dessert this time?"

"Ooh," Sarah said. "Sounds very … provocative."

"Shut up," Margaret said, even though she thought it sounded provocative, too.

"What are you going to say back?"

"I'm going to tell him I'm out of town."

"That's it?"

Margaret activated the voice-to-text and said, "I'm in Seattle."

She sent it.

"That's it?" Sarah said.

"What do you mean?" Margaret said.

"You didn't tell him whether you wanted to do dinner."

"Well," Margaret said. "I don't want to do dinner."

"What? Why not?" Sarah said. "You liked him. I could tell. Amelia could tell. We could all tell."

"That's true," Margaret said. "I did like him. But I've already decided that was a one-and-done."

"What? Is that a thing?"

"It absolutely *is* a thing."

"Well, it's a stupid thing. Do you do this often? This, 'one-and-done'?"

"Let's start on the kitchen," Margaret said. "Just don't pack up the coffeemaker. We're going to need that in the morning."

She led the way into the kitchen, Sarah following her.

"You do, don't you?" Sarah said.

"I'll start with the big stuff. The food processor, the blender. Do you think I'll even need those at Mama Katherine's?"

Margaret set her phone on the counter and dragged a box across the floor to the cabinet where she kept her kitchen appliances.

"You're going to have to start calling it home, you know," Sarah said. "If you use them here, you'll use them at your new home. And don't change the subject. How often do you go on second dates?"

"Second dates? Once every four or five guys, I'd say. The thing is, I usually date when I'm traveling. I'm not around long enough for subsequent dates. Anyway. There's not, like, a formula, or anything. Sarah. I don't need a man. I enjoy men. I enjoy their company, talking to them, sleeping with them. But I don't need one on hand all the time."

"I understand that," Sarah said. "And nobody's saying a second date with Ethan-Leroy will lead to a lifelong commitment. All I'm saying is, why won't you go on another date with him? You *liked* him."

"I did like him," Margaret said. She pulled the blender out of the cabinet and set it in the box. "Which is exactly why I won't date him again. I've evaluated the situation and there is simply too much risk involved."

"What? This makes no sense. No sense at all."

"It makes perfect sense," Margaret said. "At this point in my life, the last thing I need is to have to worry about some guy. Plus, it's unfair for me to expect him to stick around for any length of time during this transition."

"Hmm," Sarah said.

Margaret said, "'Hmm,' yourself. Now, help me with this food processor."

Sarah didn't answer for a moment, and when Margaret heard her voice, it was from the other side of the room, and it was activating the voice-to-text on Margaret's phone.

"But, I'll be back in a few days and I'd love to do dinner. You should know, though, that I don't do dessert until at least the fifth date."

Margaret and Sarah finally called it quits around midnight, when the last of the wine was gone and the majority of Margaret's things were packed. Sarah settled herself into the guest bedroom, and Margaret sat on the edge of her own bed, thinking about Ethan.

What could she do? She could hardly admit to him that her kid sister had hijacked her phone and agreed to a second date. And she definitely couldn't tell him she didn't want a second date. At least, not at this point.

Ethan's response to Margaret's text—he wanted to know what she was doing in Seattle—startled Margaret. Not only because it was late, but also because she'd just been thinking about him. Sarah would call it a sign or Fate. Or something. Margaret figured she may as well get the worst part of this conversation out of the way.

"I'm moving back home, to Wyoming. My Mama's getting older, and—"

She deleted the "and" (he didn't need to know that she was running back home because she needed help, too), and sent the message. Then she slipped out of her leggings, turned off the light, and got into bed.

Ethan's response came in just as she closed her eyes: "So we're going to be neighbors."

Something about the sentence—even though it came in the form of her phone's robotic voice—made her feel aroused. Or, maybe it was lying here alone, in the dark, the silky sheets against her legs. The sheets were about eight million thread count and might not fit in at the Seedling Homestead.

Unless, Margaret thought, she bought eight million thread count sheets for her mom and sisters, too. That's what she'd do. She responded: "Yes. We're going to be neighbors. Out in the country."

Maybe she'd buy Ethan some eight million thread count sheets, too.

She closed the texting app and clicked onto the Internet app. The details on the screen were too blurry to see. She turned on the lamp on her nightstand. It was another piece that wouldn't fit in on the farm. Its delicate blown-glass base and filmy shade were meant for city life. Maybe she'd leave it here for the apartment's next occupant. She settled back onto her pillow.

When she found the sheets she wanted—in a bright coral for Mama, a deep royal blue for Hannah, and a light summer yellow for Sarah and Donny—she found her finger hovering over the steel gray she imagined Ethan would choose.

At the last minute, she clicked, "Add to Cart."

A few seconds later, she was confirming her order.

And seven hours after that, when she woke up with a headache only coffee could fix, she regretted that she'd ordered sheets for Ethan-Leroy. But it was too late—they'd already shipped.

And, almost as if he knew, Ethan had sent her a text, that, when her phone read it aloud, made her tingle in the most inappropriate of places: "I have a feeling you're going to like country living. It's like nothing you've ever done before. I'll show you."

Still tingling, Margaret made her way to the kitchen.

Why had she bought him sheets?

She knew why.

She wanted to see if country living really could be as good as city living.

Pouring herself coffee, she chuckled. And she was still chuckling when Sarah emerged from the guest bedroom.

"What's funny, besides the fact that I have the first hangover I've experienced in years, thanks to you?"

"Ha," Margaret said. "Means it was a good night. You're welcome."

"You're crazy."

Coffee mugs full, they sat at the kitchen bar in silence for a few moments. Margaret's mind drifted to Ethan and the sheets. The fix was as easy as sending them back, wasn't it? They were in her order, they were going to Mama Katherine's house, and he never had to know she'd bought them.

"You think we'll be done today?" Sarah said.

"I do," Margaret said. "You're so efficient. You're inhuman. Seriously. I couldn't have done this without you."

"How are you doing?" Sarah said.

She reached over and massaged one of Margaret's shoulders.

"I'm fine," Margaret said, "as long as I think of this as temporary."

Sarah sighed. "You know, I wish I had something reassuring to say, something that would give you a glimpse of some light at the end of this tunnel. But I don't. This sucks. It's scary. It's stupid that it's happening to you. "

Her voice broke, and Margaret felt her own throat constricting. Then Sarah went on: "Just know that I'm here for you. I want to help you make the best of this. And sometimes, no matter how terrible something seems, there *is* a silver lining. I'm going to help you find it."

Margaret couldn't respond with anything other than a nod.

## CHAPTER EIGHT

"THERE'S A PACKAGE FOR YOU," Hannah said, before Margaret had even climbed down from the moving truck two days later. Something in her voice put Margaret on alert. It was a barely-contained excitement, an about-to-bubble over giddiness.

For a fraction of a second, Margaret had thought the package might be her sheet order. But Hannah's behavior made her think it was something else. And besides, the sheets weren't due to arrive until tomorrow.

How did anyone even know to send her something here, at Mama Katherine's? She thought of Sarah, saying she was going to have to start thinking of this as her home, too, and she corrected herself. How did anyone even know to send her something here, to her new home?

She didn't like the sound of that.

"Who's it from?"

"Your secret admirer," Hannah said. She giggled.

"There it is," Margaret said.

"There what is?"

"That giggle. I could hear it, right on the edge of your voice."

"Where's the package?" Sarah said.

"Inside," Hannah said.

A growing sense of unease had Margaret saying, "Shouldn't we unpack, first? We have to return this truck tomorrow, and I'd like to get it in first thing in the morning."

This, she realized, was another downside to not being able to see.

Not only could she not do anything on her own, but it would also force her to be bossy.

"We'll get to it," Hannah said. "Come on. I've been dying to see what's inside this box."

"Who did you say it was from?" Margaret said. With sheer persistence, she could almost always get Hannah to give up her secrets.

But not today. Hannah was already walking away, up the path to the door.

"Just come inside."

The cardboard box sat on the dining room table, just like their birthday gifts had when they were little. Mama Katherine would wrap them the night before, and when the girls woke up, the presents would be waiting—mysterious packages drawing their attention throughout the day. They weren't allowed to open them until after dinner. The girls would often find themselves in the dining room, staring at the birthday gifts, as if there was some kind of magnetic pull.

Now, Margaret felt a similar stirring of excitement in her chest. The first thing she noticed was that the package wasn't properly addressed. Her first name was printed on one corner of the top, in big, bold letters she could read without squinting or getting within inches of the handwriting. Next, she noticed there was no return address. Finally, she noticed that the box wasn't taped shut. It was folded closed, flaps overlapping.

"Well, well," Sarah said.

"Open it!" Hannah squealed.

"Wait for me," Mama Katherine said, coming into the dining room from the back of the house. "I've been waiting to see this."

"I hope you're not disappointed," Margaret said. "The build-up is almost too much."

Margaret grasped the corners of the lid and pulled. She peered down into the box. It was too dark to see. She reached in and felt the object, instead.

Her fingers explored the smooth wood with its gnarled knots and immediately, she knew what it was: the lamp she'd been admiring at the farmer's market.

At the time, she'd loved it. She'd wanted it. But she hadn't bought it because she didn't think it fit in with her sleek, contemporary apartment. And there was one person who'd seen her looking at it, touching it, and even reaching for her wallet at one point, only to tuck it back inside her purse before walking away.

"Ethan-Leroy," Margaret whispered.

"I guess you'll need a second date, after all," Sarah said, "to thank him."

Margaret had almost forgotten she wasn't alone in the dining room.

"And I think that second date might just include dessert," Hannah said.

"Very funny," Margaret said. Even though she'd infused her voice with sarcasm, the feelings she experienced when she realized the gift was from Ethan *were* very funny. Very funny, indeed.

And now, she had to decide what to do about them.

As it turned out, Margaret didn't have to do anything about those feelings—at least, not right away—because Ethan was doing all the doing.

He showed up at Mama Katherine's house the very next day, at the precise moment when Margaret just happened to be heading outside to finish unpacking the moving truck.

"Got your text last night," he said as he came around the side of the truck.

Startled, she jumped, then placed a hand over her heart. "Geez, Leroy. You really know how to get a woman's heart pumping."

"You know," he said, coming toward her and hooking his hands in his pockets, "I've heard that before. Actually, what I think I've heard is that I really know how to get a woman's blood flowing. Aren't those one and the same?"

"Sadly," Margaret said, "I'm afraid they're not."

"Anyway," Ethan said, "I thought I'd come say, 'You're welcome,' in person."

"Ah," Margaret said. "That was sweet of you. I thought surely you were too busy to answer yesterday evening. Country living keeps you busy, if I remember right."

"True," he said. "Although I wasn't too busy. I was simply looking for the next stop on the Road to Margaret's Heart. I think you're going to like it."

"There's a next stop? And wait. You're on that road?"

"I am, yes," Ethan said. "Absolutely. And yes. There is another stop."

"I'm intrigued." Margaret hefted the back door of the moving truck and it rolled up. She pulled out the ramp, set it down, and walked up into the back of the truck. "It wouldn't happen to be helping me get these boxes to the shed, would it?"

"I suppose I could make that a pit stop. You know, for fortification. Fuel. That kind of thing."

"You gonna need fuel?"

"I have a feeling I am," he said.

"It's my icy disposition, isn't it?"

"Ice cold."

She maneuvered the dolly under a stack of boxes and started rolling it towards the ramp.

"Doesn't look like you need help," Ethan said.

She could see his silhouette at the edge of the open doorway.

"Just wait until I start going down the ramp."

"Isn't that the easy part?" Ethan said.

"I'm afraid not."

"Gravity should help you."

"Oh, it helps me," Margaret said. "Maybe too much."

Sure enough, once she rocked the wheels of the dolly over the space between the floor of the truck and the ramp itself, gravity pulled—hard—and she found herself practically running to keep up with it.

"That looks dangerous," Ethan said.

Margaret laughed. "I know. I almost killed myself yesterday."

"Weren't your sisters helping you?"

"Ha," Margaret said. "They know better than to offer. I can be ..."

"Independent?" Ethan supplied.

"You could call it that. Or, you could call it what my sisters do: stubborn."

"I could see that," Ethan said.

He followed her as she rolled her stack of boxes to the shed, and then again as she walked back to the truck to retrieve another.

"Your whole life fit inside this space?" Ethan said as she pulled the dolly up the ramp.

"No," Margaret said. "My whole life did not fit inside this space. The contents of my apartment did. I prefer to live light."

"Hmm," he said. He walked up the ramp and took the dolly from her, then slid it under the next stack and wheeled it down the ramp in a way that looked totally effortless. At the bottom, he turned around and said, "Would you like to wheel it to the shed?"

"Sure," she said.

"Why won't you let your sisters help?"

Margaret shrugged. "I don't know. They have their own stuff to do. Sarah's moving here, too. And Hannah—well, Hannah doesn't have anything to do. But it's not really fair for me to ask her for help and not accept help from Sarah. So. It's just me."

"And me. Why are you letting me help?"

"Well, if you haven't got anything better to do than show up here early on a weekday morning, then I might as well put you to use, right?"

"I suppose so."

They'd reached the shed and Ethan wheeled the dolly inside, setting this stack of boxes next to the last one.

"Knickknacks?" he read off the side of a box. "You don't strike me as the kind of woman who'd buy knickknacks."

"That's a box of sex toys," she said. "I just didn't want my mom and sisters to know what kind of woman I really am."

With that, she walked back to the moving truck, leaving Ethan standing in the shed. He caught up a few seconds later, and moved the final two stacks of boxes in silence.

"I'm sure you're wondering why I came by today."

He spoke only once Margaret had put the ramp away and rolled the truck door back down.

"You said it was to say, 'You're welcome,' in person." She turned to face him and put her hands on her hips.

"It was," Ethan said. "It was also to say that the only way to thank me properly is to let me take you out to eat." He looked at his watch. "How about breakfast?"

So there would be a second date. Margaret knew she'd agree to go before the words even left her mouth.

She went inside to tell Mama Katherine she was going out to breakfast with Ethan.

"Ethan-Leroy?" Mama said.

Margaret couldn't make out Mama's expression, but she knew exactly what it looked like: her right eyebrow quirked up into that seagull shape, and the right side of her mouth quirked up into a smirk.

"One and the same," Margaret said.

She knew what her own expression looked like too: a goofy, toothy smile that she'd better wipe off before Ethan saw it.

"So," Ethan said as he backed down the driveway of the farm. "Country life, huh?"

Margaret watched the blurry image of her childhood home get smaller and smaller. "Yeah."

"I can't tell if that was a resigned, 'Yeah,' but I know it wasn't an excited, 'Yeah,'" Ethan said.

"I can't decide, myself," Margaret said. "I mean, I've done country life. I grew up doing country life. And I moved away because I love the faster pace of city life. I love the hustle and bustle, the diversity, the dynamics."

"You're a country-mouse-turned-city-mouse?"

"Ha," Margaret said. "I guess so."

"Do you have to move back?" he said.

"Well, no," Margaret said. "But I evaluated the situation and it does seem like the best option."

"You might like it."

"I might."

"Did you grow up at your mom's place?"

"Yeah," Margaret said. "I'm sure you'll be surprised to hear this, but I was always the one getting muddy, chasing frogs, climbing trees, coming home with scraped elbows and bruised knees."

"I'm not surprised at all."

"I moved here when I was six. My first memory of this place is picking a tomato. I thought Mama Katherine was going to beat me, but she just took me inside and we cooked it right up."

"Where were you before that?"

"Cheyenne. My biological mother was a nut job. I barely remember living with her, just snatches, you know? But I do remember being alone a lot. The adoption process took a while, and I remember over-hearing my social worker talking to someone else—a police officer, maybe—about how I was used to fending for myself, and she hoped I could acclimate to family life."

"Independence isn't a bad thing," Ethan said.

"I don't know about that," Margaret said.

As a kid, she'd had several scrapes with danger because she never thought to ask for help. She'd never had anyone to ask. That's why it seemed reasonable that when she needed a cup for milk, she'd climb onto the kitchen counter to get it. It seemed perfectly normal that she'd reheat leftover chicken pot pie in the microwave (along with her fork)—until Mama Katherine walked in, shrieked that the microwave was on fire, and sat her down to talk about electricity and arcing. And then there was the time Margaret had decided she wanted to go fishing in the creek. She'd left the house without a word, and gone hunting for a proper stick with which to make a fishing pole. Then she'd needed string, and a hook. And before she knew it, she was starving. She'd eaten a mushroom she found growing next to the big tree at the creek's edge. That's when Mama Katherine found her—mouth covered in mud, hands full of crumbling mushroom.

"If you want to go fishing, just ask me," Mama Katherine said then. "If you're hungry, just tell me. I'll feed you. Don't go wandering all over God's creation, eating poisonous mushrooms. I thought you'd left us."

Margaret remembered being bewildered by all the fuss. Eventually, though, she'd learned to ask for help when she needed it. But she rarely thought she needed it, and many times she asked only out of courtesy.

"Anyway," Margaret said. "Even though I had a great childhood, I've always felt drawn to the big city. Every time we went in for shopping or the movies or anything, I felt like I belonged there. I felt myself just come alive, you know? And it was all I could do to wait until I was eighteen and I could get out on my own."

"Did you ever miss the quiet?"

Margaret shook her head. "I visited often enough. I could come here to get my fill whenever I needed it."

"Well," Ethan said, "now, you can go to the city whenever you need it. You can stand on a busy city street and listen to all that noise. Horns honking, people yelling, trucks driving through."

"Ahhh," Margaret said. "Now you're speaking my language."

Still, she couldn't help but remember that moment when she'd almost been run down by the gray sedan because she hadn't turned her head to look for traffic before crossing the street. She remembered her papers fluttering to the ground, her coffee splashing on them, her heart beating a crazy near-death rhythm, thanks to adrenaline.

"We're here," Ethan said, bringing her back to her new life in the country. "Sally's Diner. Best buttermilk pancakes in Wyoming."

"This is a far cry from the egg white and kale scramble I'd get in Seattle," Margaret said.

"I'm ordering you a side of bacon, out of principle."

Inside, Ethan said, "We're supposed to seat ourselves. Want a booth or a table?"

"Booth," Margaret said. "This place smells like it has comfy booths."

"It does," Ethan said. "I come here every week with *my* mama."

"You do?" Margaret said. "That's cute."

"It's not cute. She makes me." Even as he said the words, though, Margaret noticed he sounded amused rather than annoyed.

Again, he took her hand and tucked it into his elbow, then walked between the rows of tables to a booth in the corner, all the while chatting about his mom in a tone of voice that sounded equally exasperated and adoring: "She's always insisted that we have a weekly date. Ever since I was a teenager." Now he mimicked her voice. "'You may be growing up, son, but you still need mothering.' Then it just became kind of a tradition, I guess."

"I love that," Margaret said.

She didn't say, out loud, what she was thinking: that she'd never heard such a sweet story from a man, not in all the men she'd dated. Then she thought, *am I* dating *Ethan?* Two dates didn't really qualify as "dating," did they?

She sank down into the booth and noticed right away that it was comfy.

"You were right," she said. "This feels like the perfect place to have a tall stack of pancakes and a side of bacon. I'm going to double my body weight living in the country."

She ordered a tall stack of pancakes and sides of bacon and sausage, just for good measure.

The bell above the door jingled, and Margaret heard a man saying, "It'll be two new houses and a few improvements to the existing structure, including a whole new roof. That's three roofs for your guys. I was going to call Barry Whittle to do the windows."

"Where'd you say it was?" the man's companion said as they walked past Margaret and Ethan's table.

"The old Bradley place. You know it? Down by the creek? The oldest daughter, Hannah, still lives there with the mom, Katherine. And the two younger daughters are moving back."

"Ethan," she hissed. "They're talking about our place."

"Sure are," Ethan said. "Why are you whispering? They're contractors. A couple of local guys. Tanner Lucas and—"

Margaret gasped. "Tanner Lucas?!"

"Yeah," Ethan said, his voice conveying he had no idea why she was reacting this way.

"Want me to introduce you?"

"No introduction necessary," Margaret said.

Tanner Lucas was a name Margaret would recognize anywhere—a name she hadn't heard since Hannah started college.

"Boy, is Hannah going to be pissed."

"Who is it?" Ethan said. "Old flame?"

"Something like that," Margaret said. "Tanner Lucas has been at once a thorn in Hannah's side and the combustible that lights her panties on fire since she was in high school. I'm positive she has no idea that's the contractor Donny hired."

"Didn't you say Donny went to school with you? Wouldn't he know about their history?"

"He did," Margaret said, turning the idea over in her mind. "And maybe he did this on purpose. We—all of us—always thought Hannah had a thing for Tanner Lucas. Whenever his name came up, her face would turn the color of beets. She hated him. Fiercely."

"She hated him fiercely, and that convinced you all that she had a thing for him?"

"Exactly," Margaret said.

"Well," Ethan said. "He's the best at what he does, I can tell you that. He's really made a name for himself around here."

"Is it possible that Hannah really doesn't know he's still in town? She said she didn't know whatever became of him," Margaret said. "We were just talking about this the other day when—well, we were just talking about this."

"When, what?"

Margaret smiled. She'd brought up Tanner's name when Sarah and Mama Katherine were grilling her about her first date with Ethan. But she didn't want Ethan to know their first date had been fodder for conversation.

"Oh, nothing. Anyway. How's your bacon?"

---

HANNAH WAS in the chicken coop when Ethan dropped Margaret back at the farm.

"How was it?" Hannah said.

"Interesting," Margaret said.

"Well, that's a strange way to describe a date."

"Guess who's in charge of building our commune?"

"Would you stop calling it that?"

"Are you irritable today?"

"No," Hannah said.

"So? Are you going to guess?" Margaret said.

"No."

"You already know, don't you?"

"Know what?"

"You already know Tanner Lucas is building our commune."

"Stop calling it a commune," Hannah said.

"Did you know?"

Hannah sighed, a short, impatient huff of air. "I knew, yes."

"Why did you say you didn't know what had happened to him?" Margaret said.

"I wanted to not know what had happened to him," Hannah said. "But he's been popping up in my life ever since high school. Just when I think I've seen him for the last time, he reappears. And now this."

"Didn't Donny hire him?"

"Yes. Which I will be talking to him about."

"Talking to Donny about what?" Sarah came around the corner of the coop.

"About why he hired Tanner Lucas to build our commune," Hannah said.

"Hey, you just told me not to call it that," Margaret said.

"Anyway," Hannah said. "Your husband hired Tanner for our project."

"He *is* the best at what he does," Sarah said, in the know-it-all voice she'd developed around age ten. "Everybody knows it."

"Wait," Hannah said, and Margaret said, "You knew about this?"

Then, in unison, they said, "Why didn't you tell us?"

"If I'd told you before they signed the contract, you would have wanted Donny to find someone else. But I know you both want the best for us. Enough about that. It's a done deal. How was your date, Margaret?"

Margaret could hear the humor in Sarah's voice. Entertained, herself, she told her sisters about Ethan's weekly meals with his mom, and about the way he'd fed her a bite of his fruit-filled crepes across the table.

"So, it sounds like you had dessert," Sarah said. She added, "When is the third date?"

"That wasn't dessert," Margaret said, noticing that her own voice sounded almost as prickly as Hannah's. "And there won't be a third date."

"Oh, I'll just bet there will," Hannah said.

"You're having way too much fun with this," Margaret said, and Hannah responded, "Only as much fun as you're having with the Tanner Lucas project."

Still smiling, Margaret went inside to get a drink. Walking through the dining room to the kitchen, she nearly tripped over Mama Katherine, who was lying on the floor.

"Mama!" Margaret's heart was in her throat.

"I'm all right," Mama Katherine said. "Just help me up, will you?"

Margaret knelt down to help her into a sitting position, and water from the floor soaked through the knee of her jeans.

"The floor's wet," she said, hooking her arm through Mama Katherine's and pulling. "Did you slip?"

"Don't you dare tell your sister about this," Mama said.

"Which one?"

"Hannah," Mama Katherine said. "She already worries. This will only make things worse."

Margaret stood, then offered her hands to Mama Katherine and brought her to her feet.

"I'll dry the floor," Margaret said. "Why don't you sit down for a minute until then. Are you sure you're okay?"

"I'm not made of china, you know," Mama Katherine said.

She sounded as irritable as Hannah had.

"Did you and Hannah get into it?" Margaret said. "The two of you sound like a couple of mad hens."

Mama Katherine sighed and straightened her shirt. "Yes, we got into it. She's like a *lead* hen, top of the pecking order. She doesn't want me to do anything on my own. Says she's afraid I'm going to hurt myself. Hurt myself, repairing the chicken coop. Well, I never. And then I slip and fall here, in the dining room, doing nothing more complicated than walking to the restroom. I'm eighty years old."

"Not twenty-nine? Remember how you used to always tell us you were twenty-nine? I think *I* was twenty-nine by the time I caught on."

"You weren't, either. You were nine, if I recall. Couldn't keep that secret forever, unfortunately. But we can keep this one. Don't tell your sister about this."

"I won't, Mama. But only if you let me help you with the chicken coop."

"You're scared of the chickens."

"True."

"You know what I've always loved about you, Margaret?"

"What's that? I keep your secrets, and no one else's? Like the time I woke up in the middle of the night and you were making cookies?"

"And I asked you not to tell anyone—"

"And I didn't."

"And you didn't," Mama Katherine said. "And I ate the whole batch by myself."

"Except for the one you used to bribe me, to keep me quiet."

"That's right," Mama Katherine said. "I suppose a cookie wouldn't work now, would it?"

"It just might," Margaret said.

"But that's not what I love about you," Mama Katherine said.

"Well, there *are* many things to love," Margaret said.

"True. But the one thing I've always loved, the one thing I've learned from you, is that if there is something I want to do, why then, I ought to just do it. And that's that. And right now, I want to fix that chicken coop. Whether Hannah wants me to, or not. But first, I'm going to the restroom. I'll be right back."

Mama Katherine walked away, and Margaret went into the kitchen to get a towel. When she was a child, coming to live with Mama Katherine had seemed magical in every way except one, she thought as she dried the floor. His name was Robert, and he was Mama Katherine's prized rooster.

He was one of the first things Margaret noticed the morning after her arrival, for obvious reasons. She'd never heard a rooster crow, except for on cartoons. It woke her up out of a sound sleep, right at sunrise, and she was beyond excited. She leapt out of bed and ran outside in her bare feet. There he was, stalking around the coop, his beak open and lifted toward the sky, his iridescent tail feathers shining in the morning light.

Of course, Mama Katherine was already up. She was in the coop collecting eggs, and when she saw Margaret she jumped, just a little.

"That's old Robert," she said. "He's making quite a ruckus, isn't he?"

"Sounds just like on TV," Margaret said.

"Come on in, you can see him up close."

Later, Hannah would say, "Well, everyone knows roosters are ornery, Margaret. Why'd you get that close?"

But at the moment, inspecting Robert seemed like exactly the right thing to do. Mama Katherine came to the door of the coop to let Margaret in, and Margaret clung to her hip, hiding behind her leg.

"Go on, now," she said. "Go on up to Robert and say hello."

Margaret was scared. Robert was big, almost as big as a dog one of Margaret's old neighbors had. Yes, the dog was small enough to fit inside a backpack, but still. It was a dog.

"Go on," Mama Katherine said again. Margaret obeyed, easing out from behind Mama to approach Robert. He stopped crowing for long enough to examine Margaret, pinning her with a reddish eye, tilting his head to one side and then the other to look at her head and then her feet.

Margaret laughed. Mama Katherine laughed.

And then Robert struck. Wings spread, mouth open, he lunged at Margaret and pecked her right on the cheek. And he didn't stop there. He backed up, wings still flapping, that musical crow having morphed into an angry clucking sound, and he readied himself to lunge again.

Mama Katherine scooped Margaret up by the waist before he could make a second contact. Margaret had brought her hands up to her face in an automatic response, and when she took them away, they were red with blood. Which, of course, made her face hurt worse.

"That mean old rooster," Mama Katherine said as she carried Margaret into the kitchen to clean her up.

Of course, the screaming woke Hannah, who walked straight out to the coop to yell at Robert. Margaret had been wary of the chickens ever since. When Robert died a few years later, Margaret continued to treat the flock with extreme caution.

Even now, as Mama Katherine came back from the bathroom, Margaret said, "Please tell me I don't have to go inside the coop for this project."

"No, you can stand outside and babysit me," Mama Katherine said.

As they walked outside, Margaret said, "This ought to be interesting—the blind woman and the twenty-nine-year-old octogenarian."

"Funny, Margaret," Mama Katherine said. "Very funny."

# CHAPTER NINE

ALTHOUGH HER VISION was getting worse by the day—by the moment, even—Margaret decided to throw herself into her work before she couldn't work any more.

She hadn't quite figured where to set up her workstation. In fact, she'd sold her old desk because she didn't think it'd fit anywhere inside Mama Katherine's house. They all ate together at the dining room table each evening and her bedroom was too small.

Even though Margaret hadn't planned on interacting with Ethan any more than was strictly necessary, he sent her a text message one morning while she was sipping her coffee.

And she could have turned him down, if Hannah wasn't standing right there, sipping her coffee.

The robotic voice on Margaret's phone said, "Hey, I ran into Donny yesterday at the Hammer and Nail. He said you wanted to set up a workstation. I'll stop by later today, take a look. Oh, and leave room for dessert."

Hannah set down her coffee and clapped her hands together.

"Wait," Margaret said. "Are you jumping up and down right now?"

"Yes," Hannah said, her voice a squeal. "That's awesome! We love Ethan. And he said dessert."

The reference had even Margaret's mouth forming a smile.

That afternoon, Margaret was harvesting tomatoes, wondering why Mama Katherine had insisted on buying twelve different varieties, when she heard Ethan's truck rumbling down the driveway. She couldn't deny the quick flutter of anticipation she felt in her stomach.

She wiped her hands on her shorts as she walked around to the front of the house. Ethan cut the engine. The driver's door opened and shut. She'd always loved the movie, *Dirty Dancing,* and she had an insane vision of her, running to Ethan and him, lifting her above his head where she'd arch up like a bird.

"Are you giggling at me?" Ethan said.

"No," Margaret said. "Just thinking about *Dirty Dancing.*"

"You're into that?"

"The movie."

"Right."

"You didn't have to come over," Margaret said.

"I know," Ethan said. "But your mama said she'd feed me dinner. I can't resist a good meatloaf or a good woman. So. I'm here."

Margaret didn't ask which woman he was referring to. Instead, she said, "You talked to Mama Katherine about this?"

"I did. I knew you'd be skittish about accepting my help."

"Well, you're right about that. And now I can't turn it down, not if you talked to my mama about it. Come on in."

He followed her back, into the dining room, where she stopped and held out her arms. "This area's obviously off-limits. But I can work almost anywhere else where there's space. Preferably somewhere—"

"With lots of light."

"Exactly."

"Give me a tour."

Something about the quality of his voice turned her insides to liquid and made her shiver. It was deep, like he'd smoked cigarettes for years, and smooth, like river water shaping stones.

Margaret took a deep breath and when she would have walked past him, he took her hand. The callouses on his palm sent tingles up her arm.

"The bedrooms are that way," she said, inclining her head. "And the living room's this way. I can't fit a workstation in my bedroom, not with all the boy-band memorabilia in there."

"Oh, you were a fan of those boy bands, huh? I have to say, I pegged you as more of an alternative girl."

"Yeah, I was more into alternative in high school, but the junior high version of myself wouldn't let me give up the life-sized cardboard standup Brian Beatty."

"You're going to have to show that to me. He was the idol of adolescent boys back then."

"I'm not quite ready to allow you into my bedroom."

"Does that mean you plan to be ready at some point?" he said.

Margaret shrugged, but her body was already imagining what that would feel like. Sleeping with him was probably a terrible idea. No, definitely. It was definitely a terrible idea.

They were in the living room now, and Ethan said, "Why don't we set you up in here?"

"In the living room?"

"Why not? There's plenty of room for a desk, I think. Let me take a couple of measurements."

"I need a big desk."

Ethan released her hand and walked toward the window. Immediately, she missed the connection. And right after that, she kicked herself for missing the connection.

He took several measurements—in the corner, in the nook of the big bay window. Although she couldn't quite make out the details, she enjoyed watching him work. His movements were fluid and easy, almost graceful.

Unexpected.

Then, he stood back from the window, angled his body to one side, and said, "Here. It's going to go right here. That'll give you plenty of light in the morning, and it won't be too hot in the afternoon."

Margaret couldn't help but be delighted. It was perfect. She preferred working in the mornings, when she was fresh and had caffeine flowing through her veins. Afternoons were for researching or revising designs or looking through magazines.

"Perfect," she said. "It's perfect."

"Okay. I'll set it up. Be right back."

"What?" she said, but he was already gone.

He came back a couple of minutes later, with a big box on a dolly.

"What's that?" she said, but she knew: it was a desk. He'd brought her a desk.

"It's a desk," he said.

"Of course it is," she said. "You bought me a desk."

"I did," he said. "Ordered it online. Read all the reviews. This is supposed to be the best one."

"You didn't have to do this."

"I know. I wanted to. I'll just get it set up. Assembly required."

Margaret couldn't explain the emotion that clogged her throat as she watched him set the box flat, pull the dolly out from under it, and start cutting the tape with his pocket knife. It was silly. Ridiculous. Was she on the verge of tears over a desk?

No, she realized. She was on the verge of tears over a man. A sweet, kind man who had gone out of his way to do something for her. Something meaningful.

She cleared her throat. "Let me help."

For the next hour, Margaret played assistant. She held up legs and ends and corners, and Ethan put it all together. While they worked, she ran her hands over the surfaces: glass here, metal there, wood there. It was heavy and sturdy, the high quality she'd have bought herself.

When they were done, she stood back and admired it. The tilt of the working surface was perfect, and the adjustable legs meant she could work standing or sitting.

"I love it," she said. She reached out to give Ethan's arm a squeeze.

"I'm glad you do," he said. "I'll admit, I wasn't too sure if I should make the commitment, you know. I thought you might turn me away and I'd have to ship this thing back."

Although she'd sworn there wouldn't be a third date, she found herself saying, "Let me take you to dinner. As a thank you."

"Well, I won't turn you down."

"Tomorrow," Margaret said.

Again, Ethan did something totally unexpected: he turned towards her, put his hands on her shoulders, and said, "I'm going to kiss you, now."

He gave her a full second—enough time to protest, if she wanted to—and then he leaned in and covered her mouth with his.

Just after their lips met, Ethan cupped the back of her head with one hand, his fingers diving into her hair. The movement was so sweet, so tender, that when he ended the kiss, her knees felt weak.

Then, he said, "Tomorrow, then," and walked out of the house.

It was a sleepless night, one during which Margaret relived that kiss over and over again, where she imagined the kiss turning into something more. She considered what would have happened if she'd asked Ethan to stay.

But she couldn't ask him to stay; not yet. Sleeping with him in her childhood bedroom, knowing her mom and sisters were in such close proximity, would be weird.

She contented herself instead with imagining that her new house was built, and that she'd bought a giant bed, big enough for two, and that Ethan shared it with her. Just for one night. It couldn't turn into a longer-term relationship. Was it a relationship? It couldn't last longer than a night because it would become too easy to depend on him.

The next morning, she decided that she wouldn't take him to dinner. She'd make dinner, and set up a picnic outside and they could eat alone.

She bribed Hannah to take her to the store, offering a bottle of wine in exchange for the chauffeuring services.

"So, you're making him dinner," Hannah said once they were on the road.

"I hear that twinkle in your eye," Margaret said. "It's just dinner. Don't get all emotional on me."

"How often do you make dinner for a man?"

"Rarely."

The real answer was never. Margaret never cooked for men. It was too intimate. If a man happened to sleep over, which was also rare, she'd order dinner in, and in the morning, she'd brew some coffee and send him on his way.

"What's different about Ethan?"

*What's different, indeed*, Margaret thought.

"I can't put my finger on it," she said. "He's ... different."

And maybe that was it. Ethan was not pretentious like many of the men she met in the big city. He wasn't afraid to get his hands dirty. He was thoughtful, present, focused.

"Hmm," Hannah said. "What are you cooking?"

"Haven't decided. What would you cook?"

"No idea," Hannah said. "I've never cooked for a man."

"Never?"

"Never."

"Why don't you cook for Tanner Lucas?"

Margaret should have expected it, but Hannah caught her off guard with a quick smack to the shoulder.

"Hey!" Margaret said, rubbing the offended area. "That was uncalled for."

"Not from where I'm sitting," Hannah said. "You should cook something that goes well with wine. Italian, maybe? Lasagna? Spicy spaghetti?"

Margaret nodded. "Good thinking."

SHE COOKED lasagna and bought an expensive bottle of wine. The cost came nowhere near what Ethan had probably spent on that beautiful desk, but hopefully he'd appreciate the gesture.

An hour before he was set to arrive, Margaret put the lasagna in the oven and opened the wine to let it breathe. Ethan showed up smelling like soap and pine trees, which reminded her of that kiss.

"I hope you brought your appetite," Margaret said.

"It always shows up when you're around."

Again, Margaret felt that little thrill in her core, and thought that maybe she'd give in and have dessert tonight. Maybe. Everything in moderation.

"So, tell me about computers," Margaret said once they were seated at the picnic table under the quaking aspen tree next to the house.

"Computers are simple," Ethan said. "Not like people, you know? They speak a certain language. There are no nuances."

Intrigued, Margaret leaned forward. "No nuances, huh? Nuances like—"

"Like the way a woman tilts her head when she tells a man to choose where they're going to eat dinner. Or the way she smiles when she tells him she doesn't mind doing the dishes. That kind of thing."

"I take it you've got experience with these nuances."

"Some," Ethan said. "Good wine, by the way. Great lasagna."

Possibly that was a touchy subject, Margaret thought. She said, "So, was it a nuance when you used, 'Good' to describe the wine and 'Great' to describe my homemade lasagna?"

"It was," he said. "Absolutely."

"How long have you lived with your mother?" Margaret cringed before she even finished the sentence. Certainly that could prove a touchy subject as well. Worse, what if he'd lived with his mother forever? What if he'd never left?

"Going on a year, now," he said. "I was married before. Not something I usually discuss over dinner with a beautiful woman, but then I haven't had many dinners with beautiful women in the past year. Anyway, long story short: I grew up in New Mexico. Albuquerque. When my siblings and I—there were five of us—got out of the house, my parents moved here, to Wyoming. I stayed in Albuquerque. Got married. Got divorced. Ran away. Came here to lick my wounds. And I found that I felt settled here. I stayed."

"I can understand that," Margaret said.

The story made her curious. Why would someone divorce Ethan?

He seemed genuinely thoughtful and kind. And his *voice*. If she ever heard that voice in pillow-talk mode, she'd never be able to walk away.

"I never thought I'd live with my parents, but I guess that's what you call it when you've been there a year. When I moved in, I found a lot of things they'd neglected. I've spent some time making repairs. The gutters needed cleaning, the roof needed patching, the weeds needed pulling. Time just passed, you know? I've actually been looking for a place."

That gave Margaret a little start, which only cemented the fact that looking for any kind of permanency with Ethan, or any man, was a mistake.

"Back in New Mexico?" she said.

"Nah," he said. "I'd like to stay here."

Margaret felt a rush of relief. She wanted to kick herself.

"That's nice," she said.

"What about you?" he said. "It must be hard coming back here when you consider yourself a city girl."

"It is. It's hard. I've always enjoyed being independent, you know? It's easy to settle into those family patterns—like being treated like the youngest child—when you're surrounded by family again. Especially when your whole family thinks you're becoming an invalid."

"Do they really think that, or are they trying to help you?"

"Ah," Margaret said. "Excellent question."

She took a sip of wine as she considered the answer.

"I know they're trying to help me," Margaret said. "But I'm not great at accepting help. Hannah wants me to go to this school for the blind. She found a video somewhere and she forced me to watch it. Then she forced me to order the materials to apply. A packet or something."

"And you don't want to go?"

"It's not that. It's just—no. I don't want to go. I feel like going to a school for the blind is like admitting, to myself, that I am going blind. Not that I don't already know that. But somewhere deep inside, I think I'm holding out for a sudden change. Enrolling in that school almost feels like giving up."

She'd never said those words aloud, or even formulated that thought in her conscious mind. Maybe she'd never even realized she felt that way. But now, having verbalized those feelings, she felt somewhat liberated.

"I understand," Ethan said, and she believed that he did. "But what if you took a different approach? What if, instead of looking at the school like it signaled you were giving up, you looked at it as a method for retaining control? Being proactive rather than reactive?"

This was a good point, and Margaret told him so.

"Does it earn me dessert?"

"We'll see."

Then, because she needed some time to think, and a little mental space, she suggested they go for a walk along the creek.

Ethan took her hand in his, and she realized that she'd been foolish to believe she could get any thinking done when he was around. Her mind took note of his palm against hers, his body next to hers, his voice telling her about how much fun he was having with his nieces and nephews here in Wyoming.

Her body reacted.

He talked about terrorizing his sister with crawdads and frogs and giant bugs, and she thought about sex.

By the time they returned to Mama Katherine's house, Margaret knew that Ethan's sister and one of his three brothers lived nearby. She also knew that she was going to have dessert. Her imagination had worked her body into a state she hadn't experienced in quite awhile.

"What's for dessert?" Ethan said when they approached the picnic table.

"Fresh strawberries and homemade cream," she said.

Even that sounded sexy.

"Sounds delicious," he said.

"Want to eat out here, or inside?"

"I think this picnic table will be sufficient."

Margaret heard him run his palm across the surface. Every nerve ending in her body was on high alert—and all this over a few words about strawberries and cream.

"I'll just go get it," Margaret said. "You can wait here."

*That way I can take a cold shower before I come back out.*

"What's wrong with you?" Hannah asked when Margaret came into the kitchen. "You look like you've just seen a ghost."

"Nothing," Margaret said. "Just getting dessert."

Simply saying the words made Margaret shiver again. Hannah was leaning against the counter, and Margaret nudged her out of the way and opened the fridge.

"Ethan still here?" Hannah said.

"Oh, yeah," Margaret said. Her voice echoed, and she held back the laughter when she realized how excited she sounded."He's still here."

"And not only are you having dessert with him, but you *made* dessert."

"That's right," Margaret said. "I did."

She took out the tray of oversized strawberries and set it on the counter. As she arranged them to make room for the bowl of cream, she said to Hannah, "What are you doing in here, anyway, besides lurking around, spying on me?"

"That's all," Hannah said.

"Liar."

"I'll tell you later," Hannah said.

"Fine. But I'm holding you to it."

"Fine."

Margaret lifted the tray and walked back outside.

"Well that looks awesome," Ethan said.

"I couldn't resist the strawberries," Margaret said. "They're the size of apples."

She set the tray in front of Ethan, then sat down across from him.

"Here," he said. "Let me."

She knew what was coming. Ethan picked up a strawberry, holding it by the stem. He took his time swirling it through the cream, and when he held it up, he said, "Perfect. Close your eyes."

Not that it made a huge difference, she thought, but she obeyed.

"Open your mouth."

Now *that* sounded sexual. No doubt about it. Normally, Margaret would find this kind of activity contrived. But for some reason, with Ethan, she found it incredibly arousing.

She felt the cream on her lips, and then the tip of the strawberry. She bit down, and she felt his fingertips on her lips. Which made her shiver. Again.

He fed her the berry, bite by bite, each time, using a finger to wipe extra cream off her lips or chin. By the time it was gone, her body ached from tension. Then, he said, "Happen to have a napkin?"

Speechless, all she could do was shake her head. She reached across the table to take his hand, and then she licked his fingers clean, one by one.

"Fuck the strawberries," he said, and before she realized what was happening, he had moved around the side of the table and was beside her, his hands on her shoulders and his mouth on hers.

The kiss wasn't gentle. It bordered on desperate and she realized his body probably felt as tightly wound as hers did right now. Which only turned her on more. His tongue was in her mouth, and her body was softening against his.

They broke apart and Ethan, his voice rough, said, "Shit. I want you, Margaret. And I'm going to have you. Just let me know when you're ready."

Then, he kissed her again, softly this time, and tucked a strand of hair behind her ear. "I've got to go."

She listened to him walk down the gravel path, get into his truck, and drive away.

She was still frozen in place when she heard someone coming up behind her.

"Didn't Ethan like the strawberries?" Hannah said.

"Oh, he liked them, all right," Margaret said. "In fact, he liked them so much we almost had sex on the picnic table."

"So what went wrong?"

"First of all," Margaret said, "I told him I wasn't going to sleep with him."

Hannah gasped, and before she could share her opinion on that one, Margaret plowed ahead: "Second of all, I'm sure he didn't want to make love in my childhood bedroom with a cardboard cutout of Brian Beatty looking on."

"Couldn't you think of an alternate location?" Hannah said.

Margaret just sighed. Sure she could. She'd had sex in Mama Katherine's garden, once, hadn't she?

"Third of all, he bought me a desk."

"Ohhh," Hannah said. "And you're thinking you want him to bend you over that desk and—"

"No!" Margaret said, bumping her shoulder against Hannah's. "That's not what I meant. It's just that right now, it's a desk. Then it's lasagna—"

"Which was your idea."

"Which was my idea. And then there's Ethan feeding me strawberries in an experience so sensual my panties were smoking."

"Which doesn't sound like a bad thing."

"Which isn't a bad thing. Until the thing that happens next, which is that we have sex, I fall in love with him, and he leaves me."

"Wow," Hannah said. "You took that story from act one, scene one to final curtain and made it a tragedy."

Margaret shrugged. "It is what it is. Help me finish these strawberries."

"If you insist," Hannah said.

Once she had her sister captive, Margaret said, "Now, spill. What were you doing in the kitchen earlier? You were acting guilty, like I caught you with your hand in the cookie jar."

"I was eating cookies."

"Liar. Why don't you want to tell me?"

"I don't know."

"Just tell me."

"Tell you what?" Sarah joined them at the table, and Mama Katherine came next.

"Didn't Ethan like the strawberries?" Mama Katherine said.

"Liked them too much," Hannah said. "Margaret had to send him packing after he incinerated her panties."

"But right now, we're talking about your guilty behavior in the kitchen," Margaret said.

"Wow," Sarah said. "We leave for a couple of hours, Mama, and look at all we miss."

"Did you pick out the materials for the countertops?" Hannah said.

"Stay on track," Margaret said.

"Right," Hannah said. "I was cyber-stalking Tanner Lucas."

"In the kitchen?" Margaret said.

"Stay on track," Sarah said, and Margaret said, "I knew it! You're curious."

"Aren't *you*? He's going to be building your house."

"Oh, I'm curious, all right," Margaret said.

"What'd you find out?" Sarah said.

"How is it possible that you still talk with your mouth full?" Hannah said.

"Stay on track," Mama Katherine said. "What'd you find out?"

"He's just as good-looking as ever," Hannah said. "Which means he's probably still a jerk."

"Well, I guess we'll find out tomorrow," Mama Katherine said. "He's coming by for a meeting with Donny at noon."

---

TANNER LUCAS *WAS* as good-looking as ever—according to Sarah and Mama Katherine, anyway. And actually, Margaret found him delightful.

When he pulled up in front of the house, Donny said, "I'll bring him in to make introductions," and Sarah snorted. "We've all been cyber-stalking him, Don. There's no need for introductions."

But Donny walked out, anyway. Hannah stood up and began to make her way toward the bedrooms, but Mama Katherine stopped her with one sharp look.

"You will not avoid this man forever," Mama Katherine said.

Hannah's voice sounded sulky when she said, "But I could at least avoid him for now." She sat on the couch next to Margaret.

When Donny walked back in, Tanner at his side, Margaret could tell he was still tall and lanky. But Hannah must have noticed something more, because she did a quick intake of breath.

Margaret stifled a giggle as they all stood up to shake Tanner's hand.

"I told Donny there's no need for introductions—"

"That's what I said," Hannah grumbled.

"—as Hannah, here, makes up a good ninety percent of the memories from my teenage years. And I could never forget her lovely sisters, either."

"Nice to see you again, Tanner," Mama Katherine said, and Hannah snorted.

Margaret fought off another chuckle.

"These your drawings, Margaret?" Tanner said.

"Oh!" Margaret said. "Yes, they are. I meant to put them away before you came."

"Why would you do that?" he said.

"I don't know," Margaret said. "We do almost the same thing. I'm kind of rusty, and…"

She let her voice trail off.

"These are great," Tanner said. "I love the lines on this one. What is it, a coffee shop?"

"If it says 'Sixth Street Coffee Shop' on the plans, then it's probably a coffee shop," Hannah said.

Margaret rolled her eyes. Tanner seemed to ignore Hannah, and Margaret wished she could see his expression. Was he embarrassed? Did he find Hannah's comment challenging, in a good way?

"I wanted to talk to you about something, Margaret," Tanner said.

"Me?" Margaret said.

"Yeah, you," Tanner said. "I wanted to offer you the chance to design the houses I'll be building for you and for Sarah and Donny. I've seen your work, not just here, but online. And it's good. Real good. Now, Donny tells me you're slowing down a bit when it comes to designing buildings, but I wanted to give you the first shot."

Margaret felt like someone had punched her right in the gut. Or, like she'd fallen out of the branches of a tree and landed flat on her back, the wind knocked out of her. She'd never been punched in the gut, but she had fallen out of a tree, and she knew how that felt. She couldn't breathe.

"Me?" she said again.

"Yeah, you," Tanner said again. "From what I've read, it seems like you're the go-to architect for all the big names."

Margaret licked her lips. They'd gone dry. "From what you've read?"

"Yeah," Tanner said. "You know. Online."

"You read?" Hannah said.

Margaret elbowed her.

"Yes, Miss Hannah. I read. And from what I've read about your sister, here, we'd all be missing out on an amazing opportunity if we didn't at least offer her the chance to design these houses."

Margaret didn't know what to say. She could hardly see. It was nearly impossible that her designs would turn out well. She and Sarah would be living in these houses for years to come. What if they hated them?

"You don't have to decide right now," Tanner said. "We have time. We've got to go through the permit process to get the acreage split. And then there's some excavating and leveling to do, before we build."

"Okay," Margaret said. "Let me think on it."

"We're going to walk the property, decide on the best spots for these two houses," Donny said. "Anyone want to come?"

"I'd like to come," Mama Katherine said, and Sarah said, "Me, too."

"I've got to run to the store," Hannah said.

Margaret joined the rest of them to walk the property. Tanner had solid ideas. He gave them several different options for where he'd build the houses, and Margaret thought each one had merit.

"I like the option where both houses sit next to the creek," Tanner said. "But that's going to mean they're pretty close together."

"Yeah," Margaret said. "I'm not sure the sound of the creek running will drown out the sound of Sarah and Donny."

Sarah nudged her, and Donny said, "That's right. We might need to put Margaret's house on the creek and our house a ways back. Like up against the property line."

In the end, they settled on the first option, and, Tanner said, "We'll put the master bedrooms on opposite sides. Besides, from what I hear, Margaret's not going to be single for long."

Immediately, Margaret thought of Ethan. In her new house. In her bed. And she blushed so hard and fierce she had to walk to the creek's edge and splash water on her face.

# CHAPTER TEN

WHILE MARGARET PONDERED Tanner's offer, she decided to drum up some new projects, just to see if she still had it. She set up a computer desk beside her drawing table and reached out to old clients, asking if they needed anything done, or if they could refer her to their colleagues.

Some of them asked for new designs, and she created a library for a small town in Arizona, a clubhouse for a new golf club in Monterey, and a hotel lobby for a resort in Jamaica.

And even when she completed those projects and didn't have a new one in the chute, she laid out giant sheets of paper and drew. She designed beautiful new houses and bookstores and art galleries that would likely never be built.

Margaret hadn't wanted children; her legacy would be buildings. And not just buildings, but all the things that happened inside those buildings. People would step into a space and immediately feel something. Maybe they'd notice the way the wide windows and high ceilings let in the light at a certain time of day, or the way the shape of the room allowed a certain kind of flow.

Or maybe they wouldn't even notice the building itself. Maybe they'd just notice how everything seemed right.

People would experience moments in her spaces: children would hear wonderful stories for the first time in that library. A man would propose to a woman in that glorious hotel lobby. The coffee shop would provide the background for a pair of best friends to have weekly conversations, to talk about their love lives, their problems, their triumphs.

This was her legacy, she thought one morning as her hand arced across the blank paper, the contrast of her pencil marks bringing relief. At least she could see that, for now, for today.

If she didn't have this, she didn't have anything.

She buried herself in that living room, creating enough drawings that she had to set up another table where she could stack them. Maybe if she worked hard enough, helped out enough, someone—God, the universe, some grand puppeteer in the sky—would let her keep her vision just a little bit longer.

Maybe if she used it, it wouldn't go away.

She helped out around the house. She fixed a toilet and replaced the doorbell. She built a new rack for Mama Katherine's pea plants and she harvested tomatoes. She canned cherries.

There was no fourth date with Ethan, although he continued to call and send her messages. She spoke with him on the phone, responded to his messages, but held him at arm's length. Dating someone was pointless, even if she could picture him, clearly, sitting next to her on the front porch of the new house, sipping iced tea in the early evening light.

Maybe they could be friends—she was going to need friends in this new phase of life—but that was it. No romance. Nothing she'd come to rely on, nothing where she could develop expectations.

But still, exactly as she'd anticipated, her body knew moving back home was like giving up: her vision deteriorated to the point where she had more bad days than good. Complete vision loss, which had once seemed laughable, now seemed probable, maybe even imminent.

Margaret always anticipated drawing up building designs well past the prime of her life. She had mental images of herself sitting at her drafting desk, a pencil in her gnarled hands, her name in college textbooks where they talked about the masters. She'd be like the Shakespeare of architecture; mentioned everywhere, a household name.

She'd be filthy, filthy rich, and although she'd eventually want to live in a house or an apartment building of her own design—and maybe designing the two new houses was a good idea, in that respect —it wouldn't be anything fancy. That way, she'd have a ton of money to leave to her nieces and nephews. And if neither Sarah nor Hannah produced any nieces or nephews in addition to Amelia, well, then, all the more for Amelia.

Of course, she'd leave some money to the field of architecture, too. Maybe she'd start a scholarship fund for students who showed potential but couldn't afford schooling. Or maybe she would start a whole new school.

Always, always, she thought she had time. Now, though, she realized she didn't have time at all.

Acceptance set in like a rainstorm in Seattle: its wide, gray edge moving over Margaret's consciousness until it covered everything, water dripping out of the soggy sky. Everything was gray and cold and dreary.

The help her sisters offered only made things worse, highlighting the fact that soon, she'd no longer be able to do things for herself. Sarah offered to cook and Hannah offered to do laundry. Mama Katherine, who should have been relaxing, started to decline Margaret's offers to help with chores.

Not only did Margaret have nothing to do, but she also experienced a growing need to get out of the house. When she finally listened to the video Hannah had found for her—the one about the school for the blind—Margaret was thinking of it as a potential for escape, rather than a necessary education. She even called Hannah into her living room office to fill out the online application form.

"I think it's stupid you have to apply for an application to get in," Margaret said.

"Well, I suppose they just want to make sure the school's a good fit for you," Hannah said. She added, "I'm just glad you decided to do this. It's going to be good for you."

Margaret merely grunted as she listened to Hannah typing, muttering, typing again.

"I know you don't want to go," Hannah said.

"No, no," Margaret said. "I do want to go. I'm sure it will be great."

"They want to know if you have a seeing-eye dog."

"Well, I don't," Margaret said. "Can you imagine?"

"Wait," Hannah said. "I thought you'd want one."

"Why?" Margaret said. "I have you."

"I'm clicking the yes box."

Margaret growled. She could always change that when she showed up at the school. As an afterthought, she said, "Wait, why? Are you going to run off with Tanner Lucas?"

Hannah elbowed her.

"Very funny. That guy's a jerk."

"Mama likes him."

"She's blinded by those dimples."

"You noticed those, huh?" Margaret said. She remembered noticing them in high school, and thinking those dimples made him a lady-killer.

"Shut up."

"What?" Margaret said. "Mama wouldn't stop talking about them. Anyway, he seemed nice. Which you'd know if you'd stuck around rather than 'running to the store.'"

"He seems nice until you get into an actual conversation with him."

"I did," Margaret said. "And he came across as very thoughtful. Charming, even. We tossed around some ideas, and he was pretty flexible. Maybe he's grown up some."

"Doubt it," Hannah said. "Let's get off this train, okay?"

"Fine," Margaret said. "But he's going to be around a lot, from the sounds of things."

A few seconds later, Hannah said, "Okay, all done. They're going to send you an application packet. Should arrive within seven days."

# CHAPTER ELEVEN

T<sup>HE</sup> A<sup>PPLICATION</sup> P<sup>ACKET</sup> arrived on a cool Thursday morning. Hannah came bouncing into the house to give it to Margaret, who was in the living room, pretending not to sketch out designs for the new houses.

"Ooh," Hannah said. "Are those for the new houses?"

"Nah," Margaret said. "Just playing."

"I like them. But I'm not here to invade the living room. Here."

She held it out and Margaret could tell she was proud of herself. She pictured her big sister, legs together, shoulders back, chin up. She took the envelope—noticed it was heavy—and set it on her computer desk.

"Need help reading it?"

"I can manage," Margaret said. "Plus, I think you said there was a CD. Thanks, though."

She went back to drawing.

"Aren't you going to open it?"

"Yes," Margaret said. "When I'm done with this."

"Oh," Hannah said. She turned to leave and Margaret felt a pang of guilt.

"Hannah," she said.

Hannah stopped inside the doorway.

"Thank you. Really. I'm going to read it. I promise."

The truth was that Margaret didn't want Hannah to see how much effort reading required these days. Margaret would have to set the papers on the table in the brightest room possible, and then lean over them with a giant magnifying glass. It was humiliating, and Margaret would prefer to do it in private. Yes, she could listen to the CD, but she'd always preferred reading.

An hour later, the first sketch complete and the second one well underway, her phone dinged and said in its robotic voice, "Text message from Ethan-Leroy."

Emotions zinged like electricity through her body. Her phone played the message: "Hey, I'm planning to stop by in a little while. I've got something for you. If you're busy, just let me know and I'll come by another time."

"Well, I'm intrigued," Margaret said.

What could it be? He certainly wasn't bringing another desk. They hadn't spoken in a couple of days. She had every intention of responding, saying she was busy. But she simply went back to her sketching. And she ignored the way those electric currents picked up when he walked in a while later and said, "Wow. You're even more beautiful when you're working."

Friends didn't call friends, "beautiful," did they? Still, she smiled up at him and couldn't help but think of the way he'd kissed her after feeding her that strawberry.

"If we're going to be friends, then you're going to have to come up with a different adjective."

"Friends, huh?" he said. "In that case, how's … smokin' hot?"

Margaret felt heat creeping up her neck.

"Or how about super-sexy?"

"Ha," she said. "I love hearing you add 'super' as a modifier. It sounds so … manly."

"I can keep going," he said. "But I won't. I brought you something."

"Do friends buy friends presents?"

"Of course they do."

"When's the last time one of your friends bought you a present?"

"Yesterday," Ethan said. "Tanner. Bought me a beer."

"Is that considered a present?"

"I believe so," Ethan said. "A beer is a gift, right? It's the gift of refreshment, relaxation, and, if you're friends, a good conversation to accompany it."

"And what did you and Tanner talk about?"

"Well, that's obvious, isn't it?"

"I don't think so."

"We talked about the beautiful, mysterious Bradley sisters."

"Of course you did. And, as my beautiful, mysterious sister,

Hannah, would say, this train is getting off-track. Let's see that present."

"It's outside."

"It is? It had better not be alive."

"Why not?" Ethan said.

She could hear the humor in his voice and decided to forego an answer. He wouldn't have bought her a puppy. They walked outside to where there was a big flatbed truck sitting in the driveway. A man Margaret assumed was the driver stood at the back, and together, he and Ethan lowered the gate. Then, Ethan came toward, her, took her hand, and led her around the truck. He placed her palm on the surface of the present, and she recognized it immediately as she ran her fingers along it.

"You bought me a tree." For some reason, Margaret was overcome by emotion. It welled up inside her chest and she thought she might actually cry.

"For the new place. I know you're still deciding on locations, but Tanner said you knew where you wanted the house. I bought it in a big container to give you time to decide where to put it. It can survive here for a few months."

"What kind is it?"

"Cherry. Symbolizes new beginnings."

Margaret's throat was too tight for any words to come out. She nodded. Then she squeaked out, "I love cherries."

"I know," he said. "And I know you've already got one cherry tree here. But your mama said it's a Bing, and this is a Rainier. So."

"So," Margaret said. "You've got to be the most thoughtful man I know."

"We've just got to unload it. Figured we could put it over there, next to the creek. And then later, Mike here will come back and help us move it, get it planted next to your new house."

"Are you trying to win over my cold, cold heart?" Margaret said.

What she didn't say, was that it was working.

"Just being a good friend," Ethan said.

Matt, whose body looked short and stocky, like a wrestler's, even to Margaret's failing eyes, used a forklift to unload the tree and drive it over to its temporary home. Ethan directed him, walking alongside the forklift. And for a moment, Margaret was able to envision the tree as an ornament in the front of her new house. Then, she had that vision again: the one where she and Ethan sat on the porch, drinking iced tea, the leaves of that cherry tree fluttering in the breeze.

"Friends drink iced tea on their friends' porches, right?" she said.

She didn't realize she'd spoken aloud until Ethan said, "Absolutely."

Matt drove away, the rumbling of his truck's engine fading into the warming day, and Ethan said, "Thinking about going back to school?"

"What?"

"I saw that packet on your computer desk."

Margaret just shrugged.

"Hannah sent for it, didn't she?"

"Yeah. She thinks I should go before—well, before I've completely lost my independence, I guess."

"Seems reasonable."

She could tell he was treading lightly.

"Out with it," she said. "You're thinking more than you're saying."

"I think it's a good idea, is all," Ethan said. "You're going to have to make some changes. Why not get support, and information, too, from experts? It's what you'd do if you were designing a building under completely new circumstances."

He had a solid point, and she told him so.

"Want moral support while you read through it?"

"How do you know I haven't read through it already?"

"That packet was brand new. Didn't have a fingerprint on it. Or a wrinkle. In fact, I think it was still in a plastic wrapper."

"That's very observant of you."

"Would it help if we read through it over a beer?"

In every scenario Margaret could imagine, she'd want to read through the packet alone. She didn't need anyone sitting next to her, helping her through it. But for some reason—some reason other than the beer—Margaret answered before she even realized what she was saying: "Yeah, that'd be nice."

"I just happen to have a six-pack in my truck. I was going to take it home and sit by the river, but I'd be happy to crack open a couple right now."

"Are you sure?" Margaret said. "Reading through an admission packet doesn't seem nearly as relaxing as sitting by the river."

"But I get to read through the admission packet with you."

When Margaret didn't answer right away—she was too stunned to know what to say—Ethan said, "I'll get the beers. You get the packet. Then we can go sit in the shade of your new tree."

Ethan spread a blanket on the ground at the site of Margaret's new home, and once they were settled she took a moment to enjoy the sound of the creek.

"This really is going to be a nice spot for my new house," she said.

"I think so, too," Ethan said. "I'm looking forward to seeing how it turns out."

Again, Ethan's words surprised Margaret. The men Margaret typically associated with didn't often refer to the future. She spread the admission materials out in front of them.

"*Start here*," Ethan read, picking up a folder. "Looks like a nice place. Not sure you'd be impressed with the architecture. But that aside, the campus looks nice."

"Hmm," Margaret said. "What's it say on the inside?"

She heard Ethan open the booklet, and he started reading: "*Losing your vision comes with many challenges—physical and emotional. At the Mary Thompson School for the Blind, it's our mission to help you navigate these challenges with dignity and even fun so you can maintain your independence. Since 1978, we've delivered expert training to more than five thousand people.*"

He paused, then said, "Keep going?"

"Independence is good," Margaret said. "Sure, keep going."

"*We offer several different programs to meet your needs: Mobility Training, Life Skills Training, and Guide Dog Training.*"

Margaret nodded. Would she need mobility training living in the country? She wouldn't be using public transportation, but there was a lot more to mobility than hopping on a city bus or a subway. In fact, downtown Walker did have crosswalks and stores. And she'd have to grocery shop, go to the dentist, take showers. She wasn't even sure what Life Skills Training was, but she should probably find out. And she definitely didn't want a Guide Dog.

"There's a little blurb on each of those programs," Ethan said, "and then a whole, separate pamphlet on each one, too."

"That's a lot of reading for you," Margaret said.

"I don't mind," Ethan said. "I'm in great company. Which should I read first?"

Margaret sipped her beer and considered.

"Read the Mobility Training, I guess."

As he did, Margaret listened more to the sound of his voice than to the words he was actually saying. She didn't know why, exactly, but she found that she'd already made the decision to go to the Mary Thompson School for the Blind. If both Hannah and Ethan thought it was a good idea, it probably was.

# CHAPTER TWELVE

Hannah and Sarah insisted on taking Margaret to the Mary Thompson School for the Blind when the next session started two weeks later, even though Margaret said she could grab a taxi.

"We'll make a fun overnight out of it," Sarah said.

"Yeah," Hannah said. "It'll be a slumber party. Just like the old days."

"Fine," Margaret said, "but I'm not sleeping with either one of you, because just like the old days, you'll keep me awake."

"We know," Hannah said. "You need your beauty sleep. But just FYI, I stopped singing in my sleep years ago."

"Did not," Sarah said. "We heard you on our road trip. What was she singing, Margaret?"

"I think it was *Rudolph the Red-Nosed Reindeer*."

"Was not," Hannah said. "It was *Jingle Bells*."

"Whatever it was," Margaret said, "I get my own bed."

They agreed, and when they checked in, the hotel receptionist gave them a suite with two queens and a sofa pull-out.

"I know why you didn't want us to bring you," Hannah said. Margaret heard her flopping down onto one of the mattresses in the main bedroom. "You wanted Ethan to bring you, because you wanted to have hot hotel sex with him."

Margaret arched an eyebrow at her. "Hotel sex loses its luster when that's all you do."

"But," Sarah said, "notice how she didn't say anything about the Ethan portion of that comment."

"Have you guys done it yet?" Hannah said.

"I'm scandalized," Margaret said. "And no. We haven't. And it's not a 'yet.' We just haven't."

Her mind flashed her a memory of the way Ethan had fed her those strawberries, and she couldn't help but notice the warmth flowing down to her core.

"You're getting all hot and bothered," Sarah said. "You want to do it with him."

"Do not," Margaret said.

"Liar," Hannah said. "I'll bet it's good, too."

"Oh, my gosh," Margaret said. "You're thinking about sex with Ethan? That's just weird."

"He has those big, workman's hands," Hannah said.

"And I'm pretty sure he knows how to use 'em," Sarah said.

"That's enough of that," Margaret said, her face blushing madly. "We're going out."

They had dinner and wine and listened to live music, and of course her sisters couldn't—or wouldn't—stop making sex jokes about Ethan.

"We'd stop talking about it if you'd stop blushing," Hannah said. Margaret remained silent, and blushed some more.

She had such fun that evening she almost forgot why they were there. But eventually, the band packed up, the wine ran out, and the sisters went back to the hotel room. Once they were all in bed with the lights out, Margaret said, "You guys?"

"Yeah?" Sarah said. Margaret could tell she was on the verge of sleep.

"While I'm here, maybe you guys could research what happened to Mama Katherine's old husband. Philip."

She heard Hannah sigh. "Part of me is curious. Beyond curious. I mean, he's my father. But part of me feels like looking him up would be a betrayal."

"Would it?" Sarah said.

"I don't know," Hannah said.

"I almost feel like she betrayed you, by not telling you," Margaret said. "But the truth is, she probably thought she was protecting you."

"We can't protect our children from everything," Sarah said.

"Isn't that the truth," Margaret said.

Then, despite being alone in the bed, with no one talking or singing in their sleep, she laid awake all night.

---

ETHAN WAS RIGHT: Margaret was not impressed with the architecture of the office at the Mary Thompson School for the Blind. In the bright morning sunlight, she could make out its boxy structure: gray cinderblocks on bottom with a blue metal box on top.

"Function over form," she said, and her sisters—one standing on either side of her—gripped her hands simultaneously.

"I'm just proud of you for enrolling," Hannah said.

"It's going to be great," Sarah said. "You'll see."

Margaret nodded. "I'm nervous."

The sunlight bounced off the front door of the building as it opened, and someone walked towards them. Margaret took another deep breath, and her sisters squeezed her hands again, then let go.

"Margaret Bradley?" the woman said.

She nodded, and the woman extended a hand. "Grace Lancaster. Come on in and we'll get your paperwork filled out."

Margaret felt panic swoop in as she imagined herself filling out paperwork. How would that even work? How would she read the forms? How would she write small enough to fit the text in all the proper places? She'd be on her own. Maybe Hannah or Sarah could stay and help her.

"Don't worry," Grace said. "You'll be fine."

Margaret nodded, licked her lips. "I feel like it's my first day at a new school."

Hannah laughed, and Margaret realized she was nervous, too. "It *is* your first day at a new school."

"Right," Margaret said. "I guess this is it, ladies. This is where you drop me off and tell me to behave myself and have a good first day. I'll call you later."

"Behave yourself and have a good first day," Sarah said, hugging her. "It's going to be great."

With that, Margaret was on her own. She followed Grace into the ugly (*make that functional*, she corrected herself) building, and into a small room where Grace pulled out a chair. "Have a seat and I'll grab you a drink. Coffee? Tea? Water?"

"Coffee, please," Margaret said.

"I'll be right back."

When she was alone, Margaret sighed. Loudly. Then a man's voice came from behind her: "First day, huh?"

Margaret turned around to face the door. "Yeah," she said. "Did my nervous sigh give me away?"

The man chuckled. "Yep. I'm pretty sure I felt the same way on my first day. Now, they can't get me to leave. I hung around here constantly, and they went ahead and gave me a full-time job. Brian Singer, welcoming committee."

She stood up to shake his hand. "Margaret Bradley. Is that really your job title?"

He laughed. "Nope. My official title is grand master of student orientation. We'll be spending some time together today."

"I see you've met Brian." Grace, a coffee cup in each hand, squeezed past Brian and came around to sit across from Margaret. "He'll be showing you around after we finish filling out your paperwork. Let me just fire up the computer for you."

"So, Margaret," Brian said. He sat beside her. "What's your story?"

"Which chapter?" she said.

"The one that brings you here."

"Well," Margaret said. She took another deep breath. She hadn't shared this story with very many people.

"I noticed my peripheral vision was getting worse. I thought it was just aging, or my imagination. I wanted it to be. But then one day, I was in downtown Seattle, going to meet a client. I had a folder full of papers. Drawings. I'm—*was*—an architect."

She remembered the moment with clarity: the honking of a horn, the fluttering of those papers, the realization that she'd had no idea she was about to be run over. Even now, her hands trembled. She took a sip of coffee.

"I went straight to the doctor after that," she said. "I'd been putting it off. And he diagnosed me with retinitis pigmentosa."

"And then you went to another doctor, right?" Brian said.

"How'd you know?"

"I did the same. I got a second opinion, a third opinion, and a fourth opinion. When all four opinions matched, I realized I really was losing my vision. Best thing that ever happened to me."

"Really?" Margaret said.

"Really," Brian said. "I was a high-powered executive back then, working seventy-hour weeks, closing deals, wining and dining potential business associates, leading meetings, signing contracts. I was a big hitter. And I was miserable. I didn't realize that at the time. And, truth be told, when I first started to lose my vision, I was pissed. I was angry. I had things to *do*, man. Wheels to turn, lines to sign. I didn't realize how miserable until I came here. I discovered a whole separate side of life I didn't realize existed. Instead of mergers and acquisitions, I'm actually helping people."

Margaret simply nodded. She could relate on some level. She felt like she had things to do. But in some ways, her situation was the opposite. She'd been happy. Fulfilled. She wasn't working seventy-hour weeks—well, not really. Those longer weeks didn't feel like work. And she *was* helping people—giving them beautiful spaces in which to create memories.

"Anyway," Brian said. "I'll leave you in Grace's capable hands and I'll be back in a bit to give you a tour."

Grace was true to her word: Margaret was fine. Grace walked her through filling out her paperwork on a computer with an extra-bright screen, on a form with an extra-large font.

"All done," Grace said. "Let's go meet up with Brian, and you can get that tour. And then he'll get you settled into your apartment. As you know, classes begin tomorrow. Which means you'll have some time to relax. We offer Happy Hour every afternoon at four p.m. in the lounge. It's a great time."

Brian stood in the main office with what Margaret thought was a small group of people. "Ah, there she is. Margaret, meet your class-mates. James, Isabel, and Michael."

After the pleasantries and hand-shaking, Brian opened the front door. "Let the tour begin."

Margaret was surprised at how small the campus was; just a school building and a residential building in addition to the office.

"A lot of the learning takes place off-campus," Brian said when Margaret commented on it. "Think of it like a set of field trips. We take you downtown, to crosswalks and restaurants and the city bus."

"The city bus. Wow." It was Isabel, the only other woman in the group. She had a deep, sultry voice and an accent Margaret couldn't quite place. "It's been ages since I rode the city bus. Do we have to?"

"I thought they invented taxis to save us from the city bus," Margaret said. There was a small bark of laughter from Isabel, and Brian, his voice chiding, said, "Now, now, ladies. Taking the city bus is a life skill. A rite of passage for those losing their vision. All right. Let's check out the school building."

As they fell into line behind him, Isabel, her accent lyrical, whis-pered to Margaret, "You and I can just share a taxi when they take us downtown. That's a life skill too, right?"

Margaret snickered. Isabel snickered. And Margaret felt like she'd made a new friend. They stuck together during the tour of the school building, where they learned about the modified classroom and the kitchen ("No cooking for me," Isabel said. "I thought the silver lining to losing my vision was that I could just order in from now on").

"Tell me the residential building's better-looking than the office building," Margaret said to Isabel as they walked across campus.

"I can't," Isabel said, her voice brimming with more laughter. "I can't see it."

"Oh," Margaret said. "Right. Well, I guess that's a silver lining, in and of itself."

"Yes, in this case I suppose it is," Isabel said.

The apartments were nothing special, because they didn't have to be. They were functional, utilitarian.

"You've got your bedroom here, in the corner, and your living area here," Brian was saying.

Margaret leaned against the counter while he talked about getting around the campus, and she thought about what it would be like to live in a world where things of beauty—people, buildings, the views in high-rise apartments—weren't important. That wasn't Margaret's world. She loved things of beauty.

"You don't have to worry about whether you can see those grease spots on the stovetop," Isabel said, her voice close to Margaret's ear.

"Just when I was starting to get depressed that this place didn't have a good view—and that it no longer matters whether a place has a good view."

"Ah, yes," Isabel said. "I hear you. I realized I'll never see the faces of my future grandchildren and it nearly broke me apart. But what can you do? We've got to soldier on, right?"

Margaret took a deep breath, leaned her shoulder against Isabel's for a brief moment. "Right."

At precisely four p.m., Brian led the group down to Happy Hour. If Margaret didn't suspect they were standing in yet another utilitarian room, with cheap laminate tiles on the floor and wine in clear plastic cups sitting on a folding plastic table, she'd have felt like the Happy Hour at the Mary Thompson School for the Blind was a typical, restaurant-style Happy Hour: people talked and laughed, and music was playing. It sounded a bit tinny, not like you'd get with a live pianist or band, but Margaret decided she'd make herself enjoy it— this almost-normal slice of life in an increasingly abnormal world.

Someone offered her a glass of wine, and when she accepted and the person pressed the cup into her hand, she realized how dangerous being non-sighted could be. She'd always had a keen sense of personal safety. Mama Katherine had drilled rules into her mind when she left for The Big City: never accept an opened beverage from a stranger at a bar, never leave your drink unattended, don't hitch a ride home with a stranger. She couldn't very well monitor her drink if she couldn't see it.

"Well, you seem very deep in thought, Miss Margaret."

"Isabel," Margaret said. "You surprised me."

"Always be aware of your surroundings," Isabel said, and just when Margaret was thinking she sounded an awful lot like Mama Katherine—or an awful lot like she'd been listening to the monologue in Margaret's mind—she chuckled. "Our world is changing, my friend. Want to sit?"

Of course, the lighting in this place was brilliant, and Margaret could see a bank of cushy chairs against the wall. They sat in two of them, and didn't speak for a few moments.

"When I first realized I was losing my vision, I wrote it off," Isabel said, her voice cutting through the surrounding din. "I thought, this couldn't possibly be happening, and especially not to me." Her voice turned wry when she added, "I'm a high-powered career woman. I'm important."

She paused, and just when Margaret was about to ask what Isabel did, she said, "I'm an attorney. A prosecutor. I've put people in prison for lifetimes. Combine my sentences and you have centuries. I lived my life like a checklist: college, law school, marriage, prosecutor, children. According to that checklist, I'm supposed to go into private practice next. That's where the money is, you know. I thought I had everything that was important."

"Same here," Margaret said. "Only, a husband and children weren't on my list."

"No?" Isabel said. There was no judgment in her voice—only curiosity.

"No," Margaret said. "And now I think I may be past that point."

"It's never too late for love," Isabel said. "Although, to hear my mama tell it, it is too late for bearing children. Your eggs dry up."

Margaret laughed. "I'm sure mine dried up a long time ago."

"What do you do, Margaret?"

"I was an architect. Same as you—an *important* architect. I never put anyone in prison, but I put lots of people in beautiful buildings."

"You *were* an architect?"

"I retired."

"Surely you're not more than forty. You can't retire already."

"Ever heard of an architect who can't see?"

"You may have a point," Isabel said. "I don't know how long you've been on this journey, but I can tell you that I've been through all the stages of grief. Now, looking back, I can see that the things I thought were important? They're not. Don't get me wrong, being a prosecutor is noble work. Especially for the crap pay. But I wasn't doing it for altruistic reasons. I was using it as a rung on a ladder, and I worked hard, long hours. Because of that, I haven't always been the wife, or the mother, I should be. And those are days you don't get back, right? I hired nannies to pick my children up from school, take them to soccer practice and ballet class, and cook them dinner. And I've missed out on a lot: wiggly teeth, big school projects, school shopping. And what do I have to show for it? The end of my career. I'm going blind. They don't put legal paperwork in braille, I'll tell you that."

"Surely there are other non-sighted attorneys. There must be a way to make it work."

Isabel made an "Mmm," sound, and Margaret imagined her shrugging. "I'm sure. But it almost seems like this is a sign from the gods to slow down. Spend time with my children before it's too late. Do you know they're already locking themselves in their bedrooms at eleven these days?"

"I didn't realize," Margaret said. "I wouldn't know how to handle it. I guess it's a good thing my eggs are drying up."

"They are not," Isabel said. "You're young yet, no? How old are you?"

"Thirty-two."

"Ah! Maybe this losing your vision thing is a sign from the gods that you need to go out and be fruitful. Actually, I think there's something in the Bible about that."

Margaret shook her head and drained her glass. "More wine?"

Over the course of the next several days, Margaret found that she settled into kind of a rhythm at the Mary Thompson School for the Blind: she'd get up early and sip on coffee while listening to an audiobook. At some point, she'd go for walks while she did this, but she had to perfect her use of the cane, first.

Then she'd shower and get dressed and go to class, where she practiced cooking and crossing the street, and where she learned about the resources that make life without sight easier. After class, Margaret and Isabel went to Happy Hour, where they sat in the same chairs every evening, chatting about the past and the future, debating the pros and cons of seeing eye dogs. And then they'd eat dinner. Most nights, they took turns cooking, but every Friday they ordered in. By the time dinner was over, it was practically time to go to bed. Almost every night, Ethan would send a check-in text, asking how the day had gone. Sometimes, Margaret talked with him while she was still with Isabel, and Isabel joined in the conversations. And other times, Isabel would leave early, and Margaret would call Ethan and talk with him while she lay in bed. Although Margaret was accustomed to her alone time, she found herself enjoying Isabel's company, the talks they had, and the friendship that was developing.

One day, they visited downtown Cheyenne, an experience radically different from what it had been before Margaret began losing her sight. When they stepped out of the school's van, Margaret could hear it all: the cars zooming by, people talking and laughing and shouting, doors opening with the sound of a bell. She could smell the city smells: fresh-baked bread, almost-burnt coffee, asphalt, perfume.

And although she could make out shapes and colors, she couldn't really see the things she knew were there: bright yellow taxis, turn-of-the-century buildings, the pretzel vendor, the fresh flowers in their stand outside the flower shop.

It would be easy to sink back into depression, Margaret thought. She loved those sights. She loved *many* sights. But then it came time to ride the city bus, which both Margaret and Isabel found moderately amusing.

"Quick, Margaret," Isabel said as the bus belched a diesel-scented cloud of exhaust at them. "Call a taxi."

Margaret laughed and climbed the steps onto the city bus, noticing the cool metal of the hand railing and the smooth plastic of the seats as she made her way to an empty one. Isabel sat next to her. Out of habit, Margaret turned her face toward the window. She heard the doors shut with a *whoosh*, and the bus began to move. The city passed by, a changing blur of light and shadows. Margaret closed her eyes and sighed, and when Isabel whispered, "I know, my friend," and squeezed Margaret's hand, Margaret squeezed back.

---

MARGARET TOLD herself she didn't want a seeing eye dog. If she couldn't see, how could she take care of a dog? How could she clean up after it, and vacuum up its fur?

"Get a Roomba," Isabel said. "Get a dog. You'll love it. You'll see."

So, Margaret got a dog.

Duke was a Labradoodle, which Margaret had always thought of as a trend in which she'd never partake. But the dog was sweet and calm, and took to Margaret right away, laying his head on her thigh when she sat down and producing a kind of purr when she stroked his ears.

Margaret quickly realized how helpful he could be: he seemed to anticipate what she needed, and when she didn't need anything, he lay at her feet quietly enough that she could almost forget he was there. She may have forgotten, if he didn't maintain constant contact. He kept one paw on her foot every time they sat down. Normally, Margaret would find this sort of thing a bit annoying, but in this case she found it endearing.

Isabel was paired with Duke's littermate, George, who seemed a little rambunctious for Margaret's taste—but who suited Isabel just fine.

"He's wonderful," Isabel said, over and over again. "I just love him."

Just as she had at the Mary Thompson School for the Blind, Margaret settled into acceptance when it came to her relationship with Duke. It was nice to be among other people who were experiencing a transition similar to hers, who at one point had felt like something was being taken from them. Although some of them were professionals— lawyers, nurses, school teachers—others were students or parents or retirees. Margaret found she had more in common with them than she would have expected.

Margaret and Isabel continued to eat dinner together every evening. One night, over spaghetti and French bread, Margaret said to Isabel, "Promise me you'll come visit. I'd love for my family to meet you."

"Ooh," Isabel said. "An invite to meet your family? This friendship is getting serious."

Margaret worried that maybe she'd crossed some sort of line, but then Isabel said, "I'm just joking, Margaret. Of course I'll come, as long as I don't have to take the bus. Can I get a taxi from the big city?"

<h1 style="text-align:center">CHAPTER THIRTEEN</h1>

IN A WAY, Margaret dreaded going home. She loved her mom and sisters, of course, but they were so accommodating, so helpful, that she felt like the more time she spent with them, the more quickly her independence would disappear. She wasn't sure how to convince them that she could operate on her own.

She was surprised when she arrived at Mama Katherine's and no one came to greet her as she got out of the taxi. Not that she'd expected a parade, but the lack of any greeting whatsoever was strange. Duke paused, and Margaret supposed it he was getting a sense of these new surroundings. Inside, the house was silent.

"Where is everyone?" she said aloud as she went from room to room, calling their names. No one had said anything about being gone when she got home. They all knew she was coming. In the empty air, the loud ticking of the grandfather clock and the humming of the icemaker sounded ominous and Margaret experienced a weird sense of doom.

She sat on the couch and pulled out her phone, which didn't light up when she pressed the home button. Of course. She'd left it off after her flight. No wonder she hadn't received any calls or texts in a few hours. She turned it on and waited while it booted up … then waited some more while the messages came rolling in, her phone making too many notification sounds for her to count. Impatient, Margaret drummed her fingers on her thigh.

Why hadn't she remembered to turn on her phone? Why did she have all these messages?

When the notifications stopped coming in, she began to play them.

From Sarah: *"Call me ASAP."*

From Hannah: *"Where are you? Your plane should have landed by now. Call me. Or Sarah. Just call home."*

From Sarah: *"We're taking Mama to the hospital. She fell and she's pretty banged up."*

From Hannah: *"We're in the ER. Doctors think she's going to need surgery."*

From Hannah: *"She's going into surgery. Call me, please. Where are you?"*

Although her phone's robotic voice didn't convey any sense of urgency, Margaret's body created its own: her heart was beating fast, her hands were shaking, and her stomach was swirling with nerves. She knew there were more messages, but she didn't listen to them. Her voice cracked the first time she attempted to give her phone the voice command to call Sarah (Hannah would be a disaster).

After clearing her throat, she tried again. Sarah picked up before Margaret even heard a ring.

"Margaret. Thank goodness." Her voice was quiet and scratchy, the stress barely controlled.

"What's going on?"

"Mama's in surgery," Sarah said.

"What happened?"

"She fell. We were in the kitchen. From what we can tell, a piece of ice fell on the floor and melted. She slipped. It was awful, Margaret. The sound of her hip hitting the floor—"

Margaret cut her off: "What's happening now?"

Sarah let out a breath. "Surgery. She somehow managed to break her ankle and crack her pelvis. And she probably has a few other strains, too."

"I—should I come there?"

Sarah didn't answer right away. When she did, she sounded uncertain. "How will you get here?"

"Take a taxi?"

"That's going to cost a small fortune."

"It's fine. I have a small fortune in savings."

"I mean, you don't have to come now. They said the surgery will take as long as three hours. And it's only been one ..."

Did they not want her to come?

"Margaret," Sarah said. "Why don't you just stay there and hold down the fort? I'm sure one of us will have to come home soon, after Mama's out of surgery, and we can bring you back."

"There's nothing to hold down at this fort. Why don't you want me to come to the hospital?"

"I mean," Sarah said. Her voice trailed off. "It's just that it seems like such a hassle for you. You know?"

A flame of indignation flared up inside Margaret's consciousness. She'd anticipated this—this phenomenon where other people made decisions for her. No matter how good Sarah's intentions were, this exact scenario was one Margaret had to fight against. She didn't want to be cut out of family matters because she couldn't see. And losing her vision did not have to mean losing her autonomy.

Duke shifted, put his head down on her foot next to his paw, and Margaret reminded herself that she wasn't exactly autonomous when she was attached to this dog. But close enough.

"I'll see you soon," Margaret said to Sarah. She hung up and put her hand on the dog's head. "Duke," she said. "We're going to the hospital."

Like all plans made in haste, getting to the hospital included a few obstacles Margaret hadn't anticipated. When the taxi showed up, she remembered from class that she should have warned the person at the switchboard that she was traveling with a service dog.

But Duke settled in the seat next to her, with only one fur-related comment from the driver, and they were off. Time seemed to move slowly, and Margaret didn't have any way to distract herself; she couldn't scroll through social media on her phone or read a book. And she hadn't remembered to bring headphones to listen to music or an audiobook. She sat, tapping her toes on the floorboard and fidgeting with her purse strap.

Margaret knew the hospital was only thirty miles away, but the ride felt interminable. She thought of all the worst-case scenarios: Mama Katherine dying during surgery, or being paralyzed, or dying during recovery. What if she caught pneumonia while she was in the hospital? Or that flesh-eating bacterial infection?

What if she never recovered completely and couldn't garden or collect eggs or get around the house? Margaret sat in that taxi, her hands clasped tightly together between her knees, her teeth chattering.

When they finally pulled up, and the taxi driver read her total off the meter, Margaret gasped. Sarah had been right: it was astronomical.

"I know," the driver said. "And I don't take installments."

He'd meant it as a joke, but Margaret bristled as she pulled out her credit card. Duke led her to the Emergency Room entrance like a pro, and although she knew she shouldn't feel surprised when the doors whooshed open and she was walking into the triage area, she did. She scratched Duke behind the ears.

Only, now what? She'd expected Hannah or Sarah to notice when she came in and to come collect her. But they didn't. She made her way to the desk, which she could make out, straight ahead.

"May I help you, hon?"

Before she started losing her vision, Margaret hadn't paid much attention to people's voices, to the timbre, the rich quality of each syllable. Now, though, she assigned a personality type to everyone based on how they sounded. This woman belonged in a New Orleans jazz bar.

"I'm looking for Katherine Bradley," Margaret said.

"Let me see," the woman said. She did something on her keyboard, made a few humming noises, and then said, "Here she is. They took her up to surgery. Third floor."

Margaret froze. She had no idea how to instruct Duke to get her to surgery, third floor.

The woman must have seen Margaret's panic, because she said, "Just a minute, hon. I'll walk you to the elevator."

She came around the counter in a rush of vanilla-scented air and began walking. "This way."

Duke followed her, and within a few seconds, the nurse said, "Here we are. Just take it up to the third floor. When you get out, hang a left. You'll walk straight up to the desk in the surgery department. Waiting area's to the left."

Margaret took a deep breath and nodded. "Thank you. I appreciate your help."

She and Duke walked into the elevator and turned around to face the doors, which closed quickly with minimal sound. Only then did Margaret remember she'd have to locate the right button for the third floor.

The doors opened again as she was running her fingers over the button panel, feeling for the ground floor button, which she'd use as a starting point to find the third-floor button. She considered getting out of the elevator and asking where the stairs were, but then she heard the nurse's voice: "Let me press that three for you."

Another few seconds later, and Margaret was again enclosed in the elevator, which was kind enough to announce the second and third floors as it arrived at each. She'd barely stepped onto the third floor when she heard Sarah and Hannah talking.

"I mean, she just graduated. She hasn't had any time to practice. She shouldn't be coming all this way, alone."

It was Sarah. Hannah said, "Well, you know Margaret. She's independent. I think she just has to prove to herself that she can do this."

Margaret nodded, to herself. That was true. She did have to prove to herself that losing her vision didn't mean the loss of her independence.

"I know," Sarah said. "I just—"

"Margaret!" Hannah said.

"Oh, do go on," Margaret said. "I was curious to see what Sarah was going to say."

"You made it!" Sarah said.

"Did you doubt that I would?" Margaret said.

"I should have known better," Sarah said, and Hannah added, "She was just worried about you. We both were. Oh, is that your new dog?"

"No," Margaret said. "This is my new boyfriend."

"He's adorable!" Hannah was practically squealing. "His eyes! Can I pet him?"

"You can, but he bites on command," Margaret said.

"Does not," Hannah said.

"He really is cute," Sarah said. "But I don't think we're supposed to pet him, are we?"

"It's fine," Margaret said. "He's such a good dog. Got us up here with no problems. I think he deserves some lovin'."

"Don't be mad, Margaret," Sarah said. "We were just worried, that's all."

"I'm not mad," Margaret said.

"Liar," Sarah said.

"I'm frustrated," Margaret said.

"I knew it!" Hannah said.

"You would be, too," Margaret said. "I know you have good intentions, but I am an adult, perfectly capable of making my own decisions."

"I know you are," Hannah said. She stood up, put a hand on Margaret's arm. "I know. We were just already scared for Mama, you know? And then we were worried about you, too."

Anticipating Margaret's reaction to this, Sarah jumped in. "And only because you just graduated, Margaret. Not in general. We just thought you could use a little more practice getting around, you know? Add your beginner status to the stress of Mama Katherine being in the hospital, and, well …"

"I understand," Margaret said, and she meant it, although the frustration lingered. "Any updates on Mama?"

Sarah sighed. "Not yet. It's a short surgery, relatively speaking, and we don't anticipate they'll give us an update until it's over. They told us to grab a cup of coffee, make phone calls, whatever, and they'll come get us when she's out."

"Do they serve cocktails?" Margaret said.

"I wish," Hannah said. "But actually, I was just going down to get us some beverages. Want to come, or do you want to wait with Sarah?"

"I'll wait with Sarah," Margaret said. "Truth be told, that first elevator ride with the dog was pretty dicey."

Hannah left, and Sarah and Margaret walked back to the waiting room and sat down.

"Was Mama still conscious when you guys were driving here?" Margaret asked. "Was she scared?"

"She was conscious, but kind of out of it," Sarah said. "And you know Mama. She may have been scared, in fact, I could tell she was. But she put on a brave face. She didn't want to worry us."

Margaret nodded. "I'm sure that's true."

"It was scary, Margaret. All the worst-case scenarios flashed through my mind, you know?"

"I do know. Same thing happened to me."

"What will Hannah do without her, Margaret? She'll be devastated."

The same thought had run through Margaret's mind innumerable times during the taxi ride. Hannah depended on Mama Katherine now almost as much as she had when they were children. Not in the same way, of course. They'd reversed roles. She depended on Mama Katherine's presence, more than anything else. She thrived on taking care of her.

"She'll survive," Margaret said.

"But she doesn't have anything else," Sarah said.

"She has us," Margaret said, and Sarah said, "I just hope that's enough."

# CHAPTER FOURTEEN

WHEN MAMA KATHERINE WOKE UP, she whispered, "My girls."

The dim light of the hospital room forced Margaret to rely on her hearing to tell her Hannah had immediately made her way to Mama's beside.

"How do you feel, Mama?"

"Like shit," Mama Katherine said, and Margaret pictured her face breaking into a wide grin, her eyes sparkling. "Like absolute shit."

Sarah nudged Margaret with an elbow. Even from her chair in the corner, Margaret could tell Hannah's shoulders sagged with relief.

"I'm sorry, Mama," Hannah said. "This is my fault. I'd just gotten ice a few minutes before you slipped. I hit my elbow on the freezer door and knocked a bunch of it on the floor. I thought I'd picked it all up, but I obviously missed a piece."

Mama Katherine *tsk*ed, dismissing Hannah's apology. "It's not your fault, and you know it. It's no one's fault, except that of a clumsy old lady who can't maintain vertical position after a tiny slip. I would have recovered from that like Ginger Rogers back when I was your age. In fact, remember the time you girls went on a Wyle E. Coyote kick? You set booby traps all over the house for a week, straight. You thought it would be hilarious."

"That's right," Margaret said.

"I never would have done that If I'd known," Hannah said. Although Margaret couldn't make out her facial features, she suspected Hannah's expression had grown grim.

"Oh, Hannah," Mama said. "You were just kids. But you know the one I'm talking about."

"The one where we spread soap in the walkway between the dining room and the kitchen," Sarah said.

"We thought we were really clever," Margaret said.

"And you were," Mama said. "It would have worked well, too, if Margaret hadn't been giggling like a loon when I said I was going to go inside and make lunch."

"I've always been terrible at keeping secrets," Margaret said.

"Oh!" Mama Katherine said. "There he is. You brought your dog. Where are my manners? I completely forgot you were coming home today. Introduce me to that handsome boy. And then tell me all about your school."

Margaret walked Duke up to the other side of Mama's bed, and he leaned his head against it. Her hand came down to his head, and he made that funny purring sound.

"This is Duke," Margaret said.

"Well, I'll be," Mama said. "You named him after John Wayne."

"Yeah," Margaret said. "I figured John Wayne isn't long for this world, so—"

Margaret stopped short. She could practically feel Hannah giving her a sharp look, and Sarah rolling her eyes.

"Sorry," Margaret said. "I just meant that Duke could carry on the legacy, that's all. He won't be a great farm dog or chicken herder like John Wayne is, but I wanted him to know he has standards to live up to."

"It's perfect," Mama said. "Just perfect."

Sarah came up behind Hannah and sat on the edge of Mama's bed.

"Girls," Mama said. "I'm glad you're here. I don't think I've mentioned it yet, but it means a lot to me to have you all together."

Hannah sniffled.

"I hope that when I'm gone—"

"Mama," Hannah said.

"I'm not at death's door, Hannah," Mama said. Her voice was laced with just a little impatience. "But when that time comes, I hope you'll spend time together."

"We'll be forced to, Mama," Margaret said. "We'll be neighbors. Forever. Pretty cozy, if you ask me."

Mama Katherine chuckled. "That was all part of my master plan. I can't believe you're all going to be living under one roof—well, not one roof, but one slice of sky—again. It's amazing."

The Bradley sisters agreed Hannah would stay overnight with Mama. Since it was Duke's first night at home with Margaret, things would be easier if she brought him back to the house, where she didn't have to use an elevator every time she wanted to take him outside. And Sarah, a morning person, said she'd rather come back with the sunrise.

As Margaret and Sarah prepared to leave, one of the nurses came up to give them a final update. She said Mama was stable, and the pain medication seemed to be doing its job—as if Mama's goofy grin and weepy countenance hadn't been evidence enough.

"And since Dr. Lane, the surgeon, didn't get a chance to talk with you earlier, she would like a quick word with you before you go," the nurse said, and when she walked away, Hannah said, "Dr. Lane, the surgeon, looks like she's about twenty. She has a blond cheerleader ponytail and Bambi eyes. I'm not sure we can trust her."

Margaret found that she liked Dr. Lane right away. Her steps were brisk, her handshake was strong, and she spoke with confidence.

"Your mom's surgery went well," she said. "We were able to stabilize her hip and ankle. Although she may experience significant pain initially, especially since she has a few sprains and strains in addition to the breaks, I do expect her to have a full recovery."

"As long as nothing goes wrong," Hannah said.

"Complications do happen," the surgeon said. "Blood clots, infections—"

Margaret held up a hand. "Say no more. You'll have Hannah in a fit of nerves."

Beside her, Hannah sighed. "She's right."

"Your mother is strong and healthy," Dr. Lane said. "As you've seen, she's already alert. The night staff will get her up and moving as soon as possible. And, especially once she gets home, I anticipate things going very well for her."

Margaret nodded. It sounded reasonable. But Hannah gripped Margaret's arm.

"You think she'll be okay?" she said.

"I do," Dr. Lane said.

Mama Katherine may not be at death's door, but Margaret couldn't stop the thought that entered her mind, then: she was in her eighties. And just like all humans, she would die, eventually. And when she did, Hannah's world would be turned upside down. Margaret only hoped she could help right it again.

Sarah and Margaret said good-bye to Mama Katherine and

Hannah, and as they walked down the hallway towards the elevator, Sarah said, "So, do I need to do anything, like, guide you and Duke out of here?"

"I can just tell him to follow you," Margaret said. "And that should be it."

"Amazing," Sarah said. She started to walk, and Margaret followed just a half-step behind.

"I know," Margaret said. "These dogs go through some serious training."

"That's not what I meant," Sarah said. "I meant that I never thought I'd see you with a seeing eye dog."

"Why not?"

"You know. You're independent. You've never even wanted a fish."

"This is different," Margaret said. "Duke's not a pet."

"We're at the elevator," Sarah said. "I know he's not a pet. But still. You'll have to feed him, water him, take him outside. And you'll actually have to depend on him. At least a little. That's the whole point, right?"

"It is," Margaret said. She stepped into the elevator. "And I know. The wonders never cease."

Before Sarah had a chance to respond, Margaret's phone announced, in its robotic voice, "Message from Ethan."

Sarah made a humming noise, and Margaret rolled her eyes.

"Wait. Aren't you going to check it?"

"Not right now," Margaret said.

"But why not? Don't you want to know what it says?"

"Can't a girl get some privacy around here?"

"Afraid not. What happened with Ethan while you were gone?"

"What do you mean?" Margaret said. She loved playing dumb with her sisters. "Nothing happened. He wasn't there."

"You know what I mean," Sarah said.

The elevator came to a stop and the doors opened. Margaret and Duke followed Sarah into the hospital's main entrance, and out into the parking lot. When they were in the car, the dog in the backseat, Sarah said, "I mean, did you guys talk? Do you still want to sleep with him?"

"We talked," Margaret said. "And I don't know."

"They say absence makes the heart grow fonder."

"They do say that," Margaret said.

And she thought of some of those moments, when, after a long day of learning and practicing and socializing, she'd lain in bed and wondered what it would be like if Ethan laid beside her. She thought of those evenings when she'd wanted to call him to tell him about Duke and Isabel and re-learning how to cook.

But then she thought of other moments—moments when she stumbled, or failed all together. There was the day she'd come out of her apartment at the school, tripped over the toe of her own shoe, and fallen flat on her face. Not that something like that couldn't or wouldn't happen if she had full vision. But if she had full vision, she would have recovered without scraping her palms and knees like a five-year-old. Then there was the day when she'd walked right into a wall and smashed her nose. Of course, that was before Duke. But no man on Earth would want to be with a woman for whom disaster lurked around every corner.

It was because of these moments that Margaret had initiated a certain conversation with Ethan the night before she was set to come home. She decided she wouldn't tell Sarah about it—her sister believed romance was everything and Margaret was already doubting her own decision.

So, not for the first time, she replayed that conversation in her mind.

Her first mistake was calling Ethan instead of texting, but she couldn't bring herself to say good-bye to him via text, especially when she was forced to use voice-to-text and listen to responses in the phone's robotic voice. But calling him meant she had to hear his voice, deep and rich and sexy.

"Margaret."

The sound of him speaking her name made her want to hang up, to cancel the conversation she'd run through again and again throughout the day. But she had to follow through. She had to end this. She didn't want to subject Ethan to her increasing weakness.

"Ethan."

There was a pause. He was perceptive. He could probably hear the dread in her voice.

"How are you?" he said.

Damn it if that single question didn't cause a lump to form in her throat and lodge itself there.

"Fine. I'm fine. How are you?"

"Are you okay?"

Margaret took a deep breath, focused on opening her airway. "I'm doing well. Really well. Duke and I are coming home tomorrow."

"Your sister told me."

Her sister? Which sister? How had he talked to either one of her sisters?

"I saw Hannah at the farmer's market," he said, as if he could read her mind. "Seems to be her hangout. And mine too, apparently. How's the dog?"

"Ethan, I need to say something."

"This sounds serious."

She tried to laugh, but failed, and the sound that came out instead was a cross between a choke and a cough.

"I really enjoyed our time together."

"I do, too," he said. "And your use of the past tense, combined with the tone of your voice, gives me a feeling there's a 'but' coming."

Again, he was incredibly perceptive. It threw her off.

"This whole thing is pretty overwhelming," Margaret said. "When I get home, I have a lot of adjusting to do."

"Of course," Ethan said. "I understand. Whatever you need."

She sighed. He was perceptive *and* accommodating. A tiny part of her thought that maybe—just maybe—she could give things between them a try. He was so good. So good for her. But he'd be better for someone else, someone who could be good for him, too.

"I need space, Ethan. This isn't the time to start a new relationship. Duke and I will be busy. Adjusting. Practicing. Vacuuming. I really need to focus."

Another long pause.

"I understand," he said again.

"Thank you," she said, managing to croak the words out without bursting into tears.

"But, Margaret? Will you do me a favor?"

She nodded, licked her lips, and said, "Sure."

"Call me when you're ready. I'll be waiting."

Even now, as Sarah drove Margaret home from the hospital, tears threatened. She bit her lower lip to keep them from falling, and she turned her face toward the window even though she couldn't see anything beyond it. For now, Margaret would content herself with being alone and taking care of herself—just like she always had.

---

ALL THREE OF the Bradley girls had been to therapy, but Margaret and Sarah had been to the most. Margaret remembered Dr. Spencer telling Mama Katherine that children from tough situations (he always used that euphemism) were so used to chaos that they almost couldn't help but create it.

For Margaret, that chaos took the form of a forced independence. Mama Katherine told Margaret countless times that she'd help her if she needed it. But because Margaret had always done things for herself, it never occurred to her to ask for help.

One day, about a month after Margaret came to live with Mama Katherine, Margaret woke up before everyone else. This was unusual; Mama Katherine was always up before the sun, doing chores and cooking massive breakfasts. But Margaret had a nightmare, and even though she was still tired, she was afraid to go back to sleep. She didn't want to see her first mother's face, slightly grayish and doughy, again. And she definitely didn't want to see those eyelids flip open to reveal black emptiness. She got out of bed, rubbing her own eyes, and went into the kitchen. Usually, by the time the girls got up, Mama had a big plate of pancakes set out. Or a pile of scrambled eggs. And bacon. But not today.

Margaret dragged a chair from the dining room into the kitchen. She used it as a stool to climb onto the counter, and from there, she tried to reach the cereal boxes on top of the fridge. Mama Katherine walked in just as Margaret was teetering, just slightly off-balance.

"My goodness, child!" Mama Katherine said. "Why didn't you ask for help?"

At that very moment, Margaret regained her balance, snatched the box of cereal off the fridge, and, still standing on the counter, turned around to face Mama Katherine.

"Because I didn't need it."

"Child, if you have to climb onto the kitchen counter to reach something, you need help. I can't have you falling and breaking your arm."

"I won't," Margaret said. "I've done this lots of times."

"Not here, you haven't," Mama Katherine said.

Even as this conversation was happening, Margaret had set the cereal box on the counter and then turned around—still standing on the counter—and was retrieving a bowl from the cupboard. Of course, this required her to lean way back to open the cabinet door. Mama gasped.

"Margaret!"

Margaret got the bowl and closed the cupboard, leaning way back again, and then turned around, sat down and hopped to the floor. By now, she was giggling.

"Mama Katherine," she said between bouts of hysteria. "It's fine. I'm *fine*."

Mama Katherine watched Margaret pour her cereal and her milk, and then came to sit with her at the table while she ate it. When she slurped as she took a bite, Mama gave her a stern look but didn't say anything. When Margaret was about halfway through the cereal, Mama finally spoke.

"Margaret. Listen to me. I know you're accustomed to doing things on your own. I know you're capable of it, too. You're a very brave and independent little girl, and that will serve you well as you get older. But here's the thing. When the state sent you to live with me, they trusted me to take care of you. If you end up getting hurt, they'll believe it's because I wasn't supervising you well enough. And they'll take you away."

Even as the words started to sink in, Margaret said, "I won't get hurt, Mama Katherine. I've done this lots of times. Thousands, even."

"I know you don't think you'll get hurt," Mama Katherine said. "None of us ever think that until it happens. In fact, I have a story about that."

Mama Katherine put her elbows on the table.

"When I was a little girl, older than you, I'd say—probably eight? I decided I was going to run away from home. You see, my parents said I had to clean my room before I could play outside. It was a glorious fall day. You know those days. It was warm but not hot, and I could just smell the fall in the air. I wanted to be outside. I *loved* to be outside."

Mama Katherine smiled, and there was a faraway look on her face that Margaret knew meant she was remembering something.

"Hold on. I've got to get some coffee."

As Mama Katherine got up to get coffee, Margaret tried to imagine what she'd been like as a little girl. Did she have those same long legs? Those same bony elbows?

"But," she said, having come back to the table, "My parents said I had to clean my room. My daddy said he was putting his foot down. And I hated when he said that because I had no idea what it meant. His foot was down."

Margaret giggled. It was funny to think of Mama Katherine this way, as an ornery little girl.

"I was spittin' mad, Margaret. I thought that if I went to live alone, you know, off the land, that I wouldn't have to answer to anybody. I wouldn't have to clean my room or do chores or *anything*. I packed my bag. I had this little duffle bag, and I could barely fit my pajamas in there. I didn't pack a toothbrush because if I lived outside, nobody would be there to tell me to use it. I set out. I left them a note. It said, 'I'm leaving.'"

"That's it?" Margaret said.

"That's it," Mama Katherine said. "And I left. I can still remember that feeling I had as I marched down the driveway. The air was crisp. The sun was perfectly warm. Everything seemed promising. I realized immediately that I didn't want to go too far, you know. I found this tree, one where, if I climbed high enough, I could still see my house. I figured that as long as I could still see my house, I was safe. Only, guess what?"

"What?"

"I had to get really high to see the house. I mean, *really* high. And this was the very same kind of tree my parents always told me not to climb. 'The branches are too thin,' my daddy'd say. 'They can't support you,' my mama said. 'You'll fall and break an arm.' That was Uncle Jeb. Anyway. I thought to myself, 'I won't get hurt. I'll be fine. I've climbed trees a million times.'"

Margaret did not miss the fact that Mama used the very same words she'd used earlier. She smiled. And Mama Katherine rewarded her with a tiny return smile.

"I set to climbing. I thought I was being smart, testing each branch before I stood on it. My confidence increased. I went higher. And higher. Before I knew it, I was so high that when I looked down, I felt a bit spinny. I stopped looking down. I kept testing and climbing, testing and climbing. And by now, the sun was starting to set, just a bit. You know what happens in the fall when the sun starts going down?"

"It gets dark."

"And cold."

Margaret nodded. That made sense. Fall was probably the time of year when Margaret's other mama had burned all the food wrappers in the fireplace and made a bed on the floor in front of it. They slept there, and called it camping.

"I decided maybe being at home wasn't as bad as I thought it was," Mama Katherine said. "But I was a stubborn little cuss. I kept climbing. Finally, I could see my house. By this time, my fingers were numb. My nose was numb. And my feet must have been numb. Because you know what happened next?"

"No," Margaret said. "What happened?"

"I tested the next branch. It felt sturdy. I'd climbed enough trees that I knew to step as close as possible to the trunk, and I did that. To my surprise, that branch didn't hold."

"And you fell?"

"My sweet child, I fell. I fell, one branch at a time. *Whack! Whack! Whack!*"

It was impossible to imagine that happening to Mama Katherine now, her long arms and legs spinning in a cartwheel motion as she fell.

"Were you hurt?"

"Boy, was I. I had bruises in places I didn't even know it was possible to get bruises. I landed flat on my back on the ground, and do you know what I saw when I looked up?"

Margaret couldn't imagine. She shook her head.

"My bag. The strap on my duffle bag caught on a branch. Just laying there, the wind knocked out of me, I could tell it was beyond my reach. There was no way I could get it back without climbing that blasted tree again."

"What did you do?"

"I had a choice to make," Mama Katherine said. "If I left it there, went home and didn't tell my parents, they'd eventually find out that my bag was missing, and I'd be in a world of trouble. If I went home and told them it was up in the tree—and the circumstances by which it got there—I'd be in a world of trouble. If I climbed back up in the tree to retrieve it, well…" She shrugged.

"You climbed back up," Margaret said.

"I did. After a long, long conversation with myself."

"Did you make it?"

"Well, I got the bag, if that's what you're asking."

"What happened?"

"If you can believe it," Mama Katherine said, "I fell again. I fell hard. And this time I wasn't as lucky. I landed funny on my arm and broke it."

Here, she held up her arm and pointed at a spot somewhere between her wrist and her elbow. "Both bones. And let me tell you something. That hurts. That was the worst pain I'd ever felt. And until that first fall, I thought I'd be safe. I thought I could handle that climb, that it was impossible for me to fall."

Margaret felt her eyes open up, wide, and she said, "Did the people from the state take you away?"

"No," Mama Katherine said. "For two reasons. First of all, the people at the hospital just viewed the fall as an accident. And there was no social worker coming to our house to check on me every month. Also, things were different back then. There weren't as many rules and regulations."

Margaret let this sink in for a minute. "But they would take me away?"

She remembered the social worker's car, the way it smelled of mothballs, and the way that smell made the fluttery feeling in her stomach even stronger.

"They could," Mama Katherine said. "If they don't think I'm supervising you well enough. Think about it this way, Margaret. The people who work for the state just want you to be safe. That's why you came to live with me in the first place. Now they're trusting me to make sure you're safe and well cared for. And if they think I'm not doing that, then they'll take you to someone who will."

"Where would I go? If they took me away?"

"To another house, with a different family."

"Without Hannah?"

"Right," Mama Katherine said.

"I want to stay here," Margaret said.

"Then I need you to let me help you, Margaret. If you want to get the cereal yourself, we'll put it on a lower shelf. But it's not really just about the cereal. I need you to ask for help when you need it. This is actually a life skill, honey. Because as you get older, there are going to be times when you need help. Sometimes asking for it can be hard, especially when you're used to doing everything on your own. Practice here, now, with me and Hannah. And I promise, it will become easier. Okay?"

Margaret nodded. "Okay."

# CHAPTER FIFTEEN

DURING THE WEEK Mama Katherine spent in the hospital, Margaret was so busy adjusting to having Duke around that she didn't remember to ask whether Hannah had done any new research on Mama's ex-husband, Hannah's father, Philip Carlisle.

When she did remember, she was sorry she'd asked.

Hannah snapped, "I've closed that book, Margaret, and you should, too. It would only upset Mama to know we've been talking about this."

Maybe Mama *was* too fragile to handle the emotional turmoil. Margaret didn't know, but when Mama came home, the point was moot. Hannah fretted and flitted around, a little bird tending to her young. Sarah worried but pretended not to, finding excuse after excuse to go into Mama Katherine's room: she needed a needle and thread, she should really fill Mama's water glass, she forgot she'd already collected the laundry.

For her part, Margaret used Mama's being laid up in bed as a distraction from her own ailments. She threw herself into Mama's chores with an abandon that allowed her to forget—or at least pretend not to notice—that her potential romance was gone, along with her vision. As the bad days (the ones where she could not see more frequently than she could) began to outnumber the good (the ones where she could make out shapes and shadows), she collected eggs, harvested vegetables, and washed and folded laundry, creating new systems for getting around.

From the dining room door, the chicken coop was fifteen steps out and twelve to the right. The laying boxes were seven steps from the entrance of the coop, straight ahead. The corner of the garden was twelve steps past the coop. From there, Margaret picked down one row and up the next: corn, squash, cucumbers, tomatoes, strawberries. The regular wash cycle was two clicks from the top, and to dry clothes for an hour, she had to turn the knob exactly ninety degrees from its zero position.

Mama Katherine protested, saying Margaret shouldn't have to do it all, and Margaret waved a hand and carried on. Besides, she wasn't doing it all. She let Hannah do the cooking and Sarah, the errands.

Meanwhile, Ethan texted occasionally, staying in touch but keeping a friend-like distance, which Margaret appreciated. But even while she appreciated it, she found herself missing him. And even though she wasn't one to regret her decisions (instead, she put them squarely where they belonged—in the past), she did wonder several times what would have happened if she'd handled things differently.

In general, Hannah, Margaret, Mama Katherine, Sarah, and Donny all settled into a rhythm while Mama Katherine learned how to get around on her crutches—and how to let her daughters take care of her, for once.

None of these developments much interested Margaret, but the one that did was the relationship between Tanner Lucas and Hannah. Although Donny managed most of the building-related interactions with Tanner, both Hannah and Tanner seemed to find an increasing number of ways to interact with each other.

Margaret may not be able to see, but she could feel the tension when they were in the same space together. One morning, Margaret and Hannah were in the kitchen. Margaret was washing dishes, and Hannah was making iced tea. Margaret could hear her tearing the tea bags out of their paper packets. She could hear the tiny hiss of the flame under the teapot.

And she could hear someone's footsteps coming into the kitchen— and Hannah's immediate intake of breath. Margaret's ears perked up.

"Good morning, ladies," Tanner said. He spoke like a cowboy, Margaret thought, his words slow and easy and accompanied by a bit of a twang.

"Morning," Margaret said.

"Tanner," Hannah said.

"Hannah," Margaret said. "Where are your manners? Offer the man some iced tea. He's building our houses."

"He's building *your* house," Hannah said. "And he hasn't started yet. Iced tea?"

"I'd love some iced tea," Tanner said.

Margaret could hear the humor in his voice—and the irritation in Hannah's. She smiled and kept her head down as she scrubbed the pan from last night's casserole.

"It's not ready, yet," Hannah said.

"When do you think it will be?" Tanner said.

"I'm not sure," Hannah said. "But I'll let you know."

"Would you, please?"

"Be happy to."

With that, Tanner Lucas walked back out of the kitchen. After the door closed, Margaret said, "Were the two of you really talking about iced tea?"

"Of course," Hannah said. "What else would we be talking about?"

Margaret just shrugged, rinsed the baking dish, and set it on the drying towel. She picked up a pot and started washing that. "Why did he come in here?" she said after a moment.

"What?" Hannah said.

Her movements had stopped. Margaret imagined her leaning against the counter, watching Tanner out the window over the sink.

"Why did he come in here?" Margaret said again. "I mean, did he come in just to say good morning? He didn't say anything about the project."

"Huh," Hannah said. "You're right. You know, I don't know."

"Think the iced tea's ready? I'd like to hear you guys have another conversation."

"What are you talking about?"

"The tension was literally palpable. I could've wrapped myself up in it," Margaret said. "Tell me that's not true."

"I don't know what you're talking about."

Margaret said, "When you're forced to listen—and I mean, really *listen*—you hear a lot more than what's on the surface."

"There's nothing below the surface," Hannah said.

"Uh huh," Margaret said. When Hannah didn't answer right away, Margaret said, "Tell me. Is he as good-looking now as he was back in the day?"

"Iced tea's ready. I'm going to bring some outside."

"I knew it," Margaret called after Hannah. "He *is* good-looking. You have a crush on Tanner Lucas!"

The door shut. Margaret laughed out loud. She knew she was being juvenile, but it felt good. And she'd love nothing more than to experience her sister falling in love.

She finished scrubbing the dishes, and her thoughts drifted from Hannah and Tanner to Ethan. And not just Ethan, but Margaret and Ethan. What would she hear if she forced herself to really listen to whatever was between them? Would she hear that same tension she heard between Hannah and Tanner?

She would hear kindness, she knew. She would hear thoughtfulness. And she would hear desire. Because try as she might, she couldn't help but want Ethan. And, she thought, this was the very reason to remind herself that you don't always get what you want.

It was only a few hours later that life decided to challenge Margaret. She and Duke were walking along the bank of the creek. She was practicing, starting and stopping and turning around.

Without warning, he spoke: "Margaret."

Margaret's heart responded by thumping loudly in her chest, and she imagined the echo inside her body. Yes, he'd startled her. But also, hearing his voice sent shivers skittering across her skin.

First of all, she told herself, she was going to have to learn to listen a lot more carefully. One of the instructors at the Mary Thompson School for the Blind had said something about being aware of your surroundings, and this was a perfect, real-life example of that. Ethan had sneaked right up on her.

Secondly, what was he doing here? Hadn't she made it clear she wasn't going to get involved with Ethan, or anyone else? She'd listened to a news article recently (was it on the flight home?) about how adults in America were having less sex. Researchers believed this phenomenon was thanks to a wide selection of high-quality sex toys, an increased availability of instant-gratification entertainment, like TV shows you could stream whenever you wanted, and women taking a stand. Okay, the article hadn't said, "taking a stand," but it had said something about women finally speaking up for themselves; saying, "No," to their significant others when they didn't want to get intimate.

Margaret jumped a little when she realized she had started this whole thought process to justify the fact that she didn't want a boyfriend of any type, and ended it thinking she did want to have sex with Ethan. Whom she still hadn't said hello to.

"Ethan. Hi."

"You took such a long time to answer, I was afraid you didn't recognize me."

"Oh, I recognized you," Margaret said, the words out of her mouth before she realized she'd drawled them like a bawdy barmaid—or worse, a woman of the night speaking to a repeat customer. Things got even worse when she added, "I'd recognize your voice anywhere."

And again when she realized goosebumps had risen on her arms.

She could hear the smile in his voice when he said, "Well, that's a relief."

"May I ask to what I owe the pleasure?"

Well, this was an odd experience. If she could see, she'd have the opportunity to watch him, his body language, his facial expressions, the way he looked in this early-afternoon light. Instead, she was forced to wait, and then pick up clues from the tone of his voice.

"Oh. Uh, yeah. Tanner asked if I could come over and have a look at something. At Sarah and Donny's house. I guess she wants a built-in desk, similar to the one I bought for you. Since I set up yours ... Anyway. I saw you down here and thought I'd say, 'Hey,' since I hadn't seen you since you got back."

"Hey," she said. "We're not already at the built-in desk stage, are we?"

He laughed, just a chuckle, and her body reacted as if he'd touched her. Provocatively.

"Not yet, no. Although they're planning to pour the foundation next week, I think. For Sarah and Donny's. And then at your place the following week. Tanner just wanted me to do a walk-through now that they've got the place all laid out on the ground."

"Seems a bit premature, if you ask me," she said, although she didn't really think so.

"I'm never premature," he said.

Now it was Margaret who laughed loudly enough to worry Duke, because he licked her hand.

"So, this is Duke," Ethan said. "I didn't get a formal introduction."

"Yeah, this is Duke," Margaret said. "You can pet him, if you like."

Margaret felt, rather than heard, Ethan approach. It was almost like his body put off some kind of vibration to which her own body reacted. It was somehow magnetic. He was kneeling in front of her now, his face on level with Duke's.

"Hey, buddy. I'm jealous you get to spend all this time with your new mama, here. You're a good-looking dog, you know."

Margaret heard Duke's collar jingle and she knew Ethan was scratching his neck. The dog made his purring sound, and Margaret smiled, despite the slew of emotions running around inside her brain.

"He's well-behaved, too," she said. "At the school, someone said they'd had to give up their first dog because of behavioral issues. But I think Duke's going to do just fine."

"He knows he's got a good thing, here," Ethan said. "He doesn't want to risk losing you."

"Wow," Margaret said. "You're reading a lot into his doggy psychology after having known him for a very short time."

"I recognize a kindred spirit." Ethan straightened up; when he spoke again, his voice was level with Margaret's face. "Look, Margaret. Could we have dinner again sometime? I'd love to hear about your school and your training with Duke."

On one hand, Margaret thought, *What could it hurt?* Even if she didn't want romance, she could have friends, right? But could she be friends with Ethan? Or would her traitorous body always be magnetically attracted to his sexy one? Would she always be thinking of the chocolate-covered strawberries and the way his voice seemed to actually touch her skin?

"I don't know," she said, as much to herself as to him.

"It's just dinner," he said. "I'm not asking you to move in with me."

He was right. It was just dinner.

"Fine," she said. Then, realizing that sounded a little petty, she added, "That would be nice."

"Okay," he said. She could hear the relief in his voice. Had he been nervous, afraid she'd say no?

"Ethan," she said. "I really like you. I enjoyed the time we spent together before I went to school. Right now, I just need to focus on my new life, here."

"I get that," he said. "I really do. And I can respect that. For now."

"That sounded like a threat," she said, laughing.

"It was," he said. "I can be patient, Margaret. I can wait. But just know, that when the time is right, I'm going to make my move."

He sounded serious, but she couldn't help laughing again. "Okay. I hear you."

Now he reached out and squeezed her free hand. "Good. I've got to get back to Tanner. He's waiting for me."

"Speaking of Tanner," Margaret said. "What can you tell me about him and Hannah?"

"Not much to tell, far as I can see," Ethan said. "She won't give him the time of day. He watches her, though, real carefully. And he finds reasons to talk to her. Even though she acts prickly about it, she doesn't turn him away. Which makes me think there's hope for Tanner, yet. But I guess we'll have to wait and find out. Why? What can you tell me?"

"Oh, nothing," Margaret said. "Hard to tell, I guess."

Ethan waited for more, but Margaret didn't offer it.

Margaret walked into the house a few minutes later and heard Mama Katherine, in a grumbly voice, saying, "I won't hear of it. You need to go back to work as much as you need to breathe, Hannah Mae. And you will. I'll be just fine, here. There are still two more weeks until you go back, which gives me plenty of time to get up to speed. I'm getting more mobile every day. Feeling better every minute. Besides, your sisters can help me if I need it."

"Who, Margaret? Sarah's going to be running her new business, and Margaret—"

"Margaret will be just fine," Mama Katherine said.

"She can't even *see*, Mama. How is she supposed to—"

"She'll be just fine," Mama said again. "You've always been such a caretaker, Hannah, and I love that about you. But it's time to put your own needs first. You need to teach. You need to work. You need to get out of this house once in a while."

"I just don't understand how you believe Margaret can help you."

Margaret cleared her throat. "I'm blind, not incapable."

She experienced a tiny victory when she heard Hannah jump, her hand or arm hitting the dining room table.

"Margaret," she said. "I'm not saying you're incapable. I'm just—"

"That's exactly what you're saying," Margaret said. "You don't think I can help Mama Katherine if she needs it."

"I know you can, Margaret."

"Now, now, girls," Mama Katherine said. "I feel a bit offended that the two of you are even talking this way. I am perfectly capable of taking care of myself, here. When the two of you have to give me sponge baths and wash my hair with dry shampoo, that's when you should start to worry. Okay? Now run along, both of you. I've got to take a real shower and shampoo my hair. And then I've got a doctor's appointment."

Hannah sighed, loudly, and stomped off, mumbling something about how Mama was going to get to her appointments when Hannah went back to school.

Margaret turned to leave, too, and Mama Katherine called her back. "I'm really proud of you, you know. This has been difficult for you."

"Lots of people have gone through it, Mama," Margaret said. "It's no different for me than it is for anybody else."

"But I know you," Mama Katherine said. "I know you hate having to rely on other people, being slowed down. All I'm saying is, you've settled in spectacularly. I expected you to buck the system, to—I don't know, continue living life just as you always did, fast and adventurous and—"

"And reckless?"

"I've never thought you were reckless. I just worried, that's all." Margaret knew Mama Katherine shrugged before adding, "It's what mothers do."

"Well, thank you for the compliment," Margaret said. "I think. And just for the record, I know you don't need as much help as Hannah thinks you do. But I can dry shampoo like nobody's business."

Mama Katherine chuckled. "And I know that if I do need a dry shampoo, I can come to you, honey. Now go do something useful, would you? Your sister's hovering is starting to make me batty."

"She's just worried, Mama. It's what daughters do."

"I know. But right now, the only reason for her to worry is that she's going to make me batty. No go on. Get out of here. Why don't you call that Ethan fellow and have him take you on a date?"

"We're just friends."

"Oh, I know," Mama Katherine said. "It's plain to see. Plain as day."

"Hmm," Margaret said. "I wouldn't know. I'm going to cook dinner."

# CHAPTER SIXTEEN

IT WAS CHILDISH, she knew, but Margaret's offer to cook dinner stemmed not from altruism, but from the need to prove she was independent and capable. How did she know it was childish? Because it was exactly like the time she'd done the same thing when she was ten. She'd nearly burned the house down.

Margaret remembered it with such clarity, it was almost like reliving the entire experience. In an instance as rare as a solar eclipse, Mama Katherine was sick. Laid up with the flu. The girls were left to fend for themselves (although, Margaret thought now, not really: Mama had felt the flu coming on and spent an entire day preparing meals they could later reheat for themselves). Hannah, a mother hen even back then, had insisted on caring for Mama Katherine, day and night. She remained at her bedside, leaving the room only to use the bathroom or heat broth to spoon into Mama's mouth.

After two solid days, Margaret had offered to sit with Mama to give Hannah some time to rest, and Hannah said something about how Margaret wasn't responsible enough to take care of herself, let alone Mama Katherine.

"I am," Margaret said. "I am responsible. I can show you. I can prove it."

Of course, there'd be no proving it; Hannah would never believe anyone but she could take care of Mama Katherine. Somehow, Margaret convinced Hannah to go take a shower and a nap. "Just for an hour," Margaret said. "Two, tops."

Hannah, greasy-haired and exhausted, said, "You'd better not mess this up, Margaret."

"I won't. I promise."

Only, she had.

She'd decided that, while Mama Katherine and Hannah both napped, she would cook a real meal for Mama Katherine. She didn't need to heat up something that was already made. She could make something from scratch. Looking through the pantry, she'd spotted tortillas and beans, and thought they had all the fixings for enchiladas. Mama loved enchiladas. And she could make Mexican rice on the side.

Things went spectacularly, at first. Margaret measured out water and brought it to a boil for the rice, and then dumped the rice in and stirred it. She found cooked chicken breast in the fridge, and shredded it, then put it into a pot with enchilada sauce and beans. By now, the rice had returned to a boil. She put the lid on and moved the rice to a back burner. She stirred the chicken mixture and shredded a block of cheddar she found.

Even as she stirred the chicken mixture again, she thought about her next steps: heat the tortillas, assemble the enchiladas, put them in the oven. Chop lettuce and tomato for toppings. Easy as pie.

Only, as soon as she put the first tortilla on the pan, she realized she'd forgotten all about the rice, and as rice is known to do, it boiled over. Big, shiny bubbles pushed at the lid, and smaller bubbles leaked out, sizzling on the stovetop.

"Crap," Margaret said, although she wasn't panicking, yet.

She grabbed a dish towel out of the drawer and swiped at the bubbly water running down the sides of the pot. She shoved it under the pot, hoping to catch all the liquid. The last thing she wanted was for Hannah to wake up to a huge mess.

Only, what happened next was worse than a huge mess: because Margaret hadn't turned off the flame under the rice, the dish towel caught fire. Before she realized what was happening, the flames were crawling up the towel towards her hand.

She shrieked and dropped the burning towel on the floor, and immediately realized her mistake. The rug next to the stove was, apparently, extremely flammable.

Now she was standing barefoot on a burning rug. In the milliseconds that followed, Margaret ran through her options for fixing this situation. She could try to stomp the fire out. That would probably be the quickest solution. But that might hurt. She could grab the iced tea pitcher, fill it with water, and dump it on the rug and towel. But how long would it take to fill the pitcher? By the time she did that, the entire kitchen would be engulfed in flames. Wasn't there something about throwing flour on a fire? Or was that just for a grease fire? Was this a grease fire? The flames had moved towards her. They were advancing across the rug, an army leaving nothing but blackened fabric in their wake.

She shrieked again and jumped backwards.

There was a thundering sound, then. At first, Margaret thought the fire must have gotten into the walls, and was going to burn the house down. Then she realized it was Mama Katherine, running. Forehead beaded with sweat, tendrils of hair escaping her bun, she ran into the kitchen, retrieved the fire extinguisher from the bottom shelf of the pantry, and sprayed the fire right out.

The flames were gone, replaced by foam.

Unfortunately, the chicken enchiladas were covered with foam, too.

By this time, Margaret was in the deepest throes of disappointment. She'd wanted badly to help Mama, to give her a break, and she'd ended up forcing her to play firefighter. For her part, Mama stood there, chest heaving, fire extinguisher in one hand, which hung at her side.

"Well, Margaret," she said. "You sure made a mess of that one."

Margaret was too shocked to cry (at least, at that point). She simply stood there, staring at the aftermath. Before she had a chance to apologize, to wrap her arms around Mama Katherine's waist, Mama Katherine set the fire extinguisher down and walked back towards the bedroom.

"Get that mess cleaned up, honey. Find some work gloves, though. I imagine there'll still be some hot spots." When she reached the entrance to the hallway, she turned around. Margaret thought that Mama must really be sick, because her body swayed before she spoke. "Oh, and Margaret? Let Hannah do the cooking next time, would you?"

That comment hurt more than anything else Mama Katherine could have said. And the worst part was that she had a point. Margaret dutifully cleaned up the mess, scooping the foamy rug remnants into a garbage bag along with the entire meal on which she'd worked terribly hard.

Of course, Hannah had come in a few minutes later, giving Margaret only a brief, disapproving glance before making them all gourmet turkey sandwiches. Margaret didn't eat hers. She hid in the garden while everyone else ate and then she went for a long walk along the creek.

Remembering it now, twenty-five years later, Margaret experienced the same feelings of inadequacy all over again. But this was different. She was an adult. She'd cooked hundreds—thousands—of meals. And she hadn't started a single fire after that.

But she still had the same need to prove herself. Wishing, hard, that this was a better day for her vision, she walked into the kitchen. She had Duke lie down at the end of the counter where he'd be out of the way. Then she went to the refrigerator and opened it. The bright light there did enable her to see shapes and fuzzy outlines; she could make out the gallon of milk on the bottom shelf and the rotisserie chicken, in its black and clear plastic container next to it.

She knew they had the supplies to make lasagna but that seemed pretty complicated. When they were kids, Mama Katherine always kept ingredients on hand for staple meals like chicken pot pie, spaghetti, and tortilla soup.

"Chicken pot pie, Duke. I could make that in my sleep."

Hearing his name, the dog lifted his head—Margaret heard the movement of the tags on his collar. Then, realizing he wasn't needed at the moment, he flopped his head back down—there was a quiet thumping noise.

By feel, Margaret found the pie plate in the cupboard. She set it on the counter.

"You know, if Mama ever decides to switch things around in here, I'll be lost," she said.

Now more than ever, she could appreciate Mama's penchant for keeping pre-made basics on hand. There were pie crusts and already-chopped onions, as well as frozen vegetables. The hardest part of making a chicken pot pie would be cutting and cooking the chicken, and cutting the potatoes.

The pie crusts were in their normal spot: freezer, top shelf, right side. She tore the wrapper off one and put it in the microwave to defrost, then unrolled it into the pie dish. Then, she felt around for the package of chicken breasts in the fridge. She cut the breasts into bite-sized cubes, found a pan and the oil, and got the chicken cooking on the stove, hoping she'd set the flame at an acceptable size.

She located and washed some potatoes, then cut them, carefully, only nicking her finger once.

She wished she could train Duke to read; it would be handy to have him show her which frozen vegetables were the peas and carrots. Come to think of it, though, she could figure that out by feel, too.

The process took longer than it would have when she could see, but she did it: at least an hour after she started, she slid the pot pie with its mashed potato topping into the oven. Then she turned to Duke and flung out her arms. "Ta da!"

His tail thumped on the floor.

"Smells good in here."

She'd recognize that voice anywhere, any time. "Ethan. What are you doing here?"

"Well, now," he said. "That's a nice greeting if I ever heard one."

She could hear the humor in his voice, but there was something else, too. Sadness, maybe? Resignation?

"I'm sorry," she said, and she meant it. "I wasn't expecting you, that's all. You surprised me. I thought I was alone, and here I am, talking to the dog."

"Nothing wrong with talking to a dog," he said. "Can I pet him?"

"Of course."

"Tanner sent me in here. He's got a leftover bay window from one of his other projects—homeowner changed her mind and went with something else—and he thought you might like it."

Before she could answer, he said, "Now, I know. You haven't even designed the houses yet—"

"I'm not even sure I'm going to design them. And ... in case you've forgotten, I probably won't actually *see* the window."

"Right. But Tanner says it's a beauty, and he wanted to offer it to you."

"I can't see any of it. I don't care what he gives me." Realizing that answer sounded ungrateful, she blew out a sigh and offered another apology. "I mean, what do you think?"

"It's a nice window. The bottom half opens, I guess. If you put it in the front of the house like Tanner's thinking, you'd be able to open it and hear the creek. Which I think makes it worth the trade. I'd take it."

Margaret nodded, considering. "Okay, then. If you'd take it, I'll take it."

"I'll let him know."

His footsteps retreated. She wanted to call out to him, to stop him, to talk to him for longer, but she didn't know what to say.

*Want some chicken pot pie?*

*I'd like to talk to you.*

*I miss you.*

*Stay for dinner.*

*Feed me strawberries.*

The door shut behind him, and he was gone.

Margaret had no idea how long she stood there, willing Ethan to come back. But she hadn't set the oven timer and realized she'd have to check the pot pie. She slid it out of the oven and tapped its top gently. It wasn't quite done.

"Another five minutes," she told Duke. "And then it's done."

Five minutes pass slowly when you're pining away after a man, Margaret thought. And that's exactly why she wasn't pining away after a man. Or, was she?

The pot pie's mashed potato topping boasted a nice crispy finish, and Margaret supposed it was golden brown and delicious. She pulled it out, set it on the counter, and turned off the oven.

"You know," she told Duke, "your namesake, John Wayne? He used to steal food off the counter. I remember once, Mama Katherine left a whole chicken on the counter while she went to light the barbecue. She came back and John Wayne was standing over it like some wolf in the wild."

"Boy, was I mad." Mama Katherine was making her way into the kitchen.

"Mama, you're up. Feeling any better?"

"I was, until you brought up the John Wayne incident."

Margaret laughed. "That was not funny."

"Agreed. But Duke here would never do that, would you, Duke?"

Duke's tail thumped on the floor.

"This pot pie looks beautiful, Margaret. Did you mean to use sweet potatoes instead of regular?"

"What? No! Did I?"

She'd checked to make sure the potatoes had rounded ends, not pointy.

"No," Mama said, on the verge of laughter. Her hand came to rest on Margaret's upper arm. "Just giving you a hard time, sweetheart. It looks great."

"Now, to see how it tastes," Margaret said. "Think anyone will eat it?"

They ate it, and to Margaret's relief, it tasted great. Hannah had seconds, which she rarely did, and Donny polished off the lone slice that remained in the pie plate before licking his fingers like he had when they were teenagers. Margaret could hear the sounds from across the table.

"Ouch," he said. "Don't elbow me."

"Mind your manners," Sarah said, "or Mama Katherine won't let us eat in here. Remember how she used to threaten to send us outside to eat?"

"She wouldn't do that now," Donny said.

"Try me," Mama Katherine said. "That turned out wonderfully, Margaret."

"It did," Hannah said. "And you've put me in my place. I'll never again imply that you can't cook. In fact, I've got dishes and cleanup."

While Margaret sat at the table, reveling in the success of the pot pie experience, she began to formulate a plan. Cooking dinner was one thing, but what if she went big? What if she devised a way to prove—to her sisters and Mama Katherine, and to herself—that she was still a strong, autonomous woman?

What would that look like?

If she were still footloose and fancy-free, she might decide to go on a trip. Somewhere she'd never been, somewhere beautiful where she could get a penthouse suite and sweeping views of a big city skyline. But now, the view would be wasted on her. And besides, the possibility existed that taking a trip was going *too* big.

In the kitchen, the water ran and Hannah and Sarah chatted about recipes. Mama Katherine and Donny talked about the upcoming football season. Dishes clinked. Cupboards opened and closed.

In all the reading Margaret had done on personal development, experts said a goal should really stretch you beyond your comfort zone. Taking a trip would certainly do that, Margaret thought. But at the Mary Thompson School for the Blind, the experts had said that you should trust your gut—and that you shouldn't push yourself too far beyond your comfort zone.

"Going blind is beyond my comfort zone," Isabel had quipped when one of the instructors said that.

But what was too far? Margaret wondered as she listened to her family in the kitchen. Could a person measure her comfort zone by the size of a state? Colorado wasn't too far, was it? It was just one state south. It was beautiful at this time of year, she thought, and wasn't July the peak of wildflower season?

Then she remembered it didn't matter if she went somewhere beautiful. Maybe there was something interesting to hear in Montana or one of the Dakotas.

*Or*, a mean little voice said from the back of her mind, *maybe trav-*

*eling is pointless now. Maybe you should just settle down and resign yourself to a life at home in Wyoming.*

That was a thought. Settling down was definitely outside of her comfort zone.

Surrounded by the normal, happy noises of her family, and her new dog beside her, Margaret sighed.

# CHAPTER SEVENTEEN

IN THE END, Margaret decided to go big, to step way beyond her comfort zone. She'd take a trip to Montana—just one state north—and visit the Glacier Symphony. According to its website, which she listened to on her phone, the symphony's headquarters were in northwest Montana against the backdrop of Glacier National Park. She had never been and although she wouldn't be able to see the majestic mountains and sparkling lakes, she would be able to hear the music.

"We'll just make it a quick trip," she told Duke that evening. "Two days. Three, tops. I'll hire a car. That way we don't have to take a taxi all the way up there. Then we'll get a hotel, spend a day in Whitefish, Montana, which I'm sure is lovely, and come back."

When Duke didn't answer, Margaret said, "I'll take your silence as consent."

She went to bed and dreamed of towering, snow-capped mountains against a bold blue sky, and brightly-colored, delicate wildflowers on a lush bed of green grass. When she woke up the next morning and was cruelly reminded that she couldn't actually see, the disappointment tasted bitter.

Still, she planned the trip, using voice commands on her phone when she could and a magnifying glass with her laptop when she had to. Sitting in her childhood bedroom, cross-legged on the bed, she researched, made reservations, and bought tickets. And she wondered if she was going crazy.

The car would pick her up on Friday, and drive her to Whitefish. It would cost a small fortune. A medium fortune, actually. There really was no point to sightseeing. She'd immediately go to Pine Lodge and check in. The hotel had a restaurant, which meant she could eat in the dining room or order room service. She'd decide when she got there.

After dinner, she could take a dip in the pool or the hot tub, and then she'd go to bed. Saturday morning, she would eat breakfast and maybe walk around Whitefish, although, again, it didn't seem like much fun to walk around a new place when you couldn't see it.

Just the thought of walking around a busy downtown made her chest constrict as images of that morning, months ago, paraded through her mind: the car honking, her palm on its hood, her coffee spreading out onto her drawings on the asphalt. Margaret reminded herself that she didn't actually have to walk around downtown. She could stay in her room or lurk around the hotel lobby and get a cab to the symphony performance when the time came.

"I can do this," she said.

"You can do what?" Sarah said from the doorway.

Margaret snapped her laptop shut.

"Nothing," she said.

"Ohmygosh, really?" Sarah said. "You sound like a six-year-old. You *look* like a six-year-old. What are you up to in there?"

"I'm not a six-year-old," Margaret said. "I'm a grown woman. Which is why I expect some privacy in this house."

"Well, that's fair," Sarah said. "I'll leave you alone in there. Watching porn. I've never seen porn you needed a magnifying glass for."

"Very funny," Margaret called as Sarah's footsteps receded down the hallway.

She stood up and closed her bedroom door all the way, then, after a moment's hesitation, locked it. She'd have quite a bit of time to kill in Whitefish on Saturday morning, since the symphony didn't perform until late evening.

"I can do this," she said again.

No one answered this time.

The Whitefish Performing Arts Center was just down the street from the hotel, which meant a quick (and cheap) taxi ride to and from the concert.

By the time she got back Saturday night, it would be time for bed. Then, on Sunday, her hired car would bring her back to Walker, where she'd make a triumphant return, having proven that she was as self-sufficient as ever.

"Easy-peasy," she said, even as her stomach churned at the idea.

The first step: packing. Margaret pulled her carry-on suitcase out of the closet and laid it on her bed. Feeling especially grateful for Hannah's wardrobe-organization skills, she chose two outfits with shoes to match, a pair of pajamas, and her swimsuit. Then she sneaked into the bathroom and dug through the cabinet under the sink until she found a travel-sized toothpaste. Hotels always offered free sundries, she thought, but she'd have to figure out how to figure out which was which. It would be just her luck to wash her hair with body lotion.

"Cross that bridge when we get to it, Duke."

She zipped the suitcase and put it back in her closet.

There. No one would suspect a thing. Now, all she had to do was keep her head down for a couple of days to avoid tipping anyone off.

There were some close calls. Several times over the course of the days that followed, Margaret thought someone would out her plan. Everyone seemed suspicious, especially Sarah, and it was all Margaret could do to keep it a secret.

At dinner that first night after she planned her trip, Sarah cleared her throat and said, "Margaret was acting very suspicious today. I caught her looking at porn in her bedroom."

Mama Katherine gasped, and Margaret laughed, too loudly and for too long.

"She's just kidding, Mama," Margaret said. "I was just chatting with some of my blind school friends."

"Well, since she turned Ethan down, she's probably feeling pretty needy," Hannah said, surprising Margaret not only because she steam-rolled along as if Margaret hadn't offered an explanation for what she was doing, but also because under normal circumstances, she'd never play along with a porn reference.

Margaret just shook her head.

The next morning, Margaret was outside, walking Duke, when Hannah said, "You're sure acting weird, Margaret."

Margaret didn't know what to say. She just shrugged one shoulder and didn't say anything.

Later that day, Donny came up while she was pouring herself a glass of water, and said, "Hey. Everything okay?"

He'd always been very perceptive, Margaret thought. He was the one who caught her smuggling vodka into her bedroom when she was fifteen—not because he'd seen her hiding it in her purse, but because he could tell, from the look on her face, that she was hiding *something*. By that time, he was like a brother to her, and her behavior worried him. With a few pointed questions, he'd gotten her to admit she had the contraband, and with a few pointed comments, he'd convinced her to dump most of it down the bathroom sink.

"Everything's fine," she told him now. She leaned against the counter, hoping she looked casual. She took a sip of her water.

"Are you sure?" Donny said.

She wished she could see him: his wrinkled forehead, his eyes searching hers for signs of a truth different from what she was sharing.

"I'm sure." She reached out to squeeze his arm.

"Okay," he said. "But if you need to talk … "

"Thanks, Donny. I mean it."

And then, on Thursday night as Margaret was getting ready for bed, Ethan texted.

Her phone read the text in its robotic voice: "Hey, Margaret. It's Ethan. Obviously. Anyway, I was just texting to, you know, see how you're doing. Ah, I guess, text me back. Or call me. I would have called, but I didn't know if this was a good time and I didn't want to bother you."

"What's the meaning of this, Duke?" Margaret said.

She climbed into bed and picked her phone up off the nightstand. There were hundreds of things she wanted to say to Ethan. She wanted to tell him about the next day's trip. She wanted to ask him whether he'd ever been to Montana or heard the Glacier Symphony. She wanted to invite him to join her. Yes, she really did want to have hot hotel sex with him, and what better place than the Pine Lodge? Surely the sex with Ethan would be hot. They could turn the trip into a bonafide road trip. Would he accept her invitation? Probably. Would they have a great time? Most likely. But no matter how she imagined it —the two of them singing along to crappy songs on the radio, eating gas station junk food, walking hand in hand down the sidewalk in a quaint downtown, having killer sex on the huge hotel bed, holding hands in the vast symphony hall—the ending was always the same. He'd realize she was a burden, that she couldn't experience life fully anymore, and he'd bid her farewell.

In the end, all she said in response to his text was, "I'm fine, thank you for checking in on me. Have a great night."

There, she thought. That ought to send him a pretty clear message. He may not know it, but she was protecting him. Now, she could hop in that car tomorrow and head to Montana, where she'd have plenty of time to think—and to get used to being alone.

## CHAPTER EIGHTEEN

When Margaret's alarm went off at four-thirty a.m., the sunlight was already starting to seep into her bedroom. She could tell only because it came through as a medium gray, gentle and promising. Experiencing equal parts excitement and anxiety, Margaret got up right away and pulled on the clothes she'd laid out the night before: jeans and a soft green sweater she'd identified by the feel of the fabric.

Not wanting to wake anyone, she planned to ask her driver to stop at a restaurant along the way. She could grab a coffee and food to go. And because she didn't want her mom or sisters to be alarmed by her absence, she wrote a quick note, hoping her handwriting was legible, and left it on the dining room table:

*I'll be gone for a couple of days - back late Sunday afternoon. Don't worry, it's just a quick getaway. Margaret xo*

Then, a minute before the car was supposed to get there, she walked outside to wait for the car. It was already there.

"Good morning, ma'am," the driver said. "I'm Jack."

From the sound of his voice, she'd guess he was older, probably in his late sixties.

She wished him a good morning and he took her suitcase. The trunk slammed shut, and she felt the driver walk past her.

"Go ahead and get in, ma'am, if you're ready to go."

He took her elbow to guide her, and she breathed a sigh of relief. She'd chosen this limo company because it was expensive, which usually meant the drivers were courteous and professional and most importantly, that they didn't ask questions.

Duke hopped in beside her, and, as if he'd been doing this for years, he turned around once and then curled up on the seat. Margaret reached out and stroked his head.

"So, all the way to Whitefish, Montana, ma'am?"

"Yes, thank you. And please, call me Margaret."

"Will do, Margaret. What's in Whitefish?"

So much for not asking questions. "Going to hear the Glacier Symphony," she said.

"You're going all the way to Whitefish, Montana, just to hear a symphony?"

"Yep."

"You know there are symphonies in Wyoming."

"I know."

After that, Jack didn't speak again for a while. They drove along in silence, and Margaret imagined that the sun's edge was coming up over the horizon now, red and shimmery. The light would be golden, slanting between the leaves on the trees, making the rivers sparkle. Mornings were spectacular in Wyoming, and very different from mornings in Seattle.

It was unfair, Margaret thought. Nature was cruel. Her eyes filled with tears, and she thought it was stupid that her eyes still worked to cry, but that they couldn't watch the sun rise or the geese flying along the water.

"Are you all right, Margaret?"

She cleared her throat. "Yes, I'm fine. Thank you, Jack."

"Are you running away from home?"

She hadn't expected, or wanted, to converse with her driver. But there was kindness in his voice, and compassion. She was almost relieved to answer: "Yes. As a matter of fact, I am."

"Man troubles?"

"I wish it were that simple," she said. "But unfortunately, no. I just need a little time, that's all. Could we stop for breakfast?"

"Sure thing," he said. "What are you running away from?"

"I don't even know, to be honest. My real problem—the fact that I'm losing my vision and therefore my identity—is coming with me. I think I just needed to get away from everything else for a couple of days, you know?"

"Oh, I do know about that. Here we are. It's a cute little diner. No idea if it's good, but they have a fluorescent 'Hot Coffee' sign in the window."

"Sounds perfect," Margaret said, and then, even though she knew it wasn't customary, she said, "Would you like to have breakfast with me, Jack?"

There was a brief silence while he considered.

"I think I'd like that," he said.

He opened the door for her, and rather than take her elbow, he took her right hand and tucked it into the crook of his arm. Margaret called Duke to her other side, and the three of them walked into the diner, linked.

"So, how do you typically order, when you go out and have to read a menu?" Jack said once they were seated.

"That's a good question," Margaret said. "I haven't gone to many restaurants since I finally admitted that I couldn't see. I suppose I could ask my breakfast companion to tell me what's on the menu. Or, if I didn't have a breakfast companion, I could ask the server what's good. Right now, I smell bacon."

Jack made an appreciative noise. "Smells good, doesn't it?"

"Sure does," Margaret said. "I think I'll order that and some pancakes with my coffee. That should be pretty easy, right?"

"Should be," Jack said. "And the pancakes look delicious, too."

Jack ordered an omelet, and when the server took their menus and walked away, he said, "Tell me, Miss Margaret. What are you really running from?"

She sighed and leaned back against the squishy booth seat. Duke licked her hand. "Everything."

"You know you're going to have to come back, eventually, right?"

"Right," she said. "I think I just needed a break, you know?"

"I do know," Jack said. "I ran away from home once, too."

He sipped his coffee. Margaret waited.

"I was tired," he said. "Really, really tired. I was working hard. This was before I was a driver, mind you. This is my retirement gig. Can you believe I'm seventy-nine years old? I'll be eighty next month. Anyway, I was working such long hours. And I'd get home and my wife—she stayed home with our kids—she'd leave. Go shopping, go to the library, go to a movie, get her nails done. At the time, I couldn't understand why she needed to get away. I didn't mind taking care of the kids. You know, feeding them dinner, finishing up homework, getting them to bed. But I felt like my wife—Susie—didn't want to be home with me. I'd worked hard all day long, and then I came home and worked hard again while she went out and relaxed. I felt like the very life force was being drained out of me. I later realized that Susie was tired, too. She was exhausted from running all over creation with those kids. She just needed a break. The day I left—I remember it well. I finished up my workday, and I walked out to my car. I sat down in the driver's seat and I thought, 'You know, I'm not gonna go home. I'm just gonna drive.' And I did. I drove all night long. We lived in a suburb just outside of Portland back then, and when the sun came up the next morning, I was south of San Francisco. I spent the first several hours of that drive in self-righteousness, thinking about how I deserved this. I deserved to get away. I considered never going home. I was a smart man; I could make myself disappear. I'd send Susie and the kids money, but I wasn't going back."

There was a break in Jack's story while the server delivered their food. Margaret thought Jack was lucky he'd been able to drive all night. At least he had the autonomy to do that.

"I know what you're thinking," Jack said. "You're thinking I'm lucky I could drive, myself. You're thinking you had to hire a driver to get away."

Margaret smiled. "You're right. That's exactly what I was thinking."

"Well, let me tell you what happened when the sun came up and I was all the way south of San Francisco," Jack said. "I'd had all night to think. And sometime during the second half of that drive, I came to my senses. I realized that even though Susie kept trying to tell me that she needed a break, I wasn't really listening to her. You know? I was *hearing* her. I could hear the words she was saying, but I wasn't really listening."

Margaret used her fingertips to find the edge of her plate, and she picked up a piece of bacon.

"She tried to tell me. She said, 'Jack, why don't we get away for a weekend?' or 'Jack, why don't we let someone else watch the kids while we just sit home and have a cocktail?' But I always thought she was implying that *I* needed a break. And that somehow made me feel inadequate. When the sun came up that morning, though, I had an epiphany: Susie was exhausted, too. You know what I did?"

Margaret shook her head.

"I stopped at a payphone. This was in the days before mobile phones, right? I stopped at a gas station payphone, and I called Susie, and I said, 'Honey, I am sorry. I am coming home.' And you know what Susie said?"

"What did she say?"

"She said, 'Jack, you're crazy. Don't come back here unless it's to pack up your stuff'."

"That's what she said?"

"No," Jack said. He laughed. "She told me to get my ass home. And I did. Best thing I ever did, Miss Margaret. Sometimes the very thing you need is right in front of you. Going home was the best thing I ever did. Now. I'm going to eat my omelet. You eat those pancakes. We've got to get back on the road."

The rest of the drive to Whitefish, Montana gave Margaret several hours to think about what Jack said. And maybe he was right. She did have what she needed at home: her mother, her sisters, and a wonderful man who wanted to be more than friends.

But what she didn't have—what they couldn't give her—was her old life back. They couldn't give her the independence she needed to survive.

And if she didn't have that, then what good was she to them? On the other hand, did she even need to be good to them? Was just being herself, being Margaret, any kind of contribution? Maybe, she thought. Maybe it was. But—and this was the kicker—she wasn't actually Margaret, any more.

---

ACCORDING to her online search results, the Pine Lodge was an "exquisite piece of architecture," renowned for its "elegant-yet-rustic design" and it's "breathtaking, scenic location."

Margaret had scoffed when those words came out of her computer's speakers; not because of the description, but because for her, now, all of it was pointless. Nevertheless, the lodge had wide, easy-to-navigate stone steps leading up to the front doors, and she could tell from the way the sound bounced around that the entryway was tall and grand. Inside, the carpet was thick under her feet. She couldn't help but consider what kind of pattern an interior designer would choose to create an elegant, rustic look. Jack offered to walk her in, and he took her up to the front desk.

"I set your bag right here," he said to her. Then, he surprised her by giving her a quick kiss on the cheek. "You remember what I said, now, okay?"

"Okay," she said. "I will. I promise."

After a hotel staff member led Margaret to her room, Duke plodding along like the perfect gentleman he was, Margaret explored, trailing her fingertips over every surface. Alone, she didn't feel any sense of embarrassment or failure as she walked slowly around the bed, feeling the soft bedspread. There were two nightstands, and in the corner, a sitting area with a round table and two cushy chairs. A huge TV hung on the wall over a long, low dresser. The bathroom had a wide entrance, and it was easy enough to find the shower knobs, the curtain, the toilet, and the sink.

Feeling confident that she could navigate this small space on her own, Margaret walked back to the bed, flopped down, and put on an audio book Isabel had recommended: *The Truth About Vision Loss.*

"Losing your vision may feel like a loss of life as you once knew it," the narrator said, and Margaret said, "Amen to that."

She expected the narrator to say something like, "But it doesn't have to be."

When he said, "And it is," Margaret expelled a sigh of relief. She should have known Isabel wouldn't recommend a book that pussy-footed around.

"The challenge," he said, "is to learn the skills, and more importantly, the mindset, to create a new life."

Margaret started to groan, and the narrator cut her off by saying, "I know. It sounds impossible. But hear me out."

She laughed out loud and made a mental note to text Isabel later.

For the next hour, she listened to the audio book, and found herself experiencing the tiniest bit of hope even as she alternately laughed, cried, and responded out loud to the narrator. Maybe this was the key to finding happiness again: to let go of her old life and embrace her new one.

There was a tiny problem with this idea, though: she loved her old life. She didn't want to let go of it. She had always been proud of the strong, independent woman she was, a woman who could take care of herself, who got shit done, who didn't take no for an answer.

It was dinnertime, and Margaret felt like she'd stepped far enough outside of her mental comfort zone that ordering room service (rather than going down to the lodge's restaurant) would be acceptable—and ordering a bottle of wine with it would be more than appropriate.

When her steak and seafood dinner arrived, Margaret fed Duke, arranged her food on the round table, opened and poured her wine, and called Isabel. She put the phone on speaker and set it on the table.

Isabel answered right away: "Margaret! Amiga! How are you?"

"I'm great," Margaret said. "Just eating steak and seafood at the Pine Lodge in Whitefish, Montana."

"Ooh," Isabel said. "Did you finally let that man with the sexy voice rope you in for a getaway? Steak and seafood sounds romantic."

"Ha!" Margaret said. "No, I'm alone. I took a little trip to listen to the symphony. I ordered myself room service and a bottle of wine."

"*Salúd*," Isabel said. "I'm having some wine, myself. But you're all alone, Margaret?"

"Yes—well, Duke's here, of course."

"Is that safe? You've only just learned how to get around on your own."

"Oh, it's safe." Margaret waved a hand, dismissively, more for her own benefit than for Isabel's—because now she felt butterfly wings brushing her skin. They were the very first sign of fear. Because maybe this had been a stupid idea.

"If you're sure…" Isabel's voice trailed off.

"What are you up to?"

"Oh, just the usual. You know. I've met a man, Margaret. He's wonderful."

Margaret felt a pang of jealousy. Which, she told herself, was stupid. She didn't want to meet a man. In fact, she'd met a man and turned him away.

"Tell me about it," she said, taking a gulp of wine.

Isabel didn't hesitate. "His name is Carlos. He's a chef, if you can believe it. His hands are magic, Margaret. I mean, magic. He spoils me. And I love it. Tonight he's cooking me a lasagna with his secret vodka sauce. And, of course, we're pairing it with wine. I'm having a glass now, before he comes over, and I'm just delighted you called. I was just sitting here, waiting, and time was passing slowly. Now tell me what's going on with you and that sexy-voiced man."

"I'm happy for you, Isabel," Margaret said. "It's great to hear your voice. Nothing's going on with Ethan. Although, his voice is still very sexy. I really called to thank you for recommending that book. It's great. I've just spent an hour listening to it."

"Good perspective, eh?"

"Yes," Margaret said. "Good perspective."

"Oh, I hate to cut this short, but I've got to go. Carlos is here. I'll call you soon, okay?"

"Okay," Margaret said. "Thanks again."

"You're welcome, my friend," Isabel said. "And Margaret? Be safe, okay?"

They disconnected and before Margaret had a chance to start eating again, her phone announced, "Text message from Ethan-Leroy."

She tapped the screen to play it.

"Margaret, are you okay? Your family's worried. I'm worried. Text me back. Or call me. Or call one of your sisters."

Margaret thought about the note she'd left: purposely vague, short and sweet. Of course they were worried. She took Ethan's advice and texted Hannah, Sarah, and Mama Katherine: *I'm safely at my destination. Just had a delicious steak and seafood dinner and some wine. I'm turning in for the night.*

Then, she responded to Ethan, thanking him for letting her know, and repeating what she'd said to her family.

Finally, with her stomach full and her body relaxed, she fell into a deep sleep.

---

WAKING up in a hotel room and not being able to see was a bit disconcerting, Margaret decided.

But, this was it: her chance to prove to herself that she could handle doing the things she'd always done. This day would require courage and action. Margaret took a deep breath and made her way to the bathroom.

The first thing she had to do was get dressed and take Duke outside. She'd planned her outfits carefully, bundling each one together in a little roll to make getting dressed as easy as possible.

She congratulated herself on this stroke of genius as she pulled on jeans and a sweater, and then clipped Duke's leash (which she'd hung on a hanger in the closet in another forward-thinking move).

"The elevator's to the left," she told Duke.

Even if she hadn't remembered, the darned thing reminded her all night, creaking its way up and down its cables. The receptionist had given her a room right next to the bank of elevators, presumably for better access.

Duke seemed to know just what to do: he led her to the wall, where she easily found the buttons. She pushed the one on the bottom, and waited until she heard a chime. He guided her into the elevator, and she found the Lobby button. When they made it to the first floor, Margaret took a quick moment to orient herself. The main doors were straight ahead, and Duke walked that way as if he knew the plan. Margaret felt a wave of gratitude.

"Good dog," she said.

Outside, while Duke did his business, Margaret listened. Birds were chirping. Cars were driving by. A fountain bubbled.

She jumped when someone spoke to her: "Good morning, ma'am. Is there anything I can help you with?"

The realization came swiftly: Margaret had no way of knowing whether this guy was a hotel staff member or a man off the street. She couldn't make a character profile based on the clothes he wore or whether his eyes were shifty.

Hoping her smile was genuine and her panic wasn't visible, she turned her face in the direction from which his voice had come and said, "No, thank you."

"You're welcome, ma'am."

As she and Duke made their way back to the hotel room, Margaret walking at a brisk pace that contrasted the leisurely one she'd used on her way down, she rethought her brave adventure. She should probably label it a stupid adventure.

Safe in the room, she fed Duke and ordered room service—again. She'd find her courage and head to the restaurant for lunch. Or maybe dinner. Or maybe she'd order room service for the next several meals, stay in her room all day, and take the car home tomorrow without ever stepping foot off the hotel property.

*No*, she thought. That would never do.

Maybe she needed a pep talk.

She called the one person she knew who wouldn't try to convince her to come home immediately.

"Margaret." Ethan's voice carried surprise and the huskiness of sleep, and Margaret couldn't help but imagine him in bed, and herself in bed with him. Did he sleep naked? She decided to believe that he did, and then she realized quite a bit of time had passed.

"Ethan, hi," she said. She sat down in one of the chairs next to the little round table.

He cleared his throat. "Good morning. To what do I owe the pleasure?"

"Well. I'm in Whitefish."

"Montana?"

"The one and only. At least, I think it's the one and only. I don't know of any other state where there's a Whitefish."

"Is everything okay?" he said, cutting her off.

She tapped her fingertips on the tabletop. "Sorry. I'm rambling. Yes. Everything is okay. I just had a moment of panic, though. I took Duke downstairs to go to the bathroom. You know, a dog's gotta do his business."

"Right," Ethan said, drawing the word out. "Is everything okay?"

"Yes! Yes, I'm fine. Nothing happened. But a man came up to me and asked if there was anything I needed help with. I assumed, for a split second, that he was a hotel staff member. You know, maybe the bellman or the valet. Since he was outside. But then I realized anyone could talk to me like that, with good manners, calling me 'ma'am.' And I can't see. I wouldn't know whether it was a bellman in a hotel uniform or a hoodlum disguising his voice as a bellman's voice."

"True," Ethan said. "What does a bellman's voice sound like?"

Margaret chuckled. "I don't know. He called me, 'ma'am.'"

"What did Duke do?" Ethan said.

"Nothing," Margaret said. She stood up to pace the room. "Well, nothing that I could hear, anyway. He just stood there. Actually, I felt his tail thumping my leg. He was probably like a greeting committee."

"No growling? No backing you away from the person who owned the voice?"

"No," Margaret said. "None of that."

"First of all," Ethan said, "I understand your need to do this, Margaret. But I wish you'd told someone where you were going before you actually went. You're pretty far away for anyone to get to you if you need help."

Margaret stopped walking. She bit her lip. That was the point.

She continued pacing, and Ethan continued speaking: "That being said, I think Duke can serve as a pretty good barometer of someone's intent. Dogs can sense that stuff, you know? I'll bet that if someone meant to do you harm, Duke would growl or start walking away, or maybe both."

Margaret bumped into the edge of the bed and sat down on it. She nodded. "I hear Duke's a pretty harmless-looking dog, though."

Ethan chuckled and the sound sent shivers skittering over Margaret's skin. "He is that. But he's still a dog. A big dog with a strong jaw. I like to think no one would mess with you as long as you've got Duke with you."

"Huh," Margaret said, flopping back onto the bed. "I hope you're right. I'll be back tomorrow. No need to worry. I've already got a car lined up. Anyway, what's going on there?"

Ethan told her about a new vendor at the farmer's market— someone selling homemade lavender oils—and said he'd bought her some to try, along with a new huckleberry wine.

"Why are you buying me presents?" she said. "I mean, that's awfully nice of you, but I hope you don't feel obligated."

"Of course I don't," Ethan said. "I was thinking of you. I think about you all the time, Margaret."

She blushed and was glad he wasn't there to see it.

"Thank you," she said. "I look forward to drinking the wine with you."

"And what about the soap?"

If it were even possible, Margaret's blush grew even hotter. "What about it?"

"Do you look forward to sharing that with me, maybe in the bath?"

For a moment, she couldn't speak. Fortunately, Ethan did: "I'm kidding, Margaret. Although, if you invited me to shower or bathe with you, I wouldn't turn you down. The soap smells great."

They concluded the conversation there, Margaret spluttering and Ethan chuckling again.

Even though it ended on a positive note, a pinprick of doubt had appeared in the blanket of confidence Margaret had thrown over herself. Maybe being all the way north in Whitefish, Montana, was a terrible idea after all. Who was she trying to impress, really? Her family—her mom, her sisters, Donny, even Ethan—they didn't need to be impressed. They didn't think any less of her because she was losing her vision.

But *she* did.

She sat back up, feeling as if the world was spinning around, too quickly, and she was standing still.

She was changing, evolving. Going blind may not be a part of the metamorphosis she'd expected, but it was part of her metamorphosis, anyway. Margaret supposed people didn't always get to choose how they evolved. And she didn't get a choice about whether she was losing her vision. But, like that motivational poster her high school leadership teacher had on the wall said, "Life is ten percent what happens to you and ninety percent how you react." Or something.

Margaret had a choice, here. She could choose how to react to losing her vision. She could forge a bold new path for herself, rewrite the next chapter of her life, even if it looked different from the one she'd originally imagined.

First, though, she had to get through the rest of this weekend. She'd set out to hear the symphony, and she was going to hear the symphony.

CHAPTER NINETEEN

——————

MARGARET'S entire being tingled with awareness the moment she set
foot in the Whitefish Performing Arts Center. The building emanated a
sense of reverence. She'd never designed a music hall or, actually, a
performance venue of any type, but she knew it required great skill
and care. From acoustics to seating to aesthetics, the building had to
meet numerous criteria.

And she could sense the quality of this building, in the way the
glass doors slid shut, sealing the lobby, and in the thickness of the
carpet beneath her feet. She recognized it in the wood paneling on the
walls, the velvet coverings on the seat cushions, and the way the
sound flowed as people made their way to their seats, chatting quietly.

Attending this performance was going to be the next step on her
evolutionary journey.

Here, she vowed to herself, she would focus on listening. As a
sighted person, she'd always been somewhat distracted during
musical performances. She couldn't help but notice the way a building's walls curved upward or the ornate woodwork and chandeliers
on the ceiling. She loved watching the conductor as he moved his
arms, the twirling of his baton controlling the crescendo and the fall of
each instrument's sounds.

The lights went down, and the crowd hushed. Margaret drew in a
breath, and next to her, Duke sighed, his ribcage expanding and
contracting against her calf.

And when the music started—a long, sad note from a single violin
—Margaret's heart beat just a bit faster. She could almost feel the

sound vibrating at the very center of her being. It was as if the violin was telling a story. If she wanted to get poetic, she could imagine that it was the story of this part of her own life.

Some other instruments—clarinets, maybe?—joined the violin, and the effect was haunting. Chills made their way up Margaret's torso. Even though it was unnecessary, she closed her eyes. She let the music flow over her, through her. And she smiled. Something about sitting here, in the dark, enveloped in the sound of the music, was healing. It didn't matter that Margaret couldn't see, that she'd never see again. It didn't matter that she couldn't work as an architect (at least, not in the same way). It didn't matter that she was going to have to rely on the kindness of strangers and the skills of a seeing eye dog. None of it mattered because there was more to life.

She pictured Mama Katherine, Hannah, and Sarah, the people who had always been a source of comfort for her, on levels deeper than her own feelings of inadequacy. She thought of Ethan, who wanted to be a source of comfort to her, and with whom she'd really like to explore the possibility of that working.

Yes, Margaret Bradley had always prided herself on her ability to do what needed doing, without letting anything stop her.

Why should blindness be any different?

There was still life to live, and Margaret would live it.

The music built up in intensity and volume, and Margaret pictured a phoenix rising, its wings spreading before it took flight into a wide open sky.

By the time the symphony finished playing its second encore, to a standing ovation, Margaret could feel the tears streaming down her cheeks. Metamorphoses, even unexpected ones, could bring about something truly beautiful.

She couldn't wait to get back home.

She stood up and made her way through the lobby and out into the cool evening air to wait for her car.

---

WHEN SHE MADE the car reservations for the symphony performance, the receptionist told Margaret that she'd have the same driver all day. He'd pick her up at the Pine Lodge, drive her to the Performing Arts Center, and then pick her up and return her to the hotel.

She'd scheduled the pickup for four-thirty, thinking that even if the performance ended before that, she'd take in the afternoon sunshine. Surely the building would have some nice seating areas outside.

Her phone told her it was four-fifteen, and she was surprised at how quickly the crowd thinned out and disappeared. Because she hadn't thought about how she would actually locate a bench in front of the Performing Arts Center, Margaret ended up standing there, somewhere between those swishing glass doors and the parking lot. Before losing her vision, she would have said it was silent while she waited for the car. But now, she heard many things: the summer breeze whispering through the leaves of the trees, birds flying by, chirping to one another, cars passing on the street.

Still steeping in the wonder of hearing the symphony in this new, all-consuming way, Margaret tilted her face toward the sky and enjoyed the late-afternoon sun on her skin. She'd done it. She'd taken an adventure on her own. A nagging feeling, one she might describe as hollow, started to push in at the corners of her consciousness. How different would this experience be if she'd asked Ethan to come with her? What would it be like to have him standing here, now, discussing the music or the building or the town of Whitefish?

Did being independent have to mean being alone?

Maybe it didn't. Nevertheless, she could be—and was—proud of herself for taking this mini trip. On her own.

Margaret heard what she assumed was a piece of trash, maybe a plastic grocery bag or a single sheet of newspaper, scuttling through the parking lot. And then she heard footsteps. They were coming closer. Maybe it was her driver. She hadn't heard a car pull up, but maybe he'd left it in a parking space and planned to escort her to it.

No, if this was her driver, he'd have said something by now: "Ms. Bradley," or, "Margaret," or, "How was the performance?"

But whoever these steps belonged to didn't speak. And now, she was aware of the person standing there, probably just beyond her reach.

Despite the calm she'd felt during the performance, Margaret's body stiffened. Then the person—a man—spoke: "Nice evening."

Duke, apparently just now noticing they had a visitor, stood up and turned around. Now, she could tell, they were both facing the stranger.

Margaret cleared her throat and licked her lips. "It is."

She felt Duke's body press against her leg—absent the thump of his tail. This particular visitor did not enlist a tail wag.

"Are you waiting on someone?"

"Just my driver," Margaret said.

Immediately, she realized her mistake. She should have said she was waiting on her husband. Or even a friend or a sister. Someone with whom she'd actually attended the performance, whose arrival was imminent.

"He should be here any minute," she said quickly. She knew it was an obvious attempt at making it sound like she wouldn't be alone too long.

"Ah," the stranger said.

His voice took on a creepy, knowing quality. She wished she could tell Duke to take her to safety. Her mind started painting a picture of this man who had intruded on an otherwise perfectly pleasant evening: he slouched. Men with voices like his never carried themselves with confidence. They never looked like they were supposed to be there—no matter where "there" was. He was skinny. He probably had little pouches on either side of his mouth, lines deepened by a perpetual frown. And yellowing teeth with gaps between them. Most likely, spittle collected at the corners of his lips. His face was covered in dark, splotchy stubble. His eyes were green—no, dark brown. The kind that glittered, hard enough it almost hurt to look at them. He looked like everything bad in this world: hate and fear and grime.

Margaret knew what *she* looked like: a wealthy woman who was completely vulnerable. She wore designer slacks, designer heels, and a designer sweater, and she carried a designer clutch encrusted with gemstones. And, she couldn't see anything. Which meant that not only could she not tell what this guy's body language was like, but she also couldn't tell if he was about to snatch her clutch and run. And if he did, she'd never be able to run after him or give the police a description.

She could just hand it over now. As a savvy traveler, she had only one credit card in there—one she could call and block with a couple of voice commands before he had a chance to use it. And she'd brought only fifty bucks in cash tonight, six of which she'd used to buy a glass of wine during intermission.

But what if he wasn't going to mug her? What if he just wanted to ask her something?

She waited, the drumbeat of her heart echoing in her ears, throbbing in her fingertips. She tightened her grip on Duke's harness. When the man spoke again, his mouth was close to her ear. She could feel the moisture from his breath.

"A pretty woman like you shouldn't be out here alone."

"I'm not alone," she said, even though she felt alone—very, very much so.

This time, Duke did back up, towing Margaret with him. The man straightened; the amount of space between them increased.

"Why don't you hand me your wallet?"

"I—I didn't bring it."

"Liar."

Maybe talking to him would buy her time.

"I didn't," she said. Her voice didn't sound confident. She plowed on anyway. "I'd already bought my ticket. Online."

His voice was in her ear again, and this time she caught a whiff of the stale cigarette smoke on his breath: "I'm sure you needed identification."

He enunciated each syllable of "identification," and Margaret shivered. This time, Duke growled, low and long. The words Isabel and Ethan had spoken floated through her consciousness:

*Is that safe? You've only just learned how to get around on your own.*

*You're pretty far away for anyone to get to you if you need help.*

Suddenly, the man shoved her, hard. His hands met her shoulders and she was stumbling backwards before her mind even had a chance to register what was happening. She didn't know whether letting go of Duke's harness was a conscious decision or a matter of physics, but she came down on her butt and used both hands to break the fall.

She'd dropped her clutch, but she could feel its wrist strap against her skin. That lasted only a moment, because the next thing she knew, it was being yanked roughly off. Margaret made a scrambling attempt to hang onto it, but the strap was thin and the thief was fast. Duke was barking.

Later, she'd reflect on this event and imagine the skinny, raggedy thief raising his arm to hit her. But at the moment, all she experienced was a blow to the side of the head and then a horrible pain as she fell back onto the concrete. She seemed to lose control of her body. She couldn't sit up or even move.

Through the haze, Margaret thought she could hear the man's footsteps as he ran away. She couldn't tell if she lost consciousness or not. Duke seemed confused by the whole situation. He charged in the same direction the man had gone, and then came back to lick Margaret's face, over and over.

It felt like several hours passed, during which Margaret's awareness came and went. When she was aware, she felt her palms stinging. She was sure they were scraped up. Her backside was already sore.

She felt an explosive pain radiating out from her temple. And her pride was torn to shreds.

Duke laid down next to her and stayed there, sniffing her. She put a hand on his head in an effort to calm them both.

"It's okay, Duke. I'm okay."

In snatches of coherent thought, Margaret thought about the Mary Thompson School for the Blind. When she was attending, someone had recommended buying a separate purse or pouch in which to carry a cell phone. That way, if you lost your main purse, you'd still be able to contact someone if you needed to. At the time, Margaret had done an internal eye roll. How would a person lose a purse?

Now, though, she knew. Now that she'd spent the tiniest amount of time out in the real world, she could see how it could happen, even to the most careful person. Without that visual reminder, it would be easy to walk off and leave it.

Even though, at the time, Margaret thought the separate-purse advice was overkill, she'd followed it this weekend. Her phone was in a small pouch with a cross-body strap. But whether it was because she was too out of it or because her arms wouldn't work, she couldn't manage to find it. Instead, she lay there on the ground, blinking, feeling like she wanted to scream, but knowing that if she opened her mouth, she'd cry, instead.

She heard a car—its tires on the asphalt, its engine rumbling, its brakes squeaking just the tiniest bit. And she hoped with all her being that this was *her* car. Still, she couldn't get her mind clear enough to force her body to sit up.

Throughout the whole ordeal, Duke had never gone more than a couple of feet from her side. Now, she ran a hand over his head and let it rest on his back. She heard one of the car doors open and shut. Footsteps.

Duke growled, and Margaret's stomach twisted. Now her mind was waking up. In the half-second that followed, she experienced a fear like she hadn't felt since childhood. She was already lying on her side. Now she brought her knees up to her chest and used her arms to cover her face. The footsteps came closer. Duke growled again and scooted his body closer. It was touching hers. Margaret prepared for the worst.

"Ms. Bradley!"

She recognized the driver's voice. Relief wanted to push through the panic, but it couldn't quite do so. She maintained her curled-up position and waited.

"What happened?"

When Duke growled for the third time, gratitude bloomed in Margaret's chest.

She said, "It's okay, Duke," and the driver said, "Do you think you can stand up?"

Normally, Margaret would say something like, "Of course I can."

But right now, in this moment, she really didn't know, and she said so.

"May I help you?" the driver said.

With tears filling her eyes, Margaret rolled onto her back and offered him her hands. He grasped them and pulled her to sitting. "You all right?"

A new wave of dizziness overcame her and she said, "I need a minute."

"I've got you," he said, squeezing her hands.

This kindness, and her own need to accept it, opened a raw wound at Margaret's core. After she sat there for a few minutes, she said, "I think I can stand," and he pulled her up. Again, dizziness overcame her, forced her to lean against the driver, who slipped an arm around her waist.

"I'll walk you to the car, okay?"

She nodded.

As soon as he closed the door, encasing Margaret and Duke safely in the back seat, she lost consciousness again.

# CHAPTER TWENTY

Waking up in the hospital was probably disorienting enough on its own. But waking up in the hospital and not being able to see was even more so. Margaret's other senses were on high-alert: she could smell antiseptic and bleached sheets and the bandaging on her face. She could hear regular beeping and the hush of scary places. And she could feel an oxygen tube in her nose, draped over her cheeks and around her ears.

"Duke?"

Duke's wet nose came into contact with her hand, then, and her throat closed. Was she actually crying, over a dog? This was ridiculous. He licked her fingertips.

"Good boy," she said. Her voice was clogged with tears.

Duke's head remained on the edge of her bed even when someone pulled the curtain back.

"You're awake."

The voice was honey and whiskey, Margaret thought.

"I'm Natasha, your nurse. Your driver brought you in. Said he didn't know who to call. He's in the waiting room. Is there someone I can try reaching for you?"

Margaret licked her lips.

"My phone—"

"I put it in this bag for you," Natasha said. "I'll get it. Your driver gave us your name—Margaret Bradley, is that right?"

"Yes," Margaret said. "Someone stole my purse."

"That's why you didn't have identification on you."

"Right."

"Here's your phone."

Margaret took the phone and set it beside her leg on the bed. "Thank you. Will you please thank my driver for me? Tell him I'm all right and I appreciate him scooping me up off the concrete and bringing me in?"

"Sure," Natasha said. "Would you like me to call someone for you?"

Margaret groaned.

"Are you all right?" Natasha said. "Are you in pain?"

"I'm all right," Margaret said. "I just don't want to call anyone. Although I know I should."

"Won't someone be worried about you?"

"Not yet," Margaret said.

"But they'll be upset that you didn't call," the nurse said. "If someone I cared about ended up in the hospital with a concussion, purse stolen, side of the head split open, and she didn't call, I'd be upset."

"Well," Margaret said.

"I'll leave you alone, for now," Natasha said. "Doctor says you're going to be fine. She wants to keep you overnight for observation. We've got you on some medication for the pain, and you'll want to monitor that head injury. Would you like me to find someone to take your dog out?"

"Yes, please," Margaret said, hating that she couldn't do it herself but knowing she couldn't let her pride interfere with Duke's well-being.

"I'll send someone," she said. "And then one of our registration folks will be in to get your information."

Margaret lay in the hospital bed, debating whether to call home. An overnight stay at the hospital wouldn't extend her trip; she could have her driver pick her up here first thing in the morning and drive her back to Walker, where neither Mama Katherine nor her sisters would have any inkling she'd been in the hospital.

But there was the matter of the huge bandage on her head. Margaret ran her fingertips over the gauze, which wound once around her head and covered a thick pad at her temple. Even if she took off the wrapping, she knew she had a nasty cut and an even nastier bruise. Was there any possible excuse for the injury, other than, "I was mugged by a slouching thief with a voice that sent tingles up my spine?"

"I fell and hit my head on the table."

"I slipped in the shower and hit my head on the tub."

"I was doing ballet and took a spill."

No.

She could extend her trip, tell everyone she was enjoying Whitefish and she couldn't tear herself away. Then she could hole up at the Pine Lodge, order room service for every meal, and wait for the swelling to subside. She knew, though, that the bruising could last for weeks—and the money in her bank account wouldn't.

"That will never do," she said to the empty room.

Someone with a young, cheerful voice came in to get Duke, calling him, "Buddy" and "Sweetie," and talking to him about what a great dog he was.

Margaret rolled her eyes as soon as she was sure they were all the way out of the room.

Maybe she could go somewhere else, somewhere she didn't have to stay in a hotel. She could live off the land.

That thought had her laughing, and when the candy striper (at least, that's how she was thinking of the girl who'd taken Duke out) came back in, tears were leaking out the corners of Margaret's eyes.

"Are you okay, ma'am?"

"Fine!" Margaret said. "I'm fine!"

Margaret knew Natasha was right: she'd have to call home at some point soon. If she showed up with such an obvious injury, her mom and sisters would be aghast that she hadn't called them.

But she didn't want to. This—being taken advantage of, thoroughly—was the ultimate failure. And admitting that to Mama Katherine would only burden her at a time when she should be focusing on herself.

Anyway, what would she say? Whatever it was, it had to be something that wouldn't alarm her.

The last thing Margaret needed was for the entire family to show up at the hospital.

"Don't panic, but…"

That wouldn't do. Any sentence that started with those two words would only incite panic.

"I'm fine, but…"

"When you see me, don't be alarmed."

"I may look like I was accosted and beat up, but I'm fine. Really."

Margaret decided to take a break from this line of thinking. Her head hurt and she was tired. Maybe she'd take a nap. She used the buttons Natasha had shown her to lower the head of her bed. Despite everything she'd done to convince herself otherwise, she *was* vulnerable, she thought. And this weekend, she'd been stupid. All of the resolve she'd felt just hours ago seemed like a distant memory. There was nothing to make the best of. Her old life was dead. Her old way of being was dead. It was time to let those go. It was time to mourn.

Then, somewhere between being awake and falling asleep, her mind brought up a film reel of the very moment she'd decided independence equaled survival.

This moment was like a major scene in the uncut version of her life story. Her mind had cut it from the edited version, and every time she started to remember it, every time the first frame flashed into her consciousness, she shut it down. But here it was, making her feel like she was five years old again.

---

"MAMA?"

"Hmm?"

There was no food in the refrigerator. Or the pantry. Or on the counter. There weren't even any leftovers on paper plates, or in bags from the fast food restaurants. She'd checked.

"I'm hungry."

Margaret's mama was laying on the couch, her eyes not quite closed, but not quite open, either. Margaret didn't like seeing her mama like this, drifting somewhere between awake and asleep. She was subdued, which was kind of nice. But she wasn't much of a help when it came to things like finding food.

The coffee table showed potential as a source of lunch—or was it dinnertime by now? There was crumpled-up paper and an empty pizza box and French fry container with oil stains on it. And what was this little dish, with the clear tube on it?

Margaret pinched the clear tube between her thumb and her forefinger and held it up to examine it.

Suddenly, her mom's left eye, the one that wasn't smashed into the couch cushion, opened, just a crack. Margaret could tell because she could see the shine of the white part, and a tiny bit of the bright green.

"Don't touch that," she said, her voice more clear than it had been in a while. "Put it down."

Margaret obeyed. She knew and feared what happened when she didn't. And although she was usually safe when her mama was laying on the couch or the floor, or half-laying in a chair, with her eyes in this state, something seemed different right now. Maybe it was the way that one eye had opened at the very moment Margaret picked up the clear tube. Maybe it was the stern tone of her mama's voice.

"I'm hungry, Mama."

Her mama's left eye closed again, and she murmured, "Go on out back."

Margaret stood up, and swayed from dizziness. She was only six, but she imagined her stomach, starving, trying to eat itself. Her vision went blurry around the edges, but cleared up within a few seconds. She walked to the door of the apartment and opened it. After slipping outside and noticing the brightness of the sun made her eyes water, she she closed the door as carefully and quietly as possible—Mama didn't like it if she left it open, even a tiny crack. As Margaret made her way down the stairs, she remembered the last time she'd gone out back to get something to eat.

She'd found a peach on the ground next to the trash can. It was juicy and delicious, and her hands were still slimy as she climbed the stairs. She fell once, hitting her face on the concrete step. Crying was pointless; there was no one there to help her. She wiped the blood from her mouth and continued on to the apartment. No matter how hard she tried, she couldn't get that knob to turn. The peach juice made her hands slippery. even after she wiped them on her shirt. Dark had fallen, and all the neighbors were probably asleep. There was no one to help her. She curled up on the spot where some people put a mat for wiping feet—the neighbor had one with birds on it—and she slept there all night.

The next morning, she was jolted awake when the door to her apartment opened and she fell right into the entryway. A man came out, then, and she remembered he'd come over just before she went downstairs. He tripped over her, said something like, "Geez, kid," and waited for her to stand up and get all the way inside before shutting the door.

The memory of that struggle fresh in her mind, Margaret wiped her palms on her t-shirt as she approached the Dumpster behind the building. The sun beat down on it, making that sour smell stronger than usual. Her arms were barely long enough to reach the top of the Dumpster, but she managed, and she placed her bare feet on the hot metal to climb up the side of the giant box. When Mama had realized she could do this, she started sending Margaret to the Dumpster alone.

She didn't have to go all the way in. She'd learned that if she just hooked the bottom of her rib cage on the top of the Dumpster, she could reach at least a couple of garbage bags and get them open. The first bag she opened was full of paper. It wasn't kitchen trash. If Mama was here, and awake, she'd say, "Jackpot!" when Margaret opened the second bag. At the very top, there was a chicken carcass—and someone (someone Mama would call a "dumb jerk") had left a whole bunch of meat on that thing.

Margaret pulled it out and then, straddling the top edge of the Dumpster, she picked the meat off with her fingers and ate until her stomach stopped growling. Mama would be hungry, too, Margaret thought. She tucked the carcass under her arm and scrambled back down the side of the Dumpster.

Someone—probably old Mr. Joe, the building superintendent—yelled, "Hey!" and Margaret didn't wait to see if he was yelling at her. She took off running, right up the stairs and back into the apartment. She was big enough to turn the round knob now; she'd practiced doing it a hundred times after being locked out that one night.

Mama was still lying on the couch and she didn't stir when Margaret slammed the door. Normally, she'd holler at Margaret to be quiet but she must be really tired today. Margaret put the chicken in the fridge and went back into the living room. Sometimes, when Mama slept, Margaret would build towers out of the paper garbage on the coffee table. Other times, she'd line up her stuffed animals and play school, even though she'd never been to school and didn't know exactly what it entailed. And still other times, she'd turn their space into something of an obstacle course. When they had cable TV, Margaret used to watch this show where the contestants raced through obstacle courses. Sometimes they'd fall into the water or mud and Margaret always thought that was funny.

Today, she built a tower out of Burger Giant bags and cartons, played school, and ran the obstacle course, falling into the water and the mud three times each.

And Mama still didn't wake up. Margaret figured it was close to bedtime, then. She curled up on the floor next to the couch and went to sleep.

The next morning when Mama hadn't moved at all—her hand still hung off the couch and her fingertips touched the floor, exactly as they had yesterday when Margaret returned with the chicken—Margaret started to feel a little scared. Usually when Mama took a nap, she woke up within one overnight.

Of course, Margaret's stomach ruled her life, and it was telling her now that it was time to put food in it. She'd save the rest of that chicken for Mama, which meant she had to go back outside. Mama always said Margaret had to ask permission to go outside, whether it was to get food or to find some other kid to play with.

Margaret said, "Mama?"

Mama didn't answer. Margaret came up close to her. Their faces were just inches apart. "Mama."

Still, Mama didn't answer. Margaret tapped Mama on the shoulder. Nothing. Sometimes, one eye would slit open, just the tiniest bit, and Margaret could get least a mumbled "mhmm," when she asked if she could go outside.

But not today. Margaret's stomach was starting to feel weird now; suddenly it was less hungry and more fluttery. Now, she grabbed Mama's shoulder and realized her skin felt cold. Maybe she was sick.

Which meant Margaret had to take care of her. She went into the bedroom and dragged a blanket off her own bed, pulled it into the living room, and covered Mama with it. Then, she crept outside and down the stairs, around back to the Dumpster. The same bag, the one where she'd found the chicken, was still on top. She opened it and startled when a swarm of giant black flies with iridescent eyes buzzed out, almost causing her to fall off her perch.

She pushed that bag closed and hunted for another.

"Jackpot!" she said when she found a half-eaten can of chili. Her appetite returned in full force. Careful not to cut herself on the edges of the can, she used her fingers to scoop out the chili. Even though she was hungry enough to eat until it was gone, she didn't. She'd save half for Mama.

The Dumpster was just this side of unbearably hot as Margaret climbed back down, and she told herself she'd have to wear pants the next time. There was Mr. Joe again, and she was sure, positive, that he was yelling at her. He actually said, "Miss Margaret!"

She didn't wait to see what he wanted.

Up in the apartment, she found Mama in the same position. She put the chili in the fridge. Building a tower didn't seem like much fun right now, and playing school suddenly felt strange, as quiet as it was in here. And running an obstacle course definitely didn't feel right.

Margaret stopped keeping track of time after she slept twice more and made three more trips out back. Mama's skin was turning a funny color, now, and it was colder than ever. Although trying to wake her up was tempting, Margaret didn't want to.

"How many times have I told you to leave me alone when I'm sleeping?"

Mama's words, in that shrill voice, echoed in Margaret's memory. She left her alone.

One morning, when Margaret was trying to cling to the last edges of sleep, someone banged on the door, causing everything inside the apartment to rattle.

"Cheyenne Police," someone said in a gruff voice. "Open the door."

Margaret looked at Mama. Then she looked around at the apartment.

The loud knocker banged again. "Open the door. Cheyenne Police."

One of Mama's special visitors used to yell, "Police! Open up!" whenever he came over. And if it was him standing on the other side of that door, Margaret did not want to open it. That friend had always given Margaret the creeps with his shifty eyes and the way he looked at Mama, like she was a mouse and he was a snake.

But this voice sounded different, more serious. More bossy.

With one more quick glance at Mama to make sure she wasn't going to jolt upright and tell Margaret whether or not to obey, Margaret crept over and peeked out the window next to the door.

It was the real police.

Well, what in the world were they doing here?

Margaret knew two things about dealing with the police: they always gave you a sticker, and you did what they said. Right now, they were saying, "Open up."

Margaret did. And as soon as she opened the door, the police officers (a man and a woman) started coughing. They stuffed their noses into the crooks of their elbows.

"Hey, sweetheart," the lady cop said. "I see your mama's on the couch. Anyone else here?"

Even as she asked, the man cop was walking around the apartment, looking into all the corners.

Margaret shook her head. "No, ma'am."

A few seconds later, Mr. Joe came in. "Like I said, I've seen the kid in the Dumpster for several days now, and I haven't seen Jade—uh, Ms. Wilson—at all. I was just getting worried, that's all."

If Mama were awake, she'd say, "Worried about your rent money, eh, Mr. Joe?"

But Mama didn't bat an eyelash. And, Margaret thought, Mr. Joe did seem worried. He was twisting his hands together in front of his body, and his forehead was all wrinkly. He really had always been nice to her.

The man cop nodded at Mr. Joe and said, "Thank you for calling, sir." Then he pinched the tiny black radio on his shoulder and spoke the words that would change Margaret's life. He said, "Dispatch, we have a nine-oh-one H. Subject is deceased. Looks like she's been dead for two, maybe three days."

He continued speaking, but Margaret's ears were buzzing.

She knew what dead meant. Dead was like when she accidentally stepped on a grasshopper on the sidewalk and its guts squished out of its tummy and its legs slowly twisted to the ground. Dead was like last summer when that tiny bird flew *smack!* into the apartment window and then fell onto the balcony, its wings outstretched against the concrete walkway, its eyes squinted shut. Margaret had tried to help it, but Mama, in a rough voice, said, "Don't touch that! It probably has diseases."

When Margaret had said she wanted to help the bird, Mama had laughed—a short, harsh sound—and said, "It's dead, Margaret. There's no helping it."

And now, the man cop was talking about her mama. Her mama being dead.

"There's no helping it," Mama had said.

Which meant there was no helping Mama. Mama was dead.

The pain inside of her was so intense, Margaret didn't know what to do. She ran to the couch and slid under her blanket next to Mama, seeking the warm reassurance of her body. But her body was cold and hard like it was carved out of rock. Margaret got back down and sought solace under the coffee table. There, she thought, nothing could get to her.

Lying on her side, she curled up as tightly as she could, and thought about the promise she'd made to her mama: that she'd never, ever rely on another human.

## CHAPTER TWENTY-ONE

Now, as Margaret lay in the hospital bed in Whitefish, Montana, she thought about how her life had unfolded. After finding her mother dead, the police had packed her up, along with her stuff, and taken her to the police station. More specifically, the lady police officer, her eyes sad and her voice infused with fake cheerfulness, had helped her put some clothes and a couple of stuffed animals into a plastic bag, and had then taken her hand and led her into the living room.

"Would you like to say good-bye to your mother?" she said.

Margaret looked down at her mother, her gray face visible above the edge of the blanket, and she shuddered.

"Good-bye, Mama."

She looked up at the lady police officer, who was pressing her lips together in a funny way, and then the lady police officer took her hand again and led her down to the police car.

That afternoon, a social worker delivered her to Mama Katherine's house.

During one of the countless counseling sessions Margaret attended over the course of her lifetime, her therapist suggested that she "re-parent" herself.

"Just think back to the child version of yourself," he'd said, "and feel into how scared you were, how angry, even. What would you say to to that little Margaret now, if you were her parent?"

The exercise had actually felt healing, Margaret remembered. A bit out there, a bit "woo woo," as Hannah and Mama Katherine liked to say, but healing, nonetheless.

And throughout her adult life, she'd done the "re-parent yourself" exercise countless times. Here she was, thirty-five years old, and she still felt like she needed to be re-parented.

Natasha had charged Margaret's phone for her, and now it sat on the table next to the bed. She'd reached out and run her fingers over its surface several times throughout the evening. It was Ethan's voice she heard as she imagined someone answering when she finally dialed. And his voice filled her with relief.

But still, something stopped her from actually picking up the phone and dialing.

The little girl inside of her was scared. Depending on someone else for comfort was a mistake.

Margaret imagined herself as a little girl, curly black hair in a wild halo around her head, fingernails caked with dirt, palms covered in a film of grime. She remembered feeling like there was no one in the world who wouldn't let her down, like she was the only person she could depend on. But she was an adult now, and throughout her life, a small group of people had shown that she could depend on them, too. The adult version of Margaret wanted to take comfort in that, wanted to ask someone to come to Whitefish and take care of her.

She picked up her phone, weighed it in her hand. She wanted to make the call, but actually doing it felt hard. For some reason, the fact that she was having to force her thumb to press the button for voice command made her laugh, and this seemed to push her through the barrier she'd created.

"Call Ethan-Leroy."

The words were out of her mouth before she thought about it, and when she realized she hadn't decided to call Mama Katherine or Hannah or Sarah, she didn't take the time to think about why.

And when he answered—just as she'd known he would—an unfamiliar feeling warmed every part of her being.

She told him *almost* everything: the real reason she'd planned the trip, the diner breakfast she'd eaten with her driver, Jack, how hard it was navigating unfamiliar territory, how much she'd enjoyed the symphony.

She tried to gloss over the part about the man hitting her and stealing her purse, and she finished up with how much she wanted to let Ethan be there for her now. She didn't tell him she was in the hospital—not yet.

He was silent as she spoke. When she finally finished telling the story, she said, "Are you still there, or did I put you to sleep?"

"Wait," he said. "Where are you now?"

"Whitefish Regional Hospital," she said.

Silence.

Then, "You were a bit sparse on the details, but are you telling me someone mugged you, and hurt you enough to put you in the hospital?"

"Yes," Margaret said. "But I'm fine. The doctor wants to keep me overnight for observation. Surface injuries, that's all."

"I'll be there in drive time," was all he said.

---

ETHAN WAS true to his word. A few hours after they hung up, Natasha came through the door of Margaret's room saying, "Your visitor is here."

There was something about the emphasis she put on the word, "visitor" that made Margaret smile. She might actually feel a little giddy.

"I'll leave you two alone," Natasha said.

"Thank you," Ethan said. His voice cracked, just the slightest bit, and Margaret had to wonder if he was nervous, or she looked like a mess, or both.

She heard him walk over to the side of her bed, and she felt him sit down next to her. He took one of her hands between his, and she noticed they felt warm and strong. Her body responded, practically melting right into the hospital bed.

"Coming up here alone was the stupidest thing you could have done," he said, then, his voice gruff.

That's not what she had expected. Typically, she would have reacted by pulling her hand away. But it felt good there, enveloped by his. And she'd asked him to come. And, maybe her idea really had been stupid. She nodded.

"You're right," she said.

"Still," he said, "I understand why you did it."

This was a surprise. "You do?"

"Sure," he said. "I get it. You've always been strong and independent. You've never needed anyone. And now, with these changes to your vision and your life and your autonomy, you're being forced to create a new identity. I'd be pretty pissed off, if it were me."

Margaret, amused, said, "Well, I was pretty pissed off. I was on a mission to prove—to myself, mostly—that I was still the old me. But the old me is a scared little girl, a little girl who believes, at the very core level of her being, that she cannot rely on anyone, ever. I think it's time to let the old me go."

"That little girl gave you your strength," Ethan said. "I wouldn't let her go, completely. But what do you think about letting her grow up? Teaching her that people—*some* people—can be trusted to stick around?"

Here, he lifted their joined hands and kissed her knuckles. Quite unexpectedly, Margaret started to cry. And then Ethan's arms were around her, and she was inhaling the scent of his skin and feeling his whiskers on her cheek and the muscles of his back under her hands. And she thought, she was falling in love with him.

———

ETHAN SPENT the night at the hospital. He fed Duke and took him out to go to the bathroom, and slept in the chair next to Margaret's bed. The doctor came in the next morning to discharge Margaret, and when he made the assumption that Ethan was her husband, neither of them corrected him.

The morning shift nurse, Abby, wheeled Margaret down the corridor and outside, Duke and Ethan flanking the wheelchair. Ethan brought his truck up, and when they were all settled inside, he said, "What do you think about staying in Whitefish one more night? We could get a room at the Pine Lodge, make a mini-vacation out of it?"

Margaret's insides went all warm and tingly when she thought about the implications of getting a room. She smiled, involuntarily, and reached over to put a hand on his leg.

"That sounds like a wonderful idea," she said. Then she thought about Mama Katherine and Hannah and Sarah. "I should probably call home, first, though, just to let them know I'm okay. I'm relieved you already updated them on the mugging-and-hospital part."

"I'll drive. You make the call."

Margaret decided Sarah would give her the best reception, but she quickly realized she should have waited to call until she could do it alone.

"What?" Sarah said in a near-shriek when Margaret explained that she was staying an extra night. "You're going to spend the night with Ethan in a hotel room?! You guys are going to have hot hotel sex, aren't you?"

Her voice, at its current pitch, rang through the cab of Ethan's truck. Margaret was positive Ethan could hear every word. She wished she could see Ethan's face, but she was also glad she couldn't.

"Sarah—"

"I can't wait to hear about it, Margaret. It's going to be fun!"

"Sarah—"

"I'm going to go tell Hannah right now."

"Sarah!"

"What?" Sarah said. "You can't blame me for being excited."

"We're just driving right now," Margaret said. "In Ethan's truck. If you could—"

"Ohmygosh," Sarah said, immediately bringing her voice down to a near-whisper. "He can hear me, can't he?"

"Oh, yeah."

Now Sarah cackled and said, "Good. I hope he screws your brains out."

When Margaret sat there, mouth hanging open, Sarah said, "I'll let you go. Have a *great* time."

By the time she dropped her phone into her lap, Ethan was laughing. Well, roaring, actually. Margaret couldn't help but smile, although she felt uncertain about what Ethan's laughter meant.

"Well," he said when he finally got it together. "I guess I've got my work cut out for me."

"Sorry," Margaret said. "She loves romance."

"Does your sister consider me 'screwing your brains out,' romantic?"

Now Margaret laughed out loud. "I guess so."

They rode for a few moments in comfortable silence, and then Ethan said, "We're here. Shall we get down to business?"

Margaret felt like giggling, but she managed to keep it together as she signaled for Duke to get out of the truck. When Ethan came around to her side, she said, "Actually, I'm starving. Do you think we could eat, first?"

"I suppose we'd better fortify ourselves," Ethan said. "But I'd recommend you take a shower, first."

"Oh," Margaret said. "Right. I probably look like a fright, don't I?"

"The dried blood couldn't look better on anyone else, but yeah. I'd say you should probably get cleaned up."

When Margaret woke up in the hospital, her first nurse, Natasha, had called the Pine Lodge and asked the receptionist to hold her room. They went right upstairs, following a path that had become familiar.

"Want me to run you a bath, since you're not supposed to shower for a few more days?" Ethan said. "I can get it started and then give you some privacy. Duke and I can go outside for a while."

"That's—" Margaret was going to say, "That's okay," or "That's nice of you to offer, but I can do it." But instead, she said, "Sure. That would be great, thanks."

Ethan took Duke for a walk and Margaret sank down into the hot water, a miracle in an oversized tub. Her body was sore in a few places: her right hip, which had taken the brunt of the fall, and her right elbow. She ran her fingers over the skin in those two places and sure enough, it was rough with scrapes that were probably an angry red over a base of purplish gray. Gently, she touched the spot on her head where she'd gotten stitches. Even the light pressure from her fingertips hurt enough to make her suck the air in through her teeth. Ethan had set the soap and a washcloth out for her, and she sudsed them up and scrubbed herself down, then rinsed the washcloth and carefully wiped her face.

They had agreed that he'd come back in thirty minutes, and her phone told her she had five minutes left. She was just combing her hair when she heard the door open.

Duke came up to her immediately, and gave the hotel bathrobe a good sniff.

"You look a lot better," Ethan said. "How do you feel?"

"Better," Margaret said. "Much better."

"Good," Ethan said.

The atmosphere was charged. The tension expanded between them, like air in a balloon.

"Can I help you clean that cut?" Ethan said.

That wasn't what she was expecting.

Again, Margaret's first inclination was to decline his offer, tell him she could do it, herself. Ethan cleaning dried blood off her face didn't seem very romantic, and it definitely dispelled any sense of romance she'd been feeling. She nearly choked on the words, "Sure. Thank you," but she said them.

"Let me get a washcloth," he said. "Be right back."

She heard the water running in the bathroom, and when he came back, he said, "Why don't you sit here, on the bed?"

It seemed natural for her to follow the sound of his voice. She sat on the foot of the bed and he sat next to her. The tension returned. If this moment had happened pre-vision-loss, Margaret would have been naked already.

But she felt uncertain of herself.

"Okay," Ethan said. "I'll be gentle. Ready?"

Margaret swallowed, trying to tamp down her arousal. He must have read it as anxiety, because he said, "I promise. If it's too much, just say so. I'll stop the moment you tell me to."

"Okay," Margaret said.

His hands on her skin made her insides flare up with longing. He tilted her head to one side and then went to work, using gentle pressure as he cleaned the area around her stitches.

"When you first left for Whitefish, I was worried," Ethan said. She opened her mouth to speak, but he continued before she had a chance. "I was afraid that it somehow meant you'd never give me another thought."

"Why would you want me to?" Margaret said.

"The moment I saw you, Margaret, you took my breath away. I haven't gone more than a few moments without thinking of you since that moment."

"Even though—"

"Yes, even though you've lost your vision. I thought you were striking, then. And now that I've gotten to know you, you're even more striking. You're a smart, sophisticated, self-sufficient woman. And God, you're beautiful. The whole package."

She chuckled at this, and then winced.

He went on, "When you left to come here, I thought that was it. You were asserting your independence and you'd refuse to build any kind of relationship with someone like me."

"Someone like you?"

"Let's face it," he said. "We're from two different worlds, aren't we?"

"We're both from Walker, aren't we?"

"Ha," Ethan said. "We are. But you moved away. You wouldn't be back here if it wasn't for losing your vision."

"And my mama getting sick," Margaret said. "I would have come back for her."

"But would you have stayed?"

"Probably not. But maybe this is what needed to happen. You know, for my evolution as a human being."

"I think you're pretty evolved as you are," Ethan said. "All done. You clean up good."

"Do I?"

"You do."

Even though he'd said he was done, his hands still cupped her face. Her body seemed to be extra perceptive at the moment, sensing Ethan's every movement and intention. He leaned forward and rested his forehead against hers. When he spoke, she could feel the current of his voice running through her.

"When I saw your number come up on my screen yesterday, I was ecstatic."

"Were you?"

She leaned into him.

"I was," he said. "I couldn't believe my luck. About a million thoughts ran through my mind. Maybe you were calling to ask me out. Maybe you'd changed your mind about dating."

She felt him shrug and heard the humor in his voice when he said, "Maybe it was just a booty call."

A small, throaty chuckle escaped and he went on: "But none of those thoughts was about you being in danger."

Margaret's body stiffened. This wasn't where she'd thought he was going.

"When you said you were in the hospital," he said, "I was terrified. I saw the worst possibility. I saw everything that you are—the bright, vibrant human that you are—coming to an end. I saw your wit and strength and humor being snuffed out in one moment. And I realized something. Well, I realized three things, actually. I realized that there is no way I'm ever letting you travel alone again. Before you interrupt, or interject, or argue with that, please know that it's not because I believe you can't handle it. It's because *I* can't handle it. I can't stand the thought of you being alone, like you were yesterday when that asshole assaulted you."

Margaret nodded, and tightened her grip on his wrists.

"Second," he said, "I realized that I'm in love with you."

Her body reacted again, and she inhaled, a quick, sharp breath that did nothing to hide her surprise.

"I know," he said. "Caught you off guard with that one, didn't I? I told you I'd wait for you. I told you that whether we do this thing or not is up to you, and the timing is up to you. But I want you to know that I'm not going to make it easy on you to walk away this time. And that's because of my third realization."

"What's that?" Margaret said.

"My third realization is that you're in love with me."

Margaret felt her heart stop beating, just for a split second. She could have sworn she felt the world stop turning, too. Then she realized she was just being silly. No one's heart stopped beating unless they were having a heart attack. And if the world stopped turning, they'd all be thrown from its surface.

Those feelings were the result of something else. And she knew what it was: she *was* in love with Ethan.

"You're not denying it," he said. "I knew that if you reached out to me, if you let your guard down and let yourself need someone, then you must have feelings for me. And when I walked into that hospital room, I saw relief in your expression. Plain as day. And that's because you wanted me here. You love me, don't you? Margaret Bradley is in love with me."

"I do love you, Ethan James. I'm in love with you."

"Knew it," he said, and although there was a little amusement in his voice, it was mixed into something else, something husky that made the goosebumps rise on Margaret's skin. Then he was kissing her, his lips firm and warm on hers, his hands curled gently around the back of her head. He eased her onto the bed and laid down next to her.

One of his hands ran from her hip to her shoulder and back down again, slowly, teasing her, then turning her onto her back. She felt the indentations of his knees, one on either side of her waist, and she held her breath, anticipating. That anticipation built as he ran his hands down the opening in the front of the bathrobe. His fingertips skimmed the skin along the center of her body, but he didn't open the robe. Instead, he leaned over her and kissed her again, this time with a little more force, a little more desire.

Her hips arched upward, involuntarily, and his hands were on her bare breasts. A moan escaped from her at the same time one escaped from Ethan, and she smiled against his mouth.

"Why are you still wearing clothes?" she said.

"I have no idea."

He sat up. She could feel him pulling off his shirt. Then he leaned forward, and his skin was on hers. She hummed in appreciation, and slid her palms up his torso. He kissed her thoroughly, covering her body with his.

Margaret reached for his belt, and was surprised at how quickly she unbuckled it and pulled it through the loops on his jeans.

"Wow," he said. "I'm impressed."

"Just wait," she said.

With that, she unbuttoned his pants and slid them down around his thighs, along with his underwear. When she felt him, warm and ready, it was all she could do to control herself, stop herself from flipping him over and taking him.

Ethan stood up then, and Margaret heard him stepping out of the jeans. He leaned down and pulled the bathrobe away from her body, easing her arms out of it.

For a moment, Margaret was terrified. She was laid bare, completely vulnerable. Even more, because he could see every square centimeter of her skin, and she couldn't see him at all. He must have seen the panic cross her face because he laid down next to her and said, "You can trust me, Margaret. I promise you."

This time when he kissed her and she closed her eyes, she felt a tear escape and slide down her temple. She couldn't see Ethan. She couldn't see the emotion in his expression. But she could hear the truth in his words. And she could feel the sincerity in his touch. At that moment, she came to her own realization: it wasn't until she lost her vision that she gained the ability to feel this deeply.

# CHAPTER TWENTY-TWO

"I've never experienced breakfast in bed quite like that before," Margaret said to Ethan as he pulled the truck out of the Pine Lodge parking lot the next morning.

Her body still felt warm and pliable after what had turned into a deeply relaxing and arousing session of love-making that involved fresh fruit and whipped cream. He made an appreciative noise, and she said, "I love real whipped cream."

Ethan put a hand on her thigh and gave it a gentle squeeze. "I do, too. Much better than the canned stuff."

They rode for a few moments in silence, and Margaret enjoyed the heat of the late-summer sun coming through the window. She wondered, briefly, what would happen between them when they got home. Would he still want to be with her? Would they be an official couple? Would he come and go as he pleased? Would she? Did she want either of them to come and go?

There were enough questions to drive a person crazy, and not enough answers to quell the slide off the cliff of sanity.

"I'm nervous about getting home," Margaret said. "I'm tempted to ask you to take me on a long detour. Idaho, maybe? Ever been?"

"I've been to Idaho," Ethan said. "Nice place. I'll take you some-time. But not today. I don't think it would make a good impression if I took you there instead of home."

"My family already loves you. Especially considering you called and updated them all on my situation in Whitefish."

"I'm pretty lovable. They'd love me even more if I told them how you were well enough for the breakfast-in-bed activities this morning."

She swatted his arm.

"Anyway," he said, "I can't take you to Idaho. I think your mom and sisters have a parade planned, or something."

Margaret rolled her eyes. "They do not."

"Probably not," he said. "But still. I know they're worried and I'm positive they'd like to see you, well and in one piece."

"Do I still look like a mess?"

"A little," Ethan said, then, after a pause, he added, "But you look better than you did yesterday. I think one more night made a difference."

"One more night of hot hotel sex," Margaret said.

Ethan's laugh rumbled through the cab of the truck. "We should really do that again."

So. He planned to stick around long enough to have hot hotel sex again. That was good news.

"Ethan?"

"You hate to break it to me, but you don't want to have hot hotel sex again? That was a one-time deal for you?"

Now, Margaret laughed. She uncrossed her arms—not having realized she'd crossed them—and leaned back in the seat.

"I'd love to have hot hotel sex again. Lots of it. But—and I realize I bring this up at the risk of making my former self cringe—what is this thing between us? I mean, what's going to happen when we get back?"

"Aside from hot hotel sex, you mean?"

"Right."

"Well," Ethan said.

In the half-second span between "Well," and his next words, Margaret wished she hadn't asked. She wished she'd just let things happen. But then he said, "I'd love nothing more than to explore that with you. I'd like to take you to dinner. Introduce you to my mother. Go to the farmer's market with you. Sit on your new front porch and listen to the creek go by."

Something in Margaret's chest loosened. "I'd like that, too."

THERE WAS no parade to celebrate Margaret's homecoming.

But Mama Katherine, Sarah, and Hannah came running out of the house to greet her when Ethan parked the truck. She could hear their footsteps crunching through the gravel, and the energy emanated off them.

Before she was even all the way out of the car, the three of them had enveloped her in a giant hug. And she let herself enjoy it: the way their arms came around her waist and neck, the solidity of their bodies against hers. Here, she thought, was life. She had a man who cared about her, who showed up when she needed him and did amazing things with whipped cream. Real whipped cream. And she had two sisters and a mother who loved her more than anything.

That blissful feeling lasted only another moment, because the hug ended and Sarah said, "Why the hell did you go off on your own like that?"

Before Margaret could answer, Mama Katherine said, "Now, now. Let's go inside before we interrogate her."

There was humor in her voice, but Margaret sensed worry, too.

"It's okay," Margaret said. "The answer's not long. I wanted to prove—not to you guys, but to myself—that I could do this … life. That I could do the things I've always done. If not all of them, at least most of them."

"I would have gone with you," Hannah said.

"That's not the point," Sarah said. "She wanted to go alone."

"I know," Hannah said. "But I could have been, you know, just standing by. I could have been there, after the symphony, and she wouldn't have been alone."

"But therein lies the problem," Mama Katherine said. "She had to do this alone. I don't think our independent, spirited girl, here, would have been satisfied with anything less."

"I know," Hannah said again. "But still."

"The good news," Margaret said, "is that I'm alive and well, despite my stupid idea. And, for what it's worth, I am really sorry I put you through all that."

"We forgive you," Sarah said. "Right, Hannah?"

"I guess so," Hannah said. "As long as you promise never to do that again."

"I promise," Margaret said.

"Good," Mama Katherine said. "Now that that's all taken care of, let's go in and have dinner. Donny's grilling up some burgers, and

Sarah made a salad. I've got some baked potatoes on. I think we have enough food to feed a dozen ranch hands. Ethan, you'll just have to stay, too."

As Ethan spoke, his fingers intertwined with Margaret's. "I'd like that."

DESIGNING houses for Sarah and for herself would be Margaret's final project. Before—well, before she'd started losing the one thing she needed in order to be an architect, she'd often considered what her final project would be. A final project was the signature on a long love letter. It had to be just the right building: something that showcased the way she felt about beauty, about lines and ceilings and flow. It had to be something she could stand behind, something people would see and they'd just know: "That's a Margaret Bradley." Like a Van Gogh or a Matisse.

Over the years, she had sketched ideas, concepts of which she'd be proud, potential buildings that would be worthy of capping off an incredible, visionary career.

Visionary. Imagine that.

Grand hotels with even grander lobbies. Mansions with cozy corners, thoughtful touches, and stunning ceilings. Innovative tiny houses that had it all.

Never once had Margaret Bradley figured on ending her career with two little houses on a creek in Wyoming. But that's exactly what she was doing now. She opened the blinds in her office and turned on the lamp. Ethan had already set up her supplies and she ran her hands over the paper, the texture rich under her fingertips. She could smell the pencils: wood and lead and rubber.

Memories came flooding back. She'd designed hundreds of wonderful spaces. Maybe even thousands. And although she'd always looked forward to the big reveal—showing her clients her designs— she'd also loved the process. She worked hard at it, of course. She wanted everything to be just right. Functional and beautiful.

She always told her clients, "I'll never force you to choose between form and function."

They loved her for it.

Kate and Matthew Pinkerton had hired her to design their house because the first two architects they approached told them their lot was "difficult." Margaret had called it "interesting," and she'd delivered a home they loved enough that they sent her a five-hundred-dollar bottle of champagne as a thank you.

Max Woodward, the professor of cellular biology at the University of Wyoming, hired her to design a home for his mother. He'd had exact specifications: the hallways had to be a certain width, the windows had to be at certain angles to the summer sunrise, and Margaret had to ensure Max's mother had walls on which to hang her prized Picasso paintings.

Someone referred Max to Margaret, and he told her later that when he first saw her, her doubted her ability to bring his vision to life.

"The wild hair, the sparkle in your eyes, the way you were always smiling," he said. "I felt like you didn't—like you couldn't—take me seriously."

For her part, Margaret could sense his doubt and she had seen the project as a challenge. Of course, she rose to that challenge. And Max Woodward, the stuffy, serious man who doubted her ability to create what he wanted, cried tears of joy when she showed him the plans.

"Thank you," he said, shaking her hand and then wrapping his long arms around her. "Thank you. It's just perfect."

And then there was Sophia Kensington. Just thinking about that name—utterly sophisticated!—struck fear into Margaret's heart. Sophia had hired Margaret with a great deal of reluctance after her first architect—a very nice colleague of Margaret's named Jim Baker—quit due to her demanding nature.

Jim had called Margaret and asked if she'd meet with this client, but hadn't explained all the details until Margaret agreed. It turned out Sophia was building a barn for the herd of wild horses she'd rescued from federal land in Arizona. It was a passion project, and it had to be perfect. Every i dotted, every t crossed, every single nail perfectly spaced. Margaret still remembered hearing that, and feeling absolutely terrified.

But, of course, she'd delivered on that project, too. Sophia Kensington had spent five minutes studying the plans. Five full minutes, during which she didn't speak or smile or even breathe (Margaret was sure of it).

Then, she'd taken off her Dolce & Gabana glasses and set them on the table, each movement very precise. Margaret's insides turned into a tangled ball of yarn.

"Ms. Bradley," Sophia said. "I had my reservations."

Margaret gritted her teeth, hard.

"But you've blasted them to smithereens, my dear. This is wonderful. It's perfect. Just perfect."

Then she'd stood up. Margaret did, too. And Sophia Kensington gave Margaret a hug.

The modern-day Margaret, sitting at her desk with her pencil in her hand, smiled at that memory. It was one of her favorites. Yes, she was a talented architect who could really hear a client's story, feel their feelings, anticipate their needs. She had vision. She had work ethic and ambition. But most of all, she loved design. And it was hard to say good-bye. But, she'd made a good—no, a great—run of things. And it was time.

"Are you ready?" Ethan's voice, behind her, startled Margaret, and she jumped.

"Sorry," he said. "I thought you heard me come up."

"I was in another world."

Now he was there, his arms around her, his chin on her shoulder. "Where were you?"

"Just reminiscing," Margaret said.

Ethan kissed the back of her neck, then sat down on the stool next to hers. "Should we do this thing?"

She nodded.

Designing a house without being able to see the paper or the lines clearly was going to be an entirely new type of challenge, especially since she'd be working hand-in-hand with someone else—literally. But she'd risen to countless challenges.

During the past week or so, Margaret had spent lots of time considering what she wanted this project to be, what she wanted for Sarah and Donny, and for herself.

Sarah and Donny were starting over after experiencing a rough patch and a near-divorce. Of course, they needed the obvious: somewhere for Amelia to stay when she came home from college, an office for Sarah's fledgling photography business, a great kitchen. But they needed a home for new beginnings. They needed spaces that would nurture their marriage, provide environments for connecting. What would that look like? What would it feel like?

And, Margaret realized, *she* needed a space for new beginnings, too. Her home had to flow, to enable her to easily move from one room to the next. Plenty of light was a must. And, since she wouldn't be able to see the creek, she'd have to be able to hear it. Tanner Lucas had snagged her that bay window, and she'd design it right in.

Another consideration she made was that they'd now be next-door neighbors. How would that manifest, in terms of interacting, cohabiting the postage-stamp lots? She'd have to make the houses mirror images with the living areas close together and the master bedrooms far apart.

For the next two hours, she and Ethan worked together. She described what she wanted, and, his hand over hers, they sketched out the lines, the shapes. At first, there was lots of starting and stopping as they found their rhythm. But as they kept at it, that rhythm became steady, and Margaret was able to focus not only on the design, but also on the feel of Ethan's hand covering hers on the pencil, his shoulder leaning against hers as he asked her questions, the sound and vibration of his voice.

They talked, sketched, even laughed.

Then Margaret said something about the double shower head she planned to include in Sarah and Donny's master bathroom (how was *that* for connection?), and things became very serious. Every single cell in Margaret's body became hyper-aware of Ethan's presence, of the sexual tension between them. She felt drawn to him, like she couldn't leave his side even if she wanted to.

"Everything okay?" Ethan said. His voice, huskier than normal, wasn't filled with concern, she noticed.

He'd turned his head toward her. She could feel his breath on her neck. He used one hand to brush the hair back from her face. Her body reacted so strongly she thought it might force her to strip down and take him then and there.

She couldn't do that now. He'd taken time out of his day to help her with this. There was something she could do, though, and she did it: she turned toward him, and, now that their lips were almost touching, she said, "Everything's great."

Then she kissed him, hoping to convey the deep feelings of urgency and passion she was experiencing. He kissed her back, and she let herself enjoy the sensations for a few moments before she ended it.

"Now that we've gotten that out of the way," she said.

"You expect me to concentrate now, woman?" he said. "All you did was get me fired up."

She cupped his face with one hand and kissed him again, lightly this time.

"Consider that a promise. I always keep my promises."

He exhaled, and his breath hitched. Margaret couldn't tell whether it was a laugh or frustration, but the sound turned her on even more, which she hadn't thought possible.

"I also promised Sarah I'd get these designs done. And I made that promise first. So. Let's get back to work."

Ethan cleared his throat and straightened beside her. "Yes, ma'am. But you should know that I'll hold you to that promise."

# CHAPTER TWENTY-THREE

THE DESIGNS WERE COMPLETE—WELL, the first drafts, anyway. Margaret would let them sit, steep, for a few hours or a couple of days, and then revisit them before showing them to the rest of the family. She was exhausted. It was rare that she designed an entire house in one sitting, and even rarer that she designed two entire houses in one sitting. But this was her final project, and, afraid of the potential for drawing it out perpetually, she'd decided finishing the first drafts in one sitting would be more efficient.

And now, she was famished. She stood up and stretched.

As if he'd read her mind, Ethan said, "Let me take you to dinner. I'm sure you worked up an appetite."

She didn't miss the innuendo.

"Oh, I have," she said. "That's for certain. But I'm not sure whether I'm hungry for sushi or beefsteak."

He stood up, too. "Did you just infer that I'm a beefsteak?"

She turned toward him and slipped her arms around his neck. "I did."

Then she kissed him, long and deep. "And you taste good, too."

They drove to the sushi bar downtown, and Margaret was surprised to hear how crowded it was. The sounds blended together: conversations, laughter, glasses being set down, orders being called up. The festive atmosphere reinvigorated Margaret's brain.

"You know," she said. "I'm thinking I should widen that space in the entryway to Sarah's house. They can put a little bench there, where people can sit and take off their boots in the winter. And for my house, what do you think about changing up the layout of the kitchen and dining area? I don't know if I even want a dining area. Mama Katherine has one, and Sarah and Donny have one. We can just dine at their house if we have a family gathering."

"Oh, I think you want a dining area," Ethan said.

"Why? Don't you think it's unnecessary?"

"Not at all," Ethan said. "You're going to marry me and we're going to raise a big family. We won't all fit in that kitchen."

This stunned Margaret into silence. She didn't even have a chance to respond, though. She heard the bell above the sushi bar's door jingle, and Ethan said, "Speaking of getting together, guess who just walked in?"

"Sarah?"

"Hannah."

"What does that have to do with getting together?"

"She's here with Tanner Lucas. And she doesn't look happy to see us."

Ethan sounded pretty entertained, and Margaret couldn't help but be, too.

"They're coming over," he said. "And she doesn't look happy about that, either."

Ethan and Tanner shook hands.

"How's it going, man?" Tanner said.

"Great," Ethan said. "Hi, Hannah."

"Hello," Hannah said, her voice tight.

So. Maybe there was a thing between Hannah and Tanner. Margaret imagined her sister's posture—stiff and uncomfortable—and her facial expression—something between flustered and mortified. She couldn't decide whether to give Hannah a hard time or to soften the circumstances.

"We're here on business," Hannah said.

"Oh, yeah?" Margaret said.

"Here's our food," Ethan said.

"It's been nice talking to you," Hannah said, her tone of voice totally unconvincing. Then she added, "Look, Tanner. They've got us a table. We should go."

"Enjoy," Margaret said, her own tone light and her lips twitching.

"So," Ethan said.

"So," Margaret said.

She was at once terrified and excited. Had Ethan really meant he wanted to get married? She didn't know what to think or say or feel about that. Surely, he'd been joking.

"Your sushi roll is really cute," he said, throwing her off. "It looks like a dragon."

"Ethan."

"Margaret."

"What you said earlier—"

"Yeah," he said. "That just slipped out. I'd planned to incorporate some romance into my proposal, but I got carried away. Let's pretend I never said anything, and we'll revisit that later."

Margaret nodded, and picked up a slice of her sushi roll. But she couldn't pretend he hadn't said anything; while she chewed, she thought about raising a family with Ethan.

DESPITE THE THROBBING in every cell of her being later that night, Margaret couldn't keep the promise she'd made to Ethan—the one she'd implied as they started working on the house designs. Despite the fact that the tension in the cab of his truck felt like the vibrations coming off a guitar string after it's been plucked, despite the way she couldn't stop imagining Ethan on top of her, she asked him to take her home.

She didn't use the word, "Raincheck," but she hoped he picked up on it in the way she kissed him when he walked her to the front door.

Duke greeted her there with way more enthusiasm than Margaret thought the situation called for. His tail thumped against the door jamb, fast enough, from the sounds of it, that his entire body was wiggling, too. He whined, and then the wine morphed into a funny kind of sound Margaret figured was his equivalent of speaking.

"Somebody's happy to see you," Ethan said.

"This is surprising," she said. She crouched down, her face was level with Duke's, and she scratched him behind the ears. He licked her face. "It makes me happy to see him, too."

"I'm going to be happy to see you, later," Ethan said.

Margaret stood back up and kissed Ethan again. "You are," she said. "I promise."

He left, then, and she let Duke lead her inside.

"Margaret, is that you?"

Margaret followed the sound of Mama Katherine's voice to the living room.

"Hey, Mama."

"I can hear it in your voice and see it on your face. You're in love with that Ethan fellow."

"Mama."

"Don't deny it."

"I wasn't going to. I was going to tell you that he wants to marry me and raise a big family and eat dinner in our formal dining room."

"Well, my word. Do you want to marry him and raise a big family and eat dinner in a formal dining room?"

"I do, Mama. Well, I'm not positive about the formal dining room. But for the first time in my life, the idea of marriage actually sounds appealing. The trouble is, he didn't officially propose. I suppose it was the sake talking."

"Nonsense," Mama said. "I can see it on his face, too. He'll propose."

"Who'll propose?" Hannah came into the room, then, emanating a strange energy that immediately put Margaret on alert.

"Ethan," Mama said, her tone matter-of-fact.

"What?! Is that why the two of you looked—I don't know, *weird* at dinner?"

"No, we looked weird because of sexual tension. We could have done it right there on the table. But we thought that would be inappropriate."

"Then, why are you here, instead of somewhere with Ethan, relieving that tension?"

"For the same reason you're here, and not off with Tanner Lucas, relieving some of *that* tension. I can feel it from here."

"That's not true, I—"

Mama Katherine chuckled, and Margaret felt triumphant. She was right. Hannah was attracted to Tanner Lucas, despite everything she said to the contrary.

"We had a business meeting," Hannah said. "We decided to try the new sushi bar since neither of us has been. There was—there *is*—no tension. Aside from the tension created by my extreme dislike for him."

"Mmhmm," Margaret said.

"What is that supposed to mean?"

"Now, now, girls," Mama Katherine said. "Margaret, let's get off this track. You're making your sister uncomfortable."

Margaret opened her mouth to speak, but Mama Katherine plowed on. Margaret imagined her lifting a hand, palm out, to stop Margaret from speaking and she said, "It's obvious Hannah has feelings for Tanner, but let's let her discover those on her own."

"Hannah admitted she has feelings for Tanner?" Sarah came into the living room next, and Margaret giggled—a bit maniacally.

"No," Hannah, Margaret, and Mama Katherine said at the same time.

"And I'm not going to," Hannah said.

"Stomp your foot when you say that," Margaret said. "It'll have a better effect."

"What happened?" Sarah said.

"Well," Margaret said. "Ethan and I were having sushi—"

"And bathing in sexual tension," Hannah said.

"—and who walks in, but Hannah and Tanner, cozy as thieves. I could just *feel* her discomfort."

"Because she has the hots for Tanner," Sarah said. "That's what you're implying?"

"Right," Margaret said.

"I do not," Hannah said.

Mama Katherine chuckled.

"I think you should just admit it," Sarah said. "He's hot, Hannah."

Margaret heard Hannah exhale, and she smiled. Margaret recognized this tic—Hannah was exasperated. She knew she'd been beaten. She pursed her lips, remained otherwise silent, and exhaled through her nose. Margaret had seen it a million times: when she beat Hannah at charades, when she won a debate, or when, as children, Margaret convinced her to do something they weren't supposed to do (like eat raw cookie dough out of the freezer).

"You girls," Mama Katherine said. "I am going to bed. I'd love to hear about your sex-capades in the morning."

Hannah gasped, and Margaret and Sarah laughed.

"Wait," Margaret said as she heard Mama stand up. "Before you go, I'd like to show you all something."

Margaret was nervous about showing the plans for the new houses to Sarah and Hannah. Mama Katherine would love anything she'd created; isn't that what mothers are for? But this was the house Sarah would live in. And Hannah, perfectionist to the core, was inclined to look for mistakes or weaknesses.

Nevertheless, the moment seemed right.

Margaret navigated around the couch to the corner where she'd set the rolled-up plans. Meanwhile, her heart rate increased. As she she made her way over to the desk Ethan had given her, she practiced her deep breathing.

She'd been sure to put the drawings for her own house on top of the drawings for Sarah's. She wanted hers to be the first everyone saw. She unrolled the giant paper and set it on the desk, then clipped it down and said, "Come take a look."

She felt them gather around her, Sarah on her left and Mama Katherine and Hannah on her right. They leaned down to get a better look, and then Sarah reached up to turn on the lamp over the desk.

They all leaned down again.

It felt like hours passed before all three of them, in unison, sighed.

"What?" Margaret said. "What's wrong?"

"It's beautiful, Margaret," Sarah said. "Absolutely beautiful. I can see the thought you put into this. I love this mud room. I would have loved to have something like that when I was raising Amelia."

Margaret heard the emotion in Sarah's voice, and her own throat tightened up.

"And here!" Hannah said. "Look how she's added an angle to the porch! The two of you can sit on your porches and talk."

"And here's your formal dining room," Mama Katherine said. "Where you and Ethan will eat with your big family."

"You and Ethan are having a big family?" Sarah said, her voice rising a full octave.

"Not so fast," Margaret said. "The proposal wasn't official."

"There was a proposal?" Sarah said.

Margaret shook her head and made a big show of switching out the floor plans to put Sarah's on top. As soon as she'd finished smoothing them out and clipping them down, Sarah leaned against her.

And … silence.

Sarah didn't say a thing.

Margaret pressed her own lips together, wishing she could see her sister's face, to discern what this silence meant. She knew better than to ask any questions. She waited.

Suddenly, Sarah's arms were around Margaret's waist, and her cheek was pressed to Margaret's.

"I love it," she said, and Margaret exhaled. "It's perfect. I don't know how you did that. It's exactly what I wanted."

She extracted herself from Margaret and with growing excitement, pointed out all the details Margaret had incorporated: the kitchen island, the corner bathtub, the creek-view windows in the master bedroom.

"You got it all," Sarah said. "Even things I didn't know I wanted. Like, look at this! It's a huge countertop in the laundry room. I never would have thought of that. And these built-in cabinets! I love this, Margaret. I really love it."

Relief flowed through Margaret, a balm to her nerves.

Relief turned into joy when Hannah said, "You've still got it, Margaret. You still have vision."

Even as Margaret's eyes filled with tears of happiness, she realized there was one other loose end she had to tie up.

***

ETHAN ANSWERED on the first ring, and Margaret thought he sounded nervous.

"I thought about showing up on your doorstep," she said. "But then I realized this conversation needs to happen here. Can you come over?"

She was waiting by the door, Duke at her side, when he showed up fifteen minutes later.

"Let's go for a walk," she said.

If she hadn't already known she was falling in love with Ethan, she would have realized it then. Without a question, without saying anything, he grabbed her hand and started walking. "Where to?"

"The construction site."

"C'mon, Duke," Ethan said, and the dog trotted out behind them, the tags on his collar jingling.

"I love the night sounds," Margaret said. "The crickets, the owl—hear that? The breeze just barely rustling the leaves. It's peaceful."

"It is," Ethan said.

They walked in near silence, which was broken only when Ethan gave Margaret directions: "Step up here," or "Let's take a couple of steps to the right to avoid this rut." After a few minutes, they came to the creek—she could hear it bubbling by—and he guided her over the makeshift bridge Tanner and his guys had built.

"Here we are," he said. "Standing in what, I think, will be your new living room."

Margaret had planned this out. She'd imagined this moment for hours, massaging the details in her mind. Now it was here, and she felt breathless. She turned toward Ethan. Duke walked over to the creek and had a noisy drink. Margaret was grateful for the distraction.

Ethan said, "It might actually be the formal dining room. You didn't take that out, did you?"

"About that," she said.

"You don't have to keep it. We can feed our kids in the living room. They can sit on the couches and eat off TV trays."

"I need to tell you something."

He squeezed her hands. "Okay. Why do I feel a weird sense of foreboding?"

She squeezed back, and launched into the speech she'd planned. "When we first met, I told you that I didn't want to be in a relationship. I said I didn't do relationships."

"I remember," he said.

"And that's because I don't like relying on people. Never have. As I got to know you, I realized there was an immediate danger of me coming to count on you. You gave me that amazing desk. You bought me that cherry tree and recommended I take the bay window because I'd be able to hear the creek. When I woke up in the hospital in Whitefish, you were the first person I thought of calling. I realized I was breaking my own cardinal rule. And I realized that's not acceptable. I don't depend on, or rely on, anybody. I can't start to rely on you."

Ethan inhaled, sharply, and she knew he was about to speak.

"Just hear me out," she said.

"Okay," he said.

"I can't start to rely on you," she continued. He inhaled again, and she put a finger on his lips, briefly, before taking both hands again. "That is, unless we make this thing permanent. Unless we get married and build a house and build a family. All that being said … will you marry me, Ethan?"

Ethan let go of her hands. Duke, apparently sensing this was a big moment, came over and sat down next to Margaret, leaning against her leg.

"Margaret Bradley," Ethan said, taking her face in his hands, "I would love nothing more than to marry you and build a house with you, and raise a family together."

In that moment, Margaret experienced a startling clarity. She'd thought losing her vision meant the end of her life. But it was simply the end of life as she knew it. This new life, a life with Ethan, a life in which she was able to let him in, was even better than the one she'd had before this.

Then, standing in the space that would become their living room, he kissed her. Margaret wrapped her arms around Ethan's waist and kissed him back. She didn't need her vision to feel the love, the happiness, and the fulfillment of this moment. She didn't need her sight to experience this kind of love.

THE END

# THANK YOU FOR READING!

If you'd like to be among the first to know about new releases and special offers—and which adventures I'm having when I'm not writing—sign up for my mailing list at www.hilarydartt.com.

Keep reading for a preview of the third book in The Seedling Homestead Series, The Structure of Perfection.

# PREVIEW: THE STRUCTURE OF PERFECTION

## THE SEEDLING HOMESTEAD SERIES, BOOK 3

DURING HANNAH BRADLEY'S CHILDHOOD, magic was the status quo. Growing up on Seedling Homestead was perfect. It was like living in some kind of Heaven. Before her sisters, Sarah and Margaret came, it was just Mama and Hannah. They did everything together: they walked the fence line checking for breaks, they mopped the floors while singing old show tunes, and they strolled along the creek listening for the sounds of bullfrogs and birds, identifying the meadowlarks and tree swallows by their calls.

The light always seemed to sparkle. And even when it wasn't sunny, the world was filled with a kind of wonder: rain drops making tiny ripples on the creek's surface, the snow creating a soft silence while Hannah and Mama snuggled under a blanket in front of the fire.

Of course, being a child, she took this idyllic life for granted.

Then one day, when Hannah was just learning to read, she sounded out the words on the sign that hung between the pillars on either side of the driveway:

"Seed … ling. Seedling. Home… What's that say, Mama?"

"It says homestead. Seedling Homestead."

"What's that mean?" Hannah wanted to know.

Mama took a deep breath, and she didn't answer right away. When she finally started to speak, Hannah noticed she seemed to be choosing her words carefully, as she often did when she tried to explain a big idea.

"Well, do you know what a seedling is?"

Of course Hannah did. She'd been planting seeds and transplanting seedlings for as long as she could remember. She nodded. "It's a baby plant."

"Right," Mama said. "And a homestead is a place where you make a home."

"Okay," Hannah said, drawing the word out.

"When I moved here," Mama said, "I was sad. I was looking for a place to make a home. I felt like a baby plant. Like I was starting over. Do you remember what a plant needs to grow?"

Hannah thought for a minute. "Sunlight?"

"Yes," Mama Katherine said. "And there's plenty of that here in Wyoming. What else?"

"Water?"

"Yes, and what else?"

"Soil."

"Right," Mama said. "Sunlight, water, and soil. I imagined myself as a tiny tree, and I found all of those things I needed here, at Seedling Homestead."

"But you were already a grown-up."

"I was," Mama said. "But I needed to start over."

"Why?"

"Well, that's a conversation for a different day."

"Why were you sad?"

"That's a conversation for a different day, too."

Hannah just nodded. She was used to Mama saving stories for a different day.

Some time later, when Hannah was about seven, she was playing near the creek, throwing in sticks and watching them float along. Mama came up and sat down on the creek bank.

"Hannah," she said, "How do you like our life here?"

A big feeling swelled up inside Hannah's body, one that made her want to squeal and run up and down along the water's edge. That's what she did, while shouting, "I love it!"

"Do you think another little girl would love it as much as you do?"

Hannah was so stunned by this question that she stopped running and sat right down on the wet ground at her mother's feet. She was perceptive. She knew this question was an important one. She knew it meant that maybe there was an actual little girl somewhere, one who would be part of this life, too. Also, she could tell Mama wanted her to say that yes, another little girl would love it here at Seedling Homestead.

So she nodded, and she could feel that her nod was a little slower than usual. She wondered if Mama noticed.

"I need to talk to you about something."

Hannah nodded again. Slowly. Then she stood up.

"Remember a while ago, when you asked me what Seedling Homestead means? And I told you that it was a place for new beginnings."

"Uh huh," Hannah said.

She'd picked up a stick—one she knew would float quickly along in the creek, bobbing only a little—and now she scraped shapes into the mud with it: a stick-figure girl and a dog.

"Well, I've come to know of some little girls—little girls like you—who could use some new beginnings."

"They're like baby trees?"

"Yes," Mama said, and Hannah could tell this pleased her. "They're like baby trees. What would you think about having a couple of girls come to live here? We could plant them and give them water and sunlight and we could help them grow. You and me, together."

"But … they're humans, though, right?" Hannah said. "We won't really plant them."

"It's a metaphor," Mama said.

Hannah tested the word out and found that it felt funny in her mouth.

"Anyway. We would give these girls a home. We would feed them and love them and help them grow up. They would be your sisters."

"Where are their mothers?"

"Ah," Mama said.

Hannah hoped she wouldn't say this was a conversation for another day, and she didn't.

"For whatever reason," Mama said, "their mothers can't take care of them. So they need new families."

"But why?"

Hannah found this concept scary. If other girls' mothers couldn't take care of them, did that mean it was possible that there might come a day when Mama couldn't take care of her?

"Let's sit," Mama said, and she sat right down on the bank of the creek, as wet as it was. Hannah joined her, and Mama wrapped an arm around Hannah's shoulder and gave it a squeeze.

"I can see your wheels turning," she said, "and you don't have to worry about a thing. I will always be here to take care of you. But what do you say? Do you think we could take care of a couple of girls?"

Leaning up against the side of her mother's body, tucked in like this, Hannah thought they could do anything. "Yes," she said. "I think so."

Mama nodded. "Good. I have a feeling you're going to love having sisters."

"When are they coming?" Hannah said, and Mama chuckled a little. "I'm not sure. We just have to wait for the right ones."

This made sense. Hannah had seen cartoons where a stork delivered a blanket-wrapped baby to someone's doorstep and things always seemed to work out.

"Mama?"

"Yes, love?"

"Did you always know I would have sisters?"

Something changed in the way Mama was sitting. She didn't move, but Hannah could feel a shift.

She simply said, "No, I didn't."

"Did you always know there were little girls who needed nurturing, like a baby tree?"

Mama made a little sound, like a gasp, and Hannah wondered if she'd said something wrong.

"I knew," she said. "But I didn't think about being the one to do the nurturing until recently."

"What made you think about it?"

Standing up, Mama grunted a little, and smoothed her long skirt before answering. "I'm not even sure. I just got to thinking about ways I could help out, you know? And I thought it'd do you good to have somebody to run around this place with. Besides me."

"Oh," Hannah said. "When you named this place Seedling Homestead, why did you need a place to grow?"

She still asked the question every now and then, when she sensed Mama was in a talking mood. But she always got the same answer, same as she got this time:

"That's a conversation for another day," Mama said.

Sarah, the first new seedling, arrived a couple of months later. Mama had warned Hannah that when her new sisters came to live with them, there wouldn't be much advance notice. Sure enough, one morning at breakfast the phone rang. Mama jumped. People rarely called them, especially not at this hour, when the sun was just peeking over the horizon and the sky was still a light gray.

Mama did a lot of listening and nodding and humming sounds while the caller did a lot of talking. By the way Mama dried her hands, again and again, on the dish towel that hung from her apron, Hannah knew this was a serious call. And when she hung up, Mama confirmed it: "Well, Hannah, this is it. A social worker is bringing us a little girl. Sarah."

Hannah had about a million questions: she wanted to know how old Sarah was, where her parents were, why she was coming here, whether she'd stay forever or just for a short time. She wanted to know what Sarah liked to eat, what she liked to play, and whether she would be talkative or playful or serious.

"Don't pester her with all those questions as soon as she walks in the door," Mama scolded. "Give her time. You'll find out the answers soon enough."

It seemed like days later when the strange, boxy-looking car rolled into the driveway, its tires crunching on the gravel. Mama went out to greet Sarah and the social worker, and Hannah, suddenly shy, stayed inside and watched through the window next to the front door.

The social worker was as strange and boxy-looking as the car was. She wore a weird coat, long, like Hannah imagined a spy would wear, and her hands were wide enough to use as paddles for a boat. She was probably an excellent swimmer, Hannah thought, before the social worker used one of those flat hands to open the back door of the car.

When Sarah first climbed out of the back seat, clutching a plastic bag, Hannah was surprised. She'd been expecting a little girl like her, one with the slightly chubby, sunburned cheeks of a child who played outside, one with bright eyes and a smile at the ready … one who was as excited to be here as Hannah was to have her.

But Sarah looked terrified. And, Hannah thought, sickly.

Her eyes were much too round, and they had dark smudges underneath. Her skin had obviously never seen the sun. It was pale and dingy. And boy, was she skinny! Her teeth and knuckles and elbows stood out, and her knees were so knobby Hannah thought she might need braces on them, like the little boy at the library. Even in a ponytail, her blond hair looked greasy. One stringy piece of it had come loose and was hanging in front of Sarah's ear.

The social worker laid a hand on Sarah's head and said something. Sarah nodded, and then Mama offered her a hand. Together the two of them walked toward the house. Hannah thought the social worker looked like she might cry as she watched them. Then she got into the car and backed down the driveway.

The front door opened, and when Sarah saw Hannah, she scooted even closer to Mama, hiding. Hannah offered what she hoped was a welcoming smile, but Sarah didn't return it. Mama had told Hannah about the possibility that her new sisters would take some time to warm up and Hannah was determined to make that time as short as possible.

"Want me to show you your room?" Hannah said.

Sarah nodded, and Hannah held out a hand, just as she'd seen Mama do. Sarah took it. As they walked toward the back of the house, Hannah pressed her lips together to keep from pestering Sarah with all those questions.

"Your bedroom's right next to mine," she said, pushing the door open.

After some conversation, Mama and Hannah had decided to leave the room almost plain so that whoever joined their family would be able to make it her own. Now, standing here with Sarah, looking at the plain white walls, the light blue bedspread, and the white curtains, Hannah thought that might have been a mistake.

"We left it plain so you could decorate it," she hurried to say. "You can do whatever you want. Mama said you can paint the walls black if you want."

This was enough to produce a tiny giggle from Sarah.

"Go on," Hannah said. "Bring your stuff in."

Sarah walked slowly into the room, looking around as if it were a cavernous castle or something. She walked over to the bookcase and set down her bag. She began pulling things out—a few paperbacks, some clothes, and a little box decorated with sea shells. Hannah had never seen sea shells in real life, but she recognized them from books.

"Go ahead," she said. "Put your stuff on the shelf. You can put your clothes in the dresser."

Sarah nodded. Then she proceeded to line everything up neatly, even organizing the few items of clothing by color.

"You're very organized," Hannah said, Mama having told her that giving people compliments was a great way to start a conversation.

Sarah nodded again, and Hannah wondered if she knew how to speak.

"Are you hungry?"

A nod.

"Do you eat pancakes?"

A shrug.

"Have you ever had pancakes?"

Sarah shook her head.

"What do you eat for breakfast, then?"

Another shrug.

"Come on. I'll make you some pancakes."

Maybe Sarah had never had pancakes, but she sure knew how to eat them. She devoured eight—two with syrup, three with powdered sugar, and three with peanut butter and syrup. Then she went back into her bedroom, laid down on the bed, and slept for three hours.

Meanwhile, Hannah told Mama how strangely Sarah had set up her bedroom.

"From what I understand, Hannah, Sarah comes from a very chaotic household where things are confusing and she doesn't know what to expect. When people come from chaos, they often seek order … they can be very … well, *organized* is one way to put it."

That made sense, Hannah thought. She hoped Sarah would loosen up a bit, though, and she said as much.

"Just give her time," Mama said.

After a few months at Seedling Homestead, Sarah *had* loosened up —a lot. She still organized her things (shirts by color, books alphabetically by title, toys by shape). But she was no longer silent and drawn. She laughed, a lot, and she loved to run through the fields, chasing Hannah or being chased, hollering happily as the sun turned her cheeks a rosy color. One day at lunch, when the newly-loosened-up Sarah had finished her own applesauce and was trying to sneak Hannah's, Mama got another phone call.

This one seemed different: Mama's initial hums were followed by silence, and then she looked so, so sad. When she hung up, Hannah asked what was the matter, and Mama just shook her head.

A different social worker, a tall, slender, pretty one in a maroon old-lady car, brought Margaret to the house. Margaret, with her wild, curly black hair and bright green eyes, seemed different than Sarah had. She was subdued, but, eyes alert like a cat's, she moved with a surprising confidence. Still, Hannah didn't miss the look of fear on Margaret's face when she accidentally picked a green tomato after Mama told her to pick a red one.

In her way, Mama offered to cook it up, and even while Margaret devoured it, she sat on the edge of her chair, like she was ready to run at any second. Hannah made Margaret a peanut butter and jelly, and Margaret accepted it like she'd never been offered a home-cooked meal before. She scarfed it down, at the same rate as she'd eaten the green tomato, and Hannah wondered if she'd ever been offered *any* meal before.

Margaret adapted much more quickly than Sarah had. Within a couple of hours, she was exploring the property, getting wet and muddy at the creek and swinging from the tree branches like she didn't have a fear in the world. Later on, Mama told Hannah Margaret was used to fending for herself, and that she was *adaptable*.

This was a word Hannah didn't quite understand, and it wasn't until the girls were teenagers that she could really apply it to Margaret's situation. But in those early days, Hannah marveled at how easily Margaret seemed to fit in, how quickly she made friends, and how eager she was to immerse herself in the chores and goings on at Seedling Homestead.

Just like that, they were four.

The Bradley girls became fast friends, playing and fighting like real sisters. Although each of them had her own room, they'd wind up in a single bed every night, limbs flung over one another, heads on the same pillow.

Sometimes, when Hannah described a dream she'd had, Sarah and Margaret claimed they'd had it, too. They'd elaborate on her stories, add in details. Hannah didn't recognize them at all, but the longer she let her sisters believe they were cosmically connected, the more she started to believe it, herself.

It wasn't always perfect. Sometimes Hannah would wake in the middle of the night to hear Margaret moaning, clutching the sheet so hard Hannah couldn't pry it out of her grip. Sarah would twist this way and that, turning her head from side to side as if she was trying to get away from something—or someone. Hannah would stay awake, rubbing her sisters' backs until they settled back down. They both claimed they didn't remember their nightmares, but Hannah couldn't forget. The sounds they made haunted her daytime hours.

One day, Mama kicked the girls out of the house to get some fresh air and get their wiggles out.

"Go on down to the creek and catch some crawdads," she said. "Fill this bucket and we'll boil 'em up for dinner."

Hannah got the bucket, Sarah pulled out some hot dogs for bait, and Margaret hopped and skipped between them, chattering away about how yummy the crawdads would be. They walked on down to the creek, and together, made what Hannah thought was a terrible trap: the hot dogs wouldn't stay put, the bucket kept tilting, and

Margaret repeatedly insisted on pulling it up every few minutes to check and see whether any crawdads had found their way in.

Being the oldest and the wisest, Hannah suspected Mama had known this would happen. She had likely counted on this project taking the girls hours. She had washing to do, and she wanted to mop the floor. Having the girls underfoot would make everything take longer, and she hated footprints on her clean linoleum. So she humored Margaret, pulling up the bucket every thirty seconds, adding more hot dog chunks each time.

Amazingly, by the time an hour passed, they'd collected dozens of crawdads, which moved around the bottom of the bucket in slow motion, opening and closing their shiny claws. Mama seemed a little shocked when they lugged the bucket back, water slopping over the sides, crawdads clambering to escape. But, true to her word, she filled a pot with clean water and set it on the stove. When she put the bucket next to it, though, Margaret's face twisted into a horrified expression.

"You mean, we're going to throw them into a pot of water and boil them? While they're still *alive*?"

The timbre of her voice made the hair rise on Hannah's arms, chills run up the back of her neck, over her scalp.

"That's how you cook 'em," Mama said. Hannah thought she seemed oblivious to the horror Margaret was experiencing. "That's why it's called a crawdad boil. Throw in some potatoes, corn on the cob, sausage. We'll throw it all on the table and eat it with our hands. Dip the bites in melted butter."

"No!" Margaret was crying now, tears streaming down her face. "You can't boil them! I won't let you!"

She started to pull the bucket off the counter, but she was too little to hold it. The water—and the crawdads—spilled all over the clean kitchen floor in a rush. Margaret started making a strange keening sound, almost howling, and Hannah felt compelled to try to gather up the crawdads, which were slippery and had huge dangerous claws.

The girls scrambled around the kitchen, collecting crawdads and throwing them back into the bucket as fast as they could.

"Don't let them die," Margaret wailed, on repeat.

Hannah felt simultaneously sad for Margaret and annoyed with her for causing such a ruckus. Still, she was dutiful in saving as many of the little creatures as she could.

Then, in an ironic turn of events, one of the crawdads Margaret was trying to save latched onto her thumb. She froze in the middle of the kitchen, staring at it in horror, before shaking her hand to dislodge it.

When Hannah saw Margaret's thumb turning purple, she ran to her.

"Hold still," she said, her voice more irritable than she meant for it to be. "Stop shaking it."

Margaret obeyed, her mouth still open, but nothing more than a tiny hiss of air leaking out as Hannah pried the crawdad off her skin and dropped it on the floor before it could pinch her, too. It scuttled away. In the near-silence, Sarah and Mama continued tossing crawdads into the bucket, each one making a *plunk!* sound in the remaining water.

"Where do you think chicken comes from?" Hannah said then.

From across the kitchen, Mama gave her a look, eyebrows down, and a tiny shake of her head.

"What do you mean?" Margaret said.

"Never mind," Hannah said.

"Tell me!"

As if on cue, a chicken squawked in the yard.

"Let's just get these crawdads picked up, Margaret," Mama said, giving Hannah another dark look.

"Yeah, let's," Hannah said.

Margaret carried the bucket back down to the creek, the water sloshing out with every step. She came back sniffling, vowing never to fish for crawdads, ever again. Ever.

And that night, when she crawled into Hannah's bed just after they heard Mama go to bed, herself, she whispered, "What were you gonna say about chicken?"

"Just forget it," Hannah said. "Go to sleep."

"What was it?"

Sarah came in next, sliding in on Hannah's other side. "She was gonna say the chicken we eat comes from chickens who were alive once. Just like the crawdads."

Hannah elbowed Sarah, and Sarah said, "What? She's gonna find out eventually. We can't have her going to school thinking chicken comes from the chicken factory, wrapped in plastic."

When Hannah didn't argue, Sarah went on: "They were alive, just like the chickens in our yard. And they grow up on chicken farms. And then the farmers kill them and somebody plucks their feathers, cuts them up, puts them in packages, and sends them off to the grocery store."

Silence.

Actually, it wasn't silent. Hannah could hear the crickets chirping and the bullfrogs singing outside. She could hear Margaret holding her breath, tiny grunting sounds escaping from her throat.

"Is it true?" she said, finally.

Hannah nodded. She knew Margaret could hear her head moving on the pillowcase.

"Are you nodding," Margaret said, "or shaking your head?"

"She's nodding," Sarah said. "Because it's true. So I don't know why you were so wound up about eating those crawdads."

Margaret sighed. "I won't be eating chicken any more," she said. "Ever."

The next morning at breakfast, she held up a slice of bacon, making eye contact first with Sarah, and then with Hannah, who gave a little nod and whispered, "Pigs."

Margaret gasped and put the bacon back on the serving platter.

Of course, Mama noticed and immediately gleaned what had taken place. Later that day, when Margaret was planting flowers at the base of the aspen tree in the front yard, Mama cornered Hannah in the laundry room. At first, Hannah thought she was going to get a lecture about telling Margaret where chicken came from. She'd already planned her defense, based on what Sarah had said: Margaret would have to find out sometime. She couldn't be the only kid in school who thought chicken nuggets grew on trees.

But that wasn't Mama's angle at all.

Instead, she said, "Hannah, you have to understand something. Margaret's relationship with death is … well, it's different from yours. If you're going to educate her about the facts, you're going to have to tread a little more lightly."

"She asked, Mama. What was I supposed to say?"

Mama rubbed her eyebrows with her fingertips, a gesture Hannah knew meant she wasn't sure how to answer.

"I don't know, Hannah. I'm just saying, tread lightly. When it comes to your sisters, I need your help. You're the only one who hasn't experienced significant trauma. The other two require delicate handling."

Here, she grabbed a pair of pantyhose that Hannah had just hung to dry. "Like my nylons."

Hannah simply nodded. Margaret's vegetarian phase lasted only for a few months, until Mama made her favorite meatballs one night and she couldn't—or didn't—resist eating them.

And soon, Hannah realized that Mama must have experienced significant trauma, too. It was one of the reasons she'd wanted to adopt children who needed homes. And, of course, it was the reason she'd named her new home the Seedling Homestead. At age ten, Hannah didn't know what kind of trauma Mama (or her sisters, for that matter) had experienced … but she knew they all needed to start over. Hannah was the only one who didn't. She'd grown up trauma-free. Which made her feel lonely and lucky all at the same time. But most of all, it gave her life meaning: she was a caretaker. She was the one who had the most solid foundation, the one who had the highest capacity for navigating all of life's twists and turns.

But just because she had the most solid foundation didn't mean that foundation couldn't crack.

Hannah Bradley's realization that her life was far from perfect began the summer she turned forty.

For the past twenty-some-odd years—since Sarah got married and moved away, and Margaret went off to college before becoming a jet-setting architect—Hannah and Mama had lived together on the Seedling Homestead in an arrangement she'd always considered more than satisfactory.

Yes, Mama was getting older. Yes, Hannah felt the strain of working full-time as a teacher at Walker Elementary, caring for Mama, and taking care of the property. And yes, every once in a while, when her sisters brought it up, Hannah wondered if there was *more*. But overall, life was good. She would even venture so far as to say it was perfect.

Then, this summer, three major developments took place: First, Sarah and her husband, Donny decided to move onto the Seedling Homestead again. Second, Margaret found out she was losing her vision, and that the only thing to do was to join them.

And third, Sarah made a discovery that upended absolutely everything Hannah thought she knew—about herself, about her Mama, and about her life. But Hannah was trying not to think about that.

Now, a new normal was taking shape at Seedling Homestead: all three Bradley sisters would be under one piece of sky again, living on what they were affectionately calling a commune. They'd share the bounty from the garden, the eggs from the chickens, and, hopefully, the work required to run the place.

Of course, they couldn't all live under the same roof, not with Margaret being a newlywed and Sarah and Donny being empty nesters. So they'd split the property to make room for two more houses. Margaret drew up the designs—her final project, a special farewell to her vision.

Then, they (well, Donny, if Hannah was being specific) hired a builder. Which brought Hannah to another element of this new normal: Tanner Lucas, builder extraordinaire, who had been a thorn in Hannah's side since college. And now, not only was he on the property almost every day, but also, her mother was smitten with him.

She told herself she wasn't hiding as she leaned against the trunk of the big maple, watching him lead Mama Katherine around the framed-in skeletons of her sisters' new houses. She'd just come outside to make sure spaghetti was okay for dinner, and she found herself observing Tanner (and yes, okay, *spying on him* would be a more accurate phrase, but no one had to know).

Tanner said something charming to Mama, and Mama guffawed and slapped her thigh in response. Hannah rolled her eyes. Donny had vetted Tanner before hiring him, and all of his references gave him glowing reviews. Hannah was almost positive one of the female homeowners had said something about the way he looked in his jeans. Or maybe it was something about his dimples.

Tanner had become one of the gang, helping himself to coffee in the mornings, and staying for dinner about as often as Mama's old rooster pecked the feathers off a hen's back (which happened several times a week).

Even before Sarah's discovery, Hannah couldn't figure out how she felt about any of this. Living on this commune with her sisters would be nice. They got along well. Having them here this summer had been more than fine. It had been *fun*.

It was just so *different*.

She'd always loved her life here at Seedling Homestead. It was perfect. At least, she'd thought it was (Sarah's big discovery aside). Her sisters had always had a way of getting her to question whether she was truly happy, or just content. They often talked about Hannah's future husband, even though there definitely wasn't one on the horizon. They often "encouraged" her to do something—anything —other than work and take care of Mama.

"You need a hobby, Hannah," they said, or, "Wouldn't it be fun to take a vacation?"

As if there was time.

When they talked about these things, she feigned disinterest or irritation. But the truth was that the conversations opened up new, strange desires in Hannah. Things in her brain got all tangled up. And by "things," she thought now, she meant strange ideas about whether there was more to life than what she was living … and even stranger thoughts about Tanner, himself. Not romantic thoughts, to be sure. Just … *observational* thoughts.

Somewhere between college and adulthood, he did seem to have mellowed out; he no longer debated everything everyone said. He also seemed to have aged well, which Hannah would never mention out loud to anyone. She watched him now, noticed the little lines at the corners of his eyes as he smiled at Mama, the way his hair curled over his collar.

Something about his presence made her uncomfortable, too. Maybe it was the fact that he had aged well. Maybe it was because she kept finding herself observing him, her interest growing slightly stronger each day.

"Hannah," Mama Katherine hollered. Hannah jumped, startled out of her observations on the rich, cowboy-like timbre of Tanner's voice, which carried over to where she was standing (not hiding).

She stepped out from behind the tree trunk, positive she looked guilty. Would it do any good to pretend she'd been examining the leaves? Here she was, contemplating every single detail of the completely uninteresting and unexpectedly handsome man who was, at this moment, talking to her mother not fifteen feet away in what Hannah thought would be Sarah's kitchen.

"Yeah?" She sounded meek and mouse-like, even to her own ears. She and Mama still weren't on speaking terms, not really.

"Come on over here," Mama said. "Tanner and I need your advice."

Hannah trudged over to where they stood, and even though she could feel Tanner watching her, she carefully avoided eye contact, instead looking at her mother's rain-boot-clad feet.

"I told your mother she doesn't need rain boots," Tanner said.

Hannah knew he wasn't talking about rain boots. He was letting her know that he knew she couldn't look at him. Now, she did look at him, staring straight into his eyes. She immediately wished she hadn't. They really were the most interesting color—a hazel that was more green than brown and somehow layered.

He grinned as if he could read her mind, and she felt herself smiling in response. Completely involuntarily.

"It isn't supposed to rain for two more days," they said at the same time.

Hannah flinched. Tanner grinned again. Hannah cleared her throat. "So what did you need my advice about?"

"Window placement," Tanner said.

"I thought Margaret's designs for the houses included window placement," Hannah said.

"They did," Tanner said. "But now that we're about to start framing them in, I've noticed that a tiny adjustment to the angle of this wall will give Sarah and Donny a great view—of that mountain range there, and of the maple trees, there."

"Hmm," Hannah said.

It really was thoughtful of Tanner to notice the view.

"It's a great idea," Hannah said. "You should adjust the angle of the wall."

"Okay, good," Tanner said. "Two votes in favor. I didn't want to make an executive decision."

Hannah nodded, still pretending Mama wasn't there, and found herself wondering why Tanner had gotten into building. He'd majored in education in college, same as her.

Mama Katherine beamed. "You're so thoughtful," she said to Tanner. Now he flashed that grin at her, and Hannah could have sworn she swooned.

Not for the first time, Hannah counted down the number of days remaining before the new school year started and she could escape, at least for most of every day. Three. Three more days until she could find refuge in Room Five at Walker Elementary School.

"I'm going to make dinner," she said. "Spaghetti okay?"

"Sounds great," Tanner said.

Hannah had to bite her tongue—literally—to keep from saying he wasn't invited to stay.

"Just kidding," he said. "I've got to get over to Lyla's house. She wants me to have a look at a spot in her roof. Thinks it's leaky and wants it repaired before the rain comes in. Said she'd feed me dinner if I took a look. I told her it'd better be steak. Anyway, thanks for your vote, Hannah."

With a tip of his hat and a, "Ladies," he walked away.

Then Mama spoke to her, the first casual words she'd managed in days: "You sure are smitten with that man," she said, well before Tanner was out of earshot (especially because she spoke so loudly he could have heard it from anywhere in the Walker city limits).

"*You* are," Hannah said.

She knew it was juvenile, but she didn't care. As she walked back to the house, her steps as fast as possible, she heard Mama Katherine cackle. And just underneath the sound of that bawdy laugh, was that Tanner Lucas's quiet chuckle? Hannah's face burned. She went inside and let the kitchen door slam behind her.

THE NEXT AFTERNOON, Hannah decided the wisest course of action was to make herself scarce when Tanner and his crew were wrapping things up. She told herself it wasn't because she was avoiding her family, even though she knew, deep down, that was part of it. She just couldn't face them right now. Hollering for John Wayne, she made her way through the meadow. Within a few strides, he'd caught up. She gave him a quick scratch behind the ears, and he looked up at her, smiling.

When thoughts about Mama's betrayal threatened to creep in, Hannah focused on the concrete: the end-of-summer warmth on her skin, the bright yellow of the few leaves that had turned, the way those leaves smelled. Fall. The thought of it ran a little thrill through Hannah. She looked forward to the change of seasons, which was so palpable here in Wyoming. She loved nothing more than to come home from school on a cool day, put on a comfy sweater and slippers, and drink tea while grading papers and watching the yellow-and-brown leaves flutter to the ground.

This year, along with the change of seasons would come a change in family dynamics. Margaret was set to marry Ethan James, computer programmer and likely the only eligible bachelor in the tiny mud puddle that was Walker, Wyoming, in just a few weeks. And a few weeks after that, the two of them, and Sarah and Donny, would would have completely moved in to their new houses. Then what?

Hannah had always found her role as the caretaker, the steadfast one, comfortable. As she and her sisters grew up, it seemed natural that she made sure everyone packed their school lunches, ate their proper servings of fruits and vegetables, and had enough clean under-wear to get through each week.

Looking back on it now, Hannah was positive Mama was super-vising all along, and just letting Hannah's care-taking (also known as bossy) personality flourish. When Sarah married Donny and moved out, and Margaret went off to college, Hannah had no one to mother—except Mama. And so, she'd continued to care for her ever since. Branching out, living a different life, wasn't ever a consideration.

Until now, Hannah thought as she watched a couple of birds bicker on the branch of a tree before flying off when John Wayne charged the base of their tree, giving a few half-hearted barks and sending a couple of birds flying off, chastising him in squawks.

This past summer, when Sarah and Margaret descended on the Seedling Homestead and decided to stay, Hannah had found herself in a kind of panic: would her role change now that her sisters were here to share the duties? If she wasn't the one running this place, then what was she? *Who* was she?

And not that she was interested in Tanner Lucas—not at all—but he represented something for which she'd never had space in her life: romance. If Sarah and Margaret helped around the farm, and helped care for Mama, then she would have more space in her life. What would she do with it?

She'd recently gotten just a taste of the answer to that question, which was that she didn't know. With Sarah, Donny, and Margaret here—and happy to help with chores and dinner—she'd found on more than one occasion with time to spare.

The trouble was, she didn't know how to fill it. She recognized it was there, but she often squandered it away, sitting at the kitchen table until a cup of coffee went cold between her hands, or standing at the wide back window, looking out over the property until she realized her eyes had glazed over, or sitting on the porch with a glass of wine or a beer, and more time.

Sometimes, she spent so long debating with herself about whether to do something—take John Wayne for a walk, go to the farmer's market to browse, dust the window blinds—that she ran out of time to actually do it.

John Wayne had fallen behind, and now, he streaked past her, to the creek's edge, coming to a full stop as his front paws splashed into the water. He made an abrupt right and ran along the bank. Sometimes, Hannah thought as she watched him trot along, she wasted all that time doing the unnecessary.

One morning when Sarah and Donny volunteered to help Mama with the weeding, she wiped down the kitchen counter four times before Amelia came in and pointed out that her arm must be getting tired.

Another afternoon when Margaret helped Mama repair a broken spot in the chicken coop, Hannah made three dozen cupcakes. She didn't even know who'd eat them all (actually, come to think of it, she'd put her money on Margaret), but she had been unable to think of anything else to do.

John Wayne dashed back to her, a stick in his mouth. She laughed when he dropped it at her feet. The truth was, she missed this—she loved taking the dog for walks, but she rarely did any more because she didn't want to leave Mama alone, even for a short time.

As if reminding her he was there, John Wayne whacked Hannah on the leg with the stick. She took it from him, tossed it as far upstream as she could. He charged after it, sending little chunks of mud up to hit her shins when he ran off.

In the midst of another round of fetch, Hannah thought maybe she should take this opportunity to remind herself of all the things she'd liked doing before Mama started requiring more help. How many times had she wished for someone else to help Mama with dinner, like Margaret was doing right now? And when she'd wished for that, what had she imagined doing?

John Wayne was back, offering her the stick again. She threw it, kept walking.

She could go to school and work ahead on lesson plans or redecorate her classroom, which she hadn't done in ages. Years, actually. She could take Mama into Jackson Hole and go to the mall. She could redecorate her bedroom. With Margaret's help.

Truth be told, although Hannah had been telling herself for years that she craved free time, now that she had it, she looked forward to the start of the new school year more than she ever—because it would give her structure and get her back into her routine. Back to normal.

Only, "normal" wasn't quite that any more, Hannah thought then, her mind bringing her back to the topic she'd tried to avoid thinking about. Hannah had *thought* the change in family dynamics was all she had to worry about. But then, just a few days ago, Sarah had dropped a bombshell that proved her wrong.

John Wayne came up behind her as the leaves on the trees shimmered. Hannah couldn't tell whether her tears were from hurt or anger or sadness. She decided it didn't matter. She turned back towards the house, and just as she had a million times since the bomb exploded, she went over the sequence of events that had transpired during the past couple of weeks.

When Sarah and Donny, and their daughter, Amelia, first arrived in Wyoming, Donny had just announced he wanted a divorce. After they dropped Amelia off at college, he said, they'd sell their house in Arizona. They were set to spend a few awkward weeks in Wyoming, first. One day, Hannah and Sarah went to the farmer's market, and Sarah, still in shock, bought an old metal recipe box there. She liked the colors and thought it would make a nice decoration in the kitchen wherever she ended up, post-divorce. Although Sarah and Donny had worked things out, and the topic of divorce had been shelved, Sarah's whimsical purchase had a lasting impact.

The recipe box ended up being much more than a trinket: tucked inside, Sarah found an old diary, written forty years before by someone named Hazel Rickshaw Carlisle.

Hazel detailed the tragic love story between her and her husband, Philip. Their arranged marriage started off on rocky ground. Neither of them much wanted to marry the other, but they agreed to wed because doing so meant a merger and the survival of their family orchards. Hazel was afraid getting married would mean an end to her copywriting career, but Philip encouraged and supported her. They ended up falling in love. Sarah, a romantic, loved the story so much she felt compelled to share it with her sisters.

When Hannah first read this part of the journal, she pictured the two of them dancing under a canopy of apple trees, the sky purple and twinkling with stars.

Hazel and Philip's first son was born a couple of years into their marriage, and, because Hazel preferred her career to motherhood, she always felt like a horrible mother.

Then, their son died in an accident on the orchard.

Hazel blamed herself: he'd woken from his nap, climbed out of his crib. His nanny, who was preparing dinner, didn't hear him. He wandered outside, where one of the workers ran over him with a tractor. Hazel believed that if she'd been home, mother's instinct would have warned her that her tiny son was in mortal danger.

But she was at work.

She and Philip couldn't overcome the tragedy. They couldn't speak to each other or even look at one another. Hazel believed the only thing to do was to start over. So, seeking a clean slate, she moved away from the California orchard she shared with Philip—and she didn't even tell him where she was going.

Sarah told her sisters that when she read this part of the story, a realization began to dawn. Something that had been niggling at her brain since she read the first page. The way Hazel Rickshaw Carlisle wrote, she sounded awfully familiar.

Thinking about it now gave Hannah goosebumps, even though it was too early to feel that fall chill in the air.

That's when Sarah knew. But she hadn't told Hannah, at least, not right away. Still, Hannah could tell something was going on.

She realized it one day a few weeks ago. Wanting to give Margaret an opportunity to see some of the country's best sights before she completely lost her vision, Hannah came up with the idea of taking Margaret on a road trip in Sarah and Donny's RV. Knowing she had to get Sarah's buy-in before presenting the idea to Margaret, Hannah tracked her down. She found Sarah hiding in the RV, where she'd spent much of the summer. She was reading the journal, so engrossed in the current entry that she didn't even seem to notice Hannah had climbed the stairs.

"I need to talk to you," Hannah said, and Sarah looked up, obviously startled.

"Geez," Hannah said. "You look like I just caught you with your hand in the cookie jar."

She smiled, hoping to keep the mood light so Sarah would be more receptive to her road trip idea. Still, Sarah didn't speak. Which was strange.

"Good reading?" Hannah said.

She came up the steps and looked over Sarah's shoulder. Sarah closed the journal.

"I need to talk to you, too," Sarah said. She licked her lips, which was one of her tells—she was nervous.

"Wow," Hannah said. "You look serious." She gestured to the journal. "What's happening now? Intrigue? Romance? Steamy sex?"

"You could say that," Sarah said.

Hannah should have heard alarm bells, then. Buzzers. She should have seen flashing warning lights. But she was too focused on her mission.

So she said, "Huh. Okay, well, I need to talk to you."

"So you said," Sarah said. She laid the journal on the dining table and put her hands in her lap. "All ears."

Hannah took a deep breath, and launched into her explanation about why they should take Margaret on a road trip. In the end, it didn't take too much convincing (of course, Sarah thought Margaret should focus on the practicalities of losing her vision: how she'd work, whether she needed mobility training, whether she'd want to move), and Hannah thought now that she should have been able to tell something else was going on.

It wasn't until later that Hannah found out … and her world changed completely.

ALTHOUGH HANNAH HAD CONCEIVED of the road trip for Margaret's sake, she found it was healing for her, as well. She rarely got off the Seedling Homestead and out of Walker, and it was even less often that she ventured out of Wyoming. Seeing all the sights—Zion, Bryce Canyon, Moab, Arches National Park—reminded her that there was a world outside of the little snow globe in which she lived. Maybe it even gave her an itch to explore it. Margaret seemed to have a good time, too, even if it was in part due to the constant supply of Bloody Marys Hannah kept flowing from the blender she'd packed in the RV.

And they enjoyed a new kind of camaraderie, thanks to the vulgar conversations Margaret had with Ethan via text message. Because Margaret couldn't read Ethan's texts, she played them out loud on her phone—which meant everyone in the RV participated. This provided almost unlimited opportunities for hilarity.

The first text from Ethan said, "I really enjoyed dinner the other night. Next time, we should try dessert."

Margaret gasped. Hannah gasped. Sarah said, "Wow," and Mama Katherine gave a whoop.

"Well, I can tell this app is going to be fun," Hannah said.

"What are you gonna say back?" Sarah said.

"I'm going to say, 'It's none of your beeswax, Sarah,'" Margaret said. "Just don't listen when I do voice-to-text because I'm going to tell Ethan just how much I love his dessert idea."

Then, they were all laughing—until Margaret's phone made another notification sound.

Into the silence, the phone said, "What do you like for dessert?"

"You know," Sarah said, her voice high-pitched, "you should probably change that thing's voice to one that sounds more manly, if you're going to start sexting. Especially if you're going to start sexting when we're all together."

This had Hannah practically shrieking. Margaret, lips twitching, told her phone to activate voice-to-text. Then she said, "I like cucumbers."

This stumped the other passengers in the RV, and they fell silent.

"He sent me a picture of a cucumber," Margaret said. "The other day."

"Then you should add something like, 'Covered in chocolate,'" Hannah said.

"No!" Sarah said. "Something like, 'But only when they're in my mouth.'"

"Well, I never," Mama said. "I am truly scandalized. I had no idea I was raising a bunch of harlots."

"It's not me," Margaret said. "I'm still a proper lady."

Then she activated voice-to-text and replied to Ethan: "I'm willing to try anything once."

A few seconds later, his reply came in, the feminine voice of the application breaking through the road noise: "Well. This should be interesting. I'll get a menu together."

For the seven days they spent in the RV, Hannah felt like everything was just right. In a way, she wished she could make some kind of time capsule, put the four of them inside of it, and keep living this way forever.

But real life beckoned, as it always did, and when they returned home, Sarah and Donny took Amelia off to college and Margaret became immersed in her own transition from sighted to blind. One day when everyone else was gone, Mama came into the kitchen while Hannah was washing dishes. The truth was, they weren't even *dirty* dishes. They were rarely-used items like the bundt pan and the giant blue casserole dish with the big chip on one corner from the time Margaret dropped a measuring spoon on it. Hannah, short on things to do since her sisters had taken care of most of the chores and Tanner Lucas was out on the property, taking measurements, decided a good cleaning was in order.

"We haven't used those in ages," Mama said when she saw what Hannah was scrubbing. "What are you washing them for?"

"I don't know," Hannah said. "It's just been a while. I looked into the cupboard and saw that they were dusty. I think this one even had a moth in it."

"Hannah," Mama said.

"Mama," Hannah said. "You'd've washed them too, if—"

"I need to talk to you."

Hannah's awareness perked up. Was Mama about to announce that she was sick? Dying? Maybe she had cancer or some other incurable disease. There had been an e.coli breakout a while back.

"Okay," Hannah said slowly. She dried her hands on the dish towel. Leaving the dishes in the soapy water, she gestured to the dining room table. They sat, and Mama said, "I'd like to tell you a story."

When she started talking, Hannah recognized the story as the one

Sarah had been reading in the journal. She figured Sarah had shared the story with Mama, and even though she wondered why Mama was telling it, she didn't interrupt.

Finally, she got to the part where Hazel's son died. Mama sounded a bit like she might cry, Hannah thought. Hannah hadn't yet heard this part of the story, and she was surprised at the strength of her own reaction: her stomach churned and her eyes burned. She didn't even know Hazel, or Philip, or the baby. But maybe it was because Mama seemed emotional about it. Hannah looked at the top of the table and used her thumbnail to scrape off some dried food from the night before while Mama talked about how Hazel could no longer look her husband in the eye, as guilty as she felt. If it were possible, her voice started to sound even thicker.

"So," Mama said, sighing and clearing her throat, "Hazel moved away. She moved to a place with a big sky. Somewhere about as far as she could get from the orchards and Philip and her little boy's grave. Do you know where she moved?"

When Hannah looked up at Mama, she noticed a strange intensity in her eyes.

Now, Hannah cleared her throat. "No. Where did she move?"

"Wyoming," Mama said. "To start over. She moved to Wyoming, where there's an endless sky and the freshest air. And that's when she learned she was pregnant. She hadn't known. She'd had an inkling, maybe, but she hadn't known for sure. And when the doctor confirmed it, she realized there was no other choice but to keep this new baby a secret."

Hannah's heart picked up its pace, creating a thrumming in her ears. That night when Margaret had crawled into bed asking about chickens was the first time Hannah noticed that silence is rarely actually silent. In this moment, as she stared at Mama and Mama stared back at her, everything was still. But it wasn't silent.

There was the rushing, beating sound in her ears. The cuckoo clock ticked, and the little motor inside whirred. Outside, a chicken clucked once, and then again, and the ice maker in the freezer released a load of cubes, which clattered down into the tray.

"You're—are you saying what I think you're saying?" Hannah said.

Mama continued to look at her, as if she was waiting for Hannah to come to her own conclusion. "It was the only choice," she said.

"Was it?"

Again, a moment passed where neither of them spoke. More

sounds: someone using a saw to cut some wood, a truck rumbling by on the road.

"At the time, it felt like it," Mama said.

"So I have a father," Hannah said.

She'd always known. Well, not *always*, but since the spring when she was five and she saw a pair of horses copulating at the farm down the street. She and Mama had taken one of their long weekend walks, down the driveway and out along the main road, which bordered farm and ranch properties for miles.

"What are they doing? Is that one horse trying to ride the other one?"

Hannah remembered the scene with such clarity. Her voice bordered on a giggle, as funny as she thought it was that one horse might be attempting to climb onto its friend's back. Mama hadn't bothered coming up with a clever explanation. She'd opted for the truth. Hannah had always admired her for her truth-telling. Until now, that is.

"They're reproducing," Mama said to five-year-old Hannah, who, of course, asked for an explanation. "Any time two mammals—a mommy and a daddy—want to have a baby, they do that." Here, she inclined her head toward the horses. The one that had been underneath the other one had run away now, shaking its head. Its mane shook, too.

"Humans are mammals, right?" Hannah said.

"Mmhmm," Mama said.

She took Hannah's hand and they started walking again. The sun was just a little too hot that day, and Hannah squinted, eyes watering, as she looked up at Mama.

"So, when you wanted to have *me*, did you reproduce with a daddy human to make me?"

Mama's stride faltered, just the tiniest bit, and she made a funny noise in her throat. Hannah thought it sounded a little like when she accidentally stepped on Mr. Mouser's tail. Mr. Mouser, the daddy barn cat, didn't like having his tail stepped on.

"I did," Mama said. "That's how all mammals reproduce, or make babies. But that's a story for another time. When you're older."

After that conversation, Hannah took more notice of, and a greater interest in, the makeup of families. Up until this point, when she and Mama went into town—to the library or the store—they typically saw pairs of mothers and children, or mothers with a handful of kids in tow. Hannah had never thought anything of it, because it was her normal. It was all she had exposure to.

When she started kindergarten that fall, she noticed that most of her classmates had mothers *and* fathers who came to the meet-the-teacher event and dropped them off on the first day. On the playground at recess, she heard people talk about both parents: "My daddy works at the grocery store, in produce," or, "My dad said the Broncos are going to win the Super Bowl this year but my mom, she's a Packers fan."

From the way these kids talked, their parents lived in the same house, argued over chores, and washed each other's clothes (someone's dad had accidentally turned all the whites pink when he threw a red towel into the load). As they all got older, they identified the fatherless children, but only as a matter of categorization. Hannah wasn't the only one whose mom was the sole parent: Terence Stuart lived alone with his mom and sister, and Jamie Hill's mom was raising her two daughters alone. Some kids migrated back and forth between their parents' houses.

And really, there were only a handful of instances in which it seemed to matter that Hannah didn't have a dad.

On career day, some parents came in to talk about their jobs. The grocery store dad from produce, of course, and Timmy Barrett's dad, who was a commercial airline pilot. Someone else's father was a rancher. A handful of mothers showed up: a seamstress, a nurse, and a teacher. It seemed like everyone's parents had jobs. But Hannah's mom didn't work, at least, not besides her chores on the farm. And, of course, Hannah didn't even *have* a dad. A few kids asked Hannah if she even knew who her dad was, but the teacher quickly shushed them.

Hannah could talk to Mama about almost anything. But over time, she understood that this topic, and the conversation that should accompany it, were off-limits. Every time it came up, Mama shut it down.

The last time Hannah approached it was when she was a pre-teen, in seventh grade. Some of the girls in her homeroom planned to attend a father-daughter dance their church was offering. During recess one day, they talked about it in high-pitched voices, describing the dresses their mothers had bought them and the corsages their fathers had chosen. Hannah went home that afternoon and told Mama about the dance. They were in the kitchen, and Mama was making meatloaf. As Hannah spoke, it seemed like Mama knew what was coming. She kneaded the meat mixture harder and harder, her shoulders moving up and down, up and down. After Hannah told her about the dresses and the corsages and the decorations, she paused. Mama kept kneading, and the meat made squishing sounds.

"Where's *my* dad, Mama? Why don't I have someone to take me to a father-daughter dance?"

Finally, Mama stopped kneading. Her body, which until then had been stiffly erect, drooped slightly. When she lifted her head, she didn't look at Hannah. She looked out the kitchen window, and Hannah imagined she was watching the windmill turn.

"Hannah," she said. "I just can't talk about it, okay? You probably won't ever have someone to take you to a father-daughter dance. And you know what? When you grow up and become an adult, you'll realize it was never that big of a deal to begin with. And these girls in your homeroom class, who think it's a big deal now, they'll fall into one of two categories: the first, people for whom the father-daughter dance is the highlight of their sad lives, and the second, people filled with anger and resentment and bitter disappointment because they grow up and realize their fathers aren't who they thought they were."

Hannah felt her eyes go round. Mama *never* talked like this. It seemed like Mama suddenly realized her words had become a runaway train, because she softened her tone when she went on: "But you, my dear, will be in a third category."

This was about the time Hannah had started to develop a mind of her own, and she thought—but didn't say—*a category full of fatherless children whose mothers never told them the truth.*

The two categories idea stumped Hannah. Mama rarely said anything mean-spirited about anyone.

"Hannah, you'll be among the girls who grow up strong and independent and able to think for yourselves. You won't need a man to make you happy or take care of you, because you'll know how to do those things on your own."

This answer wasn't satisfactory to Hannah. She wanted to know why he didn't care enough to be part of her life, even if he and Mama had gotten divorced.

"Now, I know this answer isn't satisfactory to you," Mama said, and Hannah wondered if her mother could read her mind. "And I'm sorry for that, but it's not going to change. I just can't talk about it. It would be really helpful to me if you didn't bring it up again."

Hannah, who prided herself on being a dutiful daughter and, above all, a helpful person, nodded. She walked out of the kitchen, her limbs numb. And she honored Mama's request: she never brought it up again, no matter how many times she wanted to. She had so many questions, questions that increased in quantity and complexity: did Mama even know who Hannah's father was? Did Hannah's father know about her? Where was he? Was he alive? Did she have any siblings, half-siblings with different mothers?

But now, here they were, Hannah more than forty years old, the topic back onstage. In the spotlight. As she replayed all those moments from her childhood, emotions began to swirl through her blood. She pictured them as colors, blooming in her veins: red for anger, blue for sadness, black for betrayal. She waited for her mother to speak.

"Of course you have a father," she said finally, her tone of voice falling somewhere right at the center of the kind-unkind spectrum.

"Well, of course I have a father," Hannah said, hoping to temper the anger she felt. "But I mean, now I know who he is. And you've always known who he is. Why didn't you tell me?"

"I couldn't," Mama said.

Again, a flash of anger. Hannah gritted her teeth. "You've said that. But of course you could. You could have told me his name, where he lives, whether he even knew about me. You could have told me the story of how you met and why you moved here. You chose not to. Not being able to do something is very different from choosing not to do something."

Mama, her elbows on the table, dropped her head into her hands.

"You're right," she said. But then she didn't say anything else.

Hannah felt like she might explode. How was this even possible, that they were sitting right here, face to face, and her mother still refused to elaborate on this story, *her* story?

She thought again about all those questions she had. She didn't know which one to ask first. Just trying to prioritize them made Hannah even angrier. But even as she clenched her teeth and balled her fists so tightly her fingernails dug into her palms, she noticed how frail Mama looked. The skin on her forearms was so thin, now, and the wrinkles around her eyes had deepened. The bones on her shoulders protruded, and, although she'd always seemed larger than life, now she looked like she'd shrunk.

What did Hannah really want to know? Which was the most important question?

"Does he know about me?"

Mama shook her head.

"He doesn't even know I exist?"

Again, a shake of the head.

"But, *why*, Mama? Why didn't you tell him? Don't you think he had a right to know? To make the choice about whether to be a part of my life? Don't you think I had a right for him to know? Or, *have* the right? For my own father to know of my existence?"

"Hannah—"

Hannah could only imagine what Mama planned to say. That she didn't know what else to do, that she didn't have a choice, that she thought she was doing what was best? It didn't matter. Hannah could think of what else to do. She could think of a better choice. And she could think of a situation far better than this.

For the first time ever, she hated her mother.

"Don't bother trying to explain," she said. "It doesn't even matter. You deprived me of my father. Who, by your own account in that journal, was a perfectly decent man. I can understand that you were going through a painful time. I can understand you thinking leaving was the only option. But what I can't understand, Mama, is that you never told me. You never came clean. You put your thoughts and feelings and explanations and secrets into a journal, and then left that journal out for someone else to find. But you never told me. And because of that, I missed out."

Hannah knew what she was implying. She was implying that her childhood had somehow been lacking. And while it had been magical, and she knew how lucky she was—especially when she lined her own story up next to Sarah's and Margaret's—she believed a father was part of some equation, where the elements came together to create a deep happiness and sense of belonging. And she knew he wasn't there.

Mama had done her best. And she'd done a good job. But she had also betrayed Hannah. Not only Hannah, but Philip Carlisle, too. And Hannah didn't know if she could forgive her for that.

# ABOUT THE AUTHOR

Hilary Dartt loves great adventures, whether she's writing, reading, or living them. The author of nine women's fiction novels, Hilary lives in Arizona's high desert with her husband, their three children, her Weimaraner and running partner, Leia, a failed barn cat, and a flock of chickens. She loves camping, exploring in the Jeep, and dance parties with her kids. Learn more at www.hilarydartt.com

www.ingramcontent.com/pod-product-compliance
Lightning Source LLC
Chambersburg PA
CBHW050344190726
48284CB00007BB/2140

9 781950 335015